Sometimes, in the midst of tragedy, beauty is born . . . .

Arye held a framed photograph of her taken with her husband on their wedding day. "You were a beautiful bride."

"It was a long time ago."

"Not that long. You're still a very beautiful woman." Peach wasn't accustomed to compliments. She didn't know what to say.

Arye's voice pierced the silence. "Can I get you a drink or would you rather wait until your husband comes home?"

She wasn't accustomed to solicitude either. "That would be a very long wait. He asked me for a divorce. I don't even know where he is."

Arye moved so close she could feel his body heat. Was he going to take her in his arms? Did she want him to?

"So you're free," he said.

"I suppose that's one way to look at it." She had read books where time stood still but never had expected to experience the sensation. Now, as her gaze locked with Arye's, she lost all awareness of the passage of time.

"I've wanted to kiss you for a long time. I know this isn't the best time—in fact, it's a terrible time—but I can't wait any longer."

He knew he ought to back off.

He knew he was taking unconscionable advantage of her distress.

He knew he deserved to be tarred and feathered for what he was doing.

He knew all those things—and didn't give a damn.

He kissed her.

Alexandra Thorne

SEASONS OF THE HEART

PINNACLE BOOKS
KENSINGTON PUBLISHING CORP.

PINNACLE BOOKS are published by

Kensington Publishing Corp.
850 Third Avenue
New York, NY 10022

First Printing: September, 1996
10 9 8 7 6 5 4 3 2 1

Printed in the United States of America

To my two personal heroes,
Lieutenant John Dane Thorleifson
and James Tracy Thorleifson.

Pilate saith unto him, what is the truth?
                                    John 18:38

Part One

There is a tide in the affairs of men,
Which, taken at the flood, leads on to fortune;
Omitted, all the voyage of their life
Is bound in shallows and in miseries.

Shakespeare, *Julius Caesar,* IV, iii.

Prologue

Houston, Texas, 1992

He hated Peach Morgan-Strand on sight.

Not exactly an auspicious beginning for a job interview, Arye Rappaport thought as he stood in the doorway of Peach's office, waiting for her to acknowledge his presence. She was studying the contents of a folder. His resume, he wondered?

Her appearance grated on his nerves like chalk on a blackboard. She looked and smelled like money—major money—Texas money.

Even his untutored eyes had no trouble guessing that the label on the back of her suit would read Chanel. Her perfume, too. Her nails, brilliant crimson and long enough to do a Mandarin proud, clearly said she had never done a lick of honest labor in her life. And her hair, a vivid strawberry blond that a television actress touted as being the color for women who were worth the very best, was Texas big.

But it was her femininity that bothered him most. It wasn't the tarted-up, cleavaged sort of womanhood he saw on those rare occasions when he ventured into a bar during the cocktail hour. Peach Morgan-Strand oozed femininity the way female insects give off pheromones. Despite the artifice of her carefully put-together veneer, she reminded him of the primal pleasures of the bed.

No one had done that to him for a long time. He didn't like the hollow ache he felt in the vicinity of his heart or the tingling sensation in his loins. Damn her to hell, he thought angrily. What in the fuck could he be thinking of, applying for a job as the managing editor of a magazine she owned!

He was on the brink of making a quick exit when she looked up. Her eyes had the shimmering irides-cent quality of the sea. Green today, they reflected her emerald outfit. He had no doubt they would look blue or grey or even purple tomorrow depending on what she wore. However their color didn't intrigue him half as much as the expression in them.

Vulnerable. Sad. Curious. Solemn. Brimming with intelligence.

He was a journalist who believed in brevity but he couldn't choose the perfect adjective to describe the look in her eyes.

She rose, came around the desk, and held out her hand. "I'm very pleased to meet you, Mr. Rappaport."

Her voice oozed over him, dark and sweet as honey from the hive. Her grip felt surprisingly firm. Cool, too, while his own palms were damp. She was heavier than he would have guessed—perhaps a size ten—and shorter. So short she could have easily walked under his chin if she chose,

Bert Hanrahan had told him she was six years older than his own thirty-one. She didn't look it, though.

"I'm pleased to meet you too, Mrs.—" he fumbled for a moment, wondering if she preferred to be called Mrs. Strand, or Mrs. Morgan-Strand.

Damn the idiocy of so-called liberated women who hyphenated their names, he mused, his mood worsening as he stumbled through, "Mrs. Morgan-Strand."

Her laughter took him by surprise. "It's a mouthful, isn't it? My husband Herbert wanted me to keep my maiden name. He said he wanted the entire world to know how proud he was to have married Senator Morgan's daughter. But my friends call me Peach. I hope you don't mind if I call you, Arye."

He minded.

She had pronounced it Are-ye instead of Ah-re. He pasted what passed for a smile on lips unaccustomed to making the effort and corrected her.

"It's Arye."

"What sort of name is that?" she asked, leading the way to an expensive-looking furniture grouping. Leather. The real thing—not naugahyde. Probably Italian.

However he wasn't here to make small talk or critique the decor. He wanted a job—not a best friend. "It's Hebrew," he replied, thinking he would run for his life if she said some of her best friends were Jewish. "It means lion."

She sank into the sofa's cushioned comfort and gestured for him to take an adjacent chair. An experienced executive would never have made that mistake. It exaggerated the difference in their heights—to his advantage. He looked down on the top of her head. Unless she'd had her hair colored yesterday, the red was natural. He wondered if she had the same shade between her legs—and felt his face heat up at the thought.

"I've read your resume," she said, "and it's very

impressive. I do have one question, though. Why would a Pulitzer-winning journalist with a national reputation want to run a regional magazine like *Inside Texas?*"

He couldn't insult her by saying he wanted a job that required so little of him he was capable of doing it with one hand tied behind his back. And he'd be damned if he'd tell her why he never wanted to return to investigative reporting. He couldn't lie to her either. That had never been his style.

"I'm not a card-carrying member of the IRE anymore."

"What's that?"

He groaned inwardly. And she called herself a publisher. "It's an association of investigative reporters and editors. Look, Mrs.-er-Peach, I haven't worked in three years and I've run through my savings. I need a paycheck. Your art director, Bert Hanrahan, told me you needed a managing editor—so here I am."

"You make it sound very simple, Arye." This time, she got the name right.

"That's the way I like to keep things—simple and unencumbered."

Simple and unencumbered my foot, Peach thought, struggling to maintain her aplomb. She read the pain in Arye's eyes as easily as she had read it in her sons' when they came to her with the physical and mental aches the most carefully sheltered childhood couldn't prevent.

She had a sudden and almost uncontrollable urge to cushion Arye Rappaport's head on her bosom, to croon the words that had eased her boys past the rough spots in the road. But she suspected nothing in the world could ease this man past the rough spot in his road.

Bert Hanrahan had told her that Arye's wife had met a ghastly death in a car bombing that had been meant for him. Bert had also told her how in love they had been. The tragedy was written on Arye's face. Somehow, it made him even more appealing.

Although she considered herself happily married, she could easily imagine less fortunate women succumbing to Arye's physical charms. Talk about tall, dark and handsome.

His height—she estimated six feet, three inches—would have made him a standout in any crowd. His shoulders were oversized, too. They strained the seams of a suit that hadn't been fashionable for years. Unfortunately it didn't nip in at a waistline that would have been worth the tailor's effort.

Arye's features were just this side of drop-dead gorgeous. He had high cheekbones, large olive green eyes screened by curly black lashes, brows that arched so perfectly they reminded her of a gull's wings, a deeply dimpled chin, and a full lower lip that promised a wellspring of sensuality.

His scimitar of a nose kept him from being merely pretty, and the well-muscled physique his suit failed to conceal attested to his apparent virility. His name suited him. He reminded her of a black-maned lion cast out from a pride.

In short, he was a man to die for. And one poor woman already had.

"As you can imagine we've had several applicants for the position," she began, then paused, waiting for his reply.

A less confident man would have taken the opportunity to tout his superior qualifications, reiterating the high points in his resume.

Arye said nothing.

The silence lengthened until she felt compelled to break it. "I should warn you I'm an absentee owner. My family, my charities, and my social life keep me busy. I gave my last managing editor a free hand and I see no reason to change that policy. However I do have some concerns about your background. Our purpose at *Inside Texas* is to show the state at its best. If you want to look under rocks—personal, financial or political—you're not the man for the job. I will not tolerate a tabloid mind-set on my staff."

"I never intend to get near investigative reporting again at any level. I'll be perfectly content to run fluff pieces."

"Fluff pieces?" she sputtered, galled by his temerity. "What's wrong with holding a mirror up to the nicer side of life?"

The lion hadn't been tamed, she realized with a start as he leaned toward her, so close she could see the golden striations in his eyes. To her surprise she found his closeness more exciting than intimidating.

Her pulse accelerated. Her palms moistened. Her blood heated. Good God, she was reacting like a turned-on teenager instead of the person in charge.

"Peach, you own a glossy publication and your circulation figures attest to a coterie of devoted readers," he said. "But between the two of us, let's not pretend that articles about Ladybird Johnson's highway beautification program, the Pasadena strawberry festival, the little old wood carver in Wimberly, or the Houston Opera Guild's latest soiree require in-depth reporting."

At least he had taken the time to read the magazine. *"Inside Texas* has a fine reputation," she countered.

"I'll do my best to uphold it." His tone was solemn, his features arranged in a submissive mold that didn't quite suit the glint in his eyes.

She chose to put her faith in what he said rather than how he looked. Her previous managing editor's sudden death had put her in a bind. The next edition needed to be finalized. If only she weren't committed to giving a cocktail party for two hundred of Herbert's best friends and to taking a trip to Oxford, Mississippi so the twins could see her alma mater before deciding to matriculate there, she could have managed to run *Inside Texas* herself for a few more weeks while she found the ideal candidate for the job.

Under the circumstances, she needed to hire some-one *yesterday.*

Like a diver about to spring off a ten-meter board, she sucked in a deep breath. "Your resume, coupled with Bert's stellar recommendation, was very convincing. Arye, the job is yours if you want it."

He smiled for the first time—and her heart took an elevator ride. Dear God, had she made the offer too hastily? A man like Arye Rappaport was bound to wreak havoc on her almost-all female staff.

"When do I start?" he asked.

One

Houston, Texas, 1995

Peach Morgan-Strand stared at her reflection in the dressing-table mirror. This was more than a bad hair day. She looked awful. Dark circles rimmed her eyes. Her skin was sallow. Terrible as she looked, she felt much worse. Her heart ached for her parents.

They had weathered the blows of outrageous fortune so far. But their strength and resilience had limits. Being vilified day in and out by the media had been bad enough. Financial security had cushioned that blow. Now, selling their home and personal possessions to satisfy their creditors, being made to arrange their affairs at the whim of a bankruptcy judge, had breached that last defense.

How could her father have fallen so low when he had been such a popular senator? "A Washington fixture" the press had dubbed him the last time he'd been reelected. Now they called him a *crook* and worse.

Peach moaned out loud, then clapped a perfectly manicured hand over her mouth to stifle the sound. Weeping wouldn't help her parents today. They needed her to be strong.

And she would be—as long as she had Herbert to

lean on. She had never needed her husband more. The sound of him moving around his own dressing room gave a sense of normalcy to this nightmare of a day. She had the urge to run straight to his sheltering embrace. But she knew he wouldn't appreciate any alteration in their daily routine. Besides, they hadn't communicated very well lately.

She covered her pale complexion with a rosy foundation, made up her eyes, subdued her unruly hair with brush and spray, dressed in a new designer dress that gave her a mental and emotional boost, then left the bedroom. As she made her way down the stairs, sunlight reflected off a massive crystal chandelier, sending rainbows of color through the two-story foyer.

Herbert had preceded her. He stood near the front door, a folded copy of the *Houston Chronicle* in his hands, watching her with a bemused expression. Although he looked better in tennis shorts and an open-necked knit shirt than any fifty-one-year-old man had a right to, they hardly seemed appropriate attire considering the gravity of the occasion.

"Have you forgotten what day it is?" she asked.

Herbert glanced down at his Rolex. "I know exactly what day it is. I've been looking forward to it all week. I'm due at the club for tennis in forty minutes."

Had he always begun every sentence with *I*? How strange to notice it now, when she had so many other things on her mind.

As if it were an afterthought, he added, "I'm doing a mammaplasty at Herman later."

The boob job didn't trouble her. The tennis did. "You're playing a match today?" Her voice rose on the last word.

"Jack Bowdoin and I have been trying to get together for months. We both had the morning free. I'm not due in surgery until eleven."

"But the auction is today." She found herself talking to Herbert's back as he headed for the breakfast room. "My parents will need all the love and support we can give them while strangers paw over their belongings."

"Senator Connally and his wife, Nellie, survived a similar auction. Your father and mother will, too," Herbert declared. Among his many gifts was a talent for making the unthinkable sound utterly reasonable.

He took his accustomed seat at the wrought-iron table they'd found on a second honeymoon in Italy so many years ago that it seemed to have happened in a novel. After pouring a cup of coffee from the insulated carafe Delia put out every morning, he hid behind the *Houston Chronicle* as if the subject of his morning activities had been settled.

She shook her head in disbelief. How could a plastic surgeon who prided himself on empathy with his patients be so unfeeling toward his in-laws?

"I know the auction won't be pleasant—however we've got to attend. My parents have always been there for us." She rapid-fired the words as if she feared they would jam in her throat if she slowed down. "Remember how Dad paid for our membership at the River Oaks Country Club when you said mingling with the members would give your practice a terrific boost—and how he made the down payment on this house long before we could have saved the money on our own?" Breathless, she paused to suck air. "All I'm asking in return is that you stand by them today."

Herbert dropped all pretense of reading. For the

first time that morning he turned the full force of his gaze on her.

His obsidian black eyes were usually inscrutable. But she had no difficulty reading the message in them this morning. His gaze was as sharp and cold as Solingen steel.

"I'm aware of the financial help your father has given us. I'm also painfully aware of the other things he's done. Influence peddling, insider trading, misusing campaign funds, to say nothing of sexual harassment, have a very unsavory ring, wouldn't you agree?"

The list of her father's supposed transgressions read like a list of political sins *du jour*. The only thing Blackjack Morgan hadn't been accused of—so far—was misconduct with prepubescent boys. And she expected to hear rumors about that any day.

The media had been in a feeding frenzy for months, pretending righteous indignation at Blackjack's difficulties as if he were some sort of monster when the escapades and peccadilloes of other Beltway insiders went unnoticed.

The only publication to ignore the scandal had been her own. Peach had never defended her father in print, but she had defended him verbally more times than she cared to remember. She never expected to defend him in the haven of her own home.

"In America, people are supposed to be innocent until proven guilty. And, in case you've forgotten, my father has never been convicted of anything."

Having spoken her piece, she sagged in her chair like a marionette with cut strings. Why was Herbert provoking her today of all days?

His scowl deepened. "Your father is a heartbeat away from being impeached."

"That's what they said about Agnew, Nixon, De-Concini, and Packwood. It didn't happen to them, and it won't happen to my father either. Besides, senators aren't impeached. They're censured."

"The end result is the same." Using his forefinger, Herbert traced a lethal line across his throat. "Damn it Peach, I've had it. I'm sick of conversations coming to a stop when I walk into the club. I'm sick of friends and acquaintances whispering behind my back. I'm sick of reading our name in the papers. It's affecting my practice. The number of new patients is in a sharp decline."

The anger and resentment welling in Peach's chest took her by surprise. Although Herbert often disappointed her, he had never infuriated her.

Admittedly, they had grown apart the last few years. At first she had attributed it to the empty nest syndrome, then to the increasingly busy schedules they maintained to fill the hours they used to spend with the twins. Hearing similar complaints from female friends, she told herself the spinning off into separate orbits was a phase all husbands and wives went through on the way to their golden years.

She hadn't realized the depth of the estrangement until this very moment. She might as well have breakfast with a stranger—and a very unpleasant one at that. Herbert sounded more like a whiny brat than a respected plastic surgeon.

"Your feelings are not the issue today, Herbert. My parents' feelings are. Since you're so determined to take center stage, have you considered what the press will write when they learn you were playing tennis today? It should make for interesting copy."

"Don't threaten me, Peach."

She hadn't known that's what she was doing until he labeled it. The knowledge sent a pleasurable frisson through her. She had never stood up to him before.

Although Herbert had been born on the wrong side of the tracks, he never let her forget that he was more mature, more intelligent, and better educated than she was and, therefore, better able to make decisions for the two of them.

She had subjugated her will, sublimated her impulses, and surrendered her sense of self on the altar of marital peace. Now those things came roaring back like an extinguished forest fire returning to unexpected life. For the first time in the twenty-one years they'd been married, she felt compelled to draw a verbal line in the sand.

"My parents are expecting you to join them—*and so am I.*"

Distaste marked Herbert's aquiline features. He heaved what could only be interpreted as a long-suffering sigh. "I hate to discuss this under the circumstances. You've left me with no alternative. Believe me, Peach, this isn't a hasty decision. I've been thinking about it for months, waiting for the right time to speak my mind."

A premonitory chill crept across her skin. "Bring what up?"

"The sorry state of our marriage. I've held off discussing it because I knew how troubled you were about your father. I guess there is no right time for a talk like this, though. The truth is, I want a divorce."

Peach's stomach heaved. For a second she didn't know whether she was going to faint—or toss her cookies. She had expected an argument, even bitter words. She hadn't expected this.

"I don't have to tell you we've grown apart," Herbert continued in such a reasonable tone, he might have been discussing what to have for supper. "It's been months since we had sex."

"I've never refused you," she burst out. She had attributed his diminished libido to her own widening waistline—not to a defunct marriage.

"It's impossible to feel romantic about a wife who is so absorbed in her father's problems that she doesn't have time for her husband."

Herbert used the authoritarian tone that worked so well with his patients.

It didn't have the same effect on her.

If she had been a more physical woman she would have taken considerable pleasure in punching him on his aristocratic nose. "Don't you dare blame my father for our troubles—sexual or otherwise."

Herbert got up so abruptly that his coffee cup fell over. A miniature brown tide engulfed the saucer, then spilled over onto the charming folk-art table cloth she'd bought in Oaxaca during a particularly pleasant vacation. Its ruin added injury to insult. Tears pooled in her eyes. But she refused to cry.

"You have some sense of timing." She looked at him, wondering if he'd told her the real reason for his decision. "Is there someone else?"

"Yes," he admitted. He didn't even have the good grace to look embarrassed.

"You—you bastard."

Herbert's lips pursed as though he'd bitten into something unpleasant. "I will not indulge in recriminations with you. Nor will I permit two decades of marriage to end in an ugly scene. I'm going to the club and then to the hospital. My attorney will be in touch."

Halfway to the door, he paused and looked back. Nothing about his every-hair-in-place exterior indicated a scintilla of inner turmoil. You'd think this was just another parting instead of the final one. "Please ask Delia to pack my things. I'll send someone for them later."

Peach sat frozen in place like one of those prehistoric mammoths the Russians keep finding in Siberian glaciers. Herbert walked out of their home and out of her life. Just like that.

Suddenly the huge house seemed preternaturally quiet. In the silence, she swore she could hear her heart breaking. Not for the death of her marriage, though. Herbert had just walked out but the truth was, he'd left her long ago. And she hadn't cared enough to stop him.

While sunlight poured through the French doors, gilding the breakfast room with cheer, Peach Morgan-Strand wept for the death of her illusions.

Senator Blackjack Morgan stood as docilely as a schoolboy while his wife knotted his tie. The long-standing ritual began on their first date forty-five years ago when Bella had commented on the sorry-looking Windsor knot at his throat.

He had challenged her to do a better job—and had stolen a kiss when she took the silk in her hands. Ever since, she had knotted his tie every morning they were together.

Such mornings had been few and far between during the years when power and its many usages had occupied his time, Blackjack recalled, wondering how he could have behaved so badly and why Bella had put up with it. He had never appreciated his wife until that bitch goddess, Lady Luck, had turned her back on him.

As prestige and money were stripped away from him like the leaves of an artichoke, he had rediscovered Bella. Now he felt as if the two of them stood, back-to-back, against an increasingly hostile world.

"There, that's done," she said, giving the paisley silk a final pat.

He planted a kiss on her brow. "How do I look?"

Bella eyed him from head to toe, taking in the shock of silver hair that rode his noble brow, the Roman nose, the florid complexion that passed for health but secretly spoke of a life given over to indulgence and vice.

He was a ruined man with a ruined face but she couldn't help caring about him and for him. Pitying him, too, although she'd die before she let him know. Her most secret wish had finally come true. Senator Blackjack Morgan needed her.

To her eternal regret, it had happened too late. He had killed her love long ago. Duty, loyalty, and her own sense of honor, were the ties that bound her to him now.

"You look very handsome," she answered with a determined smile.

"You're prejudiced." He smoothed his Saville Row suit and shot his cuffs, exposing half an inch of pristine white linen. "I suppose we ought to be grateful the bankruptcy judge didn't order us to sell our clothes, too. A few years back Bill and Hilary Clinton deducted five dollars from their income tax for every pair of

Bill's used briefs they gave to charity. Considering my current notoriety, I have no doubt mine would be worth even more." He gave Bella a rueful grin. "They say clothes make the man. Today I need all the help I can get."

"How I love your humility, even if it isn't the real article," Bella teased.

Blackjack responded in kind. "I thought you loved me because I have a big dick."

"You know what we girls say about dicks. They come in three sizes. Small, average—and oh-my-God! You, my darling, are in the oh-my-God class."

"That's one thing the bastards can't take away."

Blackjack gave Bella a wink, then took her arm and led the way from their bedroom for the last time. Tonight they would sleep at Peach's house. And tomorrow—

To hell with tomorrow. Today was all he could handle.

He looked back just once, trying to remember the good times they had shared in the room, then let the memories go.

"Would you like to go out for breakfast before we're fed to the media lions?"

By the time Peach reached the tree-lined drive in front of Belle Terre, her parents' antebellum River Oaks mansion, she had her a firm grip on her emotions. Her eyes swam in Murine rather than the tears she had shed at the breakfast table.

She had made up her mind not to tell her mother and father about the divorce. Not yet. Herbert's disaffection might be the last straw that would bring them to their knees.

While she parked, she attempted to rearrange her features in a smile. Although it felt more like a grimace, it was the best she could do.

Someone had left the front door ajar. Monsieur Armand, owner of the Horn Gallery and the man appointed by the bankruptcy court to oversee the auction, stood in the spacious foyer, admiring a Tamayo oil painting.

He turned as her footsteps echoed through the three story space. His pencil thin mustache quivered over even thinner lips. "Ah, Madame Morgan-Strand, this is a terrible day. It would kill me to part with a painting like this, let alone the rest of your parents' collection."

His French accent was as phony as his sympathy, she realized with new insight. She had bought art from him for years. Now she wondered why she had ever listened to his advice. "It's only a painting, Armand—not a member of the family. I'm certain my parents will survive its loss. Speaking of my parents, where are they?"

Blackjack Morgan sat across from his wife at a window table in Guggenheim's delicatessen, watching the traffic on Post Oak Road. The Galleria—a glitzy shopping area that rivaled Fifth Avenue or Rodeo Drive—was coming to life. He had given so many speeches in nearby hotels that he could almost taste the rubbery chicken they served on such occasions.

Despite the familiarity of the setting, he felt as alien and alienated as a newly arrived boat person. Guilt churned in his stomach at the thought of the immigrants he had blamed for what he called *the mongrelization of America.*

There were so many things he regretted doing and saying that he swore he could feel them pressing on his chest like leaden weights. Thank God he'd finally seen the light. He loved his country—and still had a chance to save it from itself.

"I don't know why I ordered so much," Bella said, pushing her plate of congealed eggs Benedict away. "I'm not at all hungry."

"Neither am I. I used to dream about having breakfast here when I was trapped in Washington by a legislative session. I suppose reality can never live up to one's memory, though. The smoked salmon isn't half as good as I thought." He rubbed his chest. "In fact, it's given me a bad case of heartburn."

"Don't eat anymore."

"I hate letting it go to waste. Who knows when we'll be able to afford to eat here again." Sighing, he too pushed his plate away. "I've been thinking about the auction. We really don't have to attend if you'd rather not."

Bella reached for his hand. Her touch still had the power to soothe him. "I wouldn't miss it for the world. Our friends have been drooling over our things for years. I want to know who gets what. Besides, Peach and Herbert are coming. I'm worried about her. She's taken our troubles very hard."

"That prick she married hasn't been any help. I never approved of him."

"Don't talk that way, darling. We may not care for Herbert, but he's Peach's husband and the twins' father."

Blackjack swallowed hard, as though he could choke down the hostility that engulfed him at the thought of the unprincipled bastard who married Peach for her family connections.

The pain in his chest had been amorphous until now—something he felt certain he could burp away. It intensified suddenly, taking form and shape as it radiated across his shoulders and down one arm. He would have given anything to go home to bed. But he didn't have a home anymore, he reminded himself.

Ignoring his physical and mental discomfort, he gave Bella's hand a comforting squeeze. "Peach will do just fine. She's stronger than you think. She has your courage, your inner strength. I couldn't have gotten through the last year without the two of you."

"I wish you'd consider resigning, the way Dick Nixon did after Watergate."

"I've never run from a fight."

Tears pooled in her eyes. Hell, if she cried he'd be a goner. He'd caused so many of her tears that he'd agree to almost anything to keep her from shedding more, anything but resigning from the Senate. If he went down, it would be fighting.

Bella took a moment to regain control. "Any law firm in the country would be thrilled to give you a partnership. We could move to a new city and start over."

"Do you recall what Nixon wrote about never giving up and never looking back?"

"Is that what you plan to do?"

Blackjack squared his shoulders. Renewed determination almost banished his pain. "Hell, no, Bella. I intend to confound my enemies. They all live in glass houses. Before I'm finished, they're going to regret throwing the first stone."

She looked askance at him. "How do you plan to accomplish that?"

"I wish I could tell you. But not yet. Not until I'm sure."

"Sure of what?"

"I have a secret weapon, Bella. I want to be certain it will work before I raise your hopes."

"What are you talking about?"

He grinned. "It's very simple. I'm going to tell the truth, my darling, the simple unvarnished truth and let the chips fall where they may."

Peach wandered through Belle Terre, feeling like a soul in purgatory as she noted the numbered stickers on the paintings, sculpture, objets d'art and antiques her parents had collected. The numbers undoubtedly corresponded to ones in the catalogue Armand had given her. But she hadn't opened it and never would.

She had no need to read the provenance of the items for sale. Their history had been written in her heart during her youth. Each treasured piece evoked memories of the time when Blackjack had belonged to his family rather than the nation.

After serving in Vietnam he'd been eager to return to hearth and home, to make up for the time he'd been away. She had an almost tactile memory of curling up in his lap, giggling over the scrape of his whiskers as he read her a bedtime story.

Her younger sister, Avery, had missed all that. Blackjack had already been infected with the virus of political ambition—the need to make sure other men didn't fight and die in wars the government didn't have the will to win—when Avery was born eleven years after Peach.

Avery had missed Blackjack's homebody period. Living in London the last two years, she had missed the recent *Sturm und Drang* too. Lucky Avery.

Peach walked into the living room where a magnificent Diego Rivera oil painting over the fireplace caught her eye. Her parents had taken her with them when they visited the artist's Mexico City studio. She could almost smell the mingled odors of turpentine, paint, and spices that filled the high-ceilinged space.

Her peregrinations finally came to a halt in the library. She sat down behind her father's massive desk, feeling the contours his body had sculpted in the leather chair. It was almost as comforting as sitting in his lap.

A dozen photographs of him with heads of state lined the walls. The inscriptions reflected the esteem Blackjack had enjoyed. God, how had he fallen so low?

She could easily dismiss the sexual harassment charges. Her father had always been a glad-hander, a politician who loved to press the flesh. In the course of half a dozen campaigns, she had seen him squeeze arms, shoulders, accidentally touching breasts in the process.

Perhaps he didn't realize how much times had changed, and that yesterday's effusive compliment or manly touch could be interpreted as an assault.

Could the other charges be summarily dismissed, too? Peach began idly opening desk drawers, as if the answer could be found inside them. Just then, her parents walked in.

"Monsieur Armand told us you were here," Bella said.

Peach jumped to her feet. "Where have you been?"

"There wasn't anything to eat in the house so we went to Guggenheim's," her mother replied. "Where's Herbert?"

Peach's stomach contracted at the prospect of lying. "At the hospital. He had an emergency—but he sent his love."

"Since when do cosmetic surgeons have emergencies?" Blackjack asked. "Did one of his face-lifts fall?"

"That's not funny. There are accidents, Dad."

"Of course there are," Bella said with admirable equanimity, "and who better to put a ravaged face back together than our Herbert?"

Peach managed to smile at her parents. Silently though, she prayed the god of tennis was turning all of Herbert's smashes into harmless lobs.

Two

Peach had to give the devil his due. Monsieur Armand certainly knew how to put on an auction. The sixty-by-thirty-foot conservatory overlooking the garden—a room that had been the scene of formal balls, charity luncheons, and huge political gatherings—overflowed with buyers. The canopy of live oaks soaring over the glass roof dappled everyone with lacy shadows. The ripe musk of warm bodies and expensive perfumes scented the air.

A red carpet running down the center of the floor added an aura of royal grandeur to the proceedings. Row upon row of gilt chairs radiated from the carpet. Collectors of every sort—art dealers, antiquarians, museum directors and their representatives had vied with Houston's elite to fill them. The bidding had been so spirited that an avaricious smile had been permanently engraved beneath Armand's supercilious mustache.

He held sway at a lectern, responding with an outstretched hand to the twitches, nods, and other arcane gestures that raised the bidding. Peach's father and mother worked the crowd at every lull, acting more like a proud host and hostess than the nation's most notorious couple.

Peach had done her best to follow their lead—but it galled her to see this flock of well-heeled vultures fighting over her parents' treasures. Although her smile never faltered, inside she howled at the injustice of it all.

It hurt even more to recall what had happened in her breakfast room just a few hours earlier. No matter how unfulfilled she'd been, she would never have asked Herbert for a divorce. Unlike other women of her age and social status, she hadn't spilled her troubles out on a psychiatrist's couch either. She had simply endured in the expectation that this too would pass.

What an idiot she had been! Her fists clenched as she thought about Herbert. He was probably inserting a saline-filled silicone bag into a flaccid boob at this very moment. She had vivid memories of the intense look he wore when operating—or having sex—as if he regarded both activities as necessary evils in his avid pursuit of the American dream.

Had Herbert ever loved her? she mused.

Although she had fallen for him like the proverbial ton of bricks when they met at a sorority party during her freshman year at Old Miss, she had never been foolish or blind enough not to see the social cachet Herbert gained from their union.

She had been so in awe of him then. To be singled out from all those beautiful coeds was as close to an out-of-body experience as she ever expected to encounter.

She had gone from this very house to her husband's apartment with only a year of college between. Giving up a degree in journalism had seemed like a small sacrifice compared to marrying her dream man.

No matter what she thought of Herbert now, he had been a good father, she reminded herself. She would have to be careful not to permit the acid of her current bitterness to etch a single line on the boys' love for their father.

At least she hadn't gone through with the face-lift he had been telling her she needed. He had used up her youth, taken her chance at an education, and destroyed her self confidence. Thank heaven she hadn't let him alter her face.

What was that saying about having the face you were born with at twenty and the one you had earned at forty? She sure as hell had earned hers.

The sound of a tumult brought her self-absorption to an end. From her position at the back of the conservatory, she looked toward the lectern to see which item had elicited the spontaneous outcry. A dozen people clustered in the middle of the red carpet, obscuring her view.

"Ladies and gentlemen," Monsieur Armand called out, waving his arms ineffectually.

What in the world could have gone wrong? Peach wondered, hurrying up the aisle. Suddenly the crowd parted to reveal a man on the floor. Her mother knelt at the man's head, cradling it in her lap. Peach heard a strangled sob and realized she had made the sound.

The man was her father.

His skin had a grayish tinge, his eyes had rolled back, and he groaned in pain. Every instinct urged Peach to race to his side. Instead she turned in the opposite direction, ran to the back of the room, found her purse and took out her cellular phone. Her trembling fingers punched in 911.

Later that day she would have no memory of making

the call, explaining the nature of the emergency, or giving her parents' address. The next thing she knew she was pushing through the dense throng to kneel at Blackjack's side.

"Get back," she commanded the gawkers. "My father needs air."

Armand stood a few feet away, wringing his hands. "Get these people out of here," she told him in a ringing tone that demanded instant obedience.

While Armand and his assistants shooed people from the conservatory, Bella and Peach loosened Blackjack's tie and unbuttoned his collar. Peach took off her jacket, folded it, and put it under his head.

There was nothing more she could do unless—God forbid—he stopped breathing. Then she could and would administer cardio-pulmonary resuscitation. Herbert had insisted she learn it along with the Heimlich maneuver when the twins were small. At least she had that much to thank him for.

"You're going to be just fine, darling," Bella crooned to Blackjack, then turned to Peach. "He complained of heartburn at breakfast. It's hard to imagine he'd get food poisoning from Guggenheim's smoked salmon but I can't think what else could be wrong."

Peach could. A heart attack could easily be mistaken for heartburn. She leaned down, took her father's wrist, and tried to take his pulse. Her hand shook so hard that it took her a minute to find it. Her own heart lurched at the thready, erratic beat.

"I called 911," she told Bella. "The paramedics should be here any minute."

Bella smoothed Blackjack's hair away from his sweat-slicked brow. "Are you all right, darling? Can I get you anything?"

"God, it hurts," Blackjack moaned.

Bella shook her head, as if to banish the sound of his pain. "I don't understand," she said to Peach. "Your father had a thorough physical last year. He was in perfect health."

Last year, he hadn't been under a strain that would fell a horse, Peach anguished. "I'm sure Dad's going to be all right."

Peach's prayers flew up to heaven. Her thoughts remained below with the man sprawled at her knees. *Don't die, please don't die. Don't leave me, Daddy,* her inner mind wailed. The wailing increased and she finally realized it was the sound of an emergency vehicle siren.

A minute later three young men in light blue shirts and dark trousers burst into the room, carrying boxes full of equipment. They didn't look old enough to know anything about emergency medical procedures, Peach despaired as she relinquished her place to one of them.

They worked quickly and expertly, getting Blackjack's vital signs, giving him oxygen and starting an I.V., talking in low voices all the while. Phrases like *ventricular fibrillation* and *the heart isn't perfusing* seeped into Peach's consciousness like an assassin slipping through an open door. Knowing what those words implied was something else she could thank Herbert for.

Her father's condition was serious.

Arye Rappaport was in his office—the one where Peach had first interviewed him—studying computer-generated layouts for the August issue of *Inside Texas*. The lead article recounted the multi-million dollar restoration of the Victorian era Rosenberg home in Galveston. Peach would be pleased, he thought, noting the stunning photographs.

A television set on the credenza spewed a talk show into the room. Arye played the portable television set all day, using the inane programming as white noise to screen out more intrusive sounds.

When he finished with the layouts, he looked up to see that Bill Balleza, a local news anchor, had replaced the story of men who cross dress while dating their secretaries, on the nine-inch screen. "Senator Morgan was stricken during the auction at his River Oaks estate," Balleza intoned with just the right note of concern. "Our on-scene reporter has told us the senator may have had a heart attack. He was taken by ambulance to the Houston Medical Center. Stay tuned to channel two for further developments."

For a second Arye flashed back to another news bulletin, the one announcing the car bombing that had killed his wife, and his knees went weak. He had been in his office then, too, working on the story that later garnered him a Pulitzer prize.

He had failed to safeguard one woman. Now he vowed he wouldn't fail another. His boss, Peach Morgan-Strand was probably drowning in a media maelstrom at this very moment.

He knew the drill, had taken part in it many times himself. Reporters would converge on the hospital from every Houston television station. Blackjack's illness, coupled with the political scandal, was news—the kind that could make a career.

A sick-bed photograph, an exclusive interview with family members, would be worth their weight in future bylines. In the quest for a scoop, reporters would interview orderlies, nurse's aides, even janitors if they couldn't talk to Peach and her mother. No detail from the doctor's prognosis to the contents of Blackjack's bedpan, would escape their scrutiny.

They would sneak onto the freight elevator or scurry up the back stairs, exploring every floor in search of the senator, as eager on the hunt as a pack of wild dogs. Arye had a vivid image of the bewildered look in Peach's eyes when one of them shoved a microphone in her face and asked the sort of questions that some reporters equated with doing a good job.

How did you feel when your father collapsed? What will you and your mother do if he dies? Do you blame Congress for your father's heart attack? In view of the scandal, wouldn't Senator Morgan be better off dead?

A shudder ran through Arye as he imagined Peach's wounded eyes, her trembling lips, her broken heart.

"Where are you going, Arye?" Cindy Downing, one of the copy editors called out as he hurried past her desk.

He didn't mind the familiarity. Every one at *Inside Texas* called him by his first name. Besides, he felt sorry for Cindy.

"To check out a story," he replied.

The office of *Inside Texas* was on the forty-fourth floor of the Allen Center in the financial heart of downtown Houston. He'd told Peach they ought to move—that their current quarters were expensive and inconvenient—that the staff spent almost as much time waiting for elevators as they did working at their desks.

He'd even found a one-story building on Westheimer that suited the magazine's needs. Peach had refused to look at it, though. Her father had offices in the Allen Center.

"If the location is good enough for a United States senator, it's good enough for the magazine," she told him with the sort of unreasoning logic that is born in the heart rather than the mind.

Peach loved her father beyond common sense. How she must be hurting now.

Arye reached the row of elevators and pushed the *down* button. By the time one of the cars arrived he was in a fever of impatience. On the way down he silently cursed every time it stopped to pick up other passengers—all of them he derisively thought of as *suits*.

Wearing his jeans, motorcycle jacket and cowboy boots, with his helmet under his arm, he knew he looked out of place. His motorcycle looked equally out of place in a parking lot full of expensive cars—but didn't give a damn.

Minutes later he raced his Harley along Smith, weaving in and out of the one-way traffic and wondering if his was a fool's errand. Would Peach welcome his arrival or regard it as an intrusion?

A sense of urgency he hadn't felt in years spurred him on. He couldn't remember the last time he had cared enough about anything or anyone to move at more than a fast walk. Yet here he was, breaking the speed limit because Peach's father had been taken to a hospital.

He barely knew Blackjack—and wasn't at all sure he'd missed much. The last year, the senator had been acting like a crusader for truth, honesty, and the American way. But Arye didn't think his transformation from one of the Senate's most accomplished pork-barrelers was anything more than a ploy for re-election in the current, *throw-the-bums-out,* political atmosphere.

To be honest, Arye didn't know Peach either. Aside from her giving a splendid Christmas party for the staff in her River Oaks mansion and her showing up at the office every few months—usually on her way to lunch—he never saw her.

Was it the sadness lurking in her eyes that drew him to her? A simple case of misery loves company? Did she even know she was unhappy—or had he misread her completely? Was she just another bored society wife? He'd spent a considerable amount of time in the small hours of the night pondering the answer.

As he approached the Medical Center the heavy traffic forced him to concentrate on his driving. He saw a pair of television trucks with thick antennas pointed skyward like phallic symbols, and he knew he'd reached the right building. He parked the Harley at an angle between them.

Like all hospitals, the building reeked of a nauseating combination of antiseptic and sickness. Ignoring the memories the smell invoked, Arye hurried to the reception desk.

"What room is Senator Morgan in?"

The approval in the woman's eyes as she studied his face belied her imperious tone. "A dozen others have asked the same question. If you're with the media, the hospital administrator is setting up a press room where you can wait for word on the senator's condition."

Years as an investigative reporter had taught Arye he could sweet-talk almost any woman into revealing what he needed to know—if he took the time. This afternoon he wasn't willing. Seeing so many members of the media increased his sense of urgency.

Retrieving his *Inside Texas* credentials from his wallet, he showed the card to the receptionist. "I work for the senator's daughter. She's expecting me. I suggest you tell me where she is."

Where there's life, there's hope.

Peach comforted herself with the tired cliché as she paced the intensive-care waiting room. The walls were buttercup yellow, the chairs and sofas upholstered in a cheerful plaid. However the decor couldn't offset the muted murmur of machines that kept people alive.

The doctor had told Peach that Blackjack's immediate access to appropriate treatment was in his favor. The senator was holding his own, he said after the initial examination. There had been no further word.

Was that good—or bad? Why didn't someone tell them something?

"Sit down, honey," Bella said from her place on the sofa. "Your pacing is making me even more nervous."

Peach collapsed beside her. "God, I wish I had a cigarette."

"You gave them up years ago. Why don't you call Herbert? You'll feel better once he's here." It was the third time Bella had asked that particular question.

"He's doing a mammaplasty."

"That's what you said this morning. He must be done by now. Really, darling, I'd like to have him here to oversee your father's treatment."

"For God's sake, he's a cosmetic surgeon, not a cardiologist," Peach burst out. Seeing the hurt in Bella's eyes, she wished she could swallow the sharp retort.

Just then, a nurse appeared in front of them as though she had materialized out of thin air.

"Is my father . . . ?" Peach asked.

Her voice faded away. She couldn't bring the sentence to its logical, *is my father dead?* conclusion.

"Your father's condition hasn't changed," the nurse was mercifully quick to reply. "A man who claims to be your managing editor is downstairs."

Peach's mouth gaped open. Arye? Here? Whatever for?

Herbert Strand hadn't been so relaxed in months. Asking for a divorce had been the right thing to do, he assured himself, even if the timing hadn't been ideal. He'd won his tennis match, the mammaplasty had gone off without a hitch and two patients who had come into the office that afternoon for check-ups had opted for more surgery.

He plucked the next patient's file from the rack on the examining door, paused a moment to read the name on the frontispiece, then smiled with satisfaction. Clotilde Dysnowski was one of his triumphs. Another good omen, he mused as he opened the examining room door and walked in.

He'd performed a series of cosmetic surgeries on her, beginning with a rhinoplasty, then moving on to cheek and chin implants and a blepharoplasty. Last, but far from least, he performed a mammaplasty on her three months ago. The results had been spectacular. He'd transformed the proverbial sow's ear into a silk purse.

He found her sitting on the edge of the examining table, swinging her legs. For a second she reminded him of a bored little girl—but only for a second. No one could look into her eyes and think about youth.

"How are you today?" he asked, studying her face for telltale signs of unfortunate complications such as migrating implants.

Her legs stilled. "Fine."

He took her chin in his hand and turned her head, examining his handiwork close up. He was a genius. No one, looking at this woman, would ever guess the extent of the changes he had wrought.

He backed off, made a few entries in her chart, then turned back to her. "How do your breasts feel?"

She began unbuttoning her blouse. "See for yourself, doctor."

He was quite accustomed to women coming on to him. However he suspected that wasn't the case this time. Miss Dysnowski had spoken of a man in her life with obvious adoration. As the blouse slid down her arms, she thrust her shoulders back to better display a perfect pair of 36-C's.

"I thought I told you to wear a brassiere," he said.

"I don't need one."

She was right. He had outdone himself, he thought, keeping his features immobile as he examined her breasts visually and then manually.

Her nipples firmed at his touch. Clotilde Dysnowski was hot to trot. "Have you experienced any of the side effects we discussed before the surgery?"

She gave him a confident smile. "Not one. I've never felt better."

He took a last look, noting the perfect symmetry

nature could never match. "You can get dressed now. When you're finished, I'd like to see you in my office."

"Is something wrong?"

"I want to talk to you about something."

"I'm not shy, doctor. I don't mind talking while I get dressed."

"Very well, Miss Dysnowski. How would you feel about accompanying me to a medical symposium in a few months?"

She gave him an incredulous look. "I'm not that kind of girl. Besides, I'm in love with someone else."

"And I'm not that sort of physician, Miss Dysnowski. I plan to use you as an example of my work."

Her entire expression changed. "Doc, I don't let anyone *use* me."

Damn all stubborn, opinionated woman. He really did want to show her off to his colleagues, though. "The convention is in Palm Springs. Have you ever been there, Miss Dysnowski? It's quite lovely, to say nothing of luxurious. I wouldn't require much of your time. In return you'd be getting an all-expense-paid, five-day vacation in the sun capital of the country."

"I don't know. My boyfriend might not like it."

"Perhaps he could get time off and travel with you? You don't need to make up your mind now. I'll have my secretary get in touch with you in a few weeks."

He walked out the door without giving her a chance to respond. After she'd had the chance to picture herself vacationing in Palm Springs, he had no doubt what her answer would be.

Miss Dysnowski had been his last patient. He had lots of time to pick up his clothes at home before going out to dinner, he decided as he opened the door to his private office.

He stripped off the long white coat he wore during office hours, picked up the phone and was about to dial his home number when he heard a knock on the door.

"Who is it?" he called out.

His office manager cracked the door open. "Do you have a moment, Doctor?"

"Make it brief," he replied curtly.

"I'm afraid I have bad news. Your father-in-law, Senator Morgan, has had a heart attack."

"Did my wife call?"

The bookkeeper shook her head. "I heard the news on television when I was on my break. Senator Morgan has been taken to the Medical Center. Do you want me to call over there and check on—"

"I'll handle it myself," Herbert replied, dismissing the woman with a nod.

Hell! He wouldn't be able to get his clothes today after all.

Arye knew a death watch when he saw one. Peach and her mother might not have admitted it yet but everything about them—their pallor, the dazed expression in their eyes, their hunched posture—told him Blackjack wasn't going to make it.

"What are you doing here?" Peach asked.

"I heard about your father and thought you might need help handling the media."

She looked dazed. "The media?"

"There are two television trucks in front of the hospital right now and a dozen reporters in the lobby. If someone doesn't give them a statement soon, they're going to start looking for you and your mother."

Peach grew even paler. "Why can't they just leave us alone?"

"Getting the news is their business."

"I can't talk to them now."

"I'll be happy to do it for you—unless Dr. Strand would rather do it himself."

Where the hell was the arrogant bastard? Anyone could see how much Peach needed him.

"That's a very kind offer," Bella Morgan interjected. "I was going to telephone my husband's executive assistant, Randolph Spurling, and ask him to fly in from Washington to handle the press. But he wouldn't get here for hours."

"How is the senator?"

"They tell us he's holding his own—whatever that means." Despair thinned Peach's voice. "We're only allowed to see him ten minutes every hour."

"Can I get the two of you anything? Coffee perhaps?"

Peach shook her head. "Not for me. It's almost time to visit Dad again."

"I couldn't swallow a thing either," Bella agreed.

"While you're visiting with the senator, I could see about setting up a press conference," Arye said. He found himself wishing he'd put on a suit and tie that morning instead of jeans. However, emergencies didn't have a dress code.

"Would you want us to be there?" Peach quavered.

He had an irrational impulse to take her in his arms. She obviously needed someone to cling to.

He wished he could mouth the platitudes people had said to him when him when Helen died. *It's all for the best. God works in mysterious ways. Your wife is at peace.*

Forget the damn platitudes, he told himself. They hadn't done him a bit of good and he doubted they would make Peach or Bella feel better either. They needed concrete help, not empty words.

"You don't need to talk to the press at all. If you like, I'll issue a statement as your family spokesman." He checked his watch. "Right now all the press wants is a few words for the five o'clock news."

Bella Morgan gazed down at her husband, shocked at how quickly illness had ravaged his features. He looked smaller and more defenseless than she'd ever seen him look. His flesh seemed to have melted away. He had an intravenous tube in one arm and wires attached to his chest. Oxygen flowed into his nostrils from a clear plastic tube.

This morning she'd been thinking how ironic it was that he finally needed her. She took his hand and lowered her cheek to his, feeling the rasp of his whiskers. He used to complain about having to shave twice a day on the campaign trail. She would give anything to hear him complain again—about anything.

His eyes slitted open. "Is that you, Bella?"

"Yes, darling."

"Are you and Peach all right?"

"We're fine. Don't talk. You need to save your strength."

"This may be our last chance."

Blackjack's words pierced Bella's mind like a mallet-driven spike. A migraine erupted behind her eyes. "The doctors say you're doing fine."

"The doctors don't know jack-shit." The warmth in Blackjack's eyes softened his barbed answer. He squeezed her hand. "I'm dying, Bella. I saw it enough in Vietnam to know it's my turn. There's so much I regret, so much I wish I hadn't done. I've been a bastard most of my life—but there's one thing I wouldn't change. When I stand at the gates of heaven to be judged, the only thing I'll say in my defense is that a good woman loved me."

He wanted to tell Bella more but the little he'd already said had left him panting. His feet felt so cold they seemed to belong to a corpse.

So much to do. So much Bella needed to know. He had to try and tell her.

"Jean—" he rasped.

A searing pain cut off the rest of the words. He felt as if something deep in his chest had broken.

Humpty-dumpty sat on a wall. Humpty-dumpty took a great fall. All the king's horses and all the king's men couldn't put Humpty-dumpty together again.

He didn't realize he'd muttered a few words of the old nursery rhyme until Bella said, "Darling, it's me, your wife."

Damn, he had no control over his body and now he was losing control of his mind, too. He had a horrible vision of Carroll Detweiler, the Vietnamese vet he had used and cruelly cast aside, beckoning from the gates to hell. A ferocious wild hog stood beside Detweiler, gnashing its fearsome tusks.

"No," Blackjack moaned. "Not that. God, not that. I've changed. I'm not the same man."

The sound of Bella's voice pulled him back from the edge of eternity. "What is it, Blackjack?" she asked urgently. "Shall I call a nurse?"

"Not the nurse. Only you. The book is in the jewels," he muttered with the last of his strength.

Bella bit her lip to keep from crying out. Blackjack was talking such nonsense.

She didn't realize Peach had come into the room until she felt Peach's hand on her shoulder. "How is he?" Peach asked softly.

"He's delirious," Bella whispered. "He called out for someone named Jean and then said something about jewels in a book."

"Does he know anyone named Jean?"

"A Jean Sinclair used to be on his staff—but we haven't seen her for years." Bella gazed off into nothingness as a feeling of unreality swept over her. She couldn't tell Peach about Jean. Not now. Not ever.

"I'll sit with Dad for a while. Try and get some rest. Arye's setting up the press conference. The waiting room is empty."

"I don't want to sleep. I'm going to ask the nurse to page the doctors. There must be something more they can do for your father." Bella got up, relinquished her chair to Peach, and hastened from the room.

She's so strong, Peach thought with awe, wishing she were more like her mother. Bella had withstood months of public humiliation with a brave smile while Peach had fallen apart this morning after a single blow.

For the next couple of minutes the only sound in the room was the beep of Blackjack's heart monitor. It comforted Peach. *While there's life, there's hope,* she told herself again, mesmerized by the rise and fall of her father's chest. Despite everything he was still the handsomest man she'd ever seen—with the exception of Arye.

The realization took Peach by surprise. Her managing editor looked better in faded jeans this afternoon than Herbert ever had in black tie. She shuddered at the errant thought, one she had no right to consider, especially at a time like this.

She couldn't seem to dismiss Arye from her mind, though. Did he go through life practicing random acts of kindness—or had some other motive brought him to the hospital? She'd been waiting for the day when he would ask permission to do a story about her father. Had that day come?

She banished the suspicion as quickly as it had appeared. Arye had held out a lifeline. She had no choice but to grab it. How terrible to think she was forced to rely on an employee's help while her own husband—who surely had heard the news of Blackjack's heart attack by now—didn't have the decency to put in an appearance.

Suddenly Blackjack's eyes opened wide and he smiled at her. "Peach, give me your hand."

He looked so alert and his grip felt so strong. It had to be a good sign. "The doctors said you weren't to talk."

"I have to. There's so much to say. I told your mother I intended to confound my enemies. I still can, with your help."

"I'll do anything you want after you get better. Right now that's the only thing you should be thinking about."

Blackjack's grip tightened. He seemed to be hanging on for dear life. Although Peach concentrated on him, she was peripherally aware that the sound of his heart monitor had changed.

"Peach, listen to me."

"I'm listening, Dad."

Blackjack reared up. The sudden motion upset his I.V. and it crashed to the floor with a clang. "Don't let the bastards get away with it," he commanded, sounding just like his old self.

Then he fell back and the monitor emitted a shrill alarm. Peach turned to look at the screen and saw that Blackjack's heart line had gone flat. She heard footsteps pounding down the hall. The door burst open and a nurse pushed a cart into the room. A man Peach took to be a doctor arrived on the nurse's heels.

Two more staff members rushed in. One of them tugged Peach from her chair and unceremoniously thrust her out the door. Peach turned to take one last look at her father but all she could see was the white-clad cadre surrounding his bed.

Three

Peach and Bella perched on the edge of the waiting room sofa, clutching each other's hands, too enervated to sit back, let alone relax. Peach felt as if they'd been frozen in place for eternity. The wall clock told her it had only been fifteen minutes.

Her heart and soul, hopes and prayers, were riveted on Blackjack's door and what was happening behind it. Her last glimpse of the room had been burned into her brain. If she closed her eyes she could relive it all. The frantic activity, the urgent commands, the indistinguishable figures dressed in white, were the stuff of nightmares.

Without warning the door opened as silently as doors do in dreams. The white-clad medical cadre came out. One of them, a doctor, she supposed, despite his youth, walked into the waiting room looking as solemn as an altar boy serving at his first Mass.

Peach knew what he was going to say before he opened his mouth. She clenched her hands, steeling herself to hear the words.

"Are you the senator's family?" he asked.

"I'm Bella Morgan and this is my daughter, Peach Morgan-Strand," Bella replied. Even *in extremis,* she behaved like a disciplined political wife.

The doctor was under no such constraint. He didn't bother to introduce himself. "I'm afraid I have very bad news. Senator Morgan passed away a few minutes ago. We did everything we could to save him but his heart had already suffered massive damage. He never had a chance."

The young physician might be trying to strike a note of sympathy. To Peach, he sounded more like he was trying to ward off a malpractice suit.

"Where is my husband's personal doctor?" Bella asked, her voice surprisingly firm.

"There wasn't time to call him," the young doctor replied. "However, if you'd like . . ."

"There's no reason to bother him now, is there?" Bella asked, a trace of hope still evident in her voice.

The doctor shook his head.

"I can't believe Blackjack's dead. He was so full of life this morning. We were talking about the future," Bella said to no one in particular. "He had plans to clear his name. You know, he wasn't the sort of man to give up."

"Would you like to see him?" the doctor asked.

Bella nodded. "Perhaps if I do I'll be able to believe he's really gone."

Peach had no trouble believing it. She had been with her father when it happened. Her mother was right about one thing, though. Blackjack hadn't let go of life easily. His face had twisted in an angry rictus when death made its final assault. She would never forget that look. Never.

"I'll wait here," she said.

As Bella and the doctor disappeared, Peach heard someone coming down the hall. Please don't let it be a reporter, she thought. She wasn't ready to deal with the press.

Arye walked into the waiting room, bringing reminders of the outside world with him. "I just gave an impromptu press conference. The reporters left to file their stories and have supper, but they'll be back."

Peach swallowed a sob. It lodged so tight in her throat she could barely push words out past it. "They'll get the story they've been waiting for. Dad's dead."

Arye crossed the floor, lifted her up from the sofa and pulled her into his arms. Had he read her mind? She desperately needed to feel the warmth of a living human being.

She trembled and he pulled her even closer. "I'm so sorry, Peach. I know exactly what you're feeling."

For a second she wondered what Herbert would think if he walked in on them. Then realizing that what Herbert thought no longer mattered, she stayed put. So many months had passed since her husband had held her in either love or lust, she'd almost forgotten the comfort that two strong arms and a solid male body conveyed.

"Cry it out," Arye said, pressing her head against his chest.

Despite her grief, the tears wouldn't come. She must have cried herself out earlier that day. Intuition told her Arye would be sympathetic, kind, and understanding—all the things a woman needed when her world had collapsed like a sand castle in a rising tide— if she told him about Herbert.

Arye felt so alive, with his breath on her hair and his heart beating against her own, he almost succeeded in banishing the specter of death hovering in the room. She clung to that life, pressing her breasts against the muscled wall of his chest, nudging her hips between his powerful thighs.

She was startled and terribly ashamed to realize she wanted Arye. In the biblical sense. Had she lost her mind along with everything else?

Thank heaven there was nothing sexual in his response to her. He acted like a brother—not a would-be lover—and a younger brother at that, she thought, as his hands kneaded the tension from her neck and shoulders.

"I'm here for you as long as you need me," he said.

She huddled in the temporary haven of his arms, letting the depleted reservoir of her will recharge until she had enough stamina to move away. Doing so seemed to take more energy than mother nature needed to move continental plates. Not until a good three feet separated them did she feel free of the force-field urging her back into his arms.

Arye was shaken by the raw need he had felt while holding Peach. For God's sake, she'd just lost her father. She needed to be comforted, not seduced. Besides, she was married—and he'd never played no-tell motel games. Where the hell was that husband of hers?

"Why are you looking at me like that?" she asked. "I really am all right."

"I'm sorry. I didn't mean to stare."

He could have told her she was fooling herself—that months would pass before she was anywhere near *all right*. He could have recounted the stages of grief— from disbelief to anger to despair to acceptance—in infinite detail.

"Where's your mother?" he asked.

"She's with my father. She wanted to say goodbye."

"And you?"

"I'd rather remember him the way he was this morning, before all of this—" Peach's voice trailed off.

He wished she would cry instead of being so damn brave. She needed the release of tears.

"I've never lost anyone close to me before," she murmured. "I don't know what to do—about the arrangements."

Arye had a firsthand acquaintance with the *pro forma* of sudden death—the thousand and one choices you had to make when you weren't in any condition to make any of them.

"You don't need to do anything tonight," he assured her. "The hospital will take care of your father. You should be thinking about yourself. You look exhausted."

His solicitude almost broke through the wall Peach had erected between herself and the day's events. Tears pooled in her eyes and she knuckled them away. She didn't dare give in to her bereavement. If she started to weep, she didn't think she'd be able to stop.

The door to Blackjack's room swung open and Bella came out. She had walked into that room under her own power. Now she staggered. Arye leapt to her side, scooped her up before she could fall, carried her back to the sofa and set her down as gently as Peach's sons had in high school when they practiced parenting skills with a raw egg.

"I don't know what's the matter with me," Bella said, looking at him. "My legs feel like spaghetti."

"No wonder. You've been through a long and terrible ordeal," Arye replied.

The doctor was scribbling something on a pad and handed it to Arye. Obviously, in the absence of any other man, the doctor took Arye to be the person in charge.

"I suggest you take the ladies home," he said. "This is a prescription for a sedative. It will help them get a good night's sleep."

Arye folded the paper and tucked it in his shirt pocket.

"I would like to go home." Bella let go a brittle laugh. "Of course, I don't really have a home anymore."

It was the first time Peach had heard her sound the least bit sorry for herself.

"You'll always have a home with me," Peach assured her. But what home and for how long, considering her own circumstances, Peach didn't know. Perhaps the two of them would wind up moving into the apartment her parents had rented.

"You will take good care of my husband, won't you?" Bella asked the doctor.

"We'll give him the very best care, Mrs. Morgan."

Bella's gaze darted around the room as though she still couldn't believe what had happened in the short time she'd spent there. "I suppose it's time to go."

Peach exchanged a glance with Arye over Bella's head, then positioned herself on one side of Bella while Arye took his place on the other. Between them, they helped her to her feet.

"We had better use the freight elevator. I don't want the two of you to run into reporters," Arye said. "I'll be happy to drive you home if one of you has a car. I rode over on my cycle."

"My Jaguar is in the lot," Peach replied.

Arye repressed a shudder. He didn't own a Harley because he was a weekend warrior suffering from grandiose visions of himself as Easy Rider. He rode a Harley because he needed a way to get around that didn't make him break out in a cold sweat.

Since the car bombing that killed his wife, he suffered from terrible claustrophobia every time he got in an automobile. Given a choice he'd tell the ladies to take a cab and follow them on the bike. But he couldn't send the walking wounded home that way— and the two women were as wounded as any injured soldier he'd seen during the Gulf War.

When they reached the Jaguar, Arye gritted his teeth, held out his hand, and asked for the keys.

The ride to River Oaks took twenty minutes. Peach spent most of it gazing out the window at a landscape that suddenly seemed so foreign, she suspected she'd have gotten lost if she'd been at the wheel. Bella seemed to be dozing and Arye had the good sense not to make meaningless small talk. When Peach looked his way, she couldn't help noticing that his jaws were clenched, as if he were in the grip of some powerful emotion.

She didn't remind him to stop to fill the prescription on the way home. She didn't need to. Herbert kept the medicine cabinet in his dressing room stocked with enough Valium, Prozac, and sleeping pills to put Kevorkian out of business.

Her home looked so normal when Arye pulled up in the circular drive that for a second, the entire day seemed like a bad dream. The lawn had been freshly mowed. Impatiens, begonias, and gazanias blossomed in tidy beds. The windows gleamed from their weekly cleaning.

It was, by any standard, a handsome house. A pretentious one, too. It clearly said its owners had *arrived*. Peach's opinion of it had always been influenced by Herbert's unbridled enthusiasm. Now, her view underwent a sea change.

Nothing about the house, from its *faux* French architecture to its *faux* stone facing to its *faux* slate roof, rang true. As it turned out, her marriage had been *faux*, too.

"If you'll tell me which room is your mother's, I'll help her there," Arye said as Peach unlocked the front door.

She nodded, then led the way to the spacious guest suite on the ground floor. By prearrangment, her parents' luggage had already been delivered.

Peach had so wanted her mother and father to feel welcome. She had asked her maid Delia to unpack for them before she left. Now, Peach saw that the everthoughtful Delia had left a pair of her father's pajamas on the bed beside her mother's nightie. Peach snatched it up and stuffed it in a drawer before Bella could see it.

"If you'll wait for me in the den," she told Arye, "I'll join you in a few minutes. The bar is fully stocked. Help yourself to a drink."

"You don't need to help me get undressed," Bella said after Arye was gone. "I'm not an invalid. But I would like something to put me to sleep."

"It's only seven. Don't you want to eat first?"

"I just want to go to sleep, honey—and the sooner the better."

When Peach returned with a sleeping pill and a glass of water, Bella was already in bed. Bella took the pill, swallowed it, and closed her eyes.

Peach closed the drapes, pulled a chair up to the bed and took her mother's hand. She waited until her mother's even respirations told her she was asleep, then tiptoed from the room. On her way to the den she made a mental list of all the things she had to do before she too could seek the oblivion of sleep.

She had to talk to her younger sister Avery, in London before Avery heard about their father's death from a stranger. Avery would undoubtedly want to rush back to Houston for the funeral, but there was no point in endangering her already high-risk pregnancy.

Next, Peach would telephone the twins at Old Miss where the two of them had just started summer school. Although she longed to see them, nothing would be gained from their leaving the campus. She would tell them to stay in class, work hard and keep up their grades. She wouldn't tell them about the divorce, though. Their grandfather's death was all the bad news they needed to handle for the time being.

There were friends to notify, Blackjack's staff to be contacted, an obituary to write, funeral plans to be made. She had never faced so many decisions without a man by her side.

A tiny part of her felt liberated.

The rest of her felt lost.

The den, all mellow paneling and masculine furniture, had been the scene of high-spirited parties when the twins were growing up. As Peach walked in she listened for an echo of their happy voices—and only heard the anxious beat of her own heart.

Arye stood by the French doors, a sweating bottle of Dos Equis in one hand and a framed photograph of Peach and Herbert taken on their wedding day in the other. He seemed oblivious to Peach's arrival until she touched his shoulder.

He put the picture down and turned to face her. "You were a beautiful bride."

"It was a long time ago."

"Not that long. You're still a very beautiful woman."

Peach wasn't accustomed to compliments. She didn't know what to say.

Arye's voice pierced the silence. "Can I get you a drink—or would you rather wait until your husband comes home."

She wasn't accustomed to solicitude either. "That would be a very long wait. He asked me for a divorce this morning. I don't even know where he's staying."

She had no idea what made her blurt it out like that—or why she felt a compulsion to confide in Arye. For the last three years their exchanges had been polite, businesslike, and even contentious when he tried to get her to move the magazine to another office. She wasn't even sure they were friends.

Arye put the Dos Equis down on the nearest table with such force that she thought the bottle would break. He looked so angry she took an involuntary step backward.

"The bastard deserves—oh hell, never mind what he deserves. He sure as hell doesn't deserve you."

Arye moved so close she could feel his body heat. Was he going to take her in his arms again? Did she want him to?

"So you're free," he said huskily.

"I suppose that's one way to look at it," she replied cautiously, looking up at him.

She had read books where time stood still but never expected to experience the sensation. Now, as her gaze locked with Arye's, she lost all awareness of the passage of time. Perhaps a minute passed, perhaps ten before he spoke again.

"I've wanted to kiss you for a long time, boss lady. I know this isn't the best time—hell, it's a terrible time—but I can't wait any longer."

Arye didn't know why this woman made him say, do, and feel things he never thought to say, do, and feel again. He only knew he was going to kiss her long and hard, until both of them forgot all the terrible things that had happened in their lives.

He gave her a last chance to voice an objection, then closed the distance between them, cupped her head in one hand, the small of her back in the other, and pulled her against him.

Her lips were as soft as he had imagined, her mouth as sweet, her body as ripe. To his intense pleasure, she didn't pull away. Was it shock that rooted her in place—or something else?

He knew he ought to back off.

He knew he was taking unconscionable advantage of her distress.

He knew he deserved to be tarred and feathered for what he was doing.

He knew all those things—and didn't give a damn. Peach had stolen into his dreams far too often the last three years. He was only stealing a single kiss.

He didn't fool himself that her seeming acquiescence had a hell of a lot to do with him. She had been wounded twice today, first by her husband's departure and then by her father's death. She was just reaching out to life in the way of beleaguered females from time immemorial.

He ached with the need to take more than a kiss—to

spill the very essence of life inside her. He pictured himself lowering her to the floor, ripping away her lingerie, freeing his erection and thrusting into her as far as he could reach.

The image was so compelling that he groaned his desire into her open mouth. Every instinct told him she wouldn't resist. Damn! If he kept on kissing her this way she would probably take off her clothes without being asked. But she would never forgive him.

More important, he would never forgive himself. Peach Morgan-Strand had all the trouble she could handle right now.

Grasping both her shoulders, he gently but firmly pushed her away. "Forgive me. I shouldn't have done that."

We did it together and it was wonderful, Peach wanted to say. Her cheeks flamed at the thought. For a few sublime moments, she had allowed herself to forget who she was. It must never happen again.

"I'm the one who should apologize. I was very needy just now. I'm terribly sorry."

"You've been through hell today. Please don't be embarrassed on my account."

Embarrassed? She wished the floor would swallow her up so she wouldn't have to face him anymore. She drew in a ragged breath, then smoothed her rumpled dress. "I'm going to have that drink. Would you like another beer?" she asked with all the *savoire faire* at her command, as though he were just another guest.

Hypocrite and idiot were a few of the names she called herself as she hurried behind the bar, bent down and opened the refrigerator, hoping the chilled air inside it would cool her heated skin.

She had never reacted to Herbert's kisses the way

she had to Arye's, never felt her bones melt along with her scruples, not even on those nights when a glass of wine suppressed her inhibitions.

But then, Herbert had never kissed her the way Arye had. Germs terrified Herbert. He didn't believe in exchanging saliva.

The sound of Arye's voice broke into her bizarre introspection. "I'll take a rain check on the beer. I'd better go. I have things to do."

Undoubtedly those things involved a shapely female, Peach thought with a jealous twinge—and immediately excoriated herself for thinking it. What Arye did and who he did it with were none of her business. He was too young, too good-looking, too sexy, too damn everything for a bereft middle-aged, soon-to-be divorcée like her.

She was grateful to him for one thing, though. At least she'd stopped thinking about her father for a few minutes. Now the memory of his death came rushing back like the tide. The pain of loss came with it.

Summoning what little dignity she could under the circumstances, she straightened up in time to see Arye heading for the door.

Halfway across the room, he stopped and turned to face her. "The press will be camped on your doorstep by morning. I wouldn't even go out for the paper if I were you."

"I was hoping they would leave us alone, now Daddy's gone."

"Not a chance." He paused and his eyes met hers. "If you like, I'll come back to help you deal with them."

If she liked?

She would like it much too much.

She wanted him there—for his expertise, she told herself, until the troublesome voice of truth that dwelled in the back of her mind put in its own two cents. She would have wanted him there if he didn't know a damn thing about the vagaries of the media.

She opened her mouth to tell him she could handle the press without any help, thank you, and was astonished to hear herself saying, "You left your motorcycle at the hospital. You can take my Jaguar tonight and bring it back in the morning."

Jean Sinclair returned to her Annapolis town house at seven, fed her two cats, then put a low-calorie frozen dinner in the microwave. She was a tall, slender, handsome woman whose upright posture and generous smile made her seem younger than her sixty years.

She ate quickly, took off her suit and put on a nightie, creamed her face, and sat down in her favorite chair with a new novel. She loved police procedurals and enjoyed shocking her friends by referring to them as *big dick books*. This one, by Robert Daley, quickly captured her attention. She was oblivious to time's passage until the phone rang after ten.

The lateness of the call startled Jean. No one ever telephoned her at this hour. The caller turned out to be a long-term employee at Jean's resume business.

After a quick exchange of pleasantries, the woman said, "Have you heard the news?"

Jean seldom listened to television. Having spent twenty years as a Washington staffer, she knew only too well how the establishment could manipulate what passed for information.

"What news?"

"You used to work for Senator Morgan, didn't you?"

"Years ago," Jean replied cautiously. Her heart skipped a beat. Dear God. Had someone found out what she—what *they'd* been doing?

"He just died. I thought you'd want to know—so you could send flowers or something," the caller concluded lamely.

Clearly, she was the sort of busybody who enjoyed being the bearer of bad news. Jean made a mental note to find a way to get rid of her—and the sooner the better, although it was almost impossible to fire anyone these days without being accused of some form of discrimination.

"That's very kind of you," Jean replied, being careful not to reveal the surge of emotion coursing through her.

She didn't give in to tears until she said good-bye. Then, putting the telephone back in its cradle, she buried her head in her hands and wept. Poor dear Blackjack.

She had known he would be the love of her life from the moment she walked into his offices on the Hill a quarter of a century ago. Their affair had lasted four years. She'd had a few other men afterward. But then, realizing none of them compared, she had given up on men altogether. Cats were a lot easier.

It had broken her heart to watch Blackjack being corrupted by power and money like so many of his peers. She'd been so sure he was better than that. She had almost refused when he telephoned last year and asked her to dinner, suggesting they meet at an out-of-the-way restaurant.

But she'd never been able to refuse him anything. For the remainder of the day she'd been foolish enough to let herself believe he might want to resume their affair. However, what he wanted proved to be even more astonishing.

Drying her eyes, she got up and with faltering steps, made her way to the small office at the back of the house and opened the safe Blackjack had bought when they began working together. She hadn't touched the four-inch-thick manuscript and the computer disks since typing the last chapter three weeks ago. As far as she knew, their existence was a secret. Blackjack had made her swear not to mention the book to anyone until he talked to a literary agent.

Did he ever have the chance?

She picked up the neatly piled pages and placed them on top of the desk. They lay there, as potentially lethal as a coiled viper. She broke into a cold sweat. What in the world was she supposed to do with them now?

Would Bella or one of the girls get in touch with her in a few days and ask for the manuscript? If they didn't should she call them—or should she just destroy everything and let sleeping dogs lie?

What would Blackjack want her to do?

He had put his heart, his soul, his knowledge of the ins and outs of government, on those pages. He called it his *secret weapon*. Jean glanced at the title page. It read "The Politics of Greed." If the book found its way into print it would shake the Beltway down to its lobby-ridden foundation.

Similar books had been written in the past but the authors were all reporters or members of think tanks. This was the first book of its kind to be written by a ranking senator. That's what made it so damaging, so dangerous. Blackjack had exposed it all, the corruption, the misused power, the wasted money, the be-hind-closed-doors deals that had made a mockery of so-called reform.

If she had an iota of sense she'd put the manuscript through a shredder and forget all about it. But she'd never had any sense where Blackjack was concerned. With a resigned shrug, she put the pages back into the safe and locked the door. There it would reside until someone asked for it, or until she herself died. Whichever came first.

She turned out the lights, walked to the window and gazed out on the back garden of her two-hundred-year-old home. Normally the feeling of history—the juxtaposition of past and present outside the window—gave her a sense of peace.

Tonight though, she felt uneasy. There was a hydra-headed monster loose in the nation's capital—a monster composed of greed, money, and unbridled power. Blackjack had hoped to help rein in that monster—and had paid for it with his reputation, his fortune, and his health.

For the first time since Blackjack reappeared in her life, she was glad her own was winding down. She had lost more than a former lover today. She had lost her hope in the future.

Peach looked in on her mother after Arye left, then went to the library to make the first of many telephone calls. She sat down behind the cherrywood desk where she usually wrote thank-you notes or addressed invi-tations, saw the message recorder's urgent blink and switched it to replay. Tucked amid the many expressions of condolence and requests for interviews, she heard a familiar voice.

"Peach, this is Herbert. I heard about your father. Under the circumstances, I thought it best to keep my distance. If you need me I've taken a room at the Houstonian. I left so hurriedly this morning that I don't have a thing to wear. I hope you didn't forget to ask Delia to pack my clothes. I'll have someone pick them up in the morning. Oh, yes, give your mother my sympathy."

Peach gagged at his unctuous tone. If he had been there she would have found a way to do him bodily harm. It took a considerable act of will to put her anger aside and dial Avery's London number.

By the time Avery answered, Peach was in control of her emotions. She stayed that way through a dozen conversations no matter how upset the person sounded on the other end of the line.

An hour and a half later, her preliminary calls complete and a pad filled with notes and reminders, Peach took a pair of scissors from the desk and made her way upstairs to Herbert's dressing room. The lingering scent of Herbert's cologne almost made her gag. Tomorrow she would ask Delia to air the room out.

Scissors in hand, she opened the door to his walk-in closet and turned on the light. Herbert adored clothes and had a penchant for expensive designers. Suits, sport jackets and trousers labeled Armani, Oliver by Valentino, and Comme des Garcons, adorned the padded hangers. Rows of custom-made shirts—all Egyptian or Pima cotton—hung opposite them. His ties were all silk and equally expensive. Herbert only wore natural fibers. He would sooner die than be caught in polyester.

Peach opened and closed the scissors just once before going to work with a will. She cut the jackets and shirts off at the elbow, the trousers at the knee, and snipped several inches from each tie. Sweaters were unraveled, underwear and pajamas slashed at the crotch. It was revenge in its purest form.

The surgery took one hour and the packing another. When she finished, she manhandled Herbert's luggage downstairs and left it outside by the front door.

Four

Cindy Downing stood nude before one of the full-length mirrors in her studio apartment, a look of rapt concentration on her face as she ran her hands over her breasts. Would he know? Could he tell the difference between silicone and flesh?

She decided that the twin globes felt as real as though they had always been part of her body. Her gaze lowered to her flat abdomen and the carefully waxed black bush between her thighs. She looked sexy, definitely sexy. Diet, exercise and financial sacrifice, had transformed her from the Pillsbury dough girl to a *Playboy* centerfold.

She was far more attractive now at thirty-five than she'd been at eighteen or twenty. Why, her own mother wouldn't recognize her—if she made the mistake of visiting the old hag.

How dare Dr. Strand take all the credit, as though her only contribution to her transformation had been to pay his exorbitant bills? Strand had merely filled the prescription she had written, giving her Geena Davis's chin, Sophia Loren's cheekbones, and Michelle Pfeiffer's nose.

Cindy had asked him to replicate his wife's eyes and he had succeeded to a point, matching their slightly almond shape. It had been up to Cindy to match their unique color. A half-a-dozen contact lenses ranging from gray through blue to emerald green did the job.

She took the gray lenses from the case on the dresser, leaned into the mirror—a movement that made her breasts sway enticingly—put the lenses in place, and her natural muddy brown vanished. The grey lenses made her look more intelligent, she decided, the green ones sexier, the blue younger.

She spent the next half hour putting on makeup, accentuating her new bony structure with three shades of foundation and two of blush. Four different shadows contoured her eyes. Four coats of mascara enhanced her lashes. She never wore false ones. They looked so artificial. Then she spent another fifteen minutes on her ebony hair, teasing and hot-curling it into a soft frame for her face.

When she finished, the woman reflected in the mirror wasn't the one she had known most of her adult life. Clotilde Dysnowski, that sorry specimen from a small town in Nebraska, had been completely erased. In her place stood Cindy Downing—up-and-coming copy editor and resident computer whiz at *Inside Texas*. And she owed it all to Arye.

It had begun with him. It had to end with him.

Had to.

She had fallen madly in love with Arye when Peach Morgan-Strand first brought him to her desk and introduced him as the new managing editor of *Inside Texas*. His gaze had flickered over her so quickly she might as well have been invisible.

Oh, he'd been polite enough—Arye was always polite. After that first meeting, he never fumbled for her name the way other new acquaintances did. But every time she saw him—and she'd made a point of doing it as often as possible—he seemed to be looking around her or through her rather than right at her.

Not that she blamed him. The man hadn't been born who enjoyed looking at her. The few times she'd made love the room had been dark and her partners never called again to ask for seconds. But Arye's lack of interest had hurt her more than all those rejections.

She'd lived with it until her nerves felt hamburger-raw. One year to the day after Arye came to work at *Inside Texas,* a voice in her ear had told her she had the power to change the situation, to change herself, to become the sort of woman he would notice—and want.

She put in for her vacation, spent it having a nose job, and paid for it by selling her new car and buying a clunker. She didn't realize how easily fooled, how gullible the magazine staff was until she returned to her job and her coworkers accepted the explanation that her residual bruises resulted from an automobile accident.

Three more surgeries had followed—and she kept all of them secret. Each time she returned to work looking better, she heard the same dumb questions. Had she changed her hair style? Was she wearing new makeup? Had she been to a spa?

After the boob job the girls in the office wanted to know if she was wearing the new wonder bra. Stupid bitches. She flexed her fingers and smiled as she imagined raking her nails across their vapid faces. She despised them all.

All of them but Arye.

She took her time dressing, relishing the feel of satin and lace as she put on a new black bra with a matching thong bikini. The strap between her buttocks made her feel especially sensual. After years of scrimping to pay off her medical bills, she relished having the money to buy pretty things.

As she dressed, other strategically placed mirrors permitted her to see herself from every angle. Striking a series of poses, she imagined she was a high-priced lingerie model. Someday Arye would see her like this. Someday soon, she vowed.

She looked up at the wall clock, realized he was due any minute, hurried to the closet and took out a DKNY suit she'd bought in a resale shop near River Oaks. She hated the rich bitches who could afford to get rid of clothes after one or two wearings—hated and envied and dreamed of being one.

Black pumps and a Chanel knock-off purse completed her outfit. Her heart pounding, she waited for the door bell to ring, imagining what she would say and do when Arye arrived. The scene came to life in her mind as vividly as though she were viewing it on television.

She would invite Arye in for coffee. He'd accept with boyish eagerness. Desire would kindle in his eyes as he looked at her. They would sit side by side on her loveseat, thighs touching, aware of each other. So very aware. Then he'd put his coffee cup down and reach for her. He was a gentleman—his kiss would be soft and sweet.

Arye Rappaport slid into the high front seat of his Suburban, silently blessing General Motors for making a vehicle so big that it minimized his claustrophobia. He eased the behemoth from the tiny garage of his West University home and turned north, wondering what had possessed him to agree to give Cindy Downing a ride to Blackjack's memorial service.

Sure, he felt sorry for her. In view of the car wreck that had left her financially strapped, and the trips she made back east to care for her ailing mother, Cindy couldn't have much of a life. But there was something off-putting about her—something unsettling about her eyes that Arye couldn't quite identify.

Still, when asked for the ride, he couldn't think of a way to refuse that wouldn't hurt her feelings. Not wanting to be alone with her, he asked Bert Hanrahan to go with them. For a man who hated being in a car, he sure as hell had committed himself to a lot of driving, he mused as he headed north toward the Heights.

Bert had spent years restoring a Victorian painted lady on Heights Boulevard, transforming it into a showplace that had been on the Heights home tour last year. Bert was that rarest of men—a heterosexual, socially acceptable, physically attractive mature person with impeccable taste, a terrific wardrobe, an endless fund of amusing anecdotes, and a genuinely caring heart.

They had met a decade ago when the two of them were employed by the same newspaper in Phoenix. A widower himself, Bert had taken Arye under his wing after Helen died, shepherding Arye through black bouts of depression and world-class drunks. He had kept Arye going when reason, logic, and a broken heart, told Arye he'd be better off dead.

Bert answered Arye's ring so quickly that Arye knew he must have waiting by the door. "A sad day, this," Bert said, leading the way into the kitchen. "I've fixed a little Irish coffee to soften the sharp edges."

Arye took his accustomed place at an antique oak table while Bert removed two mugs from the microwave.

"You ought to put some of that in a thermos and take it to Peach," Arye commented after tasting the potent brew. "She needs something to soften the sharp edges today more than I do."

"She certainly has had her share of troubles lately. How's she holding up?"

Bert's straightforward question deserved an equally straightforward answer. However, Arye couldn't give one. He hadn't figured Peach out. Although, God knew, he'd spent hours trying. He'd felt so close to her the night Blackjack died. However an unbridgeable chasm of age and circumstance had divided them ever since.

For a moment Arye let himself relive the passionate kiss they had shared—at least, it had been passionate on his part. Now he didn't know if he was crazy about Peach, or just plain crazy.

They didn't have anything in common except the magazine. Although he'd been to her home several times to deal with the media, there hadn't been another kiss. Hell, there hadn't been so much as an intimate glance.

During the daylight hours, he convinced himself it was better that way. Alone in his celibate bed, he relived that damn kiss over and over—with predictably uncomfortable results. He thought he'd outgrown middle-of-the-night wet dreams when he outgrew zits.

The sound of Bert's voice brought Arye's daydreaming to an abrupt halt. "Is there some reason you don't want to talk about Peach?"

Damn. The man was perceptive. "Of course not.

She's holding up better than I would have imagined. I just wish she and her mother had opted for a more private memorial service. The media is going to turn it into a three-ring circus."

"I don't think Blackjack would mind," Bert replied, taking a contemplative sip. "He'd like his last hurrah to be a real whoop-de-do."

"You knew him in Vietnam, didn't you?"

Bert nodded yes. "But not very well. He used to hang out with another Texan, a fellow by the name of Carroll Detweiler. The poor bastard went out of his head a few years back and died a horrible death right in front of the senator. Surely you read about it? The story made all the papers."

"As you recall I was pretty much out of my head a few years ago myself."

Bert fixed a quizzical gaze on Arye. "It's good to see you getting out with a pretty girl again."

"I wouldn't call taking an employee like Cindy to a memorial service *getting out.*"

Bert downed the last of his coffee and got up. "It sure as hell beats being the star attraction."

All things considered, Randolph Spurling was having a better time in Houston than he had anticipated when he left Washington. He had taken a limousine to his hotel, enjoyed a superb dinner at Sfuzzi, returned to his room, watched a little television and slept soundly for the first time in weeks.

On awakening he'd spent an hour working out in the Houstonian's well-equipped gym to insure that his forty-five-year-old body didn't accumulate any flab, then finished the workout by swimming twenty laps in the hotel's indoor pool. Invigorated and refreshed, he had returned to his suite and ordered breakfast from room service.

Now, showered, shaved, and wrapped in his favorite silk robe, he gazed out the window at a superb vista of modern buildings rising above the dense canopy of trees and bushes that guarded the exclusive hotel from curious bypassers.

Everything about the Houstonian, from its location to its many amenities, had been designed to appeal to a well-heeled clientele. No wonder George Bush had used it as his Texas residence during his presidency.

The arrival of breakfast interrupted Randolph's peripatetic thought process. A well-groomed young waiter wheeled in a cart laden with assorted fruits and pastries, decanters of coffee and orange juice, and a bottle of Roederer Kristal.

"Would you like me to open the champagne?" the waiter asked.

Randolph nodded.

The waiter popped the cork, then held it out for Randolph's inspection. "You have excellent taste in wine, sir."

"Is that a euphemism for expensive taste?"

The young man grinned. "You said it, sir, not me."

Randolph couldn't refrain from boasting to the rube. "It's on the taxpayer. I was Senator Morgan's executive assistant. I'm here for the service."

The waiter looked suitably impressed. "I'd like to. work in Washington someday myself. Maybe you could put in a good word for me at one of the hotels."

Randolph ignored the request. Everybody, but everybody was on the make one way or another, he mused after the waiter left. However, some people were better at it than others. He prided himself on being world class.

He filled a tall glass with champagne and topped it off with a little juice. "To Blackjack," he said, lifting the glass high.

Randolph Spurling was the quintessential public servant; well-dressed, well-educated, well-spoken, and well-traveled, all at public expense. He had paid for part of his education with an as-yet-unpaid government loan, then lived high, wide and handsome on the salary, benefits, perks and money he picked up on the side as Blackjack Morgan's top aide.

He smiled, thinking he would have to add the Houstonian to his personal list of superior hotels, along with places like the Georges Cinq in Paris and the Park Hyatt in Tokyo. A few of the trips he'd taken had actually been on government business. Most of them had been vacations thinly disguised as fact-finding junkets.

The cost hadn't been noticed in the seven-billion-dollar bill the Congress presented to John Q. Public every year for government travel—and that didn't count the two billion dollars' worth of private aircraft that Beltway bureaucrats kept handy, to say nothing of the billion-dollar-a-year tab for maintaining them.

What was it Everett Dirkson had said about how a billion here and a billion there eventually added up to some real money? Government waste, obfuscation, and fraud cost taxpayers more than the yearly budgets of most third-world countries.

He was going to miss the good life. His new job as a lobbyist, with a quarter of a million in salary, wouldn't compensate him for the goodies he had lost when the old man cashed in his chips.

He would even miss the senator, he thought as he made another mimosa. Blackjack had been a veritable cash cow before he forgot which side his bread was buttered on—and who buttered it.

Who would have imagined that one of the Senate's truly inspired wheeler-dealers—a legislator who had turned the Washington pork barrel into a two-decade-long gourmet meal—would suddenly bite the hands that had fed him. If Blackjack had continued to play the game, he would still be rich, powerful—and alive.

Randolph took a brioche from the pastry platter, bit into it, chewed a moment, then licked a buttery crumb from his upper lip. The term *public service* had become an oxymoron, he mused. *Self-service* would be more appropriate. Who was it who said that nations got the government they deserved?

Cindy Downing lived in one of the apartment complexes on Westheimer that had been built in the seventies when the oil business boomed. Since then the oil business had fallen on hard times—and so had a lot of Houston real estate. The city had been staggering toward economic recovery for years but somehow it never quite got there.

"I'll just be a minute," Arye told Bert as he parked the Suburban.

It took him a few minutes to find Cindy's apartment in the maze of buildings. She answered his knock, looking as carefully made up, coiffed, and attired as a department store mannequin. And just about as natural.

"Welcome to my humble abode," she trilled. "Would you like a cup of coffee?"

"There really isn't time. Bert's waiting."

Cindy's expectant smile evaporated quicker than dew in a desert. "I didn't know he was riding with us. How many other people have you asked along?"

"Just Bert," Arye replied, wondering why Cindy would take offense at having another passenger in a car that could easily accommodate nine adults. "I didn't think you'd mind."

Cindy's frown didn't do justice to her fury. She had counted on having Arye to herself. The expensive flowers she had purchased for the apartment, the hours she'd spent cleaning, had been a total waste. Damn Bert Hanrahan. He'd be sorry he wrecked her plans.

Seeing Arye's watchful gaze, she planted a smile on her collagen-enhanced lips. "It's not my place to mind. It's your car. Besides, you know how much I like Bert."

Her mind in turmoil, she trailed behind Arye as he led the way through the complex. Bert Hanrahan had spoiled everything. But for him, Arye would have been sitting on the loveseat in her apartment with his arms around her. They would have been kissing instead of heading off to a memorial service for a big shot who probably deserved to die.

Suddenly, a new scheme popped into her mind. She wasn't about to let a gray-haired geek like Hanrahan ruin her entire day. No, sir. No one got the best of Cindy Downing! The cracked sidewalk offered lots of places to stage an accident. At an opportune moment, she staggered and cried out. Arye whirled around in time to catch her before she actually fell.

"Oooh, I've twisted my ankle," she lamented, clinging to him for support. She even managed to squeeze out a couple of tears. "It really hurts."

For a second, Arye looked nonplussed. Then he took command of the situation just as she hoped he would. "Can you stand on it?"

She tried, then cried out again.

"I better make sure you didn't break a bone," he said, kneeling and running his hands over her lower leg.

The ecstasy she experienced at his touch made her cry out again. This time, though, the sound was genuine.

"Is this painful?" he asked, gently manipulating her foot. She knew he'd have marvelous hands!

"Just a little. I feel so silly. I knew I was taking my life in my hands, wearing high heels to walk around a place like this. But I wanted to look especially nice today—to show my respect."

He stood back up and put a supportive arm around her waist. "I'd better help you back to your apartment."

"Oh, no," she burst out. "I wouldn't miss the service for anything. I even got a new dress. Never mind my leg. I really want to go."

"You sound as though you're looking forward to what most people would regard as a rather dismal occasion."

"I am. Everyone who is anyone is bound to be there." The look on Arye's face told her she'd made a tactical error. "I mean I want to go for Peach's sake. She's been so good to all of us at *Inside Texas*. The least we can do is show our support in her time of need."

Arye seemed to accept the explanation. She continued to lean on him as he helped her to his car. Bert was standing beside the Suburban, finishing a cigarette when they joined him. He gave Cindy a bland smile. But there was something about the blue eyes beneath the shock of silver hair that made her feel he could see right through her.

She marched right up and hugged him as if he were the person she most wanted to see in this world. Then she let Arye help her into what she regarded as her rightful place in the front of the Suburban by Arye's side, leaving Bert to climb in the back.

As they drove away, she looked at Bert over her shoulder. "Do you think what's happened will change things at *Inside Texas?*"

"In what way?" Bert replied.

"I was wondering if Peach will spend more time at the magazine now she's getting a divorce and everything."

"I doubt it," Arye answered in a strained voice. "Peach is first, last and always a member of Houston society. Once the dust settles I'm sure she'll return to her luncheons and her charity work."

Arye Rappaport couldn't have been more wrong. Scandal, death, and divorce had severed the umbilical cord that tied Peach to her former life. As Peach drove Bella to the funeral home, Peach was contemplating the future.

She hadn't slept much the last three days and had eaten even less. However her resolve had never been stronger. She had made up her mind not to take a penny from Herbert. After their last conversation she couldn't stand the thought of being tied to him in any way.

"You bitch," he had screamed over the phone, "how could you ruin my clothes like that? What the fuck am I supposed to wear?"

She'd been on the brink of telling him she was sorry, that she'd been overwrought when she took the scissors to his wardrobe. At the last second she surprised herself by saying, "You're the one who wanted the divorce. If you have any complaints, take them up with my lawyer."

She shook for five minutes after hanging up. In retrospect though, she rather liked being called a bitch. People didn't use bitches for doormats.

She had instructed her lawyer to ask for the house and the Jaguar. Blackjack had made the down payment on the former. And profits from *Inside Texas,* her sole and separate property before the marriage, had paid for the latter.

"Is Herbert attending the service?" Bella asked, seeming to read Peach's mind.

"I didn't invite him," Peach replied.

The morning after Blackjack's death, Peach had no choice but to tell Bella about the divorce. She expected her mother to suggest she try everything to keep the marriage intact, from taking a second honeymoon to seeing a marriage counselor.

Instead Bella had hugged her and said, "I firmly believe every time a door closes, a new one opens. You just have to look for it."

In the press of events since, there'd been no time to discuss Herbert again.

"I thought you'd be upset about my getting a divorce," Peach said now.

"I want what's best for you, darling. The truth is, I never thought Herbert was. Neither did your father."

Peach couldn't have been more surprised. "Why didn't you ever say anything?"

"You were so dazzled by him, we didn't think you'd listen."

"Dazzled is certainly the right word. I looked up to him almost as much as I did Daddy. But Herbert wasn't anything like Blackjack. Daddy would never have left you for another woman."

A strange expression flashed across Bella's face. "You never know what's happening inside someone else's marriage."

"I should have caught on to Herbert the first time he talked about how helpful the Morgan name was going to be when he opened his practice in Houston." Peach clenched her teeth. "He's such a jerk—and I'm an even bigger fool."

"Don't be so hard on yourself. You were young and impressionable, and Herbert certainly put his best foot forward. He did everything a man can do to sweep a woman off her feet."

"You and Dad weren't fooled."

"We weren't in love the way you were."

Peach's grip on the steering wheel tightened. "I'll never be dazzled by a man again."

Bella gave her a motherly smile. "Never say never, darling."

"No, I mean it. I don't regret the years I spent being a wife and mother, but it's time I figured out what I want to do with the rest of my life."

* * *

The George Lewis funeral home on Bering had buried two generations of prominent Houstonians. But it had never seen anything like the gathering that awaited Peach and Bella. Sixty members of the media, cameras and camcorders held high, microphones clutched in sweating hands, jockeyed for position by the entrance to the chapel.

The milling throng reminded Peach of killer whales waiting for unwary seals as she turned into the parking lot. "Arye was right about keeping the service private."

"Arye is undoubtedly right about a great many things," Bella replied with her habitual equanimity, "but he wasn't right about the memorial service. Blackjack wouldn't want to leave Houston like a thief in the night."

Peach pulled in behind another car, hoping it would hide them while she figured out the best way to avoid the crowd. She shuddered to think what would happen when she and her mother got out of the car.

She cut the motor, set the brake, opened her door and hurried around the Jaguar to help her mother out.

Someone shouted, "There they are," and the press corps wheeled towards them with military precision.

"We've got to make a run for it," she told Bella.

Suddenly Peach felt a strong masculine arm sheltering her shoulders. Startled, she turned to see who had come to her rescue.

"It's you," she gasped with mingled surprise and pleasure.

Arye looked devastatingly handsome in a dark blue suit. Damn, she had just sworn not to be dazzled by a man—but he was hard to resist. Besides, he had an uncanny way of showing up when she needed him most.

His gaze met hers and she felt it in the pit of her stomach. For a second the rest of the world—the press, even her mother—faded away.

Arye's words brought her back to the present. "No matter what happens, I want you and your mother to keep going. Bert and I will take care of the crowd."

The two men hustled Peach and Bella through the media like halfbacks heading for a goal line, brushing microphones, cameras and the individuals holding them aside. They moved so quickly, Peach had to trot to keep up. By the time the funeral-home doors closed behind them she was out of breath—although whether from the hurried passage or Arye's proximity, she couldn't tell.

"I haven't moved that fast for years," Bella declared.

"Neither have I," Bert replied with a chuckle. "It certainly got my blood circulating."

Just then, an angry female voice rang out behind Peach. "Damn it. My new suit is ruined."

Considering the surroundings, the complaint seemed dreadfully out of place. Peach whirled around to see who had uttered it.

Cindy Downing stood just inside the door—and she wasn't a happy camper. Her hair was disheveled, her suit had a rip in a shoulder seam, and she had a run in one stocking. For a moment as she stared at Peach, pure venom filled her eyes. But the look faded so quickly that Peach thought she had imagined it.

"I'm so sorry," Peach said. "I didn't realize you were behind us."

"Where else would I be? I came with Arye." Cindy

pushed past Peach and dropped a possessive hand on Arye's arm.

Just then Randolph Spurling came bustling through the chapel doors, bringing the scent of floral offerings with him. "Everything's ready."

Everything but me, Peach thought as she followed Randolph inside the chapel.

Five

If rhetoric were raindrops, Peach mused, gazing around her father's Arlington grave site, it would be time to build an Ark. She had never heard so many high-flown phrases or so many empty words—but it had been some time since her last visit to Washington.

Her father had chosen the plot a few years ago. She doubted he had anticipated needing it so soon. Nearby, thousands of the nation's honored dead slept side by side. The white crosses on their graves gleamed white in the noonday sun, lending an almost joyous ambience to the otherwise somber setting.

The memorial service in Houston had been her mother's idea. The Arlington burial reflected her father's wishes. In Houston the governor had praised Blackjack's efforts on behalf of Texas—his fight to keep projects like the space station and the super-collider alive. Today's speeches had been more ambiguous.

Half a dozen of the nation's most powerful men had eulogized Blackjack. Unfortunately their speech-writers hadn't been very inventive. They all used quotes from Shakespeare's *Julius Caesar*.

"The trumpet of his own virtues, done to death by slanderous tongues," intoned the Senate whip.

"Oh, mighty Caesar, dost thou lie so low? Are all thy conquests, triumphs, spoils, shrunk to this little measure?" the majority leader boomed like an itinerant preacher in a revival tent.

A pox on both thy houses, Peach had thought at the time. Despite being a senator's daughter—or more accurately, because she was one—she had never paid much attention to politics. On this sorry afternoon she wished she had asked her father more about his vocation. Not the nuts and bolts—she had learned all that in high school civics classes.

She would have liked to have known more about the secret power plays, negotiations, compromises, pay-offs and pay-backs that were the *sine qua non* of daily business on the Hill.

What could have motivated so many *éminences grisés* to mourn a man they had attempted to ruin while blood still coursed through his veins? Was it guilt—or the need for expiation that brought them here? More important, what had her father done to warrant their joint wrath?

So many questions tumbled through Peach's mind that she didn't realize the service had come to an end until a young Marine handed Bella the flag that had covered Blackjack's casket.

"I'm very sorry for your loss," the Marine said.

"Thank you very much," Bella replied with unassailable dignity.

The doleful bugling of taps floating on the hot summer air almost broke Peach's composure. It was truly over, she mused, her features drawn with sorrow as she grappled with the reality of her father's sudden death. The door had shut on his life before he'd had a chance to clear his name.

Bella maintained her aplomb as the assembled dignitaries expressed their condolences. A few minutes later, head held high, shoulders thrown back as though she were on parade, Bella led the way back to their limousine and climbed inside with Peach at her heels.

Randolph Spurling trailed after them and leaned through the open door. A look of satisfaction rode his aristocratic features.

"The service went very well, don't you agree?" He made a statement of the words rather than a question.

"Thank you for making the arrangements," Bella replied.

"It's the least I could do—in view of everything the senator did for me. Randolph shut the car door, then as though it were an afterthought, tapped on the window.

Bella lowered it at once.

"I'd like to stop by your hotel tonight and talk to both of you. There is some unfinished business we need to discuss."

"Can't it wait? Mother and I have had a long day," Peach explained.

Weariness weighed her down. She and Bella had been in perpetual motion since Blackjack's death, manning the phones, making arrangements for the memorial service in Houston, accepting condolence calls and visits, and finally flying to Washington. Peach had counted on their getting to bed early tonight.

She saw a flicker of impatience in Randolph's eyes. "I'm afraid it can't wait," he replied.

"The Four Seasons has a marvelous restaurant, the Aux Beaux Champs. Why don't you join us for dinner at seven-thirty?" Bella suggested.

Randolph nodded his acceptance, then without a backward glance, turned and walked away.

Peach settled back onto the limousine's luxurious upholstery. "What do you suppose he wants?"

"Perhaps it's some last bit of business to do with the funeral—" Bella's voice trailed off. She looked exhausted.

"I thought you settled all that in Houston."

"So did I."

"I have a question or two for Mr. Spurling myself."

"You do?"

"I want to know why so many power-brokers were here today."

Bella frowned. "That's no secret. They all owed your father favors."

"That didn't seem to make any difference to them last week or last year for that matter. They accused Dad of every possible crime before he died."

"I suppose they wanted to show the nation the time had come to let bygones be bygones. They did the same thing when Nixon was buried."

"Do you really think it's that simple?"

"What else could it possibly be?"

"I wish I knew."

Bella gave Peach the exasperated look she had years ago when Peach asked the sort of unanswerable questions all children ask. "Honey, if there's one thing I learned as a politician's wife, it's that there are some things you don't want to know. It's too late to wonder why things happened the way they did. Nothing can bring your father back."

Peach frowned. "Don't you want to know the truth?"

"There are all sorts of truths, depending on your viewpoint."

"What's that supposed to mean?"

"You're too young to remember Lyndon Johnson's Great Society, but Democrats touted it as the best idea since Roosevelt's New Deal. It was supposed to end poverty. That was the gospel in those days. Now the very men who voted for it blame it for everything from increased teen-age pregnancy to the national debt. Times change. Opinions change. People change. Truth changes. At least it does in Washington."

"Did Daddy change?"

"Of course. Your father wasn't perfect. He made mistakes. He can't do anything about them now and neither can we. I don't mean to sound cold-blooded, honey. I cared for your father when so many others abandoned him—but it's time I got on with my life. It's even more true for a young woman like you."

Why was Bella so insistent? "Is there something you're not telling me—about you and Dad? Is that why you don't want me to—"

"There are lots of things I've never told you about your father," Bella quickly replied, as though she'd rehearsed her answer, "just as there are lots of things you've never told me about your relationship with Herbert."

Her mother hadn't sounded so stern since the time, thirty years ago, when Peach had decimated a chocolate mousse meant for a party dinner.

Their gazes locked and held while the silence stretched taut between them, vibrating with unuttered thoughts.

At last, with a little shrug, Bella said, *"Men,"* imbu-

ing the single word with all the mystery—the unknow-
ableness of the opposite sex.

"Men," Peach dutifully echoed, matching her
mother's shrug.

"There's no need for either of us to go into the
minutiae of our marriages—today or ever. That part
of our lives is over. We should be looking forward, not
backward."

Was Bella being evasive, Peach fretted—or sensible?

Despite Bella's assertions, the flame of curiosity that
had burned inside Peach during her childhood, that
made her decide to major in journalism in college,
had been reignited today. She felt as though she'd
awakened from a long trance.

She had never found out why the world was round,
why grass was green, why boys had penises and girls
didn't, but she was determined to find out more about
her father's life.

And his death.

Peach and Bella had just taken seats at their table
in Aux Beaux Champs when they saw Randolph
Spurling walking toward them with a self-important
stride that brought a waiter scurrying to ask for their
order.

Over drinks, Randolph reminisced about the years
he had worked for Blackjack, recounting anecdotes
Peach had never heard before. Randolph was, she
grudgingly admitted, a very charming man. However,
his charm was so studied it made her wary. He continued to dominate the conversation throughout the
meal. Bella occasionally chimed in, but Peach was too
busy watching and listening to talk.

In her early teens, when a bizarre combination of raging hormones and residual baby fat governed her thoughts and actions, she'd had a girlish crush on Randolph Spurling. Now she wondered what she could possibly have seen in him? He reminded her of cubic zirconium. Flash without true worth.

She toyed with her food, pushing it around on her plate and longing for the cigarettes she had given up years ago. She would have loved to light up and blow politically incorrect smoke in Randolph Spurling's face.

"You're awfully quiet tonight, Peach," he said, after the waiter brought their post-prandial coffee.

"I'm tired," she answered, making no attempt at sociability.

"I promise not to keep you up later than necessary. You need your beauty sleep."

Was he commenting on her looks, or just being condescending? Either way, she didn't appreciate it. He was the last person she'd want to stay up with. "You mentioned some unfinished business."

Indeed." He sipped his coffee. "Governor Bush called to tell me he has chosen Senator Morgan's replacement. He wants to make the announcement after a decent interval?"

"Meaning?"

"A couple of days."

"What does that have to do with us?" Peach demanded.

He gazed at her as though she had taken leave of her senses. "That should be obvious. We need to empty Senator's Morgan's office as soon as possible so the new man can move in."

The officiousness in Randolph's voice gnawed at

Peach's already frayed nerves. "Is that the royal *we*? Or do you want Mother and me to trot over to the Hill after supper and pack up Daddy's things?"

"For heaven's sake, Peach," Bella chided, "Randolph is just trying to help."

"Your mother is right. I wish we could wait until you're up to dealing with certain new realities, Peach. It's not my choice, though."

"I'm sorry," Peach made herself say.

Ignoring her apology, Randolph addressed himself to Bella. "I can have Blackjack's papers and mementos boxed up and shipped to you. Where would you like me to send them?"

Peach didn't give Bella a chance to respond. "Send them to my house. Mother and I have decided to live together for the time being."

"What about the apartment you and Blackjack rented?" Randolph asked Bella. "I thought your things were moved in the day of the auction."

"They were," Bella answered, "not that there was much left—just furniture that wasn't worth selling and a few mementos. We planned to stay with our daughter until we unpacked."

"What about all those wonderful pictures Blackjack had in his office at Belle Terre—and his personal papers?"

"They should be in the apartment. I haven't had time to look for anything yet. To be honest, I'm just not up to it."

"Then you have no immediate plans to move in?"

Bella shook her head.

"You're very wise to stay with your daughter during this difficult period of transition," Randolph intoned with papal solemnity.

"I'd like to see my father's offices before you pack up his papers," Peach blurted out.

"Come by anytime before you leave." Randolph seemed to be having trouble with his smile. It looked more like a pout.

"Our plane takes off at noon tomorrow. I could stop by in the morning."

"I'll be waiting for you," Randolph replied. "And now, if you ladies will excuse me, I have work to do."

He got up and strode away like a man with urgent business—and left them with the bill, Peach noted.

"Apparently Mr. Spurling's social graces don't extend to picking up the check," she commented.

"You don't like him very much, do you?"

"No," Peach replied succinctly. It felt good to voice an unqualified opinion without worrying about Herbert's reaction.

"You could try to be more understanding. The poor man doesn't have a job anymore, while your father's insurance left me well-fixed. I can afford a meal like this." Bella picked up the bill, added a tip, wrote down their room number and signed her name.

"Tell me about Randolph Spurling," Peach said when they were back in their room.

Bella gave her an indulgent smile. "What's there to tell? You've known him for years."

"Not well. What's he like beneath his facade?"

"You ask so many questions, you really should have been a reporter."

"Herbert took care of that dream."

"Darling, you sound as if your life is over."

"I don't mean to."

An idea had been born in the back of Peach's mind. She didn't dare give it form and substance by voicing it yet, though. She wasn't that sure of herself. "Back to Spurling. I never heard how he met Daddy."

"He spent a summer as a Senate page after he graduated from high school. Your father was impressed with his energy and initiative, to say nothing of his photographic memory. When Randolph finished law school, Blackjack offered him a job. Randolph rose through the ranks to become your father's executive assistant."

"Has he ever been married?"

"If that's your way of asking me if he's gay, the answer is no. He has quite an eye for the ladies."

"Does everyone call him Randolph?"

Bella smiled. "Can you picture anyone calling him Randy?"

Peach giggled at the double-entendre. "Not really. He strikes me as a buttoned-down yuppie who wouldn't dream of wearing loafers without tassels or suits without banker's stripes."

"That's him to a tee."

"Were he and Daddy close?"

"Not socially. However they worked well together." Bella paused. "All but the last year. Your father told me they had a falling out. Blackjack was so angry at Randolph that I couldn't understand why he kept him on."

Peach's inquiring mind pounced on the information. "What sort of falling out?"

"Your father would never tell me. You knew him, honey. He held a grudge better than most men—often for the flimsiest reasons."

"What an awful thing to say."

Bella gave Peach a wan smile. "It's the truth. I don't

want you to make the mistake of beatifying your father now he's gone."

While Randolph taxied back to Senator's Morgan's office, the rich Aux Beaux Champs meal churned in his stomach. He had counted on having days to go through Blackjack's papers. Thanks to one meddlesome female—Peach Morgan-Strand—he had less than twelve hours.

There hadn't been time to make a thorough search of the files before the funeral. Now he didn't dare pack them up until he made certain nothing in them could incriminate him. Christ, if anyone ever found out what he'd done, he'd go straight to jail without passing Go, let alone collecting two hundred dollars.

Randolph was oblivious to the beauty of the summer night or the splendor of the city's many monuments as he rode to the Senate office building on Constitution Avenue. The files he would have to search occupied his mind. He thought he knew their contents—but he couldn't risk his future on that knowledge.

He'd been poised on the edge of a precipice the last year, wondering when and if the senator would shove him over the edge. He'd presumed that Blackjack's death should have ended the threat, though. Damn Peach!

The cab dropped Randolph in front of the building at ten. Despite the late hour, eager young staffers still scurried down the corridors like so many lemmings. They all looked so damn knowing—however they didn't know shit. Maybe that's why it took so many of them to get anything done these days.

As Randolph made his way to Blackjack's office the facts and figures he'd researched for Blackjack last year scrolled through his brain as clearly as though they were displayed on a computer screen.

In FDR's day, members of the House had two or three personal assistants. Senators had four. Today a member of the House couldn't get by with less than twenty-two staffers while senators needed forty-four for a grand total of approximately 17,240 staffers for 100 senators and 535 representatives—and that didn't count the six-hundred-dollar-an-hour consultants or the fourteen thousand attorneys feeding at the public trough, let alone the staffs of all the committees and sub-committees and all the other Washington bureaucracies. It amounted to one hell of a payroll!

Randolph snorted, recalling how the Department of Agriculture employed one bureaucrat for every sixteen farmers they served while Defense couldn't get by without one civilian for 1.7 men and women in uniform. Did anyone who had the facts actually believe them?

While businesses had been downsizing, government had become the biggest growth industry in the country—and the jobs paid well. If the general public knew what was really going on, they would rise up in righteous wrath. Although, come to think of it, people who didn't take the time to vote probably didn't care if politicians gave them the shaft.

How many poor schmucks paying taxes on thirty thousand a year did it take to pay one staffer's $100,000 salary? he mused, rapidly making the calculations. The answer boggled his mind.

When it came to spending, the White House wasn't any better than the Congress. During the '92 presidential campaign, Clinton had vowed to cut his staff by twenty-five percent. He'd transferred a few people and claimed to have kept his promise. But eighteen months later he'd asked Congress for a 2.8-million-dollar increase to pay the White House staff—over and above the existing 38.8-million-dollar allowance for salaries and expenses.

Some reduction. White House spokespeople boasted about how Clinton had cut the deficit when all he'd done was cut the proposed growth in spending by a modest percent. Talk about double-speak. Only in Washington was an increase called a cut.

The government reminded Randolph of those fraudulent pyramid schemes that made lots of money for the big boys at the top and left those at the bottom sucking hind tit. Fuck them all, he mused, as he reached his destination. One of these days the whole corrupt, unworkable system was going to come crashing down like a house of cards.

He reached Blackjack's suite, walked through it to the senator's private office and flicked a wall switch. Light flooded a paneled room furnished with genuine antiques, all bought at taxpayer's expense. However Randolph wasn't about to waste another second feeling sorry for the taxpayers who paid the bills. He was already feeling very sorry for himself.

Blackjack had been much too confident the last few months not to have an ace in the hole—something that would clear his name and bury Randolph in the process. What the hell could it be? A diary? Secret tapes of their conversations?

Randolph took off his jacket, hung it over a chair, and loosened his tie. If there was anything here, he'd damn well better find it tonight.

* * *

Eleven hours later Randolph sat slumped behind the senator's desk, a glass of double-malt Scotch from Blackjack's private stock in his hand. He couldn't remember the last time he had pulled an all-nighter with so little reward. He hadn't come up with a damn thing—except the certainty that documents, and in some cases, entire files were missing.

He finished the Scotch and got up to pour another when the intercom buzzed. "Peach Morgan-Strand is here to see you," a secretary said.

"Give me five minutes before you send her in," he replied.

He'd spent the night going through the files, the drawers, the closet, turning heavy furniture over to examine the underside, even lifting the carpet at the corners. The stale odor of his labors clung to his body. His shirt and trousers were wrinkled, and he'd even managed to scuff a three-hundred-dollar pair of cordovan loafers.

He hurried into the senator's private bathroom and helped himself to Blackjack's electric razor, aftershave and other toiletries. When he finished he looked better. However his nerves felt as fragile as overcooked angel-hair pasta.

He was standing by the window, gazing out toward the Capitol, when Peach walked in. Her bandbox-fresh appearance made him feel even worse. "Good morning," he said grudgingly while she gazed around with obvious curiosity.

"I'd forgotten what a beautiful office this is," she murmured.

"You haven't been here for a long time." He made his reply sound like a rebuke.

"My father liked to keep his public and his family life separate. Unfortunately the last couple of years, things haven't worked that way," Peach shot back.

She wasn't the docile society woman he remembered. She walked over to a file cabinet, yanked it open and began reading the labels. "Are these the papers you talked about last night?"

"Those, and others."

"Where are Dad's personal papers?"

A damn good question, Randolph thought. He'd give a great deal to know the answer. "What do you mean?"

"Before I came over, Mother told me Father said something about keeping a diary the last year. She asked me to look for it."

A nerve jumped to life under Randolph's left eye. Fuck. Peach had just confirmed his worst fear. A diary could bury him. Where the hell could it be? "Your father kept personal papers in his desk."

Peach crossed the floor, sat down behind the desk, and tugged at the center drawer. "It's locked."

"Do you want me to pry it open?"

"Yes, if you can do it without damaging the wood. My mother may want to set up her own office when she buys a new house."

"I never said anything about shipping the furniture. It belongs to the government," Randolph replied, taking a paper clip from a container on top of the desk.

"I see," Peach replied.

No, she didn't, he thought, and he intended to keep it that way. Technically the furniture did belong to the government. Not that he or anyone working on the

Hill gave a shit for that particular technicality. Congress spent serious money on furniture and decorating every year. No one knew the exact figure. Certainly no inventory existed.

Blackjack had redecorated his offices every time he was reelected, giving the things he no longer wanted to favorite employees. Randolph had coveted these particular antiques for years and thought they would look quite splendid in his new office. After packing up Blackjack's papers, he intended to have the furniture delivered there.

He straightened the paper clip, leaned over Peach, and inserted it in the keyhole. It had taken him a few minutes to pick the lock last night. This morning he did it faster.

Peach opened the center drawer, took out a leatherbound appointment book and flipped through the pages, pausing here and there to read an entry. "This isn't a diary. It's a record of my father's appointments," she said.

Brilliant deduction, Randolph thought sourly.

"My father seems to have left whole blocks of time blank. Do you have any idea why he would have done that?"

"No," Randolph answered truthfully.

The past year, Blackjack had disappeared regularly without telling anyone where he was going. Randolph had assumed he was meeting with his attorneys until they called one day looking for him. Randolph still had no idea how the senator had spent the time—unless it had been with a woman.

Peach put the appointment book on top of the desk, then cut a sidelong glance at Randolph. She liked him even less today than she had last night. If his expression reflected his inner thoughts, he returned the sentiment in spades.

Herbert had always accused her of being a poor judge of character and insisted she defer to his opinions. Herbert had been dead wrong, she realized. Seeing the way Randolph shifted his weight from foot to foot and plucked invisible lint from his clothes, she had no trouble reading his mind.

He was nervous. Upset and angry, too. Did her presence bother him? Or did his barely veiled hostility have something to do with her father's papers?

She had hoped to find the answer to some of her questions this morning. Instead she added another one to her growing portfolio.

She quickly went through the rest of the desk drawers, noting the contents so she'd know what had been in them when her father's papers arrived in Houston. Then she rose, crossed the floor and opened one of the large file cabinets against the wall and started a hasty inventory.

Half an hour later, feeling dusty, she went to her father's private bathroom and opened the door. The scent of Blackjack's-after shave wafted out as though he had just used it. She had smelled the same scent on Randolph when he leaned over her to jimmy the drawer. A quick inspection of the room revealed flecks of a dark beard in the sink. Obviously, Randolph had freshened up in here this morning.

He must have spent the night.

What possible motive could he have for going sleepless that way? Had he been looking for something—something he didn't want her to find when Blackjack's papers arrived in Houston?

It didn't make sense. Randolph Spurling had access

to this office any time. Logic insisted she was making a mountain out of a molehill. Instinct screamed she was on to something.

The thrill of the hunt raised goose bumps on her arms. Deciding to test her premise, she walked back into her father's office to find Randolph stationed by the window again.

She let out a breathy sigh. "Everything seems to be in order, not that I'd know if it wasn't. I was so hoping to find something."

"What sort of something?" Randolph asked, keeping his back to her.

"I'm not sure. You see, my father said the strangest thing to me before he died."

Randolph wheeled around to face her. The skin around his mouth had a pinched look. "What did he say?"

"Don't let the bastards get away with it," she repeated, watching Randolph all the while.

The pinched look spread over Randolph's entire face. "Bastards? Are you sure he said bastards and not bastard?"

"Yes. Does it mean anything to you?"

Randolph appeared to be gazing inward at a vista only he could see. The pinched look faded. "Not really. Your mother told me Blackjack was out of his mind at the end."

So Randolph had asked Bella about Blackjack's final moments. Had he done so as a concerned friend? And if not, what could his motive have been?

Feeling as though she were shadow-boxing, Peach made one last attempt to unnerve Randolph in the vague hope he would reveal something. "My father knew just what he was saying—and I intend to find out what he meant."

She had no idea what she expected—but it wasn't the response she got. Randolph laughed, a harsh sound that had nothing to do with mirth. "I know you own a magazine but you're hardly an investigative reporter."

"That's true. But my managing editor, Arye Rappaport is."

"Rappaport? I was surprised when Blackjack told me you'd hired that drunk. My dear Peach, I sympathize with your distress. I'm sure you're burdened with a certain amount of guilt for not having spent more time with your father. However, once you adjust to his death, you'll no doubt find more productive ways to occupy yourself than snooping in your father's past. You may find things you don't like there."

He sounded so sure of himself, so utterly at ease that she didn't object when he took her elbow and guided her to the door. "I hate to cut our little visit short, but duty calls. If you need a cab, ask one of the secretaries to get one for you."

Peach Morgan-Strand was far smarter than he had ever given her credit for, Randolph fretted as he shut the office door—smart enough to go on a little fishing expedition this morning. He didn't like surprises. He didn't like Peach. However she had been no match for him.

Feeling certain he knew where Blackjack had hidden his private papers, Randolph crossed the floor, opened the door to the adjoining office, settled at his own desk and looked up a number in his Rolodex. He hadn't been a Washington insider for twenty years for nothing, he mused as he waited for the party to pick up.

He spent a couple of minutes exchanging pleasantries, then got down to business. When he hung up five minutes later he felt relaxed and on top of things again. The incident with Peach—and the more serious problems he'd had with her father—wouldn't trouble him anymore.

Six

Home. The many meanings of the word—haven, hearth, residence, dwelling, lodging, roost—percolated through Peach's mind as she pulled up in front of her house. Although she and Bella had only been gone three days, Peach felt as if she had traveled light years since she last saw it.

Coming home at the end of a day spent attending committee meetings, used to comfort her. Now she wondered if she could still afford to live here—or if she even wanted to now Herbert was out of her life and the boys were grown. She hated depriving the twins of the rooms they had lived in all their lives, but she certainly didn't need six thousand square feet anymore. Herbert had seen to that.

For once the thought of him wasn't accompanied by the nettle of bitterness, the stinging feeling that she'd been wronged. She was surprised to realize she wasn't angry with Herbert anymore.

Their marriage had been based on faulty assumptions. She had mistaken his brilliance for perfection of character, while he had married her for her name, forgetting that a living, breathing woman rather than a mannequin went along with it. Perhaps down the road, for the sake of the twins, they might find their way to friendship. She certainly hoped so.

"Am I glad to see you!" Delia called out, pushing the front door open with a resounding thud as Peach and Bella got out of the Jaguar.

Delia took Bella's luggage, gave Peach a snaggle-toothed grin, and marched back into the house, talking all the while in her gravelly West Texas twang.

"The phone has been ringing off the hook since you and Miss Bella left. All sorts of nice folks have been stopping by. You just missed that good-looking Mr. Rappaport. He left those flowers over there." A nod of Delia's head indicated a bouquet of yellow roses.

Peach's heart fluttered at the sight. How did Arye know she liked yellow roses best? she wondered before other thoughts crowded the pleasure out.

She felt guilty about leaving Delia to cope with the fall-out from Blackjack's death. However she'd had no choice. There simply hadn't been anyone else. "I hope being here alone wasn't too much for you."

Delia shook her head. "It sure beat having Mr. Herbert around. And your visitors, Mr. Arye and the other folks, couldn't have been nicer."

Peach ignored Delia's comment. She had never been one of Herbert's fans.

"My, aren't those roses lovely?" Bella commented, bending over them to inhale their delicate perfume. "You certainly hired a winner when you took Arye on."

Peach could only nod. Winner didn't seem the right way to describe Arye—but it would do for the time being. "What other folks?" she asked Delia.

"They told me they were friends of Miss Bella. They

left the things they bought at the auction. The way they talked, I thought you knew all about it."

Peach was halfway up the stairs with her suitcase. She stopped and set it down. "All about what?"

"The things they left here."

"What things?"

"Furniture, paintings and the like. I had the gardener put them in the garage where Mr. Herbert used to keep his car." Delia's tone indicated she regarded furniture as a more than fair exchange for Herbert and his Porsche.

"We had better take a look," Peach said to Bella.

A few belongings didn't begin to describe what they found in the garage. Blackjack's massive partners, desk, the dining room suite with the genuine Shaker chairs Bella and Blackjack had found in a Maryland barn, the bedroom set that was identical to the one in the Lincoln bedroom, the massive Diego Rivera oil painting that had hung in the living room, filled the space that used to be occupied by Herbert's car.

Seeing them, Bella's eyes glowed with renewed life. She ran a hand over Blackjack's desk as if it were a surrogate for the man. "A few friends said they were going to buy some things for us—but this is so much more than I expected."

Peach gulped. These were no token gifts. They had cost a small fortune.

"Did you keep a list of who brought what?" her mother asked Delia.

"I tried, Miss Bella. I knew you'd want to thank them. But they said they didn't want you feeling beholden."

Peach hadn't wept at her father's memorial service or at his Arlington burial. Now, tears began streaming down her face. She looked at Bella to see moisture oozing from her eyes, too. Even Delia—a woman from drought-ridden West Texas where hard times were more common than rain—had started to sniffle.

"Praise the Lord for making good people," Delia said with evangelical fervor.

Praise the Lord indeed, Peach silently echoed. Perhaps he hadn't forgotten them after all.

The light supper Delia had fixed, followed by a couple of hours spent watching an inane made-for-television movie, proved to be a more powerful soporific than any of the pills in Herbert's medicine cabinet. Yawning prodigiously, Peach declared herself ready for bed at nine.

She kissed Bella good-night, climbed the stairs to her room, undressed and crawled between the sheets. Sleep came so swiftly that she was unaware of closing her eyes.

The next thing she knew she was at Belle Terre, wandering through the empty rooms. Her footsteps had a hollow ring as she walked into the solarium where the auction had been held.

It looked exactly the way it did just before the auction except the gilt chairs no longer lined up like soldiers on parade. They lay tumbled across the floor like a child's game of jackstraws.

Suddenly, the red carpet began to spread in a thick crimson tide that threatened to engulf Peach. The cuprous smell of blood tainted the still air. Peach tried to scream—and couldn't make a sound. She tried to run—and her feet wouldn't move.

A shadowy form coalesced before her horrified

gaze, growing taller and more formidable with every second. The form twisted and writhed, taking on human shape. Dear God, it was her father.

His sepulchral baritone boomed off the glass walls like a doomsday bell. "Don't let the bastards get away with it."

She tried to scream again.

A shrill ringing filled her ears and jerked her from the nightmare. It was the telephone, she realized as she came awake. Still gripped by terror, she fumbled for it.

"Hello," she said shakily, so dazed that she wondered if Blackjack would be on the other end of the line.

"Is this the Strand residence?" a strange male voice asked.

The question jolted Peach. The dream had been frightening—but not as frightening as having a polite stranger call in the middle of the night. The residue of the nightmare heightened her dread.

Her first thought was that something had happened to the twins. In response, her imagination immediately conjured up the worst possible scenario. She visualized their bodies by the side of some unknown road.

She turned on the light, looked at the clock and saw it was four in the morning. "Yes, it is."

"I'm calling for the Houston fire department," the stranger said. He gave his name, then added, "I'm an arson investigator."

It took Peach's sleep-sodden brain a second to remember that the twins were away at college in Oxford, Mississippi. The call couldn't possibly have anything to do with them. Relief was instantly followed by confusion. Why would an arson investigator want to talk to her?

"I'm looking for your mother, Mrs. Strand. Can you tell me how to get in touch with her?"

"She's here, sleeping."

"I'm afraid I have bad news. Would you mind waking her?"

"Could you tell me what it is first?"

"I suppose so. There's been a fire at her apartment." The deep male voice had a hesitant quality, as though being the bearer of bad news bothered the man.

"We'll come right over," Peach replied at once.

"There isn't any need to hurry. To tell you the truth, there isn't much left of the structure or the contents. We'll be mopping up for a few hours. When you get here, just ask for me."

Peach put the phone back in the cradle, then swung her legs over the side of the bed and got up. How she dreaded telling Bella about this new calamity.

Peach helped Bella out of the Jaguar and held on to her arm as they made their way past fire trucks and over the thick hoses that littered the ground like the corpses of boa constrictors. The remnants of smoke drifted high overhead and reminded Peach of frayed netting.

She had seen the aftermath of fires on television—gutted buildings, dazed residents standing in the street, hollow-eyed spectators who were always drawn to disasters. The reality matched those images, she noted, with one addition—the acrid miasma that clung to the tropical air.

"Are you all right?" she asked Bella.

"I'm not sure," Bella replied, looking around. "This doesn't seem real."

A fireman halted their progress. Peach told him who they were, who they wanted to see, and he pointed to a man standing near the gutted building.

"I'm Peach Morgan-Strand and this is my mother," Peach said when she reached the arson investigator. "You called my home earlier."

He offered a slightly grimy hand. "I'm sorry to meet you this way. I was a great admirer of the senator."

Bella was too distracted to respond in her usual gracious fashion. The ruined apartment riveted her gaze. "Was anyone hurt?" she asked.

"Fortunately, no. A passerby called in an alarm." He paused. "That's the good news. The bad news is that someone set the fire on purpose."

His words dropped into Peach's mind like stones thrown into a pond, sending ripples in every direction. Questions chased each other through her mind. "Are you sure?"

His answer was laced with technical details about flash points and rates of burn that were lost on Peach. Her mind had already moved on. "Why would someone want to destroy my parents' apartment?" she asked when he finished.

"I was hoping you and your mother could tell me." The arson investigator turned to Bella. "Were your things insured?"

"I don't know if my husband ever got around to it. The furniture was either too old or worn to be sold at the auction. However our personal belongings were worth a great deal to me." Her shoulders lifted, then fell in a poignant gesture of loss. "I don't have anything left from forty-five years of marriage except the clothes at my daughter's house."

Sympathy mingled with repressed anger on the arson investigator's face. "Do you have any enemies, Mrs. Morgan?"

"I don't think so. My husband did, though. Most politicians do. But Blackjack's gone."

It didn't make sense. Who hated her mother? Peach asked herself. The answer came instantly. *No one.* Bella didn't have an enemy in the world. The fire had to have something to do with Blackjack. But what?

"Are you sure it wasn't an accident?" Bella was saying. "An empty apartment is a real temptation for teenagers. Perhaps they just broke in to smoke or fool around and got careless."

The investigator shook his head. "The fire was set by a pro. The place was fully involved in a matter of minutes. If we hadn't gotten here so quickly, the damage would have been much worse."

"May I see if there's anything salvageable left?" Bella asked.

The investigator offered Bella his arm. She had an enviable talent for turning the most hardened man into a courtier. "I'll take you over myself."

"For Christ's sake, be careful. That desk is worth more than you make in a year," Randolph Spurling snapped as two burly movers carried a Louis quatorze escritoire from Blackjack's office.

The two men continued on their way as if they hadn't heard him. Bastards, Randolph thought angrily. Although he had more important things to do, he felt compelled to watch their every move.

He went to the door to observe their progress, shuddering every time the escritoire bumped against something, thinking he'd be lucky if anything reached his new office in one piece. Just then the telephone rang. It took him a minute to find it in the chaos of packing boxes.

"Spurling here," he growled into the mouthpiece.

"I was afraid I wouldn't be able to reach you," came a familiar male voice. "I tried your apartment and didn't get an answer."

"I told you not to call my apartment. Where the hell are you?"

"I'm at a pay phone in Houston. It's safe to talk."

"Have you fulfilled the contract?" Randolph asked, guarding every word in case the movers returned.

"It went without a hitch. There's nothing left but ashes and soot."

Randolph's emotional state went from impatience to near euphoria. "That's good. Hell. It's more than good. It's superb. Any chance they'll be able to figure who set the fire?"

"For Christ's sake, I'm a professional." The man hadn't raised his voice but the menace in it sent a chill down Randolph's spine.

"Take it easy. I wasn't impugning your ability. I just have to be sure."

"It was a cake-walk. Once the fire got going, I called in the alarm myself."

"You what?" Randolph burst out.

"I'm no murderer, Spurling. Roasting innocent bystanders wasn't part of our deal."

He may not have been a murderer, Randolph mused, but the discredited D.E.A. agent was a bad-tempered son-of-a-bitch who needed careful handling.

"You did the right thing," Randolph managed to say, then uttered a few more placating phrases before ringing off.

He walked to the window and stared out at the splendid view, waiting for his pulse rate to return to normal. Hiring someone to burn the apartment had been a calculated risk. Thank God, it had gone well. If Blackjack had left a diary or any other personal papers that pointed an accusing finger at Randolph, they were drifting over Houston in a cloud of smoke at this very moment.

The thought tickled him so much that he did a little jig across the office. Happy days were truly here again.

He returned to the phone, dialed a number, waited until he heard an answering machine come on, then said, "Mission accomplished," and hung up.

"My hair reeks of smoke," Bella complained as she followed Peach back into Peach's house. She paused in the foyer and gazed around as if she was surprised to find herself there. "I think I'll take a shower and then write some thank-you notes. How about you? Do you have plans?"

Peach couldn't believe her ears. Bella sounded as though she had just come from a pleasant early morning outing instead of the scene of yet another personal disaster. Clearly, she was in denial.

"You might feel better if you talked about how you're feeling."

"I told you—I feel grubby."

"For God's sake Mother, that's not what I mean. It isn't good to bottle things up."

"Would you rather I spend a couple of hours in my room weeping?" Bella retorted in a rare show of temper.

"Of course not. It's just—"

"Just what?"

"You don't have anything left," Peach blurted out. "Dad's gone. Your apartment burned up along with all your possessions. How can you be so calm? I'd be madder than hell if I were you. Don't you want to know who set that fire?"

"Not particularly. Knowing won't change a thing. Besides, its a job for the fire department and the police."

"Aren't you the least bit suspicious?"

"Of what?"

"Not what, Mom. *Who.* Don't you think it's stretching coincidence to have the apartment burn after everything else you and Dad went through?"

"What in the world are you talking about?"

"A possible conspiracy, masterminded by someone in Washington."

Bella recoiled. "You sound paranoid, Peach."

"Do I? Your apartment was the only one involved in the fire. Nothing else burned. And it wasn't an accident. It was arson—a professional job."

"That doesn't prove anything."

Peach clenched her fists. Bella's habit of viewing life through rose-colored glasses could be damnably exasperating. "Think about it. First the IRS investigated Daddy for tax evasion. A few weeks later someone leaked stories about his converting campaign funds to personal use. Then a woman who had worked on his last campaign—a woman he said he hardly knew—sued him for sexual harassment. The stories about influence peddling and insider trading were all attributed to impeccable anonymous sources. And now the fire. I'm convinced someone was out to get Daddy."

Bella stared at Peach with eyes so wide open that the whites showed all around. "I think you're way off base. Even if some sort of conspiracy existed in the past—and you'll never convince me one did—your father's death ended it. It's over Peach. Why can't you get that through your head?"

Peach had never seen her mother look so agitated. But Peach couldn't drop the subject. Suspicion had its virtues. She felt alive, alert, and adrenalized. "Because I'm convinced everything that happened to Daddy the last year is tied together, including the fire. Daddy's last words to me were *don't let the bastards get away with it.* I won't rest until I find out what he meant."

Bella's lips twitched. Then her entire body trembled. "We've been all over this, Peach. Your father was irrational before he died. He didn't even know me. He'd be so unhappy if he knew what you were doing to yourself."

"I wish you could see things my way," Peach replied.

Bella's mood altered suddenly. Contrition softened her features. She reached out and touched Peach's cheek in a gesture of maternal solicitude just the way she used to three decades before when Peach came home with cuts and scrapes.

"You've been under a terrible strain. Having Herbert move out when you needed him most must have seemed like the last straw. But going on the way you are will only make matters worse. A divorce isn't the end of the world. It can be a new beginning."

"Don't change the subject," Peach replied, wondering if all mothers had the power to reduce their daughters to abject helplessness. "We weren't talking about my divorce."

"I just want you to be happy. You're still young and attractive. You may even want to remarry someday."

"Thanks for the vote of confidence, but I'm middle-aged and overweight. And no one gets married anymore. They have relationships, live-ins, significant others. I believe the politically correct term for fucking like bunny rabbits is serial monogamy."

Bella blanched. "I've never heard you swear before. You sound so cynical, darling."

"I'm just being realistic. Single women my age are as likely to get married as they are to be struck by lightning. Besides, I'm not divorced yet." Peach gritted her teeth. Why had she let Bella divert her?

"What about Arye? He's been so attentive—and he certainly is attractive."

"I pay him to be attentive. He's an employee."

"Those yellow roses tell me he'd like to be more."

"If you really want me to be happy, please don't bring him up again," Peach protested.

Having her mother romanticize the man didn't help. She had already done too much of it herself.

"I didn't mean to upset you. Have you given any thought to your future, made any plans?"

"I intend to spend more time at the magazine," Peach answered although until that moment, she hadn't harbored the thought.

Bella gave her a knowing smile. "That sounds very nice. Mr. Rappaport is such a lovely man."

"Damn it. There you go again. You can be such a bulldog. My wanting to spend more time at the magazine doesn't have anything to do with Arye—at least not as a man," Peach declared as if saying it out loud would make it so. "He used to be a crackerjack investigative reporter. I'm going to ask him to help me find out what Daddy's last words meant."

Peach had put Arye out of her mind when she realized he'd brought Cindy Downing to the memorial service. Now, thanks to Bella and a dozen yellow roses, he had roared back into her consciousness with the power of a Concorde jet taking possession of the sky.

She couldn't separate what she felt for Arye—the man—from her need for his expertise.

So he was a hunk and a half. So what?

So he'd kissed her. So what?

A single kiss didn't make a love affair anymore than a single bone made an entire skeleton. Besides, where was it written she couldn't enjoy looking at him while she picked his brain?

Seven

Arye met Bert at the Bagel Manufactory near the Rice University campus every Saturday morning at ten. While the college crowd eddied around their table, they'd schmooze over bagels, nova lox, cream cheese and Brazilian coffee, talking a little too long about nothing very much the way lonely males do. Before going home or heading out on errands, Arye always ordered a dozen assorted bagels with a variety of cream cheeses to go.

This morning, after putting two jalapeño bagels in the microwave to defrost, he stood in front of his open refrigerator, trying to decide whether chive or vegetable cream cheese would best compliment the flavor of the jalapeños.

Arye fancied himself a bit of a chef. He could make a mouth-burning, gut-churning green chili redolent with the scents of New Mexico cuisine, or a terrific chicken cacciatore that brought to mind the sun-baked Tuscan hills. But his best dishes were those he learned to prepare in his mother's kitchen. Time-consuming recipes like blintzes, kugel, stuffed cabbage, and a killer brisket, were all part of his repertoire.

He had just decided the vegetable cream cheese would best cool the fire of the jalapeños when the phone rang. He got so few calls that the sound startled him. Who the hell would want to talk to him this early?

In the cruel world Arye had inhabited since his wife's murder, the people you cared about could too easily become hostages to an uncertain fate. He had long since decided he'd be better off alone rather than risk another devastating loss. As a consequence, he had no close friends aside from Bert. And Bert wasn't a morning person.

He only had one phone, an old-fashioned black instrument that didn't take messages, log numbers, or wipe anyone's rear in its spare time. The phone resided in a living room that looked as though it had been furnished with Salvation Army discards.

He could afford better furniture but since his wife's death, he'd had no real interest in the place where he lived. He plowed across a living room floor littered with books, magazines and half a dozen out-of-town newspapers including the *New York Times,* snatched the telephone from its cradle and growled "Rappaport here."

To his surprise, a woman laughed in reply. The sound sent an anticipatory tingle along his nerve paths. Although he'd heard it far too seldom, he would have known that throaty chuckle any time, any place, any where.

"You sound terrible. Did you get up on the wrong side of the bed?" Peach asked.

"You could say that."

He'd dreamed about her last night and woke up with a rampant hard-on that transformed the sheet into a circus tent. In that condition, there was no right side of the bed.

"Arye, are you still there?"

"Sure Peach. What's up?" he answered, then grimaced at the unintended double-entendre.

"I need to see you."

Her voice sounded so close that he glanced down at his seminude body as though she had suddenly materialized in the room. He wore nothing but a brief pair of running shorts slit high on the sides—and the salt-crusted sweat from his half-hour run.

"When did you get back from Washington?" he asked, trying not to sound as eager as he felt.

"Yesterday afternoon. Before I forget, thank you for the flowers."

"I thought you might need some cheering up." Either she couldn't wait to talk to him—or she had a problem. He suspected the latter. "It's early for a social call. Is something wrong?"

"I'm surprised you haven't heard. Don't you have the television on?"

"I never play it at home."

"My parents' apartment burned down last night."

His throat tightened. "Are you and Bella all right?"

"We're fine. We were sound asleep at my house when it happened. But Mom lost every memento of her life with Dad."

Peach sounded like she needed a hug. If she'd been there, nothing on earth could have stopped him from giving her one. His jaws clenched at the inadequacy of words to express his concern. "I'm sorry to hear it. Is there anything I can do to help?"

"As a matter of fact, there is. How about joining me for lunch so we can discuss it?"

Lunch was a snap. He'd have walked across hot coals to be with her. "Just tell me when and where."

"Do you know Tony Mandola's Seafood Kitchen on Gray?"

He nodded, then realized she couldn't see him. "It's one of my favorites," he replied, trying to control the wild surge of expectation coursing through him. Peach had asked him on a date. It made him feel thirteen again—minus the acne.

"See you there at twelve." Peach said. She hung up before he could ask any of the questions that crowded his mind.

He stood in the center of the room, wondering what was on hers—and hoping it would turn out to be him. He thought her name, then said it out loud, enjoying the way the word felt on his lips.

The first time he'd heard that name, he'd concluded no intelligent full-grown woman would permit herself to be called Peach, any more than a grown man would relish answering to Billy Bob or Bubba.

However when he met her he realized how well the name suited her. With her sunset-colored hair, her golden complexion and her lush curves, she reminded him of a ripe fruit—and he often imagined how sweet it would be to consume her.

The repeated buzz of the microwave timer ended his reverie. He hurried back into the kitchen, took the bagels out, cut them in half, covered them with cream cheese, then sat down at the breakfast table to eat.

For the second time that morning he was interrupted by the telephone. This time Bella Morgan was on the other end of the line.

"Arye, I'm so glad I caught you before you went to work," she said.

"I talked to your daughter a little while ago. She

told me about the fire. Is there anything I can do to help?"

"As a matter of fact, yes," Bella replied. "I'm worried about Peach. She's been under such a strain."

"Spoken like a true mother. How are you holding up?" He liked Bella a great deal. She was a class act.

"It's sweet of you to ask. I'm fine. Arye dear, I called because I need a favor."

He suspected the ever-politic Bella could sweet-talk anyone into doing what she wanted. But he couldn't help wondering how and why he'd landed on the Morgan women's hit parade that morning. Peach had wanted a favor, too. Could one have anything to do with the other?

His curiosity aroused, he told Bella, "All you have to do is ask."

"Peach has the bizarre idea that the fire is part of some huge conspiracy to ruin her father," Bella explained.

"Isn't that a little strange under the circumstances?" Arye replied, alluding to Blackjack's demise.

"I agree. I buried my husband two days ago. Nothing—certainly not a fire—can hurt him now. Peach doesn't agree. She wants to clear her father's name. We've argued about it. I want my daughter to get on with her life but she can't seem to see her way past her father's last words to her. You'd think they had been written on stone."

"Where do I come in?"

"She wants you to help her investigate what happened to Blackjack last year. She's convinced some sinister cabal is to blame for his downfall." Bella sighed. "I want you to convince her she's wrong."

"And if I can't?"

"Refuse to help her. Peach is a wonderful woman but she's rather impractical. If you turn her down she won't know how to proceed on her own."

"I'll do what I can, Bella. But your daughter is very stubborn."

They chatted a little longer before saying good-bye. Disconsolate, Arye returned to the kitchen. His bagel and coffee were icy—not that it mattered. He'd lost his appetite.

For a few minutes he'd been foolish enough to allow himself to believe Peach wanted to see him. Now he knew she wanted to see the investigative reporter he used to be. Much as he cared for her, nothing in the world could convince him to return to his former vocation.

He was in a bad way, he mused as he cleared the table. For the life of him, he didn't know how, where, when and why Peach had gotten under his skin.

God knew, she wasn't anything like his wife. Helen had been long, lean, leggy, and so smart she intimidated him even though he had graduated magna cum laude from Berkeley. She preferred jeans to designer labels, a ponytail to a salon coiffure, and he could still picture the unadorned nails she had never been able to stop chewing to the quick.

Peach, with her couturier wardrobe, her perfect manicure and teased hair, couldn't be more different. The single characteristic she shared with Helen was a bone-deep decency.

He'd loved his wife in every way a man could love a woman. After her death he'd been sure he would never love again. But he was too old and too self-aware to fool himself about his feelings for Peach.

He loved her.

Call it a miracle, a disaster, or a royal pain in the ass. By any name the emotion scared the hell out of him. Whoever wrote *it was better to have loved and lost than never to have loved at all* didn't know what the hell he was talking about.

If he won Peach and then lost her—no matter the reason or cause—he knew he wouldn't survive.

After arranging to meet Arye, Peach spent the next few hours putting her affairs in order so she'd be free to concentrate on the investigation.

She spoke to her lawyer first. He reported that Herbert had agreed to the property settlement. She would keep the house and the magazine. Herbert would keep their considerable investment portfolio, their savings, and retain control of his practice even though her father had financed it. The settlement wasn't financially equitable but Peach didn't care. She wanted her freedom. The divorce would be final in less than three months.

Next she talked to a Realtor who specialized in River Oaks properties and made an appointment to get the house listed. She even balanced her checkbook for the first time in her life.

Somehow the things she accomplished took a back seat to the anticipation of her lunch with Arye. Every time she thought about sitting across a table from him, her stomach contracted, her pulse accelerated and her skin felt flushed. The sensations were unsettling to say the least.

She told herself her peculiar physiological reaction was due to the prospect of doing something positive on her father's behalf—but she didn't really believe it. Not for a minute. She was no more successful lying to herself than she was to other people.

When she hired Arye she'd been concerned he would raise havoc with the women on her staff. She hadn't realized one of the women would be her. Her attraction to him pulled her in one direction—the need to exonerate her father in another.

At ten-thirty she put the checkbook back in the desk drawer, then went to her room to get ready for lunch. She could dress in half an hour from shower to makeup when the need arose. This morning though, she needed all the time she had allotted.

She searched her wardrobe with a critical eye, trying to decide what to put on. The dresses she wore to charity luncheons seemed too matronly. The tailored slacks and blazers she favored for sporting events were too masculine. To add to her dilemma, everything she tried on needed to be taken in. Not too surprising since she hadn't been able to eat.

She wanted to look businesslike yet feminine. Wrong, she silently corrected herself. She wanted to look drop-dead gorgeous. She finally chose a dress she hadn't been able to get into for years, a simple linen sheath whose turquoise color enhanced her coloring.

She had missed her last appointment at the International Beauty Spot across from the Galleria on Westheimer so she put her hair up in a French twist that made her look taller and had the added virtue of being cooler than the big bouffant hairdo Herbert liked.

One month ago she wouldn't have dreamed of going out without stockings no matter how hot and humid it was outside. Going bare-legged simply wasn't done in her world. Feeling decidedly naughty, she left her pantyhose in the lingerie drawer and rubbed cream on her legs instead. Ivory sandals and a matching purse completed her casual look.

Since the most carefully applied makeup tended to dissolve in Houston's steamy summer weather, leaving the unfortunate wearer looking more like a raccoon than a *femme fatale*, she kept hers to a minimum. When she finished she stood in front of the ceiling-to-floor mirror in her dressing room and barely recognized the woman she saw reflected there.

She looked younger, thinner, and happier than she had in years—more like the Peach Morgan who had gone off to college than the staid and dignified Mrs. Morgan-Strand.

That's who she wanted to be from now on, she decided instantly. No more hyphenation for her. The next time she talked to her attorney she'd tell him she wanted to resume her maiden name.

At the last minute she retrieved a necklace of hand-carved turquoise heishi and fetish birds from her jewelry case. She had purchased it at the Santa Fe Indian Market and only worn it once because Herbert complained that it made her look like a peasant.

Now she closed the clasp around her neck, took off her wedding and engagement rings and put them in the jewelry case. The finality of the act called for a solemnity she was incapable of feeling.

Excitement, as heady as champagne, bubbled in her blood. Arye, here I come, she thought as she skipped down the stairs.

Tony Mandola's Seafood Kitchen was housed in the River Oaks shopping center, an art-deco complex that had been built in the forties when River Oaks had just become the place where wealthy Houstonians preferred to live. Despite the rarified atmosphere of its surroundings, the restaurant gave good value for the price, serving up delicious seafood with a Cajun twist and the best key lime pie this side of Florida.

Peach pulled into the parking lot fifteen minutes early. To her surprise Arye had preceded her. He sat at a banquette table sipping a Dos Equis, an expectant look on his face as he gazed toward the door. He stood up the minute he saw her, put down his beer, crossed the room and took both of her hands in his.

Her body seemed to vibrate at the contact. Warmth radiated up her arms, shoulders and neck to come to rest in her cheeks. She couldn't suppress an ear-to-ear grin even though she knew she must look like an idiot.

Arye wore a camel hair blazer over a polo shirt and well-washed jeans that hugged his hips, thighs and loins so closely the fabric could have been a second skin. God, there ought to be a law against a man advertising his masculinity that way, she thought, feeling her knees knock.

"I'm so glad you called this morning," Arye said. "I've been worrying about you. But you don't look like a lady who has been through hell. You look wonderful."

Peach felt herself blush. "I suppose disaster agrees with me."

Arye couldn't bring himself to let go of Peach's hand until they reached the table. He helped her into a chair, sat down across from her, and gazed his fill. With her red hair and memorable eyes, she had always been striking. This afternoon she took his breath away.

"You're staring," she said.

"You'll have to get used to it. I can't help it."

Before she could respond, a waiter came to take their order. Peach asked for seafood lasagna and Arye chose the snapper Tomas although food was the furthest thing from his mind.

After the waiter left, their conversation proceeded in fits and starts. They talked about the memorial service, the Arlington burial, the next issue of the magazine, occasionally stumbling into one another's sentences like teenagers on a first date. And all the while, he was wondering when she'd get around to telling him why she wanted to see him.

For his part, he was content to prolong their meal as long as possible. The crowd had thinned and the clock over the bar read one when she finally mentioned the apartment fire.

"Thank God your mother decided to stay with you. Was anyone else hurt?" he asked.

"Some one called in an alarm early enough that the fire department was able to keep the blaze from spreading. I think that someone set the fire."

Peach had never been so distracted by a man. She stared at him, tracing the line of his brow and the curve of his lips instead of thinking about what she needed to say. How could she convince him to help her when she was practically drooling? So much depended on him believing her.

"Aren't you jumping to conclusions?"

"So what if I am, as long as they're logical?"

"I've never heard of a pyromaniac calling in a fire. They are usually too busy getting off on a blaze to think about anything else."

"That proves my point. The person who set the fire didn't do it for kicks. I think the fire was part of a pattern—a conspiracy to ruin my father."

"That doesn't make sense. Blackjack's dead and buried. No one can hurt him now."

"But his private papers were in the apartment. What if there was something in them?"

"What sort of something?"

"I don't know," she answered. "But I intend to find out."

"Blackjack's life was pretty much an open book, Peach. His political beliefs, his comings and goings were well documented by the press. The last year he couldn't even take a leak without someone reporting it." Hoping to discourage Peach, Arye had used street talk for its shock value. "I can't imagine there were any deep dark secrets left to uncover."

"Dad's executive assistant, Randolph Spurling, asked all sorts of peculiar questions about Dad's private papers when Mother and I were in Washington. He looked worried when I told him Dad had kept a diary. I have the feeling Randolph Spurling has something to hide."

"Losing a job has a way of making a man look worried."

"Will you stop being so judgmental and just listen for a minute? My father's troubles began shortly after he left the Democratic party and declared himself an independent. The next thing he knew, the IRS was looking into his tax returns."

"The IRS may be as close to a Gestapo as anything we'll ever see in America, but they investigate millions of returns every year," Arye replied, hoping to pour a little oil on Peach's troubled mental waters. "Your father just happened to be one of the unlucky ones to have them look into his."

His response failed to dampen Peach's ardor. "That was just the beginning. Shortly afterward someone leaked a story to the press about Daddy converting campaign funds to his personal use. I think that someone was Randolph Spurling."

"That's one hell of a stretch. Spurling knew he'd lose his job if your father lost his. Perhaps that someone worked for the IRS. It's just the sort of thing they could have uncovered in the course of a thorough investigation."

Peach shook her head in vehement denial, loosening strands of red-gold hair. She looked a little disheveled—and utterly delicious. It took considerable effort on Arye's part to concentrate on what she was saying.

"My father was a very bright man. If he had set out to fool the IRS, he would have done such a good job they would never have known. But he would never have done anything underhanded. He was an honorable man. Every time he seemed on the brink of clearing his name, a whole new series of charges surfaced. I'm convinced he was the victim of a setup to discredit him."

"Your conclusion speaks well of your loyalty, Peach."

"This has nothing to do with loyalty—and everything to do with common sense. The last thing my father said to me was *don't let the bastards get away with it*. He wouldn't have said it unless he meant it." Peach went on to reiterate the litany of woes that had culminated in Blackjack's heart attack. "Suppose there was some sort of a cabal in Washington that went after him," she concluded. "Shouldn't it be exposed?"

Her breasts strained against her dress as she leaned toward him. She looked so earnest—and he felt so damn horny. He didn't want to talk politics, especially

Blackjack's politics. "Peach, be reasonable. All you've got is conjecture and supposition."

"The fire wasn't an accident. The arson investigator called it a professional job. What if someone burned the apartment to keep us from finding out the truth?"

"Do you have any *prima facie* evidence to prove what you're saying?"

"That's where you come in. You were an investigative reporter. You know how to get evidence. That's why I wanted to see you today."

The horniness vanished as quickly as a Saharan mirage. "Peach, do you know what happens when you tilt at windmills?"

"Are we talking Don Quixote, or reality?"

"Reality," he replied firmly. "When you tilt at windmills, the spokes have a nasty habit of coming up behind you and hitting you on the head."

The gleam in her eyes told him she wouldn't easily take no for an answer. "I happen to have a very hard head."

"A very pretty one, too. I'd hate to see it split open."

"That won't happen if you help me. Daddy's fellow politicians hounded him mercilessly the last year of his life. In the end his heart wasn't up to the strain. I want to know why they went after him. What did Daddy do to deserve their wrath?"

Translate that to who did Blackjack threaten? Arye thought bleakly, a frisson of apprehension tickling his backbone. His long quiescent reporter's intuition stirred to life. He had the feeling Peach was asking the right questions—just as he had when he began investigating Mafia infiltration of legitimate businesses in Phoenix.

He should have been more careful in view of the

fact that Don Bolles had been murdered in a car bombing when he asked the same sort of questions. He'd thought the Bolles incident was ancient history. Arye had been convinced he was smarter and tougher than the veteran reporter.

Helen had died because of that belief. He wouldn't make the same mistake again—and he wouldn't let Peach make it either. She was no match for the Washington big-boys.

"When I went to work for you I told you I'd given up investigative reporting for good. Nothing you've said has changed my mind."

"It could be the story of the decade," she declared, a cub reporter's fervor glowing in her eyes.

Hell. If he did as she wanted he'd be able to look into her eyes all day long. The temptation was great— the jeopardy even greater.

"I think you're due for a reality check, boss lady. Your father was a powerful man and yet he died bankrupt and in disgrace. If it was the result of a conspiracy—and mind you I'm not saying it was—the people involved are even more powerful than he was. What chance do you think you'd have against them?"

"Then you agree I may be right?"

"I didn't say that."

He had hoped to discourage her. However she looked more determined than ever. How could he ever have imagined she was just a bored society matron? She was a frigging lioness on the prowl. But even lionesses get killed.

"What do you think?" she asked.

He hesitated a moment, weighing his answer, choosing each word for maximum affect and wishing there was another way to bring her to her senses. "I think you're looking for something to keep you entertained now you don't have a husband in your bed at night."

Her eyes narrowed. Her fists clenched. For a second he thought she was going to deck him. "How dare you talk to me like that?"

"I dare because I don't want to see you get hurt. You're naive, Peach. You don't know a damn thing about the risks an investigative reporter can run. Hell, you don't know a damn thing about reporting either. Stick to things you do know like your charities and your dinner parties and your social life."

The look on Peach's face told him he'd stepped way over the line. She's going to fire me, he thought. So be it. He'd happily go jobless to save her from herself.

"What happened to the man who hurried to the hospital to help me—the man who came to my rescue at the memorial service?" Peach asked.

She had been so certain Arye would rally to her banner. Now she wondered what would happen if she threw her wine in his smug face. A couple of waiters would come running to mop up the mess. They didn't deserve the trouble or the extra work.

"I'm the same man."

"No, you're not. I was stupid enough to think you cared about me. Now I realize all you cared about was buttering up the boss."

She fished her wallet out of her purse, took out a couple of twenties, dropped them on the table in the most ball-breaking, ego-macerating gesture she could muster, and stalked out of the restaurant without saying another word.

For a woman who hated confrontations, she'd had more than her share lately, she thought, getting in her car. She squared her shoulders, put the Jaguar in gear and blasted out of the lot with the rubber-burning elan of an Indy race car driver.

Mrs. Morgan-Strand would have headed straight for the Galleria to seek solace in a shopping spree. But the new and improved model, Ms. Peach Morgan, had no intention of giving up or caving in because a misguided mass of muscles and testosterone wouldn't help her.

During her freshman year in college one of her journalism professors had given a lecture about primary and secondary sources of information. The primary sources—her mother and Arye—had been a bust. She would try the secondary sources, she decided, turning south on Shepherd heading toward the Rice University campus.

Eight

Damn Peach's mule-headedness, Arye fumed, glaring at the money she had thrown on the table. If she wanted to challenge his manhood, she had certainly chosen the right way to do it.

Perhaps he belonged to a dying breed, but he believed a man ought to pay for the food when he dined with a woman, just as he ought to open doors for her, help her into a car, and stay on the curb side of the pavement when they walked together. And not as a put-down, the way some feminists asserted.

He'd been raised to think treating a woman with courtesy was a way of showing respect for her sex. His daddy had treated his mother that way, he had treated his wife that way, and he'd have given the world to have treated Peach that way.

He glanced down at her barely touched platter of seafood lasagna. It seemed to glare back in reproach, as if to say *it's your fault she didn't eat, you big bully*.

And he had bullied her. Who the hell did he think he was, reassuring himself with thoughts about courtesy when he hadn't shown Peach any respect? Feeling too dyspeptic to finish his own meal, he pocketed Peach's money, planning to return it to her at the first opportunity. He caught the waiter's attention and handed over his own credit card.

The drive to the office through heavy traffic brought a series of expletives to his lips. The long wait for an elevator did nothing to improve his mood. He stormed past the *Inside Texas* receptionist's desk like Grant marching through Georgia, stalked into his own office, slammed the door with a reverberating thud, sat down at his desk and stared at the proof sheets piled on top.

They might as well have been written in Sanskrit for all the sense he made of them. He couldn't get his mind off Peach. He wasn't a cruel man and took no pleasure in the knowledge that he had wounded her. Nor was he one of those wimps who only felt masculine when he made some poor lady feel lower than a snake's belly.

He said what he'd said for Peach's own good, hadn't he?

Damn right. Under the circumstances he couldn't have said anything else. There'd been no time to come up with something that might have been easier on her pride. He'd been looking out for her. So why did remorse gnaw at his gut like a vulture working over a road kill?

Because he was a coward—a man who had never faced up to the past let alone the present, a tiny voice whispered at the back of his mind. He clenched his jaws so hard that his molars ached. What the hell kind of a mess had he gotten himself into?

If the gods were kind, Peach would call this very minute and put him out of his misery by firing him. That way he'd never have to see her again—never have to experience that hideous blend of love, longing, and stark terror that made him want to hide under his desk like a lightning-spooked dog.

On that unhappy thought, someone knocked at the door.

"Come back later," he growled.

To his dismay, the would-be visitor ignored what he said. The door opened to reveal Bert at his dapper, every-silver-hair-in-place best, a file clutched to his chest, a smile on his face. "I heard rumors about you being in a foul mood. I thought I'd come see for myself."

"The rumors are true. If that's the only reason you're here, stay at your own peril."

Bert raised his hands in mock surrender. "Don't shoot. I'm not the guilty party. The other guy did it."

"Did what?"

Bert waved the file. "Took these lousy photographs for the November cover. I don't think they'll do much for your peace of mind. Who put a burr under your saddle?"

"Peach. She's the most infuriating woman I ever met." Arye pushed his chair away from the desk so hard that it crashed into the book case at his back. He ignored the volumes that came tumbling down. "She walked out on me at lunch."

"I didn't realize you two had a date."

"It wasn't a date," Arye snapped.

Bert ignored his boorishness. "I thought Peach and Bella would be busy with other matters today of all days. Damn shame, that fire. I plan to call Bella later to see if there's anything I can do for her."

Arye was too preoccupied to see the gleam in Bert's eyes. "That's nice."

"What's nice?" Bert asked, settling in the chair opposite the desk, "the fire—or the fact that Peach walked out on you?"

Arye drew a deep breath, hoping it would calm him. "Neither. I feel so sorry for Peach. But not sorry enough to do what she wanted."

"Did you argue about moving the magazine again?"

"I wish it had been that simple. She wanted me to help her investigate her father's death."

"I thought Blackjack died of a heart attack."

"He did." Unable to sit still a minute longer, Arye got up to pace the floor. "That's not the problem. The last thing Blackjack said to Peach was, *don't let the bastards get away with it.* Now she's convinced there was some sort of conspiracy to ruin him—and she wants me to help her look into it."

"The poor bastard did have the world's worst run of bad luck last year. What did you say?"

Arye stopped pacing, looked at Bert and shook his head as though he couldn't believe Bert had asked such a stupid question. "No. I said *no!* For God's sake, I'm not an investigative reporter anymore."

Amusement twitched the corners of Bert's mouth. "I hear it's like making love. Once you get the hang of it, you never forget how."

Arye didn't appreciate Bert's humor. "I can't go back to that life. I won't. And I warned Peach not to try it on her own. Damn it, Bert. What if she's right? Do you have any idea how much danger she'd be in?"

"Are you worried about the danger to her—or to you?" Bert asked quietly.

"What the hell do you mean by that?"

Somehow, Bert managed to look smug and thoughtful at the same time. "You were smitten with the lady the first time you met her. Now she's free, it's only natural—"

"There's nothing natural about it," Arye interrupted.

"What's the matter? Do you think she's too old for you?" Bert fired back.

The question took Arye by surprise. "To tell you the truth, I've never once thought about her age."

"Is it her sons?"

"Hell, no. I've met them and they're terrific young men. It's the rest of the package. Peach and I don't have a damn thing in common. She's elegant, beautiful, rich. I'm plain as dirt. She drives a Jaguar. I ride a Harley. She wears designer clothes. I hate suits and ties. Need I go on?"

"We both know Peach isn't the sort of person who would worry about things like that. She's a straight arrow if I ever saw one. So are you. You're both caring, decent human beings with a hell of a lot to give. That's more important than clothes or cars. What's really bothering you?"

Bert knew him too well. "I think I'm in love with her—and its scares me to death."

"You poor bastard. You're afraid to care, aren't you? Afraid that something terrible will happen to Peach the way it did to Helen."

Bert's intuition was right on target, as usual. "I don't know what to do."

Bert hesitated so long that Arye could almost hear the wheels spinning inside Bert's head.

"Carpe diem," Bert finally said, "seize the day. Don't go through the rest of your life like a zombie the way you have these last six years."

Bert made it sound deceptively simple. "I don't know if I have what it takes to follow your advice."

"When we first met, nothing could have prevented you from going after something you really wanted. It's what made you one hell of a reporter."

"Yeah, sure. And it killed my wife."

It was Bert's turn to jump to his feet. His gimlet gaze caught and held Arye's. "Once and for all, will you get it through your thick head that a Mafia button-man killed Helen."

Feeling as if Bert had the power to see inside his soul, Arye lowered his glance. "That car bomb was meant for me."

"Helen's death was tragic, but it was not your fault." Bert crossed to Arye's side, grabbed him by the arms and gave him a forceful shake. *"Could have* and *should have* are damn sorry words. It's time you replaced them with *can* and *will.*"

"Meaning?"

"Call Peach. Apologize. Women like it when a man has the courage to admit he was wrong. Offer to help her." Bert cocked his head and gave Arye a crooked smile. "I imagine you're wondering who the hell I am, a widower of twenty years, to give such advice? I intend to follow it myself."

"You're talking in riddles."

"It's very simple. I've known Bella for years and I've always admired her—from afar. There isn't any reason for me to keep my distance anymore. I plan to ask her for dinner when I call her."

"Her husband just died. Isn't that pushing it?"

"Perhaps. But I'm not exactly a youngster and neither is she. We don't have a lot of time to waste. Besides, for most of their marriage Blackjack wasn't much of a husband. He spent a lot of time away from home and he was a notorious womanizer. Bella deserved better."

Bert's advice had ignited a spark inside the dark cavern that was Arye's heart. Like a moth drawn to the light, his soul winged toward it. "After the things I said to Peach at lunch, I doubt she'll talk to me."

"Make her listen. Camp on her doorstep if you have to. She's worth the fight. *Carpe diem,* Arye, *carpe diem.*" His smile deepening, Bert dropped the file on Arye's desk, walked out the door and shut it softly behind him.

Bert's words reverberated through Arye's mind long after Bert's footsteps had faded away. Seize the day!

Arye hadn't gone after anything since Helen's death. He hadn't let himself want anything for fear he'd lose it. He worked at a job that required a fraction of his skill, existed in a house he never made into a home, spent his free time riding the Harley too fast, hang gliding on days when even the pros didn't trust the wind, courting death while running from life.

Though others marveled at his daring, Arye knew himself for a coward. Death—the cessation of all feeling—would have been easy. It was living that hurt.

From this moment on he vowed to confront the pain—and the possibilities. Seize the day, he told himself as he walked over to the desk, picked up the phone, and dialed Peach's number.

It took Peach half an hour to find a parking spot on the Rice campus. When she finally did, it turned out to be a fifteen-minute walk from the library. Seeing so many shorts-clad coeds with cellulite-free legs and tight buns didn't brighten her outlook. She felt old and terribly out of place.

At the very moment that Arye sat at his desk, phone in hand, his heart drumming like the anvil chorus while hope fluttered in his brain, Peach sat hunched before a screen in the Rice Library, cursing him under her breath. If she'd had any sense, she would have fired him before she walked out of the restaurant.

He'd been insufferably rude. More important, he'd come close to extinguishing her newly awakened belief in herself. Some lion, she thought with a shake of her head. Arye Rappaport was a macho heel with testosterone running through his veins instead of blood, and a chip on his shoulder as big as a tree.

Was she destined to forever be a loser in the game of love?

Would she live the rest of her life without a man—without sex?

Should she face the facts and buy a sex toy on the way home?

Where in the world did you buy a vibrator anyway?

The question made her giggle. It took a moment to turn off her stream of consciousness and turn her attention to the job at hand. She had far more important questions to consider this afternoon.

Outrage at Arye had gotten her this far, she mused, threading a microfiche reel into the viewer. It wouldn't get her any further. She'd come to the library because a long-ago journalism professor had told her newspapers were a good secondary source of information.

But she had no idea what to look for. A needle in a haystack seemed an apt description as she contemplated reviewing reel after reel of the Houston Chronicle microfiche. She had two clues—her father's last words and the fact that his troubles began about the time that he abandoned the Democratic party and declared himself an independent.

He had been a media favorite before then. Afterward the press had used him as a target of opportunity.

"There's no such thing as bad publicity," Blackjack used to say.

How wrong he'd been, Peach thought regretfully. If he had been a less public man, he might still be alive.

The reels of microfiche she'd checked out dated from the months immediately preceding his changed political affiliation to the appearance of his obituary. She threaded the first reel into the scanner and began her search.

She didn't have to run through many editions of the *Chronicle* before she read her father's name. "Senator Blackjack Morgan Lobbies For The Space Station," the headline read. Peach fed a dime into the machine and printed out a copy of the page.

A month later another article told of her father's fight to save the super-collider project despite its runaway costs. She printed it out too, then continued scrolling forward.

Her eyes teared up when she saw Blackjack's picture on the cover of *Texas Magazine,* a popular insert in the Sunday paper. He beamed out at the camera as if he owned the world. The Vice President and world-famous model Caitlin Pride flanked him on either side. The caption read, "Caitlin Pride hosts notables at the opening of Pride's Outback."

Peach vaguely remembered getting an invitation to

the opening of the safari resort ranch herself. She and Herbert had gone to a hospital function instead. But her parents and her younger sister Avery had been in attendance. When they returned from the Hill Country, Avery had given a glowing account of the three-day gala.

Avery and Caitlin Pride had been best friends at Kinkaid. Peach and Avery's age difference and Peach's marriage to Herbert had kept Peach from knowing Caitlin well. She had been shocked when the model abandoned a glittering career and the fame and fortune that went with it, to return to Texas to transform her family's historic cattle ranch into a world-class resort and a haven for endangered species.

Peach printed out the picture, the accompanying article, and scrolled forward again. She almost missed the story tucked in the back pages of the paper several days later.

It recounted a fatal accident at the opening of Pride's Outback. Carroll Detweiler, a Vietnam veteran and former soldier of fortune, had been killed by a feral Russian boar on a part of Pride's Outback that wasn't open to the public. Her father, Cait, and the local sheriff, among others, had witnessed the death.

The name Detweiler rang a bell. Peach had an unpleasant memory of a Carroll Detweiler who visited Belle Terre a couple of years after the war. Something about him—perhaps his size, perhaps a wild look in his eyes—had frightened her so much that she refused to shake his hand. She'd heard no mention of him since. Strange, she mused, in view of what had happened.

She printed the article out, then paused to read it over. The brief paragraphs failed to mention Detweiler's earlier involvement with her father, let alone his reason for being at Pride's Outback. Either it was poor reporting, or someone had influenced the writer to stick to the bare bones of the story.

Could that someone have been her father? He had the clout. Did he also have a motive? Curiouser and curiouser, she thought, feeling a bit like Alice falling down the rabbit hole.

Peach left the library four hours later with a thick stack of reprints tucked under her arm. She had learned more about her father's political career that afternoon than she had known during his lifetime. She couldn't help wondering how Blackjack would have reacted if she'd exhibited the same interest a few years ago. Could she have prevented what happened?

As she drove home, her thoughts returned to what she now knew. Throughout his first three terms in office, Blackjack had been a politician's politician, a master at delivering pork barrel projects to Texas voters. And they had loved him for it.

Then without a word of warning, he had called a press conference, announced he didn't believe the two-party system worked anymore, and declared himself an Independent.

Shocked Democrats were quoted as calling his decision "ill-advised and "a disservice to his constituents." A prominent senator who had been one of Blackjack's closest cronies had gone so far as to describe Blackjack's action as "a political has-been's last desperate attempt to garner national attention."

The earlier incident at the Outback seemed to mark the turning point in her father's career. Afterward, as a self-avowed independent free of party affiliation, he began giving speeches about corruption in the Senate and the House. He called for smaller government, putting an end to federal mandates, enacting a balanced budget bill, term limits, a line item veto and immediate campaign reform. He asked for a special prosecutor to expose the connections between certain lobbyists, senators, congressmen, and the legislation they pushed through Congress.

What could have happened to change him into a social activist who looked beyond the borders of his own state to the state of the nation as a whole? Had Detweiler's death somehow precipitated everything that followed? Could the loss of a comrade in arms cause her father to rethink his political goals?

The first negative article showed up in the *Chronicle* two months after Blackjack became an independent. It related how Blackjack was being investigated by the IRS for failure to pay sufficient taxes. Other negative stories had followed until Blackjack had been removed from the Senate Judiciary committee. Then the Senate ethics committee—talk about an oxymoron—had appointed a special prosecutor to look into the various charges. That had been followed by talk of censure, and ultimately by Blackjack's stress-induced heart attack.

And now copies of all those stories sat on the front seat of the Jaguar next to Peach. She could almost hear Herbert telling her she had bitten off more than she could chew and that she was barking up the wrong tree. Herbert and his clichés. How could she have been convinced of his brilliance? Arye never used clichés, not even today when he'd verbally cut her to the bone.

Oh, no. There she went thinking about him again. Without realizing it her foot pressed harder on the accelerator, as if by increasing the car's speed she could run away from her own mind.

Bella was in the family room, drinking a martini and watching the evening news when Peach returned home.

"There you are, darling," Bella said brightly. "I thought you'd be home sooner. Were you with Arye the whole time?"

"Hardly," Peach replied, relieved that the tension between them had ebbed. It would undoubtedly return if Bella knew how she had spent her day. She was going to have to be very, very careful.

"Did you make enough for me?" Peach asked, pointing at Bella's martini.

"A whole pitcher. It's on the bar."

Peach helped herself to what was undoubtedly the world's driest martini—shaken, not stirred, the way both her father and James Bond liked them—then walked over to the sofa and sat down beside her mother.

"How was your day?" Bella asked.

Thank heaven she hadn't inquired *how* Peach had spent it. "Fine. And yours?"

"Very pleasant. I spent a few hours writing thank-you notes to people who sent flowers to the memorial service, visited with Delia over lunch, and then I sat out by the pool for a while. The grounds are so lovely. Will you miss the house when you sell it?"

Peach stared into her glass. "I'll never forget the years we spent here when the boys were growing up. But I won't miss the house. Herbert liked it so much more than I ever did. I can hardly wait to buy something smaller and less pretentious."

Bella nodded. "I know what you mean. I hated selling Belle Terre, but now your father's gone, I'm glad I'm not living there."

Peach gave Bella a quick hug. "I'm happy you're here. We need each other."

"Arye called while you were out. He wants to talk to you as soon as possible. He made it sound quite urgent."

Peach felt her cheeks burn. Of all the nerve. Other than an abject apology, what could he possibly have to say to her? And what in the world made him think she'd want to hear it? "He can wait until I get back."

"Back from where?"

"I've decided to spend a couple of days at Pride's Outback."

Bella gave Peach a look that clearly said she was glad Peach had come to her senses. "That's wonderful, darling. The change of scene will do you good."

"Do you mind being alone?"

"I'm perfectly self-sufficient. When do you plan to go?"

"Tomorrow morning."

"Oh." Bella's elevated brow revealed her surprise. "Are you leaving so suddenly because we argued this morning?"

Guilt urged Peach to confess the reason for her hasty trip. Knowing it would precipitate another disagreement, she kept her own counsel. "I just thought, well—"

"You don't need to explain yourself, darling. We both know the adage about two grown women living under the same roof. A little distance will do us a world of good." Bella played with her glass, twirling the stem between her fingers. "Bert Hanrahan called today after hearing about the fire. He wanted to know if he could be of any help. When I told him I'd lost all my photographs of Blackjack, he offered to use his contacts to get reprints from newspapers and magazines. Then he asked me out to supper tomorrow."

"Don't tell me you accepted!"

"Why shouldn't I?"

"But it's so soon."

"It's never too soon to see an old friend," Bella replied with unassailable logic.

Still, Peach couldn't help feeling peculiar at the thought of her mother going out to dinner with a man.

Nothing Peach had seen in *Texas Magazine* prepared her for Pride's Outback. The article had described a stay at the ranch as the closest thing to going on safari this side of Nairobi. Fifteen minutes after driving through the high double gates that guarded the entrance, Peach could easily imagine she had been transported from the Texas Hill Country to Masai Mara or some other magnificent game reserve.

Time and again, she braked for small herds of various antelope species that she associated with the African plains. As she followed signs to the main house, she passed an open-topped Range Rover that had stopped so the occupants could take pictures of a Zebra herd with a number of foals. Peach swore she recognized a famous movie star when one of them lowered a camera.

Could something have happened in this Eden—

aside from Detweiler's death—to set her father on the road to ruin?

Brochures described the main house as a shining example of historic Hill Country style. Built of buttermilk-colored limestone, it sat on the crest of a hill overlooking the Guadalupe River. Despite its size, there was nothing pretentious about its appearance.

A covered porch gave it a welcoming ambiance that was quickly bolstered when a tall man came out the front door and addressed her by name.

"You must be Peach Morgan," he called out, giving her a high-voltage smile.

"Guilty as charged."

He was undoubtedly the handsomest man she had ever seen. No, make it the second handsomest, she mused, recalling Arye's dark good looks.

"I'm Cait's husband, Comanche Killian." He beamed when he said his wife's name.

Lucky Cait, Peach thought as Comanche made an easy job of carrying her luggage inside the house.

"Honey, Peach is here," he called out before disappearing up the stairs with her bags.

An exquisite blonde materialized at the back of the wide center hall. Peach recognized her at once, not as the teenage girl who had been Avery's friend but as the model whose picture had smiled forth on dozens of magazine covers.

"It was very kind of you to let me visit on such short notice," Peach said, wishing she were tall, thin and gorgeous like Cait Pride Killian.

"It's our pleasure. We're putting you up in the main house since the guest facilities are full. You'll be staying in my old room," Cait replied with an easy smile before her expression sobered. She took one of

Peach's hands and gave it a squeeze. "I'm so sorry about your father. Losing him must have been very hard on you. My own father died a few years ago so I know what you're going through."

"I came because I wanted to find out more about my father's stay with you," Peach replied, following Cait into a living room that managed to feel cozy despite its generous proportions. "Did he visit here often?"

Cait shook her head. "Just the one time, at our grand opening. I didn't really know him that well. But I was one of his biggest fans. Without him, there wouldn't have been an Outback."

"Dad never mentioned that." Peach's heart rate quickened. On the drive out she'd wondered if the trip would turn out to be a pleasant interlude rather than a meaningful first step in her investigation. But her father hadn't just happened to be here when his old friend, Carroll Detweiler died. Blackjack had been involved with the Outback on a personal level.

She realized how anxious she must have looked when Cait took her hand again. "I hope you don't mind but I took the liberty of inviting a few people to dinner tonight. Not paying guests. They have separate dining facilities," Cait was quick to add. "My partners, Mims and Byron Neville, wanted to meet you."

Peach produced a smile. Her sleuthing could wait, she thought, as the warmth of the Pride homestead enveloped her.

Nine

"Carpe diem, my ass," Arye growsed from behind his desk as a second day wound to a close without word from Peach.

He'd followed Bert's advice and called her as soon as Bert left his office yesterday. Had he benefited from making a fool of himself? *Nein. Non. No.*

Peach might look soft, feminine and eminently cuddly but she was hard as steel inside. She would never forgive him.

The first time he tried to reach her, Delia had answered the phone. He'd swallowed his pride and said, "I'd like to talk to Peach. If she's reluctant to speak to me, please tell her I'm on my knees here."

"Whatever for?" Delia queried with a hint of laughter in her voice.

"I owe Peach a major apology."

"Miss Peach isn't home but I expect her any time now. Why don't you call back in a little bit?" Delia had suggested.

He'd waited two hours, then dialed the number again, feeling that peculiar mixture of dread and agitation he'd experienced the first time he asked a girl on a date.

This time Bella answered. "Delia told me you called

earlier. Frankly, I can't imagine what you have to apologize for considering how much help you've been. But Peach still isn't home. Shall I give her the same message, about you being on your knees?"

He swallowed. Hard. "Yes, please, with one addition. Tell Peach I'll reconsider her proposition if we can get together to discuss it."

"Dear me, if Peach propositioned you, I don't know if I'm the person you should be talking to."

"It's not what you think, Mrs. Morgan."

"Surely you aren't considering helping her with the investigation into her father's past?"

"I just want to talk to her again," he replied evenly. "About a personal matter."

"I'll have her call as soon as she gets in—and Arye, good luck."

He stayed at home close to the phone last night and even omitted his habitual run this morning for fear he'd miss Peach.

What a laugh! She wasn't going to get in touch with him. Not today, tomorrow, next week or next month. He didn't expect to see or talk to her again unless they had business to discuss.

He'd never have the chance to tell her he didn't mean that ugly crack about her being bored without a man in her bed. He was tickled pink that Herbert was out of the picture, to say nothing of Peach's bed. He said what he did because he wanted to protect her, and now he regretted every single word.

He stood up from the computer console where he'd been trying to work and walked to the bank of windows on the far wall. From the forty-fourth floor he could see all the way to River Oaks. Was Peach at home—or had she already resumed her active social life? Did she think of him at all, or had she put him out of her mind like yesterday's garbage? He frowned at the simile, however it seemed apt.

He continued to stare out the window but he no longer took in the view. He was wondering what to do about Peach. A knock at the door yanked him back to the here and now. He welcomed the intrusion. Anything was better than mooning over the woman like a lovelorn teenager.

"Come in," he called out, turning to greet his visitor.

Cindy Downing walked in carrying a stack of computer printouts. "I've completed the dummy layouts," she said throatily.

Peculiar, the way she changed the pitch of her voice when she was alone with him. "That was fast."

He gave her what he hoped was a grateful smile, although something about her made him as uneasy as the sound of chalk grating on a blackboard. But for her skills, he would long ago have considered replacing her.

She'd been the first of the staff to grasp their new computerized publishing program. He could trust her with the thorniest software task and know she'd get it done right and on time. His personal opinion had no bearing on her professional qualifications.

Instead of leaving the printouts on his desk, she crossed the floor and handed them directly to him, coming so close he could feel her body heat and smell her perfume, a musky fragrance that should have been sensual. Apparently Cindy didn't know there could be too much of a good thing. She'd made the mistake of dousing herself with it.

She stared up at him without speaking until he felt

compelled to break the silence. "How's your mother?"

She looked nonplussed. "My mother?"

"Do you plan to go home to see her any time soon?"

She shrugged. "I hadn't given it a thought."

"You've been to see her so often the last few years, I assumed you'd be leaving again in the near future. I'd like to know as far in advance as possible so I can make arrangements to have someone cover your job." Thinking he sounded a little harsh, he added, "You two must be very close."

"It's so sweet of you to worry about me," Cindy cooed although he hadn't intimated anything of the kind. "I won't be taking any more time off to visit my mother. She made a complete recovery."

"I must have misunderstood you. I thought her condition was terminal," Arye replied although he felt certain he hadn't misunderstood Cindy. He had a vivid memory of the first time she'd come to his office to ask for a couple of weeks to go back east and stay with her mother.

When he questioned her reason, she burst into tears, saying the doctors didn't hold out much hope for her mother. He'd felt so sorry for her that he'd taken her in his arms while she wept. He'd even given her his handkerchief to mop her tears. Come to think of it, she'd never returned it.

Cindy gave him a beatific smile. "Mother's recovery was a medical miracle. I've been trying to come up with some way to repay you for being so understanding about all my absences. Being a bachelor and all, you must be sick of eating out all the time. I put a roast in my crock pot this morning and as we speak, my bread maker should be turning out a loaf of rye. There's more than enough for two people. I'd love to share it with you tonight. How does seven sound?"

Terrible, he thought. He had no desire to break bread with Cindy Downing. "It's kind of you to ask, but—"

"You'd be doing me a big favor. I'll be tempted to overeat if I go home by myself and a single girl has to watch her figure." She accompanied the explanation with a peculiar wiggling motion that was almost a bump and grind. Good God, Cindy Downing was coming on to him!

"We have an unwritten law at *Inside Texas* about employees dating each other. You wouldn't want me to set a bad example by breaking it."

"Oh, come on, Arye." Her voice sounded even huskier. If she lowered it much more, she'd be a baritone. "Nobody needs to know. I won't tell if you won't."

He headed back to his desk and walked behind it, putting the solid expanse of wood between them. "I'd know. Besides, Bert mentioned something about my eating with him tonight."

Cindy's hopeful expression faded. Her lips thinned. Her eyes narrowed. For a second he detected something so venomous in her gaze that he took an involuntary step back.

She blinked the expression away the way other women blink away tears. "Perhaps some other time," she said, moving her hips like well-oiled ball bearings as she went to the door. She gave him one last lingering glance as if to say all was forgiven, then let herself out.

He breathed a sigh of relief, sat down at his desk, reached for the phone and punched in Bert's extension number.

"I just told someone we were having dinner tonight," he said after they'd exchanged greetings. "In case she checks up on me, are you free?"

"She? The plot thickens."

"It was Cindy," he explained.

Bert emitted a long drawn-out, "Ooooh," then said, "I can't help you tonight. I'm taking Bella to the River Oaks Grill. Why don't you give Peach a try? Candlelight and wine make all the difference when a man is confessing to being a horse's patoot."

"I haven't been able to reach her," Arye replied. "Do me a favor and put in a good word for me with her mother."

Cindy's high heels rat-tatted on the floor like machine-gun fire as she fled Arye's office. Too agitated to return to her own desk, she made her way to the ladies' room, pushed the door open with a shove that sent it crashing into the wall, then looked around.

Finding herself alone, she strode to the bank of sinks and stared into the mirror above them, looking at herself with a fashion photographer's minute attention to detail.

Was there something wrong with her appearance that had turned Arye off, some fatal flaw she'd neglected to fix? Could Dr. Strand do anything more to improve her looks?

A picture-perfect face stared back at her from a pair of emerald eyes. She turned from side to side, examining her profile, the fit of her dress and the shape of the body beneath it, then leaned closer and parted her lips to make sure her caps were all in place.

Her makeup and hair couldn't be improved on no

matter how much more money she spent at the beauty parlor. Her dress was businesslike but fit well enough to reveal every inch of her new curves. And she didn't see a feature that required Strand's talented scalpel. She looked as classy as any of those River Oaks bitches.

Why the hell hadn't Arye accepted her invitation? She had spent hours planning what she'd say so it would sound spontaneous. She had even gone to the trouble of buying a bread maker and learning to use it.

The thought of all that wasted effort rumbled in her stomach like an overloaded washing machine. She felt unbalanced and off center—and angrier than she could remember. It was the second time she'd gone out of her way to please Arye.

How could he turn down dinner at her place to go out to some greasy spoon with an old fart like Bert Hanrahan? She'd never liked the la-di-dah art director, never understood what the rest of the staff saw in him.

A chilling thought popped into her head. He was an artist—and artists were supposed to have a better eye than average people. What if he realized she'd had a lot of plastic surgery? What if he told Arye?

She had a horrible vision of them sitting across from each other at the dinner table tonight, having a good laugh at her expense. The thought made her so enraged, her complexion turned blotchy. She turned on the faucet and held her wrists under the rush of cold water, hoping it would cool her down.

Arye would never laugh at her—he was too kind, too understanding, she reassured herself. But Bert was another matter. Bert was Arye's best friend. He could influence Arye. She turned the water off, took a paper towel from the dispenser to dry her hands—and unconsciously shredded it into confetti.

Bert had gotten in her way the day of the senator's memorial service, and he'd done it again today. He would go right on doing it until she found a way to stop him.

She pressed her hot cheek against the cool mirror. Why did people always try to stop her from having what she wanted? Why did they take pleasure in making her unhappy? She'd grown up poor and friendless, with a drunk for a mother and a father who walked out before she was old enough to remember his face.

Girls used to make fun of her in school and boys pretended to gag when they passed her in the halls. Cindy moaned softly. How she hated Clotilde Dysnowski's miserable memories. Sometimes they crowded her brain so there wasn't room for anything else. When that happened a thousand recalled slights burned in her gut like acid.

She wasn't that helpless ugly nobody anymore. No, sir. She'd gone through hell readying herself for the day when Arye would finally realize the truth, that they were made for each other.

Yes, indeed, she'd gone through hell, she thought, baring her teeth in a feral smile.

Now it was Bert Hanrahan's turn.

Arye cooked whenever he was upset. The clatter of pots and pans, the aromas wafting from stove and oven, never failed to soothe him. The more complicated the recipe, the more he relaxed.

On the way home he stopped at the Rice Epicurean market to pick up the ingredients for stuffed cabbage.

While the cabbage simmered until the leaves turned translucent, he prepared the filling. He'd just stuffed the last useable leaf with a savory mixture of ground beef, rice, grated onion, eggs, bread crumbs and spices, when the telephone rang.

He raced to answer it, hoping to hear Peach on the other end of the line. But the voice that greeted him, although female, belonged to a stranger.

"Is Mr. Arye Rappaport there?"

"Speaking," he replied, gripping the receiver in a greasy hand he hadn't taken the time to wipe.

"I'm Detective Kern with the Houston police department. I'm afraid I have bad news. Is anyone there with you?"

"I'm alone but I promise I won't faint. Get on with it, Detective."

"Bert Hanrahan was shot in front of his home this evening. He asked us to get in touch with you."

Arye had promised not to faint. Feeling his knees begin to shake, he hoped he could keep that promise. The Heights wasn't the best neighborhood in Houston—but it wasn't the sort of area where people were gunned down in the street either.

Questions burst from his mouth like runners at the crack of a starter's gun. "Who the hell did it? Is Bert badly hurt? Where did they take him?"

"A medical evacuation flight took Mr. Hanrahan to Hermann Hospital," the Detective answered calmly. "They're operating to remove the bullet."

Arye was shaken to the core. "I'll be there in twenty minutes."

"I'll be in the surgery waiting room. Please drive carefully, Mr. Rappaport. You won't be able to help your friend if you have an accident on the way."

Arye didn't bother to reply. He hung up, returned to the kitchen long enough to wash his hands and remove the towel he'd tucked in his jeans in lieu of an apron. Ignoring the uncooked cabbage rolls on the counter, he grabbed his wallet and keys and ran out the door.

Minutes later he was on the Harley, making good time in the light evening traffic, swept by a feeling of déjà vu. How many days had it been since he raced to the hospital on Peach's behalf? Why were the people he loved in so much trouble? What the hell was going on?

Detective Kern had said Bert was in surgery—but she hadn't said how seriously he'd been injured. That they'd called in a helicopter to get him to the hospital said volumes, though. Why the hell would anyone want to hurt Bert? If ever a man lived who didn't have an enemy, he was the one.

Bert had a well-earned reputation for being a soft touch. He didn't just give at the office—he gave everywhere. He couldn't turn away from a person in need whether they approached him in his car at a traffic signal asking if he wanted them to wash his windshield, or passed him on the sidewalk schlepping all their worldly goods in a shopping cart.

Bert always volunteered to help serve Christmas dinner to the homeless so others could spend the day with their families. He'd started an art program in a homeless shelter, supplied all the materials himself and taught there every Saturday.

If they voted to choose the most popular employee at *Inside Texas*, Bert would win hands down. He wasn't a plaster saint, though. He liked cigarettes, fine wines, and the ladies too much to qualify. But he came damn close.

It would take a monster to shoot a man like that. The shooting had to be a random act perpetrated by some gang punk who pulled the trigger to demonstrate the size of his *cojones*.

In today's world, children shot other children over a pair of shoes. Gangs, drugs, murder and mayhem filled the front pages of newspapers from large cities to small towns. Society was going to hell in a hand basket and nobody seemed capable of stopping it. Certainly not Congress or the president. They were too busy playing the usual political games.

When Arye went to work for Peach, she had told him not to look under rocks for stories. But you didn't need to look under rocks to see the ugly side of society. It was right there in your face, in the newspaper every morning and on the television news every night.

He cursed under his breath the rest of the way, peeled into the hospital parking lot, braked the Harley to a rubber-burning stop and took off running. The woman at the reception desk gave him directions to the surgery waiting room. It was empty but for a lone woman wearing a tailored suit, a no-nonsense hairdo, and an aura of authority.

"You must be Arye Rappaport," she said when he walked in.

Arye nodded. "How's Bert?"

"His doctor stopped by a few minutes ago. Mr. Hanrahan is out of surgery. They removed the bullet and Mr. Hanrahan is in recovery. The doctor doesn't anticipate any complications."

"Thank God." The tightness around Arye's heart eased. "What happened? How did Bert get shot?"

"It's early in the investigation to know anything for certain, but it has the earmarks of a drive-by. Luckily for your friend, a neighbor heard the shot and called 911."

"Where was Bert hit?"

"In the chest. An inch or two the wrong way and we'd be talking about a homicide. Mr. Hanrahan was still conscious when the first squad car arrived. He asked the officer to contact you before he passed out. That's all we'll know until I have a chance to question him."

"Was the neighbor able to describe the shooter?"

"She didn't look outside until she heard the shot." The detective walked over to a group and chairs and motioned for Arye to join her. "I do have some questions for you while we wait."

"Shoot," Arye replied, then grimaced at the unintended pun.

"Does Mr. Hanrahan have any enemies?"

"I asked myself the same question on the way here. The answer is an unequivocal no."

"Does he use drugs, maybe gamble a little too much, fool around with whores?"

"That's a hell of a thing to wonder when he's fighting for his life."

"Believe it or not, Mr. Rappaport, I'm fighting for his life in my own way. I take it your answer is no."

"Bert is the finest man I know. He doesn't have any vices—except perhaps being too kind and trusting."

The arrival of a nurse interrupted their conversation. "Mr. Hanrahan is conscious. He's being moved to a private room. If you'll follow me, Detective, I'll take you there."

"I'll be coming too," Arye said.

"Are you a relative?" the nurse asked.

Before Arye could reply, Detective Kern said, "It's all right, nurse. Mr. Rappaport is with me."

They followed the nurse down what seemed like half a mile of hall, then waited at a door while she went in to make sure Bert was ready to see them. She came out a few minutes later. "He's wide awake and madder than hell. He said something about missing a date."

Although the food at the Outback rivaled a five-star restaurant, Peach was too absorbed in her dinner companions' conversation to do more than nibble. Cait's and Comanche's partners, Mims Pauling Neville and her husband Byron, proved to be two of the most amusing people Peach had ever met.

Mims regaled her with stories of the days when she owned one of New York's most successful modeling agencies and Byron proved to be equally amusing as he talked about the years he'd spent as a white hunter in Africa.

The two of them seemed as much in love as Cait and Comanche, a blissful state Peach couldn't help envying. At its best, her marriage to Herbert had never been anywhere near as affectionate, not even on their honeymoon.

While the others talked she tried to imagine how it would feel to be loved completely for herself rather than who she was. It would be heaven, she decided. But she had spent too much time in the purgatory of the last year to believe she would ever get there.

By supper's end, she felt comfortable enough with her companions to talk to them about Blackjack. "I've been looking into my father's life and trying to find out why he had such a run of rotten luck before he died. I was at the Rice University library yesterday reviewing newspapers when I came across an article about the opening of the Outback. My father was here during what appeared to be a very critical time in his life. I'd like to know everything you can tell me about his stay. Did anything unusual happen?"

"Did you find the article about Carroll Detweiler's death?" Comanche asked.

She nodded. "But it didn't give me much information. Why were my father and a man he hadn't seen in years, on this ranch at the same time?"

The four of them gazed back at her with so much sympathy that it brought a lump to her throat.

"Your father was invited," Cait said softly. "His name was at the very top of our guest list. As I told you earlier, he helped me get the financing for the Outback. I don't know what I would have done without him."

"I'm sure you and Comanche would have found a way—"

Cait interrupted Peach. "Comanche and I barely spoke in those days—and my father was very ill. I didn't have anywhere to turn—except to Blackjack. And he came through for me."

Seeing Cait and Comanche now, it was hard to imagine they had ever been at loggerheads the way Peach and Arye were. Cait and Comanche and Mims and Byron lent credence to happy endings. But Peach would never believe in fairy tales again. She could live without Prince Charming. She'd already had the frog.

"Did my father ask you to invite Carroll Detweiler?"

Comanche let go a harsh laugh. "Hardly. The man was a psychopath."

"What was he doing at the opening?"

"This Detweiler chap had been stalking Cait for a long time," Byron Neville chimed in. "I had an unpleasant run-in with him myself a few months earlier and I have to tell you, the man had blood in his eyes."

"The Prides and the Detweilers have feuded since the Civil War," Cait explained. "It's a long story and not a very pretty one. Apparently Carroll Detweiler was motivated by a need for revenge. First he tried to run me off the ranch and when that failed, he tried to ruin me financially. He trucked a huge Russian boar onto the ranch and planned to loose it in the middle of a cocktail party during our grand opening. It would have been a disaster. The Vice President had come to the gala weekend along with other celebrities, and the media was here *en masse.*"

"That doesn't sound like much of a revenge."

Comanche's arched brow gave him a sardonic mien. "Do you know anything about Russian boars, Peach?"

"Afraid not. I'm a city girl."

"Russian boars are a cross between wild pigs and domestic ones. They have the worst characteristics of both. They're big, mean, fast, and utterly unpredictable—except for one thing. When they're hungry—which is most of the time—they aren't fussy about what they eat. Russian boars have been known to attack, kill and snack on full-grown cattle. You can imagine what would have happened if one showed up at the cocktail party."

"Are you saying the pig wouldn't have confined himself to eating the hors d'ouevres?"

"Exactly," Mims piped up. "The media would have nad a field day covering the carnage. It's not exactly the way you want to launch a safari ranch. The Out-back would have been dead on arrival."

"It's a fascinating story. However I don't see what it has to do with my father—unless he was the one who foiled Detweiler's plan," Peach said hopefully.

"Not exactly. Actually the credit for that went to my father," Cait replied with obvious pleasure. "He was dying of cancer and in terrible pain. But he insisted on making a contribution to the opening. Comanche had given him a telescope and he said he'd watch over the ranch while the rest of us enjoyed the party. He saw a plume of dust from a car or a truck on a part of the ranch that was closed to vehicular traffic. Comanche and I went to see who was there. We found Carroll Detweiler."

"I saw Cait and Comanche leave the party," Mims explained. "I had the feeling something was wrong so I sent Byron and the sheriff after them."

"Your father insisted on going with us," Byron contributed. "I had the peculiar feeling he knew what we'd find. But I was wrong."

"How do you know that?"

"Your father was as shocked as the rest of us. He turned so white when he saw Detweiler that I thought he might keel over. Detweiler boasted about how he'd been stalking Cait. He said Blackjack paid him to do it, that their friendship went all the way back to the war in Vietnam."

Peach's stomach threatened to disgorge the little she'd eaten. She'd come to the Outback to begin the process of clearing her father's name, not to tar and feather what little remained of his reputation.

"As it turned out, that last bit was the only truthful

thing Detweiler said that afternoon," Byron continued. "Your father told us he and Detweiler had served in the same unit and that Detweiler had come to him a few months before the Outback opening in very bad shape. He described him as an emotional and financial mess. Blackjack gave him money to pay for psychiatric counseling. Detweiler used it to come here instead. When your father refuted Detweiler's insane claims, Detweiler lost it completely. He made a run for the truck and let the boar loose. Instead of heading over the hill to the party, the boar attacked Detweiler. It was a horrible way to die."

"How did my father take it?"

"Very badly," Cait responded. "It shook all of us. But he blamed himself for not doing more to insure Detweiler got proper psychiatric help months before."

"What more could my father have done?" Peach asked.

"Not a thing," Cait said unequivocally. "I've never understood why he felt so guilty. He put up a good front the rest of the weekend but I could see how troubled he was. He even called me a few weeks later to apologize for what had happened. He told me he'd have given anything in the world to have prevented the incident. I could have sworn he was crying."

The news startled Peach. She had never seen her father cry. Blackjack had been a fighter—and the last man in the world to resort to tearful apologies. "Did he say anything else?"

"He asked if I was going to be able to meet my financial obligations and offered to help me if I couldn't. Fortunately the opening was a huge success.

We were booked for months in advance. I was so touched by your father's offer that I started crying, too." Cait let go a heavy sigh. "I never saw him again but I'll never forget how kind he was to me."

"Did my mother or my sister know about Detweiler's death?"

"We—that is the sheriff, your father, Comanche and I—decided it would be best to keep a lid on the story until the weekend was over. It was a private matter anyway—a case of the Hatfields and McCoys that had nothing to do with anyone else."

"What happened to Detweiler's body?"

"He didn't have any family. Your father paid to have him cremated. I have no idea what happened to the ashes."

Her father must have thought a great deal of Detweiler to give him money for a psychiatrist and then pay for his cremation at a time when he was having financial problems.

"I've never known a more generous or caring man," Cait concluded.

While the others joined the conversation, Peach retreated into a thoughtful silence. Perhaps Detweiler's death—the passing of a comrade in arms—explained the profound changes her father had gone through. Clearly it had been a meaningful event for him, one he had endured in silence instead of sharing it with his family. How lonely he must have been—and how brave.

She felt euphoric at having followed a lead to a successful conclusion. She didn't need Arye, she told herself. However her elation imploded like a pricked balloon when she realized she didn't have the vaguest idea what to do next.

Ten

Peach was surprised to find a strange car—a BMW—parked in her drive when she got home. It was the sort of yuppie-buppie automobile the women in her circle drove. But she hadn't had visitors during the weeks leading up to the auction at Belle Terre and she hadn't expected any after her divorce from Herbert became public knowledge.

She'd known people would choose sides—and hers was badly tarnished by the scandal surrounding her father. Besides, presentable single men like Herbert were worth their weight in social gold while single women in their forties were a drag on the market.

She pulled in behind the strange car, got out of the Jaguar, hoisted her carry-all onto her shoulder and hurried into the house to find her trendily dressed Realtor in the foyer with an equally trendy-looking couple. Their clothes screamed status while she wore a pair of fifteen-year-old jeans that didn't even sport a designer label. They had been adequate for the Outback—but not for River Oaks.

"Here's Mrs. Morgan-Strand now," the Realtor said, looking Peach up and down as if she couldn't believe what she was seeing.

She gave Peach an air kiss, then hurriedly shepherded the couple out of the door like a harried sheepdog gathering up strays. At the last second she leaned back through the opening. "They just loved the place, darling, but they simply must have more space. Before I forget, a couple of calls came in while I was here. I wrote the names and numbers on one of my cards and left it on the bar in the den."

And then she was gone, leaving the heavy scent of Poison behind her. Peach fanned the air to get rid of it. More space? What sort of people wouldn't be happy with five bedrooms, five and a half baths, formal living and dining rooms, a family room, a den, breakfast room, kitchen and a three-car garage with servant quarters?

"Mother, I'm back," she called out, leaving her soft-sided bag sagging by the door.

No one answered.

The silence sent nervous prickles skittering over her skin. Delia didn't work weekends but Peach had counted on Bella being there. Although it was ridiculous, she felt abandoned.

She hadn't been very understanding about her mother's dinner date with Bert. Could Bella have used her absence to move out? She hurried to Bella's room to find the bed made, peered into the bathroom and was relieved to see her mother's toiletries neatly in place.

Letting go a sigh, she headed for the den. The events of the last few weeks had given her a bad case of the heebie-jeebies, she realized as she looked for the Realtor's card.

The name, Randolph Spurling, was scrawled across the top. Wondering what he wanted, she punched in his new number.

* * *

Randolph Spurling hadn't been able to convince his employers—the men who had come to him in secret when Blackjack strayed from the fold—that they need have no further concern about Blackjack's family.

"I checked through all Blackjack's papers before I shipped them to Houston," he had reported, "and I didn't find a thing. The rest of his belongings were destroyed in the fire. Bella plans to get on with her life and Peach, the Morgan's daughter, is a total airhead. We have nothing to worry about."

His assurances had fallen on deaf ears, though. He hated talking to nameless, faceless, mechanically altered voices but he didn't dare try to discover who they belonged to. He liked to think of himself as a piranha. The men who had paid him to spy on Blackjack were even more dangerous. He was smart enough to know a lone piranha wouldn't stand a chance against a school of great white sharks.

Now, as he sat in his new office surrounded by Blackjack's antiques, the money those sharks had deposited in his offshore account in his name guaranteed his continuing cooperation. He didn't agree with the need to stay in touch with the Morgan women. He simply had no choice.

The sound of the intercom jarred him from his reverie.

"A Peach Morgan wants to talk to you," his new secretary told him.

He had been wondering if and when she'd get back to him. "Put her on at once."

"How are you and your mother getting along?" he

asked, infusing his voice with warmth when Peach came on the line.

"I didn't know you cared," she replied.

He cleared his throat. "I don't know what I've said or done to offend you, but the fact I have is obvious. Whatever it was, please accept my sincere apology."

Her only response was silence.

"Is your mother there?"

"No, she isn't. I just got home myself."

"I'm glad you're getting out again. Where were you?" Although the question pushed the bounds of propriety, he needed the answer.

"Not that it's any of your business, but I spent a few days at Pride's Outback."

A film of sweat slicked his brow. Why had she gone to the Outback? Did she know more than she'd let on the last time he saw her?

"I've heard it's a marvelous place for a little R and R," he said, ignoring the gastric juices churning in his gut.

"I wasn't vacationing. I was doing research."

"For an *Inside Texas* article?"

"For me. My father's problems began shortly after he attended the opening of the Outback. I thought something might have happened there."

"I'll say this for you, Peach. You have a wild imagination."

"I prefer to call it intuition. I haven't forgotten my father's last words. I intend to keep right on looking into his past until I find out what he meant."

Randolph felt as though his heart had gone bungee-jumping, leaving the rest of his body behind. Would he never be free of her meddling? "Do you suspect anyone in particular?"

"Half of Washington is on my list."

His heart rebounded into his throat. "That's not funny, Peach. You're headed for trouble if you keep it up."

"You mustn't worry about me, Randolph. It's not good for your blood pressure," she answered with saccharine sweetness.

"I told you before, I care about you and your mother. It's only natural after everything your father did for me."

He smirked, thinking she would never know just how good Blackjack had been. A great deal of the senator's money had wound up in his bank account. Blackjack called it blackmail. Randolph preferred to think of it as a *quid pro quo*.

Peach was enterprising—he'd give her that much—or she wouldn't have gone to the Outback. But she wasn't smart enough to ferret out the truth. "I hope you'll take the advice of an old friend and give up your so-called investigation. Your father would insist on it if he were here."

"Oh, really? How dare you presume to know my father's mind when you and he didn't agree on anything the last year of his life."

"Our disagreements were political—not personal," he countered. "I thought he made a big mistake when he left the Democratic party and I told him so many times. You can imagine how he took it. In his opinion there was only one way to think. *His way.* He couldn't handle being told he was wrong. I was considering quitting my job when—" he injected a quaver into his voice, "when he died. Now I wish I had been even more outspoken. If he had listened to me, he might be alive today. The strain killed him, not the so-called bastards he raved about before he died."

He hoped her silence indicated she'd bought his rationale. And why not? The best, most believable lies always had a basis in truth.

"That was quite a lecture," she finally said. "You almost convinced me. How many times did you rehearse that speech before getting it right?"

"I didn't have to. It came from the heart. I'm worried about you. Frankly, Peach, you sound a little irrational. Perhaps you should consider counseling."

"And perhaps you should consider minding your own business."

He could hardly tell her she was his business. He dreaded calling his employers again, telling them he'd miscalculated when it came to Peach.

"Please give your mother my fondest regards. If there's ever anything I can do for either of you, don't hesitate to ask."

He hung up, then dialed a Washington number. As he waited for someone to answer, a nasty grin thinned his lips. Peach was playing with fire.

Peach listened to the line go dead with a sense of relief. Talking to Randolph made her feel as though she were looking in a funhouse mirror. He had a way of distorting things, putting a new and unexpected spin on what she said that made her dizzy.

She pocketed the Realtor's card, then surrendered herself to a world-class case of self-doubt. Was she making a fool of herself, trying to find out what her father meant? Was her investigation motivated by boredom as Arye implied? Half an hour later, Peach was still searching for answers when she heard the front door open.

"Peach, honey, I'm home," Bella called out.

"I'm in the den," Peach replied.

"I'm so glad you're home, honey," Bella exclaimed, walking into the room. "I wasn't expecting you back for another day. I imagine you heard about Bert and decided to come home sooner."

"Is there a problem at the magazine?"

"Oh, dear, then you don't know. It's been all over the television and in the newspaper."

"What's been in the newspaper?"

"Bert's shooting."

"What did Bert shoot and why in the world would the press be interested in my art director taking pictures?" Peach asked.

"This has nothing to do with taking pictures. Sit down while I fix you a drink. You're going to need one."

Bella retrieved a bottle of Courvoisier from behind the bar, filled a couple of brandy snifters and joined Peach on the sofa.

"I haven't seen a newspaper or listened to television since I left," Peach said. "Will you please tell me what's going on?"

"Someone shot Bert two nights ago."

Peach gasped. "Shot as in bang, bang, you're dead?"

"Exactly. He was on his way to pick me up for dinner when someone used him for target practice."

Bella had been right. She did need a drink, Peach thought, taking a big gulp of brandy. The liquid heat burned down her throat, warming her through and through, creating a false sense of well-being.

"Why would anyone shoot Bert? He's one of the nicest people I know. Did he—that is, will he be all right?" Peach asked, stumbling over the question.

Bella reached out and brushed the hair from Peach's brow the way she used to when Peach was small. The tender gesture was almost Peach's undoing. She felt tears gather behind her eyes—for Bert, for herself, for all of the miserable lost lonely souls in the world.

"He's fine. I just came from the hospital and he's already pestering the doctors to release him. Of course that won't happen for a few more days considering the seriousness of the wound and the blood he lost."

"Do the police know who did it?"

Bella shook her head. "No one saw a thing. And all Bert remembers is a muzzle flash."

Arye was waiting for one of the Allen Center elevators when he heard someone come up behind him. He turned to find Cindy Downing standing there, carrying a stuffed animal—a supremely ugly purple dinosaur with a broad mouth.

"I'm so glad I caught you before you left. I called the hospital to find out how Bert is doing but they won't tell me a thing. I brought this for him—to cheer him up," she said, holding out the toy.

Arye blinked, thinking Bert would have appreciated a bottle of wine or a box of cigars or even flowers a hell of a lot more. "How thoughtful," he managed to say.

"I wanted to give him something special to let him know I'm praying for him as hard as I can."

"Your prayers must be more effective than most."

Her blue eyes widened. "Whatever do you mean?"

Blue eyes? Weren't they green the last time he bothered to notice? "Your mother made a miraculous recovery. So did Bert. He should be home in a few days."

"Thank heaven for that," Cindy replied, grabbing Arye's upper arm and squeezing his bicep like a tomato she was testing for ripeness. "I've been so worried about him. Do the police have any idea who shot him?"

"Not yet. You know the seventy-two-hour rule."

"What's that?" Cindy continued to cling to his arm. Although he resented the intimacy, he was too polite to pull away.

"If a crime isn't solved in the first seventy-two hours, chances are it never will be."

"You mean the man who shot Bert is going to get away with it? How dreadful. It seems no one is safe on the streets any more."

"Why did you say man? Do you know something I don't?"

Cindy's lashes fluttered as rapidly as a bat's wings. "It was just a manner of speaking. Besides, I can't imagine a woman doing something like that."

Neither could Arye. And yet the bullet they'd removed from Bert's chest had come from a .22, and that wasn't generally a man's gun. "It may have been a drive-by shooting. It's possible some punk kid, out to prove himself, shot the wrong man." The elevator's arrival cut short the strange tête-à-tête. He tucked the dinosaur under his arm and stepped aboard. "I'll tell Bert you asked about him."

"Please do," she said, peering at him from those strangely brilliant blue eyes.

She certainly was a peculiar girl, he thought, as he

rode down to the garage level. She had never seemed as fond of Bert as the other members of the staff. But she had taken the trouble to buy him a gift. Her taste might be execrable. Her sentiments were not.

He put the dilemma of Cindy's personality out of his mind as he drove to the hospital. A poignant sense of relief swept through him at the thought of Bert's survival. He didn't have so many friends that he could afford to lose one. Hell. He didn't have any close friends aside from Bert. Hadn't wanted any, either, until Peach came into his life. Not that friendship was exactly what he had in mind when he let himself think about her.

Bert was sitting up in bed when he arrived. The I.V. and the other medical paraphernalia were no longer in evidence. His hair had been combed, his whiskers newly shaved.

"You look damn good for a man who had a close brush with the grim reaper," Arye said, pulling up a chair.

"And you look like a damn fool carrying that—that thing," Bert shot back. "If it's for me, you made a mistake. In case you haven't noticed, I'm not a member of the diaper set."

"Cindy asked me to give it to you." Grinning, Arye propped the stuffed animal on the pillows next to Bert.

Bert rolled his eyes. "The hell you say. I didn't think Cindy liked me. On second thought, that explains her gift. When you leave, give the thing to a nurse and tell her to send it to the children's ward where it will be appreciated."

Arye laughed at Bert's display of temper. It was the first time Arye had laughed since he got the call from

Detective Kern. It felt good. "You know what they say about looking a gift horse in the mouth."

"Don't you mean a gift dinosaur?" Bert grimaced. "Right now I have more important things on my mind than Cindy. I've been thinking about what happened to me."

"I imagine you have."

"I don't go along with Detective Kern's drive-by shooting theory. It's too pat."

"Do you have an alternative?"

"I know it sounds a little far-fetched but I've been wondering if my shooting could be related to the fire in Bella's apartment."

"Far out is more like it. Where the hell did you get that idea?"

Bert's gaze didn't waver. "It's a hunch. Aren't reporters supposed to follow their hunches."

"Sure. The sort of hunches that come from an accumulation of information—not from being flat on your back in a hospital bed wondering what the hell hit you and why."

"Just the same, I plan to tell Bella to be more careful in the future. Peach, too."

"Do me a favor. It's a wonder Bella and Peach aren't paranoid after everything they've been through. Don't add to their troubles."

"Then you really do think I'm off base?"

"Hell, you aren't even in the ball game."

Peach and Bella were loading dinner dishes into the dishwasher when Peach remembered the Realtor had told her there'd been two calls. She put the last dish in the bottom rack, then pulled the Realtor's card from her jeans pocket.

The name, Jean Sinclair, and a telephone number, had been written on the back. Peach searched her memory, wondering why the name sounded so familiar.

"Do we know anyone named Jean Sinclair?"

Bella paled. She dropped the glass she was holding. "Oh dear, I've broken one of your Waterford tumblers," she exclaimed, pressing a hand against her heart.

"Herbert picked out the pattern. I planned to give them to him anyway so don't give it another thought."

She took a broom and dust pan from the pantry and quickly disposed of the glittering shards. Then she poured two cups of coffee and gestured for Bella to follow her to the den.

"I'd like to know why hearing Jean Sinclair's name upset you so much," she said after they were both seated.

"It didn't upset me."

"You should have seen your face, Mother. Is she the woman Daddy talked about before he died?"

"I don't know what you mean."

"You told me father asked for someone named Jean."

"I'm sure it's just a coincidence."

"Like the fire was just a coincidence."

"Not that again," Bella lamented. "I thought you put all that behind you when you went to the Outback."

It was confession time, Peach mused, drawing in a deep breath. "I didn't go there for a vacation. I wanted to talk to Cait because I thought something that happened at the Outback played a profound part in Daddy's life."

She went on to detail what she'd read at the library and what Cait and Comanche had told her.

"You'll never stop this foolish investigation, will you?" Bella said when Peach finished, making it more an accusation than a question.

"Not until I've done what Daddy asked of me. I don't know who *the bastards* are yet, but I have a sneaky hunch Randolph Spurling is one of them. For all I know, Jean Sinclair is too. Obviously the name meant something to you or you wouldn't have dropped the glass. Level with me, Mother. Who is she and what did she have to do with Daddy?"

Bella had done her best to keep her girls from learning the truth about their father. She had wanted him to remain a hero in their eyes the way he had once been in hers. But she couldn't shield Peach anymore. Peach wouldn't let her.

"For the last time, will you please reconsider? You may not like what I have to say."

"I'm not afraid of the truth," Peach averred, her eyes shining like a would-be Joan of Arc.

She was such an idealist. Bella hated tearing down the last bastion of her innocence. Peach had learned a hard enough lesson about human nature when Herbert asked for a divorce. Now she was going to learn an even harder one.

"All right. But don't say I didn't warn you." Bella sank lower in her chair while memory carried her back to another time and place. "You have no idea how much I loved your father when we met. He was a silver-tongued devil, as handsome and shiny as a new car and twice as racy under the hood."

Peach beamed at her. "What a wonderful way to describe Dad."

"I fell for him so hard I thought I'd die of it." Bella gave Peach a probing look. "Have you ever loved a man like that?"

Peach hesitated. "I don't know."

"You would if you had. It's not something you can ignore. If it ever happens to you, I hope and pray the man feels the same way. If he doesn't he'll break your heart."

"Are you saying Daddy didn't love you?"

"I'm sure he did in his own way. But a good-looking, powerful, charismatic male like your father attracts women without even trying. I had to laugh when he was charged with sexual harassment. If anything, it was the other way around. Women were always chasing him. The trouble was, he couldn't resist letting them catch him."

Bella paused and searched her daughter's face. It was like seeing herself at the same age. "I adored your father until I was seven months pregnant with you."

"What happened then?"

Bella sighed at the lingering power of an old and painful memory. "I found lipstick on his boxer shorts. It wasn't my shade."

Peach's eyes widened in disbelief. "Don't tell me he had an affair."

"Blackjack never admitted to infidelity in so many words, but I came to know the signs. He was more attentive when he was seeing another woman. He'd bring me extravagant gifts like that double strand of pearls with the diamond clip. And he made a big fuss over you and your sister on the rare occasions when he was home."

"That doesn't prove a thing except he loved us—all of us."

"You asked me to tell you the truth. I'm asking you to have the courage to accept it. The first time I realized he was seeing someone else, I wanted to die. I even considered killing myself. But I was carrying you. You deserved a life—a happy one—and I made up my mind to give it to you. In time I was able to deal with the fact that I couldn't own Blackjack. I learned not to let him own me either. From then on I held a part of myself back—not out of spite but because I needed to stand on my own two feet."

"Did you stop loving Daddy?"

"It's not that simple. I did stop respecting him."

"Is that why you were so quick to start seeing Bert?"

"We're old friends. And we're both lonely."

"What does Jean Sinclair have to do with what you just told me? Was she involved with Daddy?"

Bella felt even worse for Peach than she did the day Peach fell out of the tree house at Belle Terre and broke her arm. The break had healed. Peach's spirit might not. She had looked up to her father, believed in him even though common sense had to tell her there must be a spark of truth behind the inferno of accusations that had engulfed Blackjack.

"Jean Sinclair went to work for your father as his personal secretary the first time he was elected to the Senate. She fell in love with him."

"How in the world can you know a thing like that? Did Daddy tell you?"

"She told me herself. She wasn't his first mistress or his last, but she was the only one to engage more than his sexual interest. For a while I thought he might actually leave us for her."

Peach trembled from head to toe. "Are Daddy's affairs the real reason you didn't want me to go digging around in his past?"

"I never wanted you to know. Blackjack was an exceptional man in so many ways. You wanted him to be a hero almost as much as he wanted you to see him that way. He loved you and your sister. No matter what happened between your father and me, that never changed."

Peach took another deep draught of brandy. This time, though, it failed to warm her. She felt so cold, she wished she could go to bed, crawl under the covers and stay there. The resolve that had compelled her to investigate her father's last words left her so abruptly, she felt achingly hollow.

She'd been a blind fool where her father was concerned, just as she had been with Herbert. Even worse, she had made her mother pay the price for her naïveté. "I don't know what to say."

"You don't need to say anything, darling. It's a lot for you to take in."

Peach couldn't meet Bella's eyes. Would she ever be able to look into them without remembering this moment. "Does Avery know?"

Bella shook her head. "I'm counting on you not to tell her. I said it before and I'll say it again. We can't change what's past."

Jean Sinclair sat in the office at the back of her house, trying to read one of her favorite mysteries—a rather good one—*Vile Acts* by Dorothy MacMillan. Despite the exciting plot and the excellent prose, she couldn't concentrate.

Her gaze kept straying to the phone as though she could will it to ring. She felt enervated yet restless, caught on a seesaw between hope and despair as the minutes became hours without any word from Bella Morgan.

Blackjack's book weighed as heavily on Jean's mind as six feet of dirt on a coffin. She hadn't slept well since his death. Her dreams had been filled with chiaroscuro images of his face. One minute he looked young and happy—and the next, a death's head with his eyes would be staring at her. Although he seemed to be speaking, she could never quite make out the words.

Jean was a pragmatic woman. She didn't believe in the ghosts, had never attended a seance, consulted an astrologer, or even read her horoscope in the daily paper. In the part of her mind where reason dwelled, she was able to ignore her dreams. But deep down where the primitive brain held sway, she believed Blackjack was reaching out to her from the grave.

He wanted her to do something with that damn book. But what? If only she could be sure.

Earlier that day she had made up her mind to turn the manuscript over to Bella. Now Jean was having second thoughts about having made the call. Talking to Bella would only dredge up a lot of unhappy memories—for them both.

Jean still regretted telling Bella about her affair with Blackjack. It had been the one shameful deed in an otherwise blameless life. But she had been so desperately in love with Blackjack, she had lost all sense of right and wrong.

The sunny afternoon sky dimmed into black night and still Jean sat in her chair, staring down at the book

in her lap without comprehending a word. She wanted
to do the right thing where Blackjack was concerned—but she wanted to do the right thing for the
living, too.

At eleven she finally accepted the fact that Bella
Morgan wasn't going to call. The decision about the
manuscript was Jean's to make. On the one hand
Blackjack's book could do a great deal of good for the
country. On the other, it would hurt Bella all over
again. Peach, too.

In the end Jean chose to act on their behalf. She
opened the safe, took the manuscript and the disks
out, carried them into the kitchen and put them in a
plastic bag. Then she carried the bag out to the alley
and left it with the rest of the trash.

Eleven

For the first time in her adult life, Peach had nothing to do—no charity luncheons or committee meetings to attend, no parties to plan, no husband coming home at the end of the day. Feeling at loose ends, she spent a couple of weeks going through all the closets and cupboards, deciding what to take when she moved, putting certain things aside for the time when the twins would set up their own households and boxing up the rest to donate to charity.

When those tasks palled she went house hunting. However her inability to make a purchase until her home sold added to her sense of futility. Her life seemed to be going nowhere.

She finally booked a flight to Oxford, Mississippi to spend some quality time with her sons. Herbert had taken it upon himself to tell them about the divorce. She wanted to reassure them she would always be there for them.

She arrived in the sleepy Southern college town to find two reasonably content, self-absorbed young men who were so caught up in their studies and their social life that they didn't have a great deal of time to spend with her. After seeing every Civil War monument in the area and exhausting all the tourist sights including

John Grisham's country manse, she flew back into the steamy heat of a waning Houston summer.

The next day she took a long look at herself in the mirror, noting the reemergence of her cheek, collar and hip bones, and decided the time had come for a new look. She called the Beauty Spot International, begged Glynnis to take her without an appointment and then spent an hour cringing as her big Texas hair fell to the floor snip after snip. A stranger with a pixie cut and enormous eyes emerged from the traumatic event.

"How do you like it?" Glynnis asked, holding up a mirror so Peach could see the back of her head.

"I didn't know a neck could look so—so naked," Peach replied.

Glynnis gave Peach a conspiratorial grin. "You need some new clothes to go with the hair—something with attitude that says you're hot, Hot, HOT!"

Peach had never associated herself with looking hot. As she drove down Westheimer to Tootsies, her favorite boutique, she found the idea intriguing. In the past she had bought the sort of conservative clothes that would get her on Houston's prestigious best-dressed list. Today she shocked the saleswomen by trying on the most outrageous size eights she could find.

She arrived home late that afternoon so laden down with packages that she had to ring the doorbell. Delia opened the door and looked her up and down. Her gimlet gaze lingered on the midriff bared by Peach's new outfit.

"The missus isn't home," Delia said in her nasal West Texas drawl, "but whatever you're selling, she ain't likely to be buying."

"Oh yes she is," Peach declared gleefully.

"Land o' Goshen, is that you, Miss Peach?" Delia demanded, her hands on her hips.

"It's not Julia Roberts."

"You sure had me fooled," Delia replied, taking packages from Peach's arms. "I don't know what all you did to yourself but it surely is flattering. You look years younger."

Peach followed Delia into the house, put the rest of her packages down and gazed at herself in a mirror, startled by the fit of her miniskirt across her newly flat stomach.

At that moment, Bella joined them. "I came to see what the commotion was all about. My oh my. You do look marvelous, honey."

"I'm not used to my hair," Peach said, running her fingers through her cropped mane. "Do you really like it?"

"I love it," Bella and Delia declared in unison.

"We really must go out tomorrow to show you off," Bella said. "How about lunch at the River Oaks Country Club?"

"I haven't been there in months."

"You're still a member in good standing, aren't you?"

"I suppose so, at least until the divorce is final."

"Go on, Miss Peach. You have to show off your new look. Those ladies you used to run with," Delia made the word *ladies,* sound like an expletive, "will eat their hearts out."

One word described the River Oaks Country Club. Money. No effort had been spared, no dollar left unspent during its planning, construction, landscaping or decorating to fulfill the members' high expectations. It was a temple to conspicuous consumption.

As Peach drove through the imposing pillared gates, she decided the club looked more *nouveau riche* than classically Greek. She pulled up in front of the main entrance, handed the Jaguar's keys over to a waiting valet, then took Bella's arm and marched up to the doors.

"I'm not sure this is a good idea," she said under her breath.

Although it was a work day for the rest of the world, Houston's elite—men and women attired in golf or tennis or designer outfits—strolled by so lost in conversation that Peach felt as if she and her mother had suddenly been rendered invisible.

Her stomach clenched at the thought that just a year ago those very same people would have fawned over the two of them. Not that she wanted fawning. A simple hello would do.

Bella however, seemed unruffled. "I'd love a bloody Mary," she said cheerfully. "How about you?"

A drink sounds wonderful," Peach replied.

A few men did a double take as Peach walked into the bar, their eyes clinging to her bare legs like limpets. What in the world had made her choose a dress with a postage-stamp skirt? she fretted.

Lifting her head as high as her five feet, four inches allowed, she pretended a nonchalance she didn't feel, as she and Bella sat down at one of the unoccupied tables. Peach had given up smoking five years ago but now she wanted a cigarette the way a drug addict craves a fix. At least she'd have something to do with her hands.

Bella glanced around, acknowledging the occupants of the nearest tables with a serene smile before turning back to Peach. "I know it must feel strange, being here without Herbert, but pretend you're enjoying yourself."

The arrival of a waiter relieved Peach of the need to answer. "It's nice to see you, ladies," he said before asking for their order.

At least someone was glad to see them, Peach mused. But then, the waiter was well paid to be polite.

A burst of laughter drew her attention across the room. She tracked the sound to see Herbert seated at a table with a woman. It was Luise Degrasse, a wealthy three-times widowed socialite who was rumored to be in her fifties. Not that anyone could tell, looking at her. Luise's taut neck and face bore the mark of Herbert's genius.

As Peach peeked at them from the shelter of her lashes, Herbert and Luise played footsie under the table. Luise had to be the other woman, Peach thought. Predictably, Herbert had left her for money and prestige rather than passion.

"If this isn't my lucky day," Peach murmured. "Look who's here."

Bella gave Herbert the sort of *noblesse oblige* wave that queens use to acknowledge their faithful subjects. "Pretend you're happy to see him."

Gritting her teeth, Peach waved too.

Although she felt certain Herbert and Luise had seen her, neither one waved back. Peach refused to ignore the snub. For the sake of the twins, she wanted a friendly divorce—if there was such a thing. She rose, headed to their table and came to a stop by Herbert's chair.

"Good afternoon," she said, acknowledging him and his companion with what she hoped was a gracious smile.

Herbert and Luise exchanged a signifigant glance. Then Luise put her hand on the table so Peach would be sure to see the huge engagement ring on her fourth finger.

"To what do we owe the honor?" Herbert asked.

Peach smiled so hard, she felt as though her cheeks would crack. "I just wanted to say hello. You're looking well, Herbert."

He shrugged. "I'm glad you like my new wardrobe. Personally though, I preferred the old one."

Guilt stirred in her stomach. However she refused to give in to it. "I always thought you had marvelous taste—in clothes, that is," she concluded, giving Luise a quick glance.

He leaned closer as though he didn't want the others to hear what he was going to say, however he failed to lower his voice. "I wish I could share the sentiment. Really Peach, don't you think that dress is too youthful for a woman of your years?"

Peach suspected she'd wake up in the middle of the night with a dozen clever rejoinders on the tip of her tongue. At the moment though, she couldn't think of one. She turned around and hurried back to her own table in full retreat.

"What's the matter, honey?" Bella asked. "Did Herbert say something ugly to you?"

"Of course. Why should he stop belittling me just because we're getting a divorce?"

"Did you ever stop to think he belittles people because he's insecure?"

"Don't make excuses for him. I was a fool to think

we could be civil to one another." Peach fished a twenty-dollar bill from her wallet and put it on the table. "I'd like to go home now."

Bella's eyes narrowed. "If you don't sit down this minute and drink your bloody Mary, you'll never be able to hold your head up in this town again."

"I don't care about this town—or the people in it."

"Me, either—but I do care about you. If you run away now you'll spend the rest of your life running. So sit down."

Peach did.

Bella opened her purse and took out a pack of cigarettes. "I thought you might need these."

Peach couldn't help laughing. "How did you know?"

"Because I used to die for a smoke every time you brought Herbert over to the house for dinner. I asked our waiter to get a pack for me. God knows where he found them."

Peach looked at them longingly. "I don't think this is a smoking area."

"All the more reason for the two of us to light up," Bella replied, taking a cigarette herself and then offering the pack to Peach.

Peach spent the next hour sipping a drink she didn't want and toying with food she couldn't eat. She felt so relieved when Bella asked the waiter for their check that she could have cried.

But she left the bar with her head held high, walking as tall as her height permitted. Bella had been right to insist on staying, Peach thought as they waited for the valet to bring the car. If she had crept away like a whipped dog, she wouldn't have been able to look at herself in the mirror.

"I'm so sorry, honey," Bella said once they were seated in the privacy of the Jaguar.

"Not for buying cigarettes, I hope. I wouldn't have gotten through lunch without a nicotine buzz."

"I shouldn't have insisted on eating at the club. It was too soon. Your divorce and Blackjack's death are still on people's minds. Next week or next month they'll have someone or something else to gossip about."

"Don't blame yourself. I could have said no." Peach shrugged. "I guess I don't fit in with the beautiful people anymore."

"I was wrong to imagine you could pick up your life where you left it when your father died. Too much has changed."

As Peach drove out through the country club gates, she was sure of only one thing. She would never return. "I've changed most of all," she said under her breath.

"What will you do now?"

"You mean now I'm a social outcast?"

Bella ignored the question. "I hear the art museum is terribly short of docents."

Peach cut a glance at her mother, taking in the serene profile, the elegant carriage, the classic clothes. She admired her mother greatly but she no longer wanted to be like her. "I don't want to be a docent or a volunteer or any of the other things rich women do to feel useful."

"What will you do?" Bella repeated.

"Go to work."

"Where?"

Peach laughed. "At my own magazine. I doubt anyone else would hire me."

* * *

When Peach walked through the Allen Center the next morning at the beginning of the work day, she felt as though she were seeing the building for the first time. Would she take her breaks in the coffee shop on the concourse level? she wondered, getting a quick glimpse of calorie laden pastries as she hurried past. And did it always take so long to get an elevator?

Another far more troubling question gnawed at her fragile self-confidence. How would Arye react when she told him her plans?

Steeling herself to deal with his displeasure, she exited the elevator on the forty-fourth floor, crossed a small lobby and opened the doors to her own little empire.

The receptionist looked up and said, "Can I help you."

What was the girl's name? Tiffany? Yes, that was it. "I'm here to see Mr. Rappaport."

"Do you have an appointment?"

"I didn't think I needed one."

"Mr. Rappaport is a very busy man, miss."

Suddenly it hit Peach. The receptionist didn't recognize her. "It's me, Tiffany. Peach Morgan-Strand."

The girl turned an unhealthy shade of alabaster, as if she feared her faux pas might cost her job. "I didn't recognize you," she sputtered.

Was that good—or bad? "Don't tell Mr. Rappaport I'm here. I want to surprise him."

"You sure will," Tiffany burst out, eyeing Peach's jeans as if she'd never seen a pair before.

Hoping to fit in, Peach had dressed down—way down. She gave the flustered girl a quick smile, then

made her way down the hall, past the offices and conference room to Arye's door. She knocked just once
before letting herself in.

Arye was seated behind his desk. At her intrusion,
he lifted his gaze, and did a classic double take. "Is
that you, Peach?"

"Who were you expecting? Ben Bradlee?"

Her attempt at humor sailed over his head. He gave
her what could only be called a what-the-hell-are-you-
doing-here? look. As if the damn magazine didn't belong to her.

He gestured at the papers piled on his desk. "As
you can see, I'm very busy. I don't have time for chitchat. What can I do for you?"

Four months ago, before her life fell apart, his icy
tone and frigid stare would have cut her to the quick.
But she'd be damned if any man would ever intimidate
her again.

"I came to talk to you about a job."

"We don't have any openings."

"Than you'll just have to make one."

"If one of your friends wants to play reporter, I suggest you forget it. I don't have the budget to pay for
a freeloader."

His eyes looked so stormy that she wouldn't have
been surprised to see bolts of lightning shooting from
them. Was there something in men's chromosomes
that just naturally made them hostile anytime anyone
questioned their authority?'

"The freeloader is me."

He burst out laughing. "Get serious."

"I am serious. I want to learn everything you can
teach me about the publishing business." Seeing his
expression harden, she added, "I'm willing to start at

the bottom. I can type and file. I'll deliver mail if I have to."

He lifted one brow. It made him look even more attractive. He probably knew it too. "You're living in the dark ages. We don't use typewriters. Our files are computerized for quick access and interoffice communications are handled by E-mail. Are you familiar with any of the current word processing programs?"

The man was relentless. "No, but it shouldn't take me long to learn. How difficult can it be?"

He shrugged again, drawing attention to his broad shoulders. "I don't mean to put you down—but I wouldn't hire you if I had a choice."

"You don't!"

"What happened to your crusade?"

"That's none of your business."

"It is if you plan to use the magazine's staff for your own purposes."

Peach felt strangely disappointed. Arye hadn't commented on her appearance. But that was ridiculous. She didn't care what he thought. "My father bought *Inside Texas* for me years ago when I told him I wanted to be a journalist someday. This is that someday. I'm here to learn about running the magazine. That's the beginning and the end of it."

When Peach had marched into his office unannounced, Arye's first thought had been she was finally going to get around to firing him. Now he realized he'd been wrong. She wanted him to teach her enough about running the magazine so she could replace him. *With herself.*

Talk about *chutzpah,* she had it in spades, he concluded with grudging admiration. He'd been hurt because she never returned his calls, hurt and angry.

Ultimately he had schooled himself to indifference. But it was impossible to be indifferent to the woman who stood before him today.

Her jeans fit as tight as a wetsuit. And she wasn't wearing a bra either. Was she deliberately trying to turn him on? If so, she had succeeded in spades. She looked incredible. Youthful. Vibrant. Exciting. Seductive. Adversity must agree with her.

Bert had kept him abreast of Peach's activities via information from Bella. But Bert had never mentioned Peach's transformation from society wife to babe.

Arye forced his gaze away from the swell of her breasts. "You're serious, aren't you."

"Absolutely."

She looked purposeful, intent, and utterly desirable. How could he endure having her around day after day? He wouldn't get much work done, that was for damn sure.

He gave her his fiercest scowl. "I think it's time you had a lesson in the way we do business around here."

"I knew you'd see things my way. What do we do first?" Peach asked, looking so eager it was all he could do not to cross the floor, take her in his arms and give her something to really get excited about.

"For starters, you can go home and dress properly. I won't have every man on the staff drooling over you. This is a place of business, not a pickup joint."

"I've seen you here without a suit and tie."

"Friday is our dress-down day. This is Tuesday. And dress-down doesn't mean flaunting your body. When you get home, call and make an appointment to see me this afternoon."

"That's the silliest thing I ever heard. I'm already here."

He hated the cliché about women looking prettier when they were angry, but it was certainly true in her case. "Is it? No one barges in on a managing editor and demands a job, not if they're serious about getting one. Are you?"

"Absolutely."

"I'll take you at your word. Don't bother calling for an appointment until you've typed up a resume."

"You're—you're—" she stuttered.

He expected her to say, *fired*. However she was full of surprises. "You're right. My approach wasn't at all professional. I see that now."

"There is one more thing before you go."

He almost laughed out loud at the sight of her struggling to rein in her temper. She would make a lousy poker player—unless it was strip poker. She'd been born for that particular game.

"What is it?"

"In the future—return your calls."

Color flared on her cheeks. Her eyes blazed. She nodded her head just once in begrudging acquiescence, then hurried to the door. The last he saw of Peach was her delightful derrière as she stalked out of his office.

Twelve

Peach returned to *Inside Texas* promptly at four in the afternoon, wearing one of her new skirts with an old blouse and blazer. The outfit wasn't chic and it certainly didn't have *attitude*—but it was as close as the contents of her closet could get to businesslike.

Arye kept her waiting long enough for her to reread her resume and decide it was the most puerile document imaginable. By the time she was admitted to Arye's office, she felt as jittery as a three-year-old who has an urgent need to go potty.

No matter how often she reminded herself she had no reason to be keyed up, that her getting a job was a given, she couldn't dismiss the sensation that she stood on the threshold of something that could change her life—and that Arye had the power to slam the door shut in her face.

This time when she entered his office, he rose from his desk and came toward her with his hand held out. She offered hers, remembering to return his shake firmly, the way her father had taught her, trying not to let him see how much his touch, his warmth affected her.

He guided her over to the very furniture grouping where she had interviewed him three years ago and gestured for her to take a seat on the sofa. He towered over her from his place in the adjacent chair. It gave him a psychological advantage.

She should have realized it the day he came to her for a job instead of letting him look down on her. She felt as though she'd gone through the first half of her life wearing blinders. But her eyes were wide open now.

"May I see your resume?"

"There's not much to it," she replied, offering him an envelope with her name and address embossed in gold script on the back. The envelope looked terribly ostentatious considering the paucity of its contents.

He took out the single piece of paper inside and read it over while she fidgeted, smoothing her skirt, patting her perfect hair, wishing she could have a cigarette. What in the world was the matter with her? Why should she care what Arye thought about the way she'd spent her life? Her getting a job was a done deal—a foregone conclusion.

But none of that mattered, her secret heart whispered in her innermost thoughts. She wanted him to respect her, to like her, to care for her. She needed it as an affirmation of her femininity. More important, she needed it because she felt all those things for him. All those things and more. Her emotions were certainly out of control.

He put the paper back in the envelope, then gazed at the window as though he couldn't bring himself to look her straight in the eyes. "Why did you leave college when your grades were so good?"

"Herbert wanted to get married before he started his residency. Look, do we have to go through all of this? We both know I never had a job."

"Nevertheless, your resume is quite impressive," he replied.

The knot in her stomach eased. "Really?"

"It takes a high level of management skills to put on the events you've chaired—an ability to plan, to delegate authority, to encourage those under you, and to get along with all sorts of people. I know lots of executives who don't have those traits."

"I never thought of it that way."

He smiled down at her and her stomach tightened all over again. "You're hired. You can start tomorrow. Our work day begins at eight and ends at five. You get an hour for lunch."

She nodded. Considering his view of her talents, she could hardly wait to hear what the job would be. His assistant, perhaps?

"You'll be starting as a trainee at two hundred and fifty dollars a week. You'll get a paycheck every other Friday."

Trainee! Had he forgotten she owned the magazine? And the pay was ridiculous. Did people really survive on so little? Herbert had spent more than that dining out every month.

Welcome to the real world, she told herself. She could hardly get angry with Arye after telling him she was willing to start at the bottom. She just hadn't known how far down the bottom could be.

"I assume that's agreeable," he said.

"You don't need to—to pay me anything."

"You'll be a better executive in the future if you understand all the ramifications of being an entry level employee. And that includes salary. Trust me, Peach. You're going to work very hard for your money. I expect you to pull your share of the load."

He got up, went to his desk, picked up the phone and said something she couldn't hear. By the time he rejoined her, Cindy Dysnowski had walked into the office. Peach had last seen her at Blackjack's memorial service. It hadn't been a pleasant encounter. But then, nothing had been pleasant about that particular day.

"Cindy, you know Peach Morgan-Strand, don't you?" Arye asked.

Cindy kept her gaze firmly fixed on his face—a worshipful gaze at that. The girl was practically drooling. Did he know it? Did he have that effect on every woman who crossed his path? The idea made Peach acutely uncomfortable.

She blinked the feeling away as Cindy said, "Of course."

"It's Peach Morgan," Peach interjected. "I've dropped the Strand."

Arye acknowledged the information with a slight lift of his brow. He had, Peach decided, the most expressive brow this side of Sean Connery.

"Peach is joining the magazine's staff. I'd like you to spend the next month teaching her our word-processing program," Arye told Cindy.

Cindy's mouth pursed. Her studied prettiness faded. She looked as though she'd taken a big bite out of a very sour pickle. "I've got an awful lot to do as it is," she murmured.

"I'll see you have extra help," Arye answered back. "If Peach is a fast learner, it may not take that long."

Then and there—although all things mechanical intimidated Peach, she made up her mind to be the fastest learner he'd ever seen. A week from now she intended to know the editing program as well as she knew the inside of her house.

"It won't be that bad," she promised Cindy. "I want you to treat me the way you'd treat any other trainee. If I mess up, don't hesitate to get on my case."

"Sure thing, Mrs. Morgan-Strand."

"It's Miss Morgan," Peach said, "or it will be soon." She rose and walked over to Cindy to shake her hand. "But I want you to call me Peach."

"Peach will report to you first thing in the morning," Arye told Cindy. When the girl continued to stand there, gazing at him as if he were her favorite food, he added, "that's all for now."

Cindy headed for the door like an obedient puppy. Peach stayed put.

"I mean you too, Peach," Arye said, giving her a dismissive nod.

She swallowed the anger that rushed up her throat. For the moment, she'd play the game his way.

Cindy fumed all the way home at the end of the day. The fact that her old car overheated and she had to stop at a gas station to put a sealant in the radiator didn't help her mood. The thought of spending a month with a woman who undoubtedly thought she peed cologne, infuriated Cindy.

The phone was ringing when she opened her apartment door and she rushed to answer it. By the time she grabbed the receiver, the line had gone dead. She kicked off her high heels, tugged her super control panties off, removed her hose and headed for the tiny bathroom. When she lowered herself onto the toilet, the phone rang again.

"Fuck," she said so loudly that the word reverberated in the tiled space. With her bladder still full, she got up and raced to answer the phone. Although the journey took seconds, it was long enough for her to imagine Arye on the other end of the line, calling to ask her to dinner as a way of thanking her for taking on the job of training Peach.

"Hello," she said in the husky voice she reserved just for him.

"Dr. Strand would like to talk to Miss Dysnowski," a female voice informed her.

What now? she fumed. She had no further use for Strand. She considered telling the woman she was too busy to talk to anyone—but she knew it wouldn't do any good. Big shots like Strand were used to getting their way. He'd just have the woman call back again and again and again.

"Put him on," she said icily.

"Miss Dysnoski, I've been trying to reach you for quite a while," Strand began without so much as a how-de-do.

"What for?"

"Surely you remember our last conversation— about the medical symposium in Palm Springs? I told you I'd give you a chance to think it over."

"There isn't anything to think about. I'm not going."

She was about to hang up when Strand said, "If you can't get away from work, I'll be happy to talk to your employer for you."

Like hell he would, she thought, feeling her anger escalate. No way did she want Arye to know what she'd been through for him. She'd see Strand dead first.

"I'm well aware some of my patients don't like their friends to know they had plastic surgery. Is that your problem, Miss Dysnowksi?" Strand continued. "If that's what's troubling you, rest assured I won't reveal your identity to anyone in Palm Springs. I just want my colleagues to see what I was able to do for you. In exchange you'll get a week in a luxury hotel."

She barely listened to what he was saying. The thought that he had the power to expose her had never really hit her before.

She had gone to him because he was reputed to be the best. Although she'd known he was Peach's husband, she had assumed using her real name would hide her new identity. She'd written her phone number down in the proper space on his office form, never thinking he'd have any reason to use it.

"Have you got a hearing problem? I said I'm not interested."

"How many opportunities do you have for an all-expenses-paid vacation in the sun capital of the world?"

The self-centered bastard. Apparently he forgot he had told her to avoid the sun.

"The answer is still no."

"I find that hard to believe. I thought you'd want to show a little gratitude considering what I did for you."

She caught a glimpse of herself in one of her many mirrors and realized her eyes still bulged when she was angry. The bastard was supposed to have fixed that. "I don't owe you a damn thing, Doctor. I paid for everything you did to me."

"Now, now, Miss Dysnowski, I didn't call to argue with you. Frankly, young lady, I'm not prepared to take no for an answer."

Anger fed on Cindy's innards like a ravenous wolf threatening to devour her from the inside out. Her eyes were so swollen and dry, she could hardly blink. Sweat oozed from a complexion that looked blotchy beneath her makeup.

Her mirrors told her the woman she fought so hard to become had been replaced by the woman she'd left behind. Clotilde Dysnowski had reappeared.

It was Dr. Strand's fault. He'd done it to her and for that, he would pay.

"Can't we meet to talk it over. I could treat you to a nice dinner at La Griglia," he said, mentioning an expensive restaurant she had never been able to afford. "Give me a chance to change your mind, Miss Dysnowski. It's the least you can do."

The least she could do? Strand didn't have a clue when it came to what she could do. But he was sure as hell going to find out.

Her lips parted over her dry teeth. "You know, you may be right," she said, pausing long enough to make him think he'd achieved his goal, "but I really don't feel like eating out tonight."

"Tomorrow night, then?"

"If you really want to talk to me, I'll be going out for a run later. We could meet at nine in the Memorial Park lot."

Peach had just gone to bed when the doorbell rang. The clock on the nightstand read ten. Whoever it was, she hoped he or she wouldn't stay long. Peach wanted to be fresh and alert her first day at work.

She got up, put on a robe and hurried downstairs to see who was there. Bella had beaten her to it. Peach found her mother in the foyer with a policeman.

"Here's my daughter now," Bella told him.

He waited until Peach reached the bottom of the stairs before saying, "There's been some trouble, Mrs. Strand. Your husband has had an accident. He's been life-flighted to Hermann Hospital."

Peach took an involuntary step back. She felt as though she were trapped in a nightmare that wouldn't end.

"I'm sorry to be the bearer of bad news," the officer said. "I know you two ladies have been through tough times lately."

Peach struggled for control. She'd been angry at Herbert after their last meeting but she had never wished him any harm. The boys. How could she tell the boys? "What sort of accident?"

"It was a hit and run," the officer said. "Your husband had parked by Memorial Parkway. He was wearing running gear. We think he planned to go jogging, however someone ran him down in the lot. He was able to get to his car phone to call for help."

"Are you sure you have the right man? My husband never jogged. He didn't like to sweat."

The cop looked at her as though she'd lost her mind. For a moment, she thought she had. Her legs went weak. She felt as incapable of staying upright as a trampled wildflower.

Bella put a supportive arm around Peach's waist. "Are you all right, honey?"

"I'm not sure. I can't believe this is happening."

Peach wondered if she would ever be all right again. She cut a look at the officer to assure herself he wasn't a figment of her imagination.

"We'll be at the hospital as quickly as we can," Bella told him.

"I don't mind waiting until you're ready to go. That way you can follow me. You'll get there a lot faster."

Were all policeman as polite as the ones she'd met? Peach wondered as she made her way back to her room to dress. Although Herbert had been life-flighted, she refused to panic. If he'd been able to summon help, his injuries couldn't be that serious. Besides, Herbert was too self-determined to let go of life without putting up one hell of a fight.

Peach couldn't have been more wrong. Although the trip to the hospital didn't take very long with a police car to clear the way, Herbert had died of massive internal injuries by the time they arrived.

As Peach stood in a waiting room listening to yet another doctor explain why he'd been unable to prevent a death, she felt tears oozing from her eyes. The sense of loss that swept over her took her by surprise. She would have given anything to have made her peace with Herbert. If only she could turn the calendar back to their meeting at the club, she would apologize for ruining his clothes and then thank him for giving her two beautiful sons.

This time she knew what was expected of her, the decisions she had to make, the relatives and friends who needed to be notified. The most distasteful task was calling Luise Degrasse. As Herbert's fiancée, she insisted on helping plan the funeral. Peach had no doubt she intended to be the star of the event. Poor Luise. She'd been widowed three and a half times.

Peach's heart constricted at the thought of telling the twins. They had loved their father as much as she loved Blackjack. She was struck anew by the enormity of Herbert's untimely death. She may not have wanted the life he'd chosen—not any more—but God knew he had enjoyed it. Who had taken it away from him?

The next morning Herbert's attorney showed up on her doorstep for what he called a preliminary talk about Herbert's will. She wasn't surprised to hear she'd been left out of it, both as heir and trustee, or that the attorney had been named to act in her place.

Instead of being upset, she was glad her sons would have such a good financial start in life, and immensely relieved to be free of the obligation to close down Herbert's practice. The names of his clients, the secrets Herbert knew about them, didn't interest her at all.

The boys' arrival, the details of the funeral, Luise Degrasse's tearful presence kept her too busy to think about the magazine—or the man who ran it. Two weeks after the funeral, she telephoned Arye to say she'd start work the next day. When he wasn't in, she left a message.

Cindy Downing was waiting when Peach stepped out of the elevator the next morning. "Arye told me you'd be coming in today. I'm so sorry for your loss," she said in a rush. "Arye wants you to know you can go home if it gets to be too much for you—being here and all so soon after the tragedy."

"I'll be fine," Peach answered with an assurance she was far from feeling.

"You're so brave."

"It has nothing to do with bravery. I'm sure you realize Dr. Strand and I were getting a divorce. So you see, I lost him long before the accident."

"Do the police have any idea who killed him?" Cindy asked.

"Not a clue. They found a chip of automobile paint

on his clothes and the forensic lab was able to identify the source, but it turned out to be a dead end."

"Really," Cindy said, leading the way to her office. "I thought they could tell what kind of car the paint came from."

"They can. The trouble is this particular car had been repainted at a nationwide chain that does cars for next to nothing."

"It sounds hopeless."

"I'm afraid it is." Feelings of sadness, guilt, and anger were so muddled inside Peach, she felt as though her innards had been churned.

"Are you all right, Peach?" Cindy's voice brought Peach back to the present.

"I was thinking about my husband. It seems something terrible has happened to everyone I care about. My father died in disgrace. A fire destroyed my mother's apartment. Bert was shot, and someone killed Herbert." Peach took a step back as she recited the mournful litany. "Perhaps you had better not get too close to me."

Cindy opened her office door, put her purse on a bookshelf, then held out her hand for Peach's. "I'm not worried. You look pretty harmless to me. Besides, I can take care of myself."

Peach paused in the doorway and looked around, noting a full-length mirror—the sort you could get at K Mart for ten dollars—hanging on one wall. Other than that she didn't see any personal decorations, no plants, posters, or photographs of family members to liven up the institutional decor.

With a start, she realized Cindy was staring at her intently.

"Do you have any idea who did those things?" Cindy probed.

Peach shook her head. "Look, I don't want to take any more of your time talking about my problems. I'm here to learn. Where do we begin?"

In response Cindy walked over to a computer console, pushed a button and the screen came to glowing life.

Arye and Bert ate at Mesa—A Touch of Santa Fe a couple of times a month. Arye thought they made the best blue corn cheese enchiladas this side of Ruidoso, and Bert favored the tamales.

The two men arrived at the restaurant at quarter to twelve, were shown to their favorite booth, told their regular waiter they'd have their usual lunch, and quickly launched into a conversation.

"Peach has been in the shop for two weeks," Bert began. "How is she doing?"

"Fine as far as I know," Arye replied, trying to keep his voice and expression noncommittal.

It had been pure hell, having Peach just a couple of offices away. He'd spent far too much time fighting the urge to go see her, and far too little concentrating on his job—had made so many unnecessary trips to the bathroom just to catch a glimpse of her that he had no doubt office scuttlebutt pegged him as a man with a prostate problem.

"What do you mean, as far as you know? I thought you'd have taken her under your wing by now. After all, she does own the company."

"That's the very reason I can't show her any favoritism. It would be bad for office morale."

"Don't you mean your morale? The way I see it, you've been avoiding Peach because you're afraid she will figure out the truth."

"And what's that?"

"We've been over this before, old horse. You're head over heels in love with the woman. I saw the expression in your eyes when you heard Herbert Strand had been killed—and it wasn't exactly mournful. You looked relieved."

Arye took a deep draught from his water glass. "It may not be good form to speak ill of the dead, but Peach is a hell of a lot better off without that man. From what I saw of him, the good doctor was a master manipulator—a user."

Bert grunted his assent. "Someone manipulated Strand straight through the pearly gates—unless of course he wound up headed in the other direction. I can't help feeling sorry for Peach, though. Bella says she's pretty conflicted over the whole thing."

Arye had learned more about Peach via second-hand reports from Bert than he had from seeing her every day. "What do you mean, conflicted?"

"That shouldn't be too hard to figure out. Peach and Herbert were getting a divorce and from what Bella has said, it wasn't exactly a friendly one. However, they did have two sons who took their father's death hard. It's a hell of a spot for a woman to be in."

Arye didn't realize he'd groaned in sympathy until Bert reached across the table and patted his shoulder. "You've got it bad."

"Bad? Basket case would be a better description. I wanted to be with Peach to help her through the funeral but I was damn sure she wouldn't appreciate my presence." He groaned again. "I sent flowers instead—flowers for a man I disliked. I've never been a hypocrite. What the hell is happening to me?"

"I believe it's called love." Bert didn't skip a beat even though the waiter arrived with their food. "You won't be able to deal with it unless you admit your feelings."

"To myself—or Peach?"

Bert's tamale-laden fork paused in mid-air. "Both."

Ordinarily a redolent plate of enchiladas would have made Arye's gastric juices flow. Today though, he was immune to epicurean pleasures. "How the hell am I supposed to do that? Do you suggest I ask her if she's mastered the computer yet, and say, oh by the way, I'm crazy in love with you?"

Bert slanted his head. With his silver hair, it made him look a bit like a quizzical borzoi. "It might just do the trick."

"Get real, Bert. I'm in a no-win situation. Peach has never forgiven the way I refused to help her look into her father's past. She's learning the ins and outs of the publishing business so she can replace me with herself. Somehow, that seems to preclude romance." Arye shrugged. "I've been thinking about beating her to it and handing in my notice."

Bert had been eating steadily. He lowered his fork to his plate with a clatter. "I never thought of you as a quitter."

"I prefer to think of myself as a realist."

"It took you a long time to put your life back together. What would you do if you left Houston? And don't tell me you'd wing it. You're too old to drift."

"I've been thinking of going back to Tucson and nailing the Mafia bastard who ordered the hit on me and killed my wife instead."

"That's a step in the right direction."

"Meaning?"

"At least you realize you aren't responsible for Helen's death. But looking into it would mean returning to investigative reporting."

Arye nodded. "It's what I do best. Much as I care about Peach, I am wearying of her idea of journalism. It's time I started looking under rocks again, holding the cretins who live there up to public scrutiny."

"You sound like an angry man."

"It beats feeling sorry for myself."

"Unfinished business, is it?"

"You could call it that." In a determined effort to put a halt to the increasingly uncomfortable conversation, Arye said, "Speaking of unfinished business, the photo spread you've got planned for the rodeo issue looks terrific."

As if by tacit agreement, the two men talked about the magazine rather than Arye's personal life throughout the remainder of the meal. As usual, they argued over whose turn it was to pay the check. When it arrived, Arye grabbed it and quickly handed it back to their waiter along with his credit card.

"I get the tax deduction this time," he exclaimed as though he'd won a major victory.

When they left he was surprised to see how dark it had gotten. Although he had lived in Houston for three years he'd never grown accustomed to the lightning-quick weather changes.

The sky had been partly cloudy when they walked into the restaurant. An hour later, it had turned the color of pumice. A howling wind prowled the sidewalk.

Bert cut a worried glance skyward. "We're in for a hell of a blow. We'd better get back to the office."

* * *

"It's time for lunch. I'm going to the underground. Want to join me?" Cindy asked Peach, referring to the five-mile mix of subterranean stores and restaurants that were Houston's best-kept secret.

"Thanks for asking me—but I'm not hungry," Peach replied.

"Don't touch the computer until I get back," Cindy warned, turning off the screen and picking up her purse. "I wouldn't want you to mess up my work."

Peach held her temper in check until Cindy was gone. Damn the girl. Although Cindy had been charged with teaching her, Peach had the feeling Cindy was doing everything in her power to hold Peach back, to make her feel inadequate at best and just plain stupid at worst. Cindy's explanations of the word-processing program seemed deliberately obtuse. She was critical and impatient with Peach rather than supportive.

At first, Peach had attributed her attitude to a natural resentment of the woman who was her boss in name if not in fact. Now though, she was convinced there had to be a deeper reason for Cindy's animus.

Peach stretched, rolling her sore shoulders. Spending eight hours a day in front of a computer was hard on the back. She walked to the window and looked out, debating the wisdom of having a solitary lunch somewhere downtown. But she wasn't hungry enough to bother. Her appetite had fled the moment Herbert asked for a divorce and nothing that had happened since had brought it back.

Impatient with her self-pity, she walked out of Cindy's cubicle and wandered down the hall with no particular destination. Arye's half-open door beckoned just ahead. Without planning it, she walked into his office and shut the door.

She had never felt like a trespasser in the room before. Today, though, she couldn't help comparing herself to Daniel walking into the lion's den. This time the lion was on a lunch break, probably gobbling up a poor unwary antelope.

Peach smiled at the analogy. Arye did mean lion, she recalled. Certainly he was as magnificently male as any lion she'd seen in a zoo. His thick black hair and well-muscled body signaled his virility just the way a lion's mane did.

Lord, was that any way for a new widow to think?

Thirteen

"I can do this," Peach thought, sitting at Arye's computer console as she made the cursor dance across the screen.

Despite Cindy's convoluted explanations about such arcane subjects as rams, megabytes and hard/soft drives—Peach giggled at what that implied—Word for Windows was a snap now Peach knew what all the funny little drawings in the boxes meant. She could move a paragraph, insert a sentence, erase a word, or create italics at will.

She amused herself by invading Arye's files, and experienced a voyeur's forbidden pleasure when she came across an article he hadn't finished. Feeling very much the way she used to when she snuck peeks at Christmas presents her mother had hidden away, she began editing, making a tiny correction here, expanding on a thought there, confident in the knowledge that the original text wouldn't be permanently altered as long as she didn't save the changes.

She had taken Arye's ability for granted. Seeing his rough draft, she realized just how talented he was. She felt as though she'd been given a diagram detailing the inner workings of his mind. She permitted herself a brief fantasy of them writing together as a team, coming up with story concepts and then pursuing them, having intimate candlelit dinners after a day spent interviewing and researching. It would be heaven to be this man's partner instead of his well-dressed serf.

The computer joined her to Arye and made them one in a way she had never imagined. She was making electronic love to him, she fancied as her fingers flew over the keyboard. It was probably as close to the real thing as she would ever get.

The further she moved into the article the more immersed she became in it. Arye had a knack for making Corpus Christi's acquisition and display of the Spanish-built replicas of Christopher Columbus's ships sound like a mini-thriller full of unexpected twists and turns that included storms at sea and being rammed by a runaway barge in the harbor.

His descriptions were so vivid, his narrative so compelling that she could almost smell the ocean's briny aroma as the Niña, Pinta, and the Santa María completed their nine-thousand-mile journey and tied up to a Texas wharf. She heard the whoosh of air being dumped from the sails and the rattle of the rigging. It seemed so real.

With a start, she realized the noise was real. It came from outside. She looked away from the screen to see a leaden sky boiling outside the window like a witch's cauldron. Amazed rather than frightened, she watched the glass bulge in, then out. She hadn't known glass could be that flexible.

Mesmerized by the sight, she froze like a deer. At last her survival instinct asserted itself. She leapt from the computer console as the glass imploded with a roar. Something hit her back, knocked the breath from her lungs, and the world went black.

* * *

Arye and Bert left the elevator at the forty-fourth floor to find the building swaying ever so slightly in the maelstrom. The sound of groaning steel was unsettling.

"If I didn't know better, I'd think we were having an earthquake," Arye said.

He gazed out a window and was horrified to see a funnel cloud coalescing a few miles away. His mind went into instant overdrive as he decided on a course of action. By now most of the magazine's employees would be back from lunch. Unless they happened to look out their windows, they would be unaware of the approaching tornado.

"We've got to get everyone into the hall," he told Bert, pushing past the doors that led from the elevator lobby to the magazine's reception area where Tiffany was on the phone.

Arye jumped over her desk in a perfect rendition of the high hurdle he had mastered in high school track meets, unceremoniously yanked her to her feet and pushed her in the direction of the interior hall.

Over her startled protest, he shouted, "We're in the path of a tornado. Get on the floor next to a wall. You should be safe there." To Bert, he called out, "Take the offices on the left side of the hall and I'll take the right. Don't let anyone stay near a window."

Arye ran for the first door, yanked it open and told the room's astonished occupants to get moving and take shelter in the hall, repeating the admonition at every door, yanking women from their chairs if they gave him a blank stare. He didn't like manhandling them but he didn't have time to worry about it.

By the time he reached Cindy's office, the building's motion, coupled with the wailing wind, must have been evident to the most preoccupied members of the staff. Doors he had yet to reach flew open and white-faced employees hurried into the hall.

Arye reached Cindy's spartan cubicle and looked inside, relieved to see neither Cindy nor Peach had returned from lunch. With luck, the two of them would have dined at one of the restaurants in the underground where they would be safe from harm.

He turned back to the main hall, saw all the office doors were open except his own, and began counting off names as his gaze went from one person to another. Then it hit him. He'd left his own door ajar when he went to lunch.

He would never be able to explain the sixth sense that sent him racing to his office. He shoved the door open so hard it banged against the far wall—and his heart lurched at what he'd revealed.

Dear God, what was Peach doing standing by his computer, looking toward the approaching vortex as though she were watching it in living color on television instead of real life. The little fool wasn't making any effort to save herself.

A vision of her body—cut and torn by flying glass—flashed across the screen of his mind. It jolted him to instant action. As the windows burst inward, he threw himself at her in a flying tackle. From then on, everything seemed to be happening in slow motion.

Wind clawed at the room like a living thing.

A burst of ozone filled the air.

Chunks of glass flew by.

Papers winged through the air like giant confetti.

All the while, he covered her body with his to protect

her from the glittering daggers that had been the windows.

The fall to the floor seemed to take forever. At last, they were down amidst shards of glass. He covered her head with his arms and ducked his neck, doing his best to imitate a turtle. Out of the corner of one eye, he saw a bird's featherless corpse land not a foot away. A hubcap flew through the shattered window like a miniature flying saucer.

It seemed as though eternity passed before the wind diminished. Debris settled to the carpet. Peach moaned beneath him. He knew he ought to get off of her but he couldn't seem to make himself let her go.

He continued to hold her close, reveling in the contact, breathing in her scent and thanking Jesus, Buddha, Mohammed, and any other spirits of inspiration whose names he could remember that he'd arrived in time to save the woman he loved.

If he didn't do anything worthwhile with the rest of his life, it wouldn't matter. Today he'd been in the right place at the right time.

Peach stirred beneath him.

"It's all right my love," he said into her ear, "you're safe."

Moving carefully so as not to hurt her, he lifted his body from hers and knelt by her side. She seemed to be in a stupor. He ran his hands down her arms and legs to make sure he hadn't broken any bones when he tackled her. Her skin was so seductively soft, her curves so primally female that he almost forgot the reason for the intimacies he permitted himself.

He withdrew his hands reluctantly. Her body was intact. He couldn't say as much for her face. She had a nasty bump on her forehead. He bent to kiss it. Then, thinking he might never have another chance, he whispered, "I love you."

Her eyes opened. She looked at him as though he was the last person she expected to see. "Did I kill you, too? Are we in heaven?" she asked in such a small voice it wouldn't have been audible if their faces hadn't been inches apart.

"Not hardly," he said, gesturing at the ruined room, "although at this minute it sure feels like heaven to me."

To his wonderment, she reached up and touched his cheek. "You're hurt."

"It's only a scratch." He couldn't help grinning. "I never felt better."

"You've looked better," Peach replied.

She struggled to a sitting position, pulled a tissue from a pocket and pressed it against his cut, then gazed around the shattered office, trying to assimilate what had happened.

There were gaping holes in her memory of the last hour. She felt woozy and disengaged, as though a transparent curtain hung between her and what she was seeing. Shock, she must be in shock.

She had to concentrate hard to say what was on her mind. "The last thing I remember is getting up from the computer. What happened?"

"A tornado passed right over the building. Maybe I should say *through* it."

Peach was struggling to take in the information when Bert came running into the room. "Thank God you're all right," he said to Arye, then noticed Peach. His eyes widened with almost fatherly concern as he hurried to her side and helped her to her feet. "I didn't know you were here."

Before she could reply, Arye rose too and a silvery shower of glass chips cascaded from his leather jacket.

"You look like you've been through a meat grinder," Bert said, circling behind him. "Your jacket's all cut up in back. You'd better take it off so I can see if your skin is still in one piece."

"Forget me. Peach has a nasty bump on her head. She might have a concussion. She needs to see a doctor."

"Me see a doctor? You're the one who is bleeding," Peach exclaimed.

Fighting dizziness, she eased his jacket down his arms, then walked around behind him and gasped as his back came into view. "There's blood all over your shirt."

Until that moment, adrenaline had kept Arye from feeling any pain. As Peach spoke he became aware of a burning sensation flaming across his back from his left shoulder to his spine.

"We'd better have a look," Bert said.

Peach began unbuttoning Arye's shirt but her hands were shaking too hard to be effective. Bert retrieved a pair of scissors from the desk and carefully cut Arye's shirt up the back.

"How bad is it?" Arye asked.

"I've seen worse," Bert replied calmly.

Bert had been a combat photographer in Vietnam. The sight of a little blood wouldn't bother him. Arye couldn't say as much for Peach. She looked as white as any of the sheets of paper littering the floor.

"I'll get the first-aid kit and patch you up before I take you to the hospital," Bert told Arye.

"I'm not going to any damn hospital. Peach is the one who needs to see a doctor."

"The two of you can go together," Bert replied. His feet crunched on the glass as he left the room.

"If you won't go to a hospital, I'll take you to see my doctor," Peach said.

"I'm not exactly a gynecological candidate," Arye replied, hoping humor would erase the lines of worry that etched her brow.

She didn't crack a smile. "Dr. Shaw is an internist."

Her hands were probing the margins of his wound. They felt as gentle as a butterfly's wings. He would have endured a lot more than a cut back to have her touch him like that. However he was much more concerned about her well-being than his own.

"Please sit down before you fall down, Peach," he said, taking her arm and guiding her over to the furniture grouping on the far side of the room. He brushed the litter from one of the chairs, then lowered her into it as carefully as though she were made of fine china.

She looked up at him. "I'm still not certain what happened. How did you know I was here?"

"I wasn't certain until I opened the door and saw you. I'm sorry about the tackle. There wasn't time to do anything else."

The instant he said it, the missing pieces of Peach's memory fell into place. She recalled seeing the window bulge inward and something hitting her in the back. That something had been Arye. She had blacked out when he knocked her breathless.

Arye had acted like the heroes in all the fairy tales Bella used to read her, Peach thought with a sense of awe. A lump swelled in her throat as she realized he had risked his life for hers. He was certainly brave enough to have done it for a stranger. However he wouldn't have roused a stranger with a kiss, let alone whispered *I love you*.

I love you. It hadn't been her imagination. He'd actually said those words. But for the weakness in her legs, she would have gotten up and danced around the room.

She drank him in with her gaze, limning his appearance on the parchment of her memory. If she lived to be a hundred she wanted to be able to summon up the way he looked at this moment, the tousled hair hanging over his brow, the pirate cut on his cheek, the way his lips seemed to promise a smile. Now she knew how Bella had felt about Blackjack when they first met—knew with every fiber of her being because she felt that way about Arye.

"I'll never be able to repay you for what you did today," she said.

"There is something you could do for me," he replied.

"All you have to do is ask."

He reached down and helped her to her feet. They stood face to face—except he was so tall she had to tilt her head to see his face. He gave her a smile that could have melted steel, let alone an object as combustible as her heart.

"I'd settle for a kiss. My mother always used to give me one when I had a boo-boo."

"I warn you, mine won't be motherly," Peach told him as she moved closer.

At that moment, the lights went out. Peach was unaware of the darkness though. Arye's selfless deed glowed like a beacon to guide her soul to his. She reached up and twined her fingers in Arye's hair, reveling in the crisp clean feel of each strand. She pressed her breasts into his chest, breathed in his scent. She couldn't seem to get close enough. If it had been possible, she would have climbed right inside his skin.

Her timing couldn't be worse. But the feelings she had repressed for months could no longer be denied. She loved this man—and maybe, just maybe he loved her back. The way he took possession of her mouth would have registered ten on the Richter scale. She parted her lips in welcome and tasted the spicy Mexican food he'd had for lunch. It only added to her pleasure.

Herbert had always insisted the two of them bathe, brush their teeth and gargle before they made love. Obviously Arye had no such compunctions. She thrilled to the erection throbbing to urgent life against her abdomen. Arye was ready for love, and from the damp heat between her thighs, so was she.

But for his injured back—and the fact that the sofa was covered with bits of glass—she wouldn't have minded if he took her then and there. Minded? Who was she kidding? She could barely restrain her passion, her yearning to be joined with him. She had wanted this for so long, wanted to be held and loved by Arye. Her hands pressed into his back to urge him even closer.

He squirmed at her touch and pulled away.

"Oh Lord. I'm so sorry. I didn't mean to hurt you," she burst out. "I forgot all about your cut."

He chuckled deep in his throat, a richly masculine sound that sent tingles along her auditory nerves. "So did I."

The lights flickered a couple of times, then came on. Peach looked toward the door to see Bert standing there. Although he had surely seen them kiss, she felt neither regret nor shame. Then she saw Cindy Downing staring at them over Bert's shoulder.

Peach had never seen a rattler in the moment before it struck but she had the feeling it would have the same look in its eyes that Cindy did. Rather than striking, Cindy turned and walked away.

"I'm sorry it took me so long," Bert said. He opened the first-aid kit and began rummaging through it.

"Let me do that," Peach said. "I've had first-aid training."

She found a small circular bandage and applied it to Arye's cheek, then opened several roles of gauze and a tube of first-aid cream. "I'll try not to hurt you," she told him.

"If you do, can I have another kiss to make it feel better?"

Bert cleared his throat. "As happy as I am to see the two of you have made up your differences, we have more important things to discuss. While I was looking for the first-aid kit, Tiffany told me the building superintendent called the reception desk to tell us we have to evacuate."

"Isn't that a little like shutting the barn door after the horse has run away?" Peach asked, daubing the cream onto Arye's back with exquisite care.

"Apparently we weren't the only ones to lose glass. The west face of the building took a lot of damage. It won't be habitable until they board up the windows and clear the debris."

"We can't close up shop," Arye objected.

"We'll worry about that tomorrow," Peach told him. "Right now, you're my only concern."

"Was anyone else hurt?" Arye asked Bert.

"I can't speak for the rest of the people in other

offices or the ones who were on the sidewalk when the glass blew out of the windows, but we were lucky. The rest of the staff came through without a scratch. Unlike the two of you, they had the sense to stay out of harm's way."

"That's a relief," Arye replied.

"I took the liberty of telling them to go home and to check with me Monday morning before coming to work."

"Do you think we'll be allowed back in the building by then?" Arye asked.

Bert shook his head. "I doubt it."

"How can the two of you can worry about business at a time like this?" Peach exclaimed, giving her anxiety a voice.

"We have a magazine to get out," they replied in unison.

She finished cleaning Arye's wound. Thank heaven it wasn't as deep as she feared. "How does it feel?" she asked him.

He turned to look at her, his gaze as intimate as a caress. "A lot better, thanks to you."

"You wouldn't have been hurt at all if it hadn't been for me."

She took a roll of gauze and started wrapping it around his chest, trying not to react to the soft pelt that covered his pectorals and trailed intriguingly lower until it disappeared inside his trousers.

However her fingers seemed to have a mind of their own. They managed to do as much caressing as they did nursing. She felt her face heat up. Arye looked flushed too, even though the room was open to the elements.

"I can see you two don't need me," Bert commented with considerable prudence. "Meet me at the front desk when you're ready and I'll take you wherever you want to go."

"I can drive," Peach exclaimed.

"Your mother would skin me alive if she heard I let the two of you go off alone after what you've been through."

What she had been through, Peach thought as Bert walked away, was the most thrilling day of her life—and it didn't have a damn thing to do with the tornado.

Bella ran out of the house as soon as Bert parked the Jaguar in the driveway. Peach reluctantly left the back seat where she had been sitting with Arye. Bella gave Peach a quick hug, moved to Arye, stood on tiptoe and kissed him on the lips, then linked arms with Bert.

"It's a relief to know my three favorite people are safe and sound. Arye, I can't thank you enough for saving my daughter's life. From this day forward, as far as I'm concerned, you're family."

Delia was waiting for them in the entry. She looked Peach up and down to reassure herself Peach was all right, then walked over to Arye, assessing him as though he were a prize piece of horseflesh. "I hear you saved Miss Peach's life. But then a man like you couldn't be stampeded by a little wind."

Arye's blush went from his hairline to the edge of the bandage on his bare chest. "Anyone would have done the same thing."

"Not the anyones I've knowed. I fixed you all a special dinner. It will be ready by the time you have one of Miss Bella's martinis."

"She's an original," Bella said after Delia returned to the kitchen. "I want to hear everything that happened, from beginning to end."

Bella continued chattering as she led the way to the den. Peach didn't mind that she and Arye couldn't get a word in edgewise. The way he held her hand as though he never wanted to let her go, spoke in a language all its own.

While Bella poured drinks for all of them, Peach went upstairs to get one of the twins' shirts to replace the one Arye had ruined. When he put it on, the shoulders were too narrow, the cuffs didn't reach his wrists and the collar was too tight, but she thought he looked marvelous in it.

After all the months of dining alone with Bella, it felt wonderful to have the man she loved sitting across the table. Delia had outdone herself. The chicken-fried steak was fork-tender, the gravy creamy, the biscuits light, and the fried okra browned to perfection. Peach found herself enjoying the food but her stomach had shrunk so much, she couldn't eat a lot.

When they reconvened in the den for coffee and brandy, Bella surprised Peach by saying, "I think Arye should spend the night."

"I don't want to put you two to any trouble," Arye objected.

"Nonsense. I said you're family and family is never any trouble. You're going to be stiff and sore in the morning. I know you men like to pretend you're impervious to pain, but a little tender loving care never hurt any of you."

Bert grinned. "You'd better listen. When it comes to playing mother hen, Bella doesn't take no for an answer. Believe me, I know. She kept me lounging around at home long after I felt ready to go back to work."

Thank you, Mother, Peach thought. She'd been dreading the moment when Arye would walk out the door. "We have two guest bedrooms. You can take your pick," she told him, thinking he had better choose the one next to hers.

"I presume you prefer a queen-size bed to a twin," she said an hour later as he followed her upstairs.

"That sounds good to me."

"The room with the queen is right here," she replied, opening the door to the room adjacent to her own.

Her cheeks heated up as she wondered if Arye saw through the ruse. "I'm afraid you'll have to sleep in your underwear. The twins' pajamas will never fit."

"The only thing I wear in bed is my skin."

Flustered by the image that conjured up, she fluttered around the room, opening the door to the bath and checking on the linens, closing the curtains and turning on the lamp by the bed.

Arye caught her by the waist and tilted her head up to his, then pressed a chaste kiss on her forehead. "You've had a rough day. Stop playing chambermaid and go to bed."

"Are you sure you want to be alone?" she asked, hoping she wasn't being too bold.

His arm still circling her waist, he guided her to the

door. "I'm sure. But one of these days, we're going to have to do a hell of a lot more in a bedroom than say good-night. And sweetheart, you can take that to the bank."

Fourteen

Peach slept in fits and starts, waking and drifting off again as her restless brain did battle with her weary body. At two in the morning her brain won. She listened to the mechanical drone of the air conditioner, feeling more muddled than refreshed and wishing she weren't alone in her bed.

Rain jangled on the roof. The sheets twisted around her legs like pretzel dough. The bottom of her baby-doll pajamas had caught in her crotch, and the top had ridden up to her armpits.

By the time she straightened the bedding, sleep seemed as far away as Tibet and as improbable as Shangri-La. She turned on the light, took a recent best seller off her nightstand, plumped her pillows, and settled down to read.

Ten minutes later she admitted she didn't care about *Smila's Sense of Snow*—or his sense of anything else—although the thought of being cold had a certain appeal given Houston's perpetual heat and humidity. What she cared about was the man in the next room.

She had married at nineteen and been a mother at twenty. Now forty-one and counting, she felt like a girl again. Jittery, excited, terrified.

She wanted so much more from Arye than Herbert had given her. She wanted passionate physical love, emotional and mental intimacy. She wanted to be Eve to his Adam, yin to his yang, pencil to his lead.

She even wanted to give him a child.

The thought jolted her from her reverie. She was really losing it, thinking about having a child when she had two grown sons.

She tried to shove the whole bizarre idea away. However, an insidious little voice in the back of her mind reminded her that lots of women in their forties were having children. If it was good enough for Susan Sarandon, who was Peach Morgan to argue?

Furious with that little voice, she stalked into the bathroom, took an aspirin from the medicine cabinet and swallowed it down with a handful of tap water. She returned to her room, shrugged into a robe that barely covered the tops of her thighs, then opened the door and tiptoed into the hall, intending to go down to the kitchen and fix herself a glass of sleep-inducing warm milk.

The next thing she knew, her hand was on the door to Arye's room. She'd just take a moment to check on him, she told herself, and make sure his bandages were still in place. If he was sleeping he'd never know. If he wasn't—well, she'd think of something.

She cracked the door open and slipped inside, moving soundlessly on bare feet. Arye must have opened the curtains and raised the blinds before he went to bed because she could see lightning dancing over Buffalo Bayou.

Widening her eyes, she waited until they were accustomed to the dark, then made her way to the bed and gazed down at him. Arye was lying on his stomach with his face cradled in one arm. Her eyes widened even more as she realized the top sheet had slipped below his hips, revealing far more of him than she had expected to see.

Raising two athletic sons to virile manhood hadn't prepared her for the sight of Arye Rappaport in the buff. The perfection of his torso would have challenged even Michelangelo's talent.

His bare shoulders looked broader, his waist smaller, and his buns a lot tighter than they did clothed. She put a hand to her mouth to stifle a moan. Something low in her stomach tightened as she pictured herself kissing every inch of his manly flesh.

A deep voice tinged with laughter broke the quiet.

"Have you seen enough," Arye asked, "or would you like me to lower the sheet even more?"

Her face heated up. Thank heaven it was too dark for him to see her crimson. "I was just checking to make sure your cut had stopped bleeding."

"It might help if you turned on the light," he replied.

Before she could respond, he rolled onto his side, reaching for the lamp on the night table.

Although the sheet slid even lower, she couldn't turn away. Did he know he was torturing her? Would he care if he did? President Jimmy Carter had said it was all right to lust in your heart. She sure hoped so.

"I tried to be quiet," she said. "How did you know I was here?"

"No one in the world smells as good as you do, boss lady."

The compliment quickened her pulse.

Arye pulled the sheet up to his waist, then grunted as his injured back made contact with the pillows.

"You shouldn't sit that way if it hurts you."

He gave her a little-boy grin. "I don't want you to have to talk to my back. My mother taught me it wasn't polite. Besides, I like looking at you, especially in an outfit like that one."

She clutched her robe tighter—although come to think of it, there wasn't much cloth to clutch.

His smile deepened. "At the Allen Center, you asked how I knew you were in my office. I didn't tell you then because I wasn't sure how you would take it. The truth is I feel so connected to you, I just seem to know when you're around."

Words to live by, she thought. If only she could believe them. "You do?"

"You got under my skin the first time I laid eyes on you—and boss lady, laid was definitely the operative word. The day your father died, I realized you'd made your way a lot deeper than just under my skin. I looked into my heart and there you were. I know it's not the time or the place to tell you this—" His voice trailed off. His gaze turned inward.

"Tell me what?" she urged.

"I said it back at the office when I thought you couldn't hear me—and I've been thinking about saying it to you ever since."

In the quiet, Peach could hear her heart thumping like a voodoo drum. "Go on."

"I love you."

He certainly had a way with words, Peach thought as her knees gave way. She sank onto the bed beside him, close enough to feel his body heat. "I hope you mean it, because I don't think I could stand it if you didn't."

"I mean it. I've only said those words to one other

woman. When she died I never thought I'd say them again. I want to make love to you so much, it's driving me up the wall."

"I wouldn't say no."

To her penultimate surprise, he shook his head. "Not here—not tonight. I want everything to be perfect our first time." He took her hand and kissed her fingertips one by one, then pressed his lips to her palm.

She felt the caress clear down to her toes. "I'm not a stickler for perfection," she said when she could get the words out. "I don't need candlelight or violins if that's what you have in mind. All I need is you."

Peach sat across the breakfast table from Arye, enjoying the intimacy of the quiet morning and wondering why in the world she'd let him convince her to return to her own bed last night. Just looking at him sent her blood pounding. She felt young and alive and foolishly happy.

Monday morning the two of them would go back to work, he to grapple with the problem of getting a magazine out with the office in ruins and she to face Cindy again. But Monday seemed to exist in another time and place. Today she wanted to forget everything but Arye and the way he made her feel.

"We need to talk," he said.

She couldn't agree more. "What about?"

"Us. Where we go from here."

"There you two are," Bella said, choosing the most inopportune moment to put in an appearance.

Bella gave them the sort of beneficent smile a minister gives a couple when he's announcing their banns.

"Did you have a restful night?" she asked archly.

"Very," Peach lied.

"I thought I'd fix breakfast but I see you beat me to it."

"Arye made French toast," Peach declared as proudly as though he'd found a new genetic marker. "He left some for you in the oven."

"If he can cook in addition to being handsome and brave, I may just go after him myself," Bella chirped before she headed for the kitchen.

"About that talk," Peach said when she and Arye were alone again, "would you like to go down to Galveston today? We could drive out to the end of Pirate's Beach and have a picnic."

Her head was instantly filled with visions of Arye in one of those band-aid sized suits competitive swimmers wear. The image was so compelling that a frisson of sexual excitement made her nipples tingle. She couldn't conjure up a better recipe for a memorable day than sun, surf, and a near-naked Arye Rappaport.

"We don't need to go out of town. I'll be content anywhere as long as we're together."

Peach controlled the desire to leap into his lap like an adoring poodle. "I still can't believe what's happened."

"Which *what* are you referring to? The tornado—or us?"

Peach was about to say *us* when Bella reappeared carrying the cordless phone in one hand and a steaming plate of french toast in the other. "A Mr. David Keller is calling from New York. He says he has some business to discuss with both of us. Why don't you talk to him while I eat."

Peach nodded, then held out her hand for the

phone. "This is Peach Morgan, Mr. Keller. What can I do for you?"

"I hope I haven't called too early," Keller replied. He had a distinct New York accent, albeit a rather cultured one.

"Not at all. What's on your mind, sir?"

"You don't have any idea, do you?"

"No."

"I was afraid of that," he said with a sigh.

"Afraid of what?"

"That your father wouldn't have mentioned me. He said he wanted to keep the whole thing under wraps until we had a deal, but I hoped he would have shared it with you and your mother."

Peach's instincts went off like a house alarm announcing an intruder. "Are you a reporter by any chance?"

"Far from it. I don't write words. I sell them," Keller replied cryptically.

"How did you get my unlisted phone number?"

"Your father gave it to me a few days before his death. He didn't have his new number yet but he said you would always know how to reach him. He seemed very proud of you."

Arye was watching her as closely as a sheepdog looking out for his flock. His concern gave her a warm feeling that spread from her center to the tips of her fingers and toes. He made her feel strong and brave and able to deal with anything—including the mysterious Mr. Keller.

"Would you please stop talking in riddles, Mr. Keller and tell me what's on your mind."

"I don't blame you one bit for being suspicious, Mrs. Morgan. Under the circumstances I would feel the same way. But I guarantee this isn't some sort of hoax. The fact is I'm a literary agent. Your father consulted me about selling a book he'd written. I told him I'd make inquiries on his behalf." Keller cleared his throat. "I have to tell you I've never had as much interest in a book and I've been in the business for thirty years. I told the senator his material was auctionable and I'm happy to say I was right. Although the senator insisted on keeping the entire project under wraps, I was able to negotiate a sale—a very large sale, I might add."

"Could you excuse me a minute." Again, Peach covered the mouthpiece with her hand. "I'd like the two of you to hear what this man has to say. His name is David Keller and he claims to be a literary agent who had dealings with Dad."

"I've heard of Keller," Arye told her. "He's supposed to be one of the best in the business—a real *mensch.*"

Peach didn't need a Yiddish/English dictionary to translate the word. Arye's body language, the way he sat forward in his chair, told her Keller was what Blackjack would have called a *stand-up* sort of guy. Her intuition went into overdrive. Goose bumps pebbled her skin.

She pushed the audio button. "I'm back, Mr. Keller. Would you mind repeating what you just said. I've got you on the speakerphone so my mother and a friend can hear."

"Certainly. As I told you, your father came to me a couple of weeks before his death to ask me to represent a book he had written. It was called *The Politics Of Greed,* and it was the most explosive exposé of what goes on inside the Beltway that it's been my privilege to see."

Exactly how much did you see? Arye mouthed the words and Peach repeated them to Keller.

"A thorough chapter outline plus the first three chapters," Keller replied. "Believe me, Mrs. Strand, I've handled a lot of nonfiction in my time but I never read anything like this. It was well written and painfully honest. I told your father he would never be reelected if the book went into print. He said he knew but he felt compelled to tell the truth. He was a remarkably courageous man. I consider his death a great personal loss as well as a loss for the country."

Peach looked at her mother to discover that Bella had turned ashen. "Excuse me again," she said to the agent, then covered the mouthpiece with her palm. "What is it, Mother? You look like you just saw a ghost."

"The last thing your father said to me at Guggenheim's the morning of the auction was that he had a secret weapon to use against his enemies. When I asked him what he meant—and I believe these are his exact words—he said, *'It's very simple, my dear. I'm going to tell the truth, the simple unvarnished truth, and let the chips fall where they may.'* He must have meant the book."

Peach shivered. She felt as though her father had found a way to reach out to her from the grave. "Please excuse the interruption and go on with your story," she told Keller.

"Your father insisted on complete secrecy. After I read the manuscript I knew why. It was political dynamite. Because of the need for circumspection, it took quite a while to set up an auction. I only showed the material to four publishers I felt certain I could trust. The auction closed the afternoon your father died. If he had lived, he would have been a rich man again. The book garnered a two-and-a-half-million-dollar advance."

Peach felt as if she'd inadvertently touched a live wire. The fine hair on her arms and the back of her neck stood straight up. "That's a lot of money."

"The publisher who bought the book believes it's worth every penny. That's really why I'm calling. He's very anxious to get his hands on the completed manuscript. We all are. Frankly, I can't wait to read the rest of it myself."

"Why didn't you get in touch with us sooner?"

"I thought I had—unless you didn't get the flowers and the card I sent for your father's funeral. I asked you to telephone as soon as you felt up to it."

"I suppose I saw your card among the hundreds we received. Since your name didn't mean a thing to me, neither did your request. And it's been months since then."

"Quite right. I was on the brink of calling when I heard about Dr. Strand's accident. I couldn't bring myself to intrude. I feel a little uncomfortable about it even now."

Peach's excitement faded away. "I presume you mean the deal fell through after my father died."

"Not at all. The publisher feels there will be even more public interest in the manuscript in view of the tragic circumstances surrounding his death—provided that you or your mother will stand in for the senator on a book tour. I hope that doesn't sound too ghoulish."

Book tour? Millions of dollars. The information had

come at Peach too fast and furious to be assimilated. "I need some time to think about what you've told me."

"That's understandable. But don't take too long. Your father wanted the book to come out during the ninety-six election campaign. He wanted voters to know exactly what goes on in Congress. The publisher agreed that would be the optimum time to release it. That means we have to get the manuscript in the publisher's hands as soon as possible."

Peach's gaze raced around the room as though she could make the manuscript appear by the force of her will. "I'll get back to you in a week if that's agreeable," she stalled.

"I was hoping we could reach to an agreement today."

"You've given my mother and I a great deal to think about. Life has just started to quiet down for the two of us. The book would put us right back in the public eye."

"I'm in sympathy with your concerns. However time is of the essence. Could we say six days? I'd like to talk to the publisher by Friday next."

"Six days it is."

Peach looked askance at Bella, wondering what her mother's response would be. Bella had been so adamant about letting sleeping dogs lie. But this was different. This was a book Blackjack had written with the intent of clearing his name, a book he had planned to publish, a book he had called his secret weapon.

The determination swelling in her chest made it hard to catch her breath. The bastards who had plagued her father to death weren't going to get away with it after all if she had anything to say about it.

Unfortunately she had very little. The decision was Bella's. A horrible thought popped into Peach's head. Had Bella known about the book all along and hidden it for reasons of her own?

Peach put the phone down, then took a few deep breaths in a vain attempt at calming her racing pulse. She would sacrifice anything to clear her father's name—except her mother's hard-won peace of mind.

Bella shoved her plate of uneaten French toast away. "I'm sure it's delicious but I'm afraid I've lost my appetite," she told Arye before turning to Peach. "I owe you an apology, honey. I should never have stopped you when you wanted to act on your father's last words. If I'd let you do what you wanted, you might have found his book before the apartment burned down. Now I'm afraid it's too late."

Peach had been thinking of compelling reasons to publish the manuscript. Now she felt as though the ground had literally shifted under her feet. "What do you mean, it's too late? All we have to do is send the manuscript to this Mr. Keller."

"I don't know where it is," Bella cried out.

One look at Bella's stricken face told Peach she was telling the truth.

Hearing about the book has sent Peach's spirits soaring. Now they plummeted back to earth like Icarus after the sun melted his wings. She was so disappointed, she wanted to jump out of her skin.

"A book called *The Politics Of Greed* ought to be published," Arye said so softly he might as well have been speaking to himself.

"I couldn't agree more," Peach told him, "and not for the money. I've never forgotten my father's last words. But I'm afraid his manuscript went up in smoke when the apartment burned."

"What makes you think it was there?"

"Where else would it be? A manuscript isn't something Dad could have hidden in his wallet."

"What about a computer disk? He could have hidden a floppy almost anywhere."

Peach groaned again. She should have thought of that.

"I know exactly what we had in that apartment," Bella chimed in. "I packed the boxes myself. Half the time, Blackjack wasn't even there. He couldn't have hidden anything in them without my knowing."

"He must have had lots of paperwork, files and records in his Washington office," Arye said. "What happened to them?"

"His assistant, Randolph Spurling, boxed them up and shipped them here. They're in the garage, along with some furniture from Belle Terre."

"Then that's where we'll start looking," Arye said.

Peach almost wept from sheer relief. It felt so good not to be alone anymore—to have someone to rely on and share things with, and a very special someone at that.

Arye got to his feet, walked over to her chair and pulled her to her feet. "Come on, Peach. Time to get to work."

"What if the book isn't in his papers?"

"I doubt he wrote it on a typewriter. Unless I miss my guess, he dictated it to someone. All we have to do is find that someone."

"You make it sound so easy. What if we don't find anything in the garage?"

"The next logical step is to go to Washington and talk to people your father knew."

"I'll help any way I can," Bella chimed in.

Bella never ceased to amaze Peach. "You're really with me on this, aren't you?"

"The only reason I wasn't with you before was my fear you would get hurt. I knew how much you looked up to your father. I didn't want to take that away from you when you'd already lost so much."

"I guess we both thought we were looking out for your best interests," Arye confirmed. "I knew your father had some powerful enemies and I didn't want you to take them on."

Peach gazed from one to another, thinking if this were an M.G.M. musical, it would be time for her to burst into a rousing chorus of "What a Difference a Day Makes." "Why should Daddy's having written a book make the two of you change your mind?"

"Because it's a weapon," Bella answered as she led the way to the garage. "I think that's what your father was talking about that last day when he asked you not to let the bastards get away with it. I think he wanted you to use that weapon."

Part II

I never give them hell. I just tell the truth
and they think it's hell.

President Harry Truman

Fifteen

Although nothing in the first-class section of the Washington-bound jet threatened Peach's sleep, Arye stayed awake to keep watch over her. Despite the shadows beneath her eyes and the frown line that seemed to have taken up permanent residence on her brow, he'd never known a more beautiful woman—nor wanted one as much.

The day of the tornado, when he realized she was in imminent danger, he had committed himself to her, body and soul—not just for a few days but for the rest of his life. He would have bartered his soul to put an end to the seemingly endless predicaments plaguing her. However, all he could do was be there for her.

His gut told him they might stir up a hornet's nest in the nation's capital. The men who had destroyed Blackjack played hardball. Could he keep Peach from harm once those men learned of the book's existence?

He didn't fear danger for himself. Hell, there had been a time when he courted it, when death would have been a blessing. Now he was torn between the desire to help Peach find the needle of the book in the haystack of Washington, and stark terror at what might happen to her if they succeeded.

Peach came awake as the plane began its descent.

She turned to him with a bemused smile. "I like waking up next to you," she said, then rolled her shoulders and lifted her hands toward the ceiling.

"I like it too—especially the way you stretch."

"What's so special about it?"

"You wouldn't understand."

"Try me."

"It's a guy thing, boss lady. When you put your arms behind your head and arch your back, I can see the outline of your nipples through your blouse."

"You're right. It is a guy thing," Peach replied with a wicked smile, then stretched again, longer this time.

The heat pooling in his groin reminded him of the more pleasant aspects of the journey. Tomorrow would be soon enough to deal with their mission. Tonight belonged to them.

The thought of spending the night with Arye made Peach's heart play hopscotch as they taxied from Dulles to the Canterbury Hotel on N Street. Arye had said he didn't want to make love to her until everything—the setting, the ambiance—was perfect. Would a room in a strange hotel be perfect enough? And what would she do if it wasn't?

She chuckled at the thought of trying to ravish a muscular man who was twice her size. Would he be horrified if he knew how much she wanted to do just that? Would he think she was sex-crazed if he knew just looking at him made her womb spasm and dampened the tender flesh between her thighs?

"Have you ever stayed at the Canterbury?" Arye broke into her thoughts.

"I usually stay at the Four Seasons," she replied.

"The Canterbury isn't as up-market but I think it has more charm. It's on a quiet tree-lined street and the suites are furnished with antiques."

"It sounds lovely." As far as she was concerned, a Motel Eight would do just fine as long as the room had a bed. She had never wanted a man as much as she wanted Arye, had never felt her insides melt the way she did every time he walked into a room.

The fact that other women seemed equally smitten made her intensely uncomfortable. The thought that Arye's interest wouldn't last, that one of these days he'd find a younger, more attractive and capable woman, made her determined to make the best of every minute she had with him.

The Canterbury exceeded his description. The street was quiet and shady, the man at the reservation desk as polite and quick to register them as Peach could have wished. One minute she was waiting while Arye handed over his credit card and a few minutes later, they were alone in a lovely flower-filled parlor.

"Your idea?" she asked, taking in the vases of yellow roses and the champagne icing in a silver bucket, "or is all this compliments of the management?"

"Did I overdo it?"

Tilting her head to look up at him, she pretended to consider the question. "Not unless a violinist knocks on the door to serenade us."

"Damn, why didn't I think of that?"

She giggled. "Because you're not as couth as I am."

"I'll work on it. Would you like to see the rest of the suite?"

"Not just yet." Although she had been dying to get him alone in a bedroom, anxiety rooted her in place as she realized how little experience she had with assignations like this. Make that no experience. She had never been alone in a hotel room with any man but Herbert.

"Are you nervous?" Arye asked.

"Enough to jump out of my pants."

He chuckled. "That's the general idea."

Blushing, she walked over to the window, pretending an interest in the street below while she enumerated her own assets—or lack there of. Arye was bound to be disappointed in her body, unless by some miracle he was into stretch marks. She certainly didn't have enough knowhow to make him her slave in bed. Disaster seemed inevitable.

"How about a glass of champagne?" he asked. "It should help you relax."

She turned around to face him. "It might take the whole bottle. I've never done anything like this before."

He handed her a brimming flute, then sat on a delicate-looking antique sofa and motioned for her to join him. "You don't have to *do* anything. There aren't any rules, Peach. I'm happy just being here with you and having a chance to talk. There's so much I want to know about you."

"Such as?"

"For starters, how did you get your name?"

"Dad took one look at my coloring after I was born and said I reminded him of a ripe peach. Fortunately, since he had planned to call me after his Aunt Hermione, the name Peach stuck."

Arye chuckled, a rich masculine sound very unlike Herbert's braying laugh. "I can't picture you as a Hermione."

She sipped her wine, then looked at him. They were

sitting so close that their thighs touched. She felt the muscles in his. His arm slipped around her shoulder. Lord, he felt good.

"What are you thinking?" he asked in a husky voice that sent anticipatory goose bumps skimming over her skin.

"I was wondering what the bedroom looked like," she replied with her habitual honesty.

"Shall we check it out?"

Her answering "Yes," was barely audible.

He got to his feet.

She kicked off her high heels and trailed after him, feeling a blush stain her cheeks at the sight of an antique four-poster bed with a downy cover that practically said, climb in.

"You must agree this is a lot better than the guest room in your house with your mother downstairs," Arye said, taking her in his arms and nuzzling her neck.

"This is lovely—but the guest room would have been fine, too. I'm not a screamer if that's what you were worrying about."

"You mean you *weren't* a screamer," he said, holding her so tight she could feel the full length of his arousal against her abdomen. And she did mean length!

"Shouldn't we talk about what we're going to do tomorrow?" she asked.

"It's a long time until tomorrow."

The slow heat of Arye's smile promised everything—and withheld nothing. He looked as expectant as a boy on Christmas morning with a mountain of packages to open. Except Arye only had one package. Her. She prayed he wouldn't be too critical.

"I'd rather talk about what we're going to do to-night."

"Do you mean choosing a restaurant?"

He bent his head and nipped at her lower lip. "We don't need to go out. We could have room service. I was hoping to have you for dessert."

"Promises, promises," she muttered before he silenced her with a kiss.

Arye devoured Peach's mouth inside and out, caressing every inch with his tongue, tasting her, breathing in her scent, needing her so much it took all his willpower not to tear off her clothes, lower her to the carpet and take her then and there.

He wanted her in a primitive "me Tarzan, you Jane" way he had never experienced before. He was so hard he hurt more than he had in his teens when he'd spent hours in the back seat of a car making out with girls whose names and faces had long since passed from memory.

In those days he had let testosterone rule his actions. But he never said words to a woman he didn't mean, or filled her head with empty promises he had no intention of keeping. Now he wanted to promise Peach the world.

He broke away from her long enough to catch his breath and rein in his runaway ardor, took her hand and drew her down on the bed by his side. "Someday when you look back on your life, I hope you'll think of the things you did with other men as foreplay."

"There's not that much to remember. There were only two of them."

The jealousy prowling his innards at the thought of her in another man's arms wouldn't be subdued. "Only two? How did the sexual revolution pass you by?" The minute the words were out, he could have kicked himself for saying them. Talk about a mood breaker.

"I was a senator's daughter. I didn't want to embarrass my father by winding up on the front page of a tabloid."

He kissed her brow, the tip of her nose, then nibbled on an ear lobe. "I know about Herbert. Who was the other man?"

"Lance Lathrop, my senior prom date."

Arye's fingers undid the buttons at the back of her blouse while his mouth found the pulse point on her throat.

"Is Lance Lathrop a real name?"

"Yes. A very important one. His parents had a fortune. I was madly in love with him for three weeks."

"That's not very long. What happened?"

She sighed. "Lance happened. I was dying to know about sex. He obliged. It was awful."

He finished unbuttoning her blouse, tugged it down her arms and let it fall to the floor. "I'm glad."

"That's not very charitable."

He slid her bra straps down her upper arms. "I give you fair warning, there isn't an ounce of charity in me when it comes to you and other men."

"You sound jealous."

"Damn right, of every man who ever looked at you." He unhooked her bra and it too fell away. Her breasts compelled his gaze. They were everything he had imagined all the times he had undressed her with his eyes. His bent his head to feast a moment while his hands undid the button that held her skirt in place. He stood and pulled her up with him, letting the skirt slither to the floor. Her half slip followed it with the sibilant whisper of silk.

"God, you're beautiful," he said huskily.

"I'm afraid I'll disappoint you."

"You could never do that."

"I'm not very good in bed."

"Who told you that?"

"Herbert."

Herbert was a damn fool, Arye mused grimly. If the good doctor hadn't already knocked on the pearly gates, he would have taken considerable pleasure in sending him there for destroying Peach's self-esteem.

"Herbert was so concerned about germs, he didn't—"

"Didn't what?" Arye growled.

"He didn't believe in French kissing or making love to me below the waist."

Arye grinned at the delicate way she had put it. Peach may have had two children but she had less experience than women half her age. He relished the thought of being the first to teach her the delights of totally uninhibited sex.

"I love germs—so long as they're yours," he said, then to prove the point pushed her panties down so they joined the rest of her clothes.

The garter belt circling her hips and the thigh-high stockings they held up made her look like a wet dream come true. The wisps of fabric drew attention to the deep auburn bush at the apex of her legs.

"You are a Peach." He groaned with desire, then fell to his knees in homage, burying his face in that crisp hair, relishing the musky female scent of her.

A gasp conveyed her astonishment. She shivered as

he kissed, then separated the petal-like folds with his fingers and tongue.

"Do you like it?"

"Like doesn't seem adequate."

He pleasured her again, longer this time. "Do you have any idea how sexy you are?"

"I'm not exactly a centerfold."

"You look gorgeous to me."

She really had no idea of her own potent femininity, he thought, as he tasted her womanhood.

Peach cried out at the intimate caress. He probed deeper, lapping her nectar, and she cried out again. This time louder. He grinned, then returned to the task he'd set himself. It hadn't been much of a scream but something told him Peach was a quick learner. She'd get the hang of it long before dark.

Peach woke up beside Arye, feeling a delicious languor. She could happily have spent the entire day in bed with him. But she couldn't ignore the call of duty. It took an act of will to get up, wake Arye and not succumb to his caresses.

She showered and dressed, then called room service while Arye got ready for the day. They discussed their itinerary and decided that Peach would have better luck getting in to see Congressmen, leaving Arye to concentrate on Blackjack's staff.

Now, as Peach hurried to yet another senator's office for what she feared would be a useless encounter like all the others that day, she couldn't help thinking she might as well have spent the day in bed.

She had called on the judiciary committee members who had been her father's closest colleagues.

Their welcome had been glacial, their stares as blank as an empty page when she asked if they knew anything about Blackjack's book.

A sense of hopelessness weighed her down as she approached Senator Perkins's office at the end of the day. She expected to be on the receiving end of another cold shoulder. To her surprise, though, after a brief wait, Alene Perkins ushered her into her private office and greeted her with genuine warmth.

"I was so sorry to hear about your father's death," the senator said after the initial social amenities had been attended to. "Blackjack was my mentor when I was elected. He showed me the ropes. I keep on expecting to see him coming toward me in one of the halls, telling me to get myself over to the Senate so I won't miss a crucial vote."

"I feel the same way," Peach replied with a catch in her voice. "I went by Daddy's office earlier today and it was all I could do not to walk right in as though he were still there."

"It must have been painful for you. Frankly, I'm surprised to see you in Washington. I take it this isn't a social call. What brought you here?"

"My father did, Senator."

"Surely you don't mean in the literal sense."

"He asked me to do something before he died."

"I didn't realize you were with him at the end. Having you there must have been a great comfort. Your father talked about you often."

At last, Peach thought with relief, she'd found a sympathetic ear. "Senator Perkins, I came to ask your help."

From her seat behind her desk, the senator looked down at her watch, then up at Peach. "I don't have any more appointments this afternoon. Would you care to join me for an early dinner?"

"There's nothing I'd like more, but I wouldn't want to impose on you."

The senator opened a desk drawer, took out her purse, and got to her feet. "You wouldn't be imposing. I owed your father a favor or two. I can't think of a better way to repay him. Besides, we have some talking to do."

And talk they did, getting to know one another as they made their way to the senator's car in the underground lot.

No wonder Alene Perkins had been elected by landslides, Peach thought as she climbed into the passenger seat of an American-made sedan. Alene Perkins was as easy to listen to as an oldie-but-goodie and as comfortable to be with as a trusted friend.

She suggested a quiet restaurant where they weren't likely to be interrupted—rather than the sort of place where being seen was as important as the food. Make that more important. Peach agreed at once, then sat back and relaxed during the forty-minute drive to Maryland.

"I hope you like Cajun food," Alene said, parking across Bethesda Avenue from the Louisiana Express.

Peach nodded her enthusiastic agreement. "We have a lot of Cajun restaurants back home."

"This place may not look like much," Alene replied, leading the way inside, "but it serves some of the best jambalaya this side of New Orleans and the prices are reasonable."

A quick glance told Peach the senator had chosen wisely. They weren't likely to run into legislators or lobbyists in a restaurant that clearly catered to a middle-class crowd.

"How can I be of help?" the senator asked after they had ordered.

Peach took a deep breath, then launched into the story that began with the auction at Belle Terre and ended with the call from David Keller.

The arrival of food and drink barely slowed the telling. To her credit, the senator didn't interrupt. She let Peach talk until she ran out of words. Only then did she say, "What an awful story. Of course I knew some of it. I always felt some forces had aligned themselves against your father. What you've told me seems to confirm my suspicions."

Peach leaned forward eagerly. "It's such a relief to find someone who agrees with me. Daddy went through hell the last year of his life."

Alene refilled their wineglasses from the bottle on the table. "Other senators have done the things Blackjack was accused of doing and stayed in power. Most of them were reelected, too. What made Daddy's case so different?"

"He did. The last year, he reminded me of an old lion. He knew more powerful males were going to kick him out of the pride but he went down fighting for the things he believed in."

"I knew he was for change. You can't get elected in the current political climate unless you promise to reform the system from top to bottom."

You certainly are your father's daughter," Alene replied. "Your father gave more than lip service to reform. He had been here a long time. He knew where all the bodies were buried. He could tie names and faces to corrupt practices like influence peddling and the buying and selling of favors. And everyone knew he had the guts to do it. The title of his book tells you that. If you ever do find *The Politics of Greed,* please send me one of the first copies. I shall treasure it."

"Did Dad ever talk to you about his book?"

"He hinted that he had an ace in the hole. He never said what, though. We weren't as close the last few years as we used to be. And he was very close-mouthed toward the end."

"Was he close to anyone?"

The senator's eyes narrowed. "I really don't know. His peers were afraid to be seen with him for fear they'd be guilty by association."

"Were you one of them?"

"I'm not running for reelection if that's what you're getting at. Two terms in the Senate should be enough for any rational person. They certainly have been for me."

Peach hadn't been a politician's daughter for nothing. She knew a soapbox oration when she heard one. "Please go on."

"I don't believe the founding fathers meant the country to be run by a professional class of political elitists. We're supposed to have a government of the people, by the people and for the people, not of the politicians, by the politicians and for the politicians. That won't change until term limits become the law. Not that I'm holding my breath." She let go a brittle laugh. "The men and women in office aren't likely to legislate themselves out of it. I'm getting out while I still have the sense to want to."

"And my father didn't?"

"Blackjack was human. Power and its privileges are far too seductive to resist forever. I'm going while my

moral center is still in one piece." Alene gazed around
the room, then turned her attention back to Peach.
"I could have dined at the most expensive restaurant
in Washington tonight as a guest of any of a dozen
lobbyists. If I wanted to fly anywhere in the world tomorrow to spend time with my constituents, there'd
be a corporate jet waiting to take me. Vacations, trans-
portation, hotel rooms—I never have to pay for any
of them unless I choose. Believe me, it gets harder to
say no with every passing year."

"What about the people who stay—people like my
father?"

"I can't speak for him, Peach—but I can tell you
this. Newly elected senators and congressmen are very
idealistic when they arrive in Washington. They know
what they hope to accomplish. And then the system
starts to work on them."

"How?"

"It's hard to ignore people who tell you how wonderful you are, how much they want to help you. Of
course there's always a caveat, a you-scratch-my-back-
and-I'll-scratch-yours hidden in the goodies. Little by
little, it erodes a new legislator's moral center. In time
they become an intrinsic part of the very thing they
got elected to change."

"You make it sound hopeless."

Alene took a final sip of her wine, then sat back. "I
don't believe that. I can't. And not just because I'm
an optimist—although your father accused me of it
often enough. He was a part of that system. He played
the game better than most. But then he changed. But
it's more than that. You know what they say about a
new broom sweeping clean. The voters brought in a
new broom last year. If it's frayed and broken by the

next election, the people can vote in a new broom. It's as simple as that."

"Are you sure you don't know anything about his book?"

Alene shook her head. "I certainly hope you find it."

"Can you tell me who was behind the attacks on my father?"

Again, the senator shook her head. "I don't think there was a formal cabal if that's what you mean. I can't and won't believe that of my fellow legislators. However, Blackjack did make a lot of people very angry."

"So they slandered him."

"Have you considered the possibility that some of their accusations may have been true?"

Peach had been sitting forward, listening to every word Alene Perkins uttered. Now she sat back and crossed her arms over her chest in an unconscious gesture of denial. "My father told my mother he was going to tell the truth, and that it would clear his name."

The light in the senator's eyes seemed to blink out. "I hope you're right, Peach. Just remember, Blackjack wasn't a saint."

"Senator Morgan was an unscrupulous, womanizing son of a bitch," Randolph Spurling told Arye.

"That's a rather harsh assessment," Arye replied.

He had spent the day interviewing Blackjack's former staffers, using every trick in his reporter's repertoire to convince them to be frank. Peach wouldn't like what he had learned.

Spurling wasn't alone in his assessment. According to the dozen or so people Arye had already seen, Blackjack had been a major prick who demanded instant and unquestioning loyalty and obedience. Not that it made him different from any other Senator.

"I did my best to protect the senator's family from the truth," Spurling continued from behind what appeared to be a genuine and very expensive antique desk. "It's a relief to finally be able to tell someone the truth."

"I gather you didn't like him."

"We were never close if that's what you mean. But there was a time when I did respect him—as a wheeler-dealer if nothing else. When his investments in Texas real estate took a tumble in the eighties, he became desperate for money. Afterward—" Spurling gazed out the window.

"What about afterward?" Arye prodded.

"It was impossible to respect a man who pulled the things the senator did."

"Such as?"

"Falsifying his income tax returns, using campaign money to pay personal expenses," Spurling fired back with righteous indignation. "It got even worse when he had to hire a bunch of Washington lawyers at six hundred dollars an hour to defend him. The last twelve months, the senator bled money."

"How do you know?"

"He bitched about it. If Blackjack hadn't passed away when he did, I would have turned in my resignation. You have no idea what hell it was, working for him near the end. I have no doubt I would have been asked to testify against him when the Senate investigation got off the ground."

"You sound like a very angry man, Mr. Spurling."

"Sure, I'm angry. My reputation was at stake, too. Blackjack damn near pulled me down with him."

"His wife and daughter claim he was going to clear his name."

"That's a laugh. He'd have to lie through his teeth to do it."

"Did he ever mention writing a book?" Arye could see the question bothered Spurling.

"What book?"

"Peach and her mother got a call from a literary agent a few days ago. Apparently Blackjack contacted him a couple of weeks before he died. According to the agent, Blackjack had written a no-holds-barred exposé of the government."

"If the senator turned the book over to an agent, why are you asking me about it?"

"He didn't send the entire book, just three chapters and an outline. The rest of the manuscript is missing."

"That's too bad. Peach and Bella must be very upset." Spurling's sympathy sounded as bogus as a three-dollar bill. The man was certainly a chameleon, Arye mused, and not a very likable one.

"So you don't know anything about the book?"

"Not a damn thing. But then, the senator didn't regard me as a confidant."

"Do you have any idea who he would have told?"

"You know what they say about *cherchez la femme.* Ask around. Maybe someone knows who he was screwing, besides the people of the United States."

"Can you give me any names?"

"I told you the senator and I weren't close."

Spurling rose to signal the end of the interview,

walked around the desk, clasped Arye's shoulder and guided him to the door.

"I wish I could have been more help," he said in a thin voice. "If there's anything else I can do, don't hesitate to call me."

In Randolph's haste to be rid of Rappaport, Randolph practically shoved him out the door. Why the hell had he agreed to see the man, Randolph agonized as he returned to his desk. Ignorance would have been such bliss.

Rappaport had confirmed his worst fears. He wasn't looking forward to passing the information on. He dialed a Washington number he knew by heart, related what he'd learned and listened attentively while an imperious voice told what to do and how to do it.

Randolph was in a sweat by the time the one-sided conversation came to an end. He waited until the vise that gripped his chest to ease, then dialed the DEA agent's Houston number and explained the nature of the new assignment.

"Do whatever you have to do to find the damn manuscript. Tear Peach Morgan's house apart stone by stone if that's what it takes. And for God's sake, don't get caught or both our asses will be in a sling."

Sixteen

Three days after leaving for Washington, Peach and Arye admitted defeat and headed back to Houston carrying an invisible burden of gloom. This time they both slept during the flight, holding hands the entire time as though they couldn't bear to be out of touch even in their dreams.

The announced descent into Intercontinental Airport woke them. They continued holding hands, offering mute comfort and support. After touchdown they retrieved their carry-on luggage from the overhead compartment, exited the aircraft and made their weary way to Arye's Suburban.

Halfway home, Arye broke the silence. "I still think you should have gotten in touch with some of your father's former lovers."

"I couldn't do that to Mother. Besides, she told me Daddy was faithful to her the last couple of years. She had no reason to suspect that his old girlfriends would know anything about the book. But I know how you feel. I hate to think we left any stones unturned."

"I'm sorry I brought it up. I didn't mean to upset you," he replied grimly. "I know you're disappointed but there's no point in beating a dead horse."

"Disappointed doesn't cover it. How about devastated?"

She lapsed into silence. Two emotions warred within her—pure bliss at discovering love when she least expected it and deep depression at being unable to fulfill her father's last request. Barring a miracle, *the bastards* were going to get away with it after all.

"Be it ever so humble," Arye said as he wheeled the massive Suburban up her drive, "you're home."

The sound of his voice jerked her from her reverie. She looked toward the house to find a Houston police car parked out front, then blinked a couple of times as if doing so would dispel the sight. "I hope that's a mirage. I've seen enough of the police to last a lifetime."

"I'm afraid it's the real thing." Arye parked behind the police car, got out and retrieved their luggage from the back of the Suburban.

Dread knotted in Peach's stomach. She jerked the car door open and bolted from the seat. The front door swung open while she fumbled in her purse for housekeys. Despite the late hour, Bella was still dressed.

"I knew you'd be upset when you saw the police car," she said, giving Peach a quick hug, "so I kept an eye out for you."

To Peach's surprise, Bert appeared behind Bella. "It's good to have you back although I'm afraid it won't be a pleasant homecoming."

"Why not? Why are the police here again?"

"You look exhausted," Bella said, taking Peach by the arm and gently pulling her into the house. "Was it a rough flight?"

"Forget the flight. What is that police car doing out front? Has something happened to the twins?"

"The boys are fine."

Peach sagged against Arye. "Then why are the police here?"

Just then, two officers walked into the foyer from a shadowed hall. The older of the two, a silver-haired man with a paunch, answered Peach's question. "There's been a break-in, Mrs. Morgan."

"Miss Morgan," she corrected him automatically.

"Come see for yourself," Bella said, leading the way to the living room.

Peach quailed at the destruction. Drawers had been pulled from end tables, their contents turned upside down on the floor. Her footsteps stirred a blizzard of feathers from down-filled upholstery that had been slashed open. Pictures had been taken off walls, books tumbled from their place on the shelves. The wall-to-wall carpeting had been pulled free of the tacking strips that had held it in place.

"Is the rest of the house this bad?" Peach asked when she could get the words out.

"Bad enough. I'm so sorry, honey," Bella replied.

If Arye hadn't kept his arm around Peach's waist as she made her way from one ruined room to another, she would have collapsed on the floor with the rest of the debris. By the time she returned to the relatively unscathed foyer, a wretched blend of rage and grief clogged her throat.

"Do you know who did it?" she asked the older policeman."

"We were hoping you could tell us," he replied: "Did you notice if anything was taken?"

She shook her head. "Just what was left of my peace of mind."

"Are you sure?"

"I just got here!" she burst out.

"I took a quick inventory while I was waiting for you to get here," Bella interjected in the cool voice of reason. "As far as I could tell, everything is still here."

"Do you have any idea when the break-in occurred?" Arye asked the officer.

"According to Mrs. Morgan, it had to have happened between seven last night and one this morning."

"Can't you narrow it down more than that?" Peach exclaimed impatiently.

"Not without a witness."

What he said finally penetrated the wall of Peach's outrage. "What about my mother? Wasn't she here?"

"She was with me," Bert was quick to say, "and you can thank your lucky stars she was."

"Mr. Hanrahan is right," the officer chimed in. "If Mrs. Morgan had been here, she could have been hurt—or worse."

"How did they get in?" Arye asked.

"Through one of the French doors. Whoever did it certainly knew their way around an alarm system. It has the earmarks of a professional job."

Peach's hold on Arye's hand tightened as she considered the implications. If the break-in was the work of a professional and nothing had been taken, the person or persons who trashed her house must have been after Blackjack's book. She spent the next ten minutes explaining the situation to the police.

"I never thought it would come to this," Bella said when Peach finished. "I should have known better than to let you go off to Washington to look for the manuscript. I'm afraid you've opened Pandora's box."

Arye's expression hardened. "If you're right, we had damn well better find a way to shut it."

Peach rounded on him. "Does that mean you've given up?"

"No. But it does mean whoever did this—or ordered it done—had better think we have." He turned back to the officers. "Is there anything you can do to protect the Morgans?"

"If you're asking if we can station an officer on the premises, the answer is no. All we can do is make sure a patrol car drives by more often."

"That's not much," Arye said sourly.

"I'm sorry, sir. I know you're upset. I would be too in your position. However my watch commander isn't likely to tie a man up on Miss Morgan's suppositions." The officer let go a nervous laugh. "To be honest, it is a wild story."

"It isn't a story!" Peach declared." My parents' apartment was torched, my art director was shot, my husband was the victim of a hit and run, and now my house has been ransacked by the closest thing to Sherman's troops on their way through Georgia I ever care to encounter."

"I'm sorry, miss. I know you've had the worst run of bad luck imaginable, but you don't have a shred of proof that any of the incidents you told me about are linked. Until you do, the police department isn't going to be able to help you."

"I understand," Bella said with her usual good grace.

"Well I don't," Peach declared, giving voice to her

frustration. If past performance meant anything, she'd be dead before Houston's finest realized she was really in danger.

She marched into the den, kicking debris aside on her way, went to the window and stared out into the night. She felt angry, hopeless, demoralized.

"You could have been nicer to those officers," Arye admonished when he joined her a few minutes later.

"Frankly Scarlett, I don't give a damn."

"Sure you do, Peach. That's why I apologized for your behavior."

"You what?"

"You heard me. Those poor guys were just doing their job, and it isn't a very pleasant one at that. They're underpaid, overworked, and unappreciated."

He walked behind the bar and took her in his arms.

She resisted her instinct to relax and enjoy it. But when his hand stroked her hair and he said, "It's all right to be angry, Peach. I know you're scared," she melted.

"It's just so hard to come home to this—this disaster after our wasted trip."

Holding her close, Arye walked her over to the only upright furniture in the room, the oak game table, pulled out a chair, sat down and pulled her onto his lap. "It wasn't wasted, Peach. As horrible as this mess is, it tells us we pushed somebody's buttons. That somebody wants the manuscript as much as we do."

"How do we know they didn't find it?"

"Because they trashed the entire house from top to bottom. Unless the manuscript was hidden in the very last place they looked—and the odds against that are astronomical—they didn't find what they came for. That means the book is out there somewhere."

"If that's supposed to cheer me up, it doesn't. We don't have the book either."

"It's bound to show up one of these days."

"Dad's been dead for months. If someone has it, why haven't they let us know?"

"Maybe they're scared." He let go a harsh laugh. "Considering everything that's happened here, I don't blame them. Since the police can't help, we're going to have to find a way to make sure you and your mother are safe."

"We could take turns watching the house," Bert said, walking into the den with Bella.

"It's a thought," Arye replied.

"Peach jumped off Arye's lap. "Hey, you two, don't I have any say? This is my house."

Arye recognized the determined gleam in her eye for what it was—a foolhardy desire to stand on her own two feet because Herbert and Blackjack had never given her the chance.

"Of course you have a say. Do you have a better idea?"

"I'm going to spend several hours on the phone tomorrow, talking to the people we saw in Washington, thanking them for their help and saying I've given up all hope of finding my father's book."

That works for me," Arye replied, even though he'd planned to do it himself. "Since it's too late to make those calls tonight, how about letting me stay?"

"No way. It's going to be hard enough to make one room livable for my mother and me."

"I can sleep on the floor."

"I know you mean well and I love you for it. But

I've been taken care of by some man all my life. It's time I learned to take care of myself."

The gleam in Peach's eyes had reached the flash point. He knew better than to supply any more sparks. Yawning as though he couldn't wait to get home to his own bed, he said, "Come on Bert. Let's get out of here so the ladies can call it a day."

"Where were you tonight?" Peach demanded, the minute she and Bella were alone.

"Bert and I had dinner."

"The policeman said the break-in took place sometime between seven and one. Were you with Bert the entire time?"

Color flared on Bella's cheeks. "I know you're tired and upset, but you're still my daughter and I won't be spoken to that way."

Peach pressed her lips together in a desperate attempt at holding her anger in. It didn't work. "Don't play mother superior with me after what you've done."

"And just what is that?"

"You've been sleeping with Bert, haven't you?"

To Peach's amazement, Bella chuckled. "So that's why you're tied up in a knot. Honey, your father died. Not me."

Peach was so furious, she would have picked up something and thrown it if she could have found anything that wasn't already damaged. "How can you be so—so disloyal to father's memory?"

Bella didn't answer. She walked behind the bar, poured two glasses of brandy, then returned to Peach and handed one over.

"I don't want a drink," Peach said, putting the glass on the game table with a thud.

"You certainly need one—either that or a good

spanking," Bella replied with such perfect equanimity, Peach could have throttled her.

Seeing the steel in her mother's eyes, though, she accepted the glass and took a small sip.

Bella sat down at the game table and gazed at Peach so intently that Peach had to look away. "I know you're having a hard time, letting go of your father, but you've got to face reality."

"Don't you mean your version of reality?"

"I haven't lied to you. I let Blackjack go a great many years ago. You know the reasons why. Now he's dead, I have to think about my future. I'm sixty-one, Peach. That may sound ancient to you but I don't feel old. I'll probably live another twenty years and I have no desire to live them alone. Can you understand that?"

Peach struggled to match Bella's composure. "Of course I understand. It's just—" Her voice trailed off. How could she explain she was having a hard time dealing with her mother's sexuality when she had just discovered the joys of her own?

"Just what, honey?"

Sighing, Peach sat back in the chair. "So many things have happened in the last few months. There's been so much to deal with, I haven't come to terms with all of it. I shouldn't take it out on you, though."

"No, you shouldn't. But you're human even if you haven't admitted it yet, and humans make mistakes. I wish you could stop seeing life in terms of black and white. It would be much easier if you did."

"What do you mean?"

"Your father wasn't a hero. Herbert wasn't a villain. Arye isn't a white knight who can solve all your problems. And I'm not a slut for finding comfort in another man's arms."

"Oh Mother, I never said you were," Peach wailed.

"But you thought it." Bella sipped her brandy. "I have one more thing to say before we figure out where we're going to sleep in all this mess. Bert has asked me to marry him."

"How did you answer?"

"I gave him a qualified yes. If he feels the same way at Christmas, we'll set the date. I hope you will find it in your heart to welcome him into what's left of the family."

Peach took a moment to collect her thoughts. "Are you sure that's what you want?"

"Very sure. Bert is a wonderful man who will do everything in his power to make me happy."

"What about love?"

"There's that too, Peach," Bella answered softly, her face glowing at the admission.

Peach had run out of questions. How could she be upset with her mother when just last night, she had been in Arye's arms, reveling in the best sex she'd ever had, screaming her fool head off from the pleasure of it.

She still loved and admired her father, but he had broken her mother's heart a long time ago. If Bert could put the pieces back together after all these years, she'd be grateful to him.

"I only have one condition," she said into the quiet.

"What's that?"

"If and when you and Bert get married, I want to be your matron of honor."

The tears pooling in Bella's eyes matched the ones

Peach felt in her own. At least one of them was going to live happily ever after.

After sending a reluctant Bert home, Arye spent what was left of the night parked across the street from Peach's house, doing his best to stay alert even though exhaustion tugged at his weary body. By dawn he had come to several conclusions.

First, he admitted his love for Peach was a given, as much a part of him as the way he looked. If the moment arrived when he could see beyond the present to plan the future, he intended to ask her to marry him.

Second, he hypothesized that what had at first glance seemed like related events weren't related after all. No wonder the police had looked at Peach as though she were hysterical when she talked about her conspiracy theory.

The fire in the Morgans' apartment and the trashing of Peach's house seemed to have been triggered by her attempts to clear her father's name. The linkage made sense. But he had been unable to find anything coupling Bert's shooting or Herbert's death to the other events.

There was no common denominator between Herbert and Bert other than Peach. In all likelihood, the things that happened to the two men had nothing to do with her and everything to do with random violence.

The realization didn't diminish Arye's feeling that Peach was in danger, but it did make the feeling more manageable. By the time the neighborhood began to stir, Arye felt certain he had come up with a way to protect Peach. All he had to do was convince her to go along with the plan.

Peach was delighted with how quickly the house had been returned to a semblance of order. The professional cleaners she had contacted—promising a large bonus for prompt performance—sent their best people. The upholsterer her decorator recommended was almost as quick to put in an appearance, carting off the slashed sofa and chairs.

Bella had taken on the job of renting furniture until Peach's was repaired. The size of the order had guaranteed speedy delivery. By four in the afternoon, the den, Peach's and Bella's bedrooms, the kitchen and breakfast room were livable again and the other rooms had been cleaned.

The knowledge failed to lift her spirits. She had promised to call David Keller on Friday and she was no closer to finding her father's manuscript than she had been when Keller first told her it existed.

She was in the den, putting books back on the shelves, when the doorbell rang. Mindful of Arye's admonition to look through the peephole to see who was there, she put her eye to the glass.

Although weariness had etched new lines on Arye's face, the sight of him gladdened her heart. She threw the door wide, intending to give him a welcoming hug, when she realized someone—or rather something—was with him.

"What in the world is that?" she asked, gazing down at an enormous black and tan dog.

"That," Arye replied, "is Archimedes von Sweibrucken."

"God bless you," Peach responded politely.

"I didn't sneeze. That's the dog's name," Arye told her.

Peach admitted man and beast, shut the door and turned to face him or rather, them. "You never mentioned owning a dog."

"I don't." Arye's gaze's traveled around the foyer and beyond. He whistled long and low. "How in the world did you manage to get this place cleaned up so quickly?"

"Money and hard work," Peach replied, never taking her eyes off the immense animal.

"If this isn't your dog," she said, leading the way to the den, "what are you doing with it?"

Arye unhooked the animal's leash, walked behind the bar and helped himself to a Dos Equis. "Would you like one?"

"You didn't answer my question," Peach objected, keeping a wary eye out for bigfoot.

It circled the room, sniffing the floor like a vacuum cleaner running at double speed, then with a sigh, settled on the area rug in front of the fireplace. Seconds later, snores reverberated through the room.

"He certainly seems at home," Arye commented, looking pleased as Punch.

"I hope he doesn't have fleas."

"He's a handsome beast, isn't he?" Arye sounded like a proud father.

I suppose so."

"You suppose so? He's got a pedigree longer than mine!"

"What sort of dog is he?"

"Archimedes is a rottweiler. A friend of mine who

has a guard dog service sold him to me. He said the dog is the next thing to a lethal weapon."

"He doesn't look very lethal now."

"Trust me. I've seen him in action." Arye reached into his jacket pocket, took out a sheaf of papers and held them out to her. "These are instructions for his care and feeding, and a list of the German commands he knows."

"That's all very interesting, but what does it have to do with me?"

"Don't you know you're not supposed to look a gift dog in the mouth."

"What in the world do I need with a narcoleptic chow hound who speaks German?"

"You need the dog because you won't let me stay here to protect you."

"I'm perfectly capable of taking care of myself." Her stern expression dissolved in a smile when a particularly loud snore reverberated through the room.

"Keep him for my sake. I'll sleep better knowing a hundred and twenty pounds of canine fury is guarding your house."

"Far be it from me to trouble your sleep," Peach replied sweetly. "Do I have to call him Archimedes?"

"He's a bright animal. He won't have any trouble learning a new name."

Peach cut another glance at the dog. He had rolled over on his back, displaying a pair of testicles that would have made most men green with envy.

"I could call him balls," she said tentatively.

"Shame on you, boss lady."

"Or I could call him Sleepy since that's what he seems to do best."

"Is your mother home?" Arye asked out of the blue.

"She's in her room."

Arye gave Peach a conspirator's grin. "If you promise not to scream too loud, I'll take you upstairs and show you what I do best."

Seventeen

In the tornado's aftermath, the rumors swirling through the *Inside Texas* offices bothered Cindy far more than the storm. When Peach and Arye didn't return to work, gossip had it that Peach planned to sell the magazine. After Bert scotched that story, another even more troubling one surfaced.

A rumor about Arye and Peach traveling to Washington D.C. together passed from office to office so quickly, it might as well have been written on the wind. Cindy overheard women in the ladies' room talking about a love affair, complimenting Peach on her taste and saying they wouldn't mind getting in Arye's pants either. Vulgar bitches.

It took all Cindy's fortitude to discount such tales. She had rationalized the embrace she'd seen after the storm by telling herself that Peach had initiated it. She even excused the trip as business and nothing more.

Deep down, she knew Arye wouldn't abandon her. Not when they were meant to share their lives. She had known it the first time she saw him when the voice whispered it in her ear.

While she waited for him to return she worked even harder on her appearance, having her hair done every other day instead of once a week and shopping for outfits she couldn't afford in expectation of the day when she would finally wear them for him.

When Cindy came to work a week after the tornado, she finally heard the words she'd been longing for.

Mr. Rappaport is back, Tiffany, the receptionist said. "He asked me to tell everyone there's a staff meeting at eleven."

Cindy was so happy, she practically floated down the hall to her own office. Her happiness faded when she saw Peach Morgan.

"No one told me you were coming back to work today," Cindy said.

"I didn't think it was necessary."

"Not that I'm not pleased to see you. Do you want to go on with your training?"

Peach continued putting her few personal belongings in a small box. "I'm done with all that."

"I guess it's been too much for you what with the storm and everything," Cindy said, turning away to hide a smile.

"The tornado didn't frighten me, if that's what you're implying."

"I wasn't talking about the storm. You were having a hard time learning the computer program. I don't blame you for giving up. And I'm sure the rest of the staff won't either."

Peach put the box down on the desk, squared her shoulders and looked directly in Cindy's eyes. "My only problem was getting enough computer time. However I was able to do some work on Arye's computer before the tornado hit. You would have been surprised to see how much I knew. You're a better teacher than either of us thought."

"But you did say you were leaving."

"I'm not going far. Arye has asked me to work with him."

Happiness at Peach's imminent departure curdled in Cindy's stomach. She had an almost irresistible impulse to hurl herself at Peach, to scratch and bite and kick. Someday, Cindy promised herself, she would do as much and more to Peach. But not today. She had run enough risks the last few months, shooting Bert Hanrahan and killing Dr. Strand when all the while, the real enemy had been Peach. Why hadn't she seen it before?

"Are you all right, Cindy?" Peach's voice seemed to come from far away.

"I was just thinking how generous Mr. Rappaport is to offer to be your mentor in addition to all his other responsibilities."

"What are you getting at?"

Cindy gave Peach what she hoped was a thoughtful look rather than one filled with hatred. "I don't think you realize how hard Mr. Rappaport works. Running *Inside Texas* is a full-time job."

"I'm well aware of his responsibilities and I have no intention of keeping him from carrying them out."

"You won't be able to help yourself," Cindy persisted. "You have so much to learn, and he has so little time to teach you. You're right about me not giving you enough computer time. If you'll give me another chance, I'm sure we can work it out."

Peach picked up the box. "I appreciate your concern, Cindy. It's nice to know an employee cares so much about the magazine. However *Inside Texas* isn't the only project Arye and I are working on. We have other mutual interests. Sharing an office will actually save time." She headed for the door without a backward glance.

Cindy's hand curled around a pair of scissors. She imagined plunging them into Peach's back and hearing her cry out in pain. What a sweet sound that would be. Damn her to hell, her and all the other rich bitches who had made Cindy's life a hell on earth.

Minutes passed before Cindy's pulse rate returned to normal. She had come perilously close to losing control. Too close. She would have to avoid Peach until she came up with a way to get rid of her forever.

Arye was at his desk when Peach walked in. Sunlight gilded his features, transforming his face into a study in gold. She paused to enjoy the sight, feeling as though she had sailed across a storm-tossed sea to arrive in a safe harbor. It had nothing to do with the place—and everything to do with the man.

Arye looked up from his work, saw her standing there, and framed her with his hands as though he planned to take her picture.

"What in the world are you doing?" she asked, carrying her box over to the bookshelves.

"I keep on forgetting how beautiful you are."

Compliments still made Peach uneasy. She turned away from him, took her books out of the box and stacked them on the nearest shelf. "You need glasses."

"Not a chance. I have twenty-twenty vision." He rose from the desk, took the empty carton from her hands, dropped it on the floor and kissed her—gently at first but then with increasing urgency.

Delicious, Peach thought. Everything about Arye was delicious. The pressure of his lips, the taste of his mouth, his scent, the muscled length of his body. Desire throbbed through her, demanding fulfillment. They could do it on the desk—or the floor—or the sofa—or even standing up, she thought eagerly.

She pulled away before a sea of desire could overcome her. "We're going to need some guidelines if we're going to work in the same room," she said.

He took a step toward her. She took a step back and put a hand on his chest to hold him off. "Don't we have a rule against employees fraternizing?"

"The rule doesn't apply in your case. You're not an employee."

Peach widened the distance between them. "Do you remember the day I interviewed you for the managing editor's job?"

"I'll never forget it."

"I knew the women on staff were going to fall in love with you—but I didn't expect to be one of them."

"One? As far as I know, there aren't any others."

"Don't be dense, Arye. Tiffany makes eyes at you all the time. So does Cindy. She's madly in love with you, and you can put the emphasis on the word, mad. There's something strange about the woman."

"Strange how?"

"She says the right things but I have the feeling she doesn't mean what she says. And then there's all the plastic surgery."

"Plastic surgery?"

Peach shook her head in amazement. "You don't have any idea what I'm talking about, do you?"

"Cindy never mentioned having surgery."

"Neither did the majority of Herbert's patients. You'd be surprised the lengths women go to, keeping their face-lifts secret. But I could always tell when he had operated on one of them. Our Cindy has had a nose job, cheek and chin implants, her eyes have been reshaped, and her breasts have been enlarged. I can't believe you never noticed. She must have taken a lot of time off."

While Peach talked, a series of expressions played across Arye's features—beginning with surprise and ending with chagrin. "I feel like an idiot. Cindy told me she had a dying mother back East. I gave her time off whenever she asked for it."

"Unless her dying mother happens to be a top-notch plastic surgeon, she was lying through her teeth. Cindy used to be a plain Jane. Now she's a beauty, in a Barbie doll sort of way. Haven't you noticed the change?"

"To be perfectly honest, I haven't paid attention to Cindy or any other woman. I was always too busy thinking about you."

Although the encounter with Cindy had upset Peach, it was hard to sustain the mood. "Is lying in order to get time-off grounds for dismissal?"

"Isn't that a little harsh?"

"Perhaps." Peach gazed out the window, taking time to sort through her feelings. "I could be overreacting. It's hard to be objective about a woman who is ga-ga over you."

"Trust me. Cindy may be off-beat but she's harmless."

"I don't agree. A woman who has suffered multiple plastic surgeries has to have a will of steel."

"Most people would regard that as a plus."

"You're in charge. I don't have any desire to usurp your authority. I just hope you're right about Miss Downing. In any case, I have more important things on my mind. I promised to call David Keller today. I should have told him I didn't have the manuscript in the first place instead of raising his hopes."

"He's a grown man. He'll handle it. It's going to be all right, Peach, really it is."

For a while, events proved Arye right. David Keller was disappointed, sympathetic, and understanding when Peach gave him the bad news. After she said good-bye, Arye assigned her to writing the restaurant listing and reviews that appeared in every edition of *Inside Texas*. Although it was journalistic scut work, Peach relished the chance to pay her dues.

As summer gave way to fall, her life took on a new shape and form. Blackjack's dying admonition finally loosened its grip. Days and then weeks passed without her thinking of him.

The twins came home for a brief visit between semesters and a whirlwind of youth blew the last of the stale old habits out of the River Oaks house. Before returning to their busy lives at Old Miss, they gave Arye their tacit seal of approval, at least that's how Peach interpreted the mumbled words, "Go for it."

Early in October, Peach woke to find that the first fall storm had blown in from the plains states. Rain rattled the windows and wind whistled around the eaves. Knowing the drive to work would take longer, she ate a hurried breakfast, kissed Bella good-bye, patted Sleepy, opened her umbrella and made a dash for her car.

She had left the Jaguar in front of the house the night before. By the time she unlocked the door and climbed behind the wheel, her clothes were soaked.

On the way to the Allen Center, the windshield wipers struggled to up keep up with the rain, and the curbs ran full.

Arye was talking on the phone when Peach walked into the office. He held the receiver out to her. "It's for you, boss lady. Your mother wanted to be sure you got here safely."

Peach told Bella she was fine, and suggested Bella not go out until the weather improved, then sat down at the conference table to work on her new assignment, writing captions for the photographs that appeared in the magazine. It was an exacting job that kept her absorbed all day.

Bella's late-afternoon arrival came as a complete surprise. Peach was the first to see her standing on the threshold, her dress dripping wet, her hair plastered to her head, two spots of red flaring on her otherwise pale face.

"Mother, what in the world are you doing here? I thought you were going to stay home today. You look ghastly. Is something wrong?"

"I'm so sorry, honey," Bella said past her chattering teeth.

Arye hurried to Bella's side, took off his jacket, put it around her sodden shoulders and helped her to the couch. "Sorry about what, Bella?"

Bella didn't seem to hear him. "I wasn't planning to go out but then I thought how nice it would be to wear my pearls to the Alley theater tonight."

"The mikimotos? I didn't realize you still had them," Peach exclaimed, joining Bella on the couch. "You said you were sorry. Did someone steal them?"

"They're in my purse."

"You've lost me, Mother. I assumed your jewelry was auctioned off along with everything else."

Arye had poured coffee while Peach and Bella talked. He handed them each a steaming mug. "Would you like me to leave while you tell Peach what's troubling you?"

"Good heavens, no. We don't have secrets from you. I found something besides my pearls when I opened the safety deposit box."

Peach could think of only one thing that would bring her mother downtown in the middle of a storm. "The manuscript?"

"No, but it's the next best thing. Your father wrote me a letter and left it in the box. I think he knew he was going to die. He told me about the book. I know who has it."

Peach's first thought was, why now? After everything she and her mother had been through, they had finally found a measure of happiness. The manuscript would change their lives again. "Who has it—and why didn't they let us know?"

Bella lowered her eyes. "She did. Jean Sinclair called the day your father died. Now I know why."

The name washed over Peach. "Dad told you the book was in the jewels before he said Jean's name. If I had gotten in touch with her when she called, or later when Arye and I were in Washington, this would all be behind us. Daddy's reputation would be restored."

"I'm not so sure," Bella said softly. "He said he was going to tell the truth. It's not exactly the same thing."

"Have you talked to Jean Sinclair yet?"

"No, honey. I drove straight here."

"Where's the letter?" Arye asked.

"In my purse along with my pearls," Bella told him.

"May I read it?" Peach asked.

Bella shook her head. "I'm sorry, dear. It was very personal. I've shared a great deal with you about your father, but not this."

"Why did he trust Jean Sinclair with the book and not us?"

"I wish I knew. The last year of his life, all those times when his staff couldn't find him, he was with her. She typed up his notes and took his dictation."

Bella looked so stricken that Peach forgot all about her own concerns. How could her father have lied to her mother again? At that moment Peach hated him for what he'd done to Bella's life—and to hers. "I had better call Mr. Keller and find out if the publisher is still interested."

"Shouldn't you get in touch with Jean Sinclair first?" Arye cautioned.

"Do you always have to be right?"

He gave her a wry grin. "It's one of those guy things."

Peach didn't know whether to hit him—or kiss him.

"I have her number here," Bella said, opening her purse and taking out a piece of paper. "She has a secretarial business in Annapolis."

Peach glanced at her watch. "It's after five there."

"Your father thought of everything. He wrote down her home number and address too," Bella replied with a sickly smile. "While you make the call, I'll go tell Bert I don't feel up to the theater tonight."

She walked out of the office with her usual quick step, her shoulders square, her head held high. Peach knew what it must have cost her, though. She had just found out that her husband, the father of her children, had never, ever been faithful to her.

"If you so much as look at another woman, I'll cut your balls off," she snarled at Arye. Then, clutching the paper in her hand, she stalked over to the phone and dialed Jean Sinclair's home number, preparing to hate the woman who answered.

The phone rang twice before a woman with a cultured southern voice came on the line. "Jean Sinclair speaking."

"This is Peach Morgan, the senator's daughter. You do remember him, don't you?" Peach spat out each word.

"I could never forget your father." The cultured voice paused. "I've waited a long time for you to return my call. What took you so long?"

"I just learned you had my father's book. I would never have called otherwise."

"I tried to get in touch with you after your father's death. The woman who answered your phone said she'd give you my message. I wanted to give you the manuscript then."

"Look, Miss Sinclair, I'm not interested in who did what, when. My mother told me all about you and Dad the day I got your message. Afterward, I didn't have the slightest desire to talk to you. I'm sure you understand."

Peach heard a sigh on the other end of the line. "Has anyone ever told you how much you sound like your father?"

"I'm not in the mood for chitchat, Miss Sinclair. I'd like to pick up the manuscript as soon as possible."

Jean Sinclair didn't respond.

"What's the matter, Miss Sinclair. Feeling a little

guilty? Does the cat have your tongue? Or are you waiting for me to offer you money for services rendered? Is that the deal you had with my father?"

Jean Sinclair rewarded Peach with a pained gasp. "If you wanted to hurt me, you've succeeded. You don't just sound like your father, you think like him too—when he was at his worst."

Arye took the phone away from Peach. "I'm sorry, Miss Sinclair. Peach is understandably upset. She's had a rough time since her father's death—however that doesn't give her the right to take it out on you."

Glaring at him, Peach pushed the speaker button in time to hear Jean Sinclair say, "And who might you be?"

"Just a friend. My name is Arye Rappaport."

"We all need friends. I lost a very good one when the senator died." Jean sounded so bereft that Peach almost forgot to be angry.

"It must have been very hard on you," Arye replied.

Peach kicked him in the shins. Didn't he realize Jean Sinclair had come close to prying Blackjack away from his family?

"It was a great loss. But Miss Morgan didn't call to exchange condolences, did she?" Jean quickly answered her own question. "Of course not. She wanted to know about her father's manuscript."

"I certainly do," Peach exclaimed loudly enough for Jean to hear her even though Peach stood ten feet away from the phone.

"I'm afraid you're in for a disappointment," Jean replied.

"Don't worry. I'm used to them by now."

"You were such a pretty little girl. I really would have liked to see you," Jean said in her Southern comfort voice. "I'm afraid you don't have any reason to come to Annapolis, though."

"What do you mean, Miss Sinclair?" Arye asked.

"The day I called, I waited hours and hours for Peach or her mother to get in touch with me, long enough to think what publication of the book would do to them. I know every word in it. It was a time bomb, Mr. Rappaport. They had been through such a horrible time, I didn't see any point in prolonging it."

"I'll just bet she was thinking about us," Peach muttered.

"What did you do with the book?" Arye asked, slowing his rapid-fire speech, something he only did when he was troubled.

"I hardly know how to tell you, Mr. Rappaport."

"A simple declarative sentence will do."

"I threw the book out. The computer disks, too."

Peach let out such a wail, it brought Arye to her side instantly.

She snatched the phone from his hand. "You what?"

"I threw it out," Jean repeated. "I'm so terribly sorry. I had no idea you wanted it."

Reason told Peach she shouldn't blame Jean Sinclair. But she did. God, how she did. "Damn you. Damn you to hell! Do you have any idea what you've done?"

"I have a better idea than you do, Peach. I typed every word. If you knew what your father wrote, you might thank me for getting rid of it."

"I can't to talk to her anymore," Peach said, handing the telephone back to Arye.

She walked over to the sofa, collapsed onto it and

lowered her head to her hands. She didn't realize her mother had returned until she felt Bella's arms around her.

"How much did you hear," Peach asked.

"All of it," Bella replied.

"Will this awful roller-coaster ride never end?" Peach sobbed.

Bella's embrace tightened. "I think it just did, honey."

"I feel like such a fool. If I had talked to that woman the first time she called, I could have saved us all a lot of grief."

"You only did what I wanted." Bella let go of Peach, took a tissue from her purse and handed it over. "Dry your eyes, honey. There is a positive way to look at what's happened. You're finally free to live your life."

Eighteen

The redolent aroma of burning oak logs and stuffed cabbage permeated the den where Peach, Arye, Bella and Bert had just finished eating.

The impromptu supper had been Bella's idea. Arye had offered to bring the main course and Bert had stopped on his way from the office to pick up a couple of bottles of Merlot, both empty now.

"Feeling better?" Arye asked Peach.

"Much better. To tell you the truth, I actually feel relieved."

Arye's brow furrowed. "That's the last thing I expected you to say."

"David Keller said Dad's book was political dynamite. Now we know the book is gone, I just want to do what Mother suggested and get on with my life."

"Me, too," Bella agreed. "I've been thinking about getting a job."

"You what?" Peach blurted out.

She had been so preoccupied with her own problems, she hadn't given much thought to Bella's needs or wants.

"You heard me, honey. I need something to keep me busy. I've enjoyed doing the things that make a house show well but it's going to sell one of these days. I'll have a lot of time on my hands afterward."

"What sort of job do you have in mind?" Peach asked.

Bella threw her hands up. "I don't have many qualifications. I could be a personal shopper or a party planner—or I could work in a boutique."

Sympathy welled in Peach's chest. She knew exactly how her mother felt. "I hate to think of you selling dresses to the women who used to be your friends."

"I wouldn't mind. They still are my friends, honey."

Peach cut a frantic glance at Arye, praying he would read her mind. His gaze met hers and he nodded as if to say, *message received.*

"Would you consider trying something else?" he asked Bella.

"Of course. I don't believe that old saw about not being able to teach an old dog new tricks. What do you have in mind?"

"Bert tells me you have a good eye for layouts."

Bella gave Bert a loving smile, then turned back to Arye. "Bert is a born flatterer. I brought a few layouts to his house when he was recovering from the shooting, but I wouldn't say I have a wonderful eye."

"You're far too modest," Bert exclaimed. "You were much more than a delivery service. I would never have finished the layouts on time if you hadn't helped. Your suggestions were invaluable."

"Bert has been asking for an assistant for months," Arye said to Bella. "If you'd consider taking the job, I'd give you the same deal I gave Peach. The pay and the hours aren't anything to brag about—but you can't beat the company."

Bella beamed at Arye, then reached across the table

and shook his hand. "It may be nepotism but you've got a deal."

"This calls for a celebration," Peach declared. "Let's forget the dishes and have champagne by the fire."

"That's the second best offer I've had all day," Bella declared.

"What was the first?" Peach asked.

"The job, honey. I don't know how to thank you."

"Thank Arye. He's the managing editor."

Peach went to the bar and took the last bottle of Dom Perignon from the refrigerator. She put it on a tray along with four hollow-stemmed glasses, carried the tray to the coffee table and set it down.

This is the way she wanted to spend the rest of her life, she mused, looking from one dearly loved face to the next while Arye popped the cork and poured. The four of them had forged a new family, one bound by love and affection rather than legal papers.

The champagne's fruity aroma brought back memories of other celebrations in this very room, but none of them sweeter than this one. "To the future," she said, lifting her glass.

By her side, Arye murmured, "L'chaim."

"What does that mean?" she asked.

"To life," he replied.

"I'll second that," Bella agreed.

"Spending an evening by a fire certainly beats going out on a night like this," Bert said, adding another log to the blaze.

Bella and Bert settled on the sofa, Arye sprawled on the floor next to Sleepy and Peach sat beside him on the raised flagstone hearth. Although wind and rain continued to assault the house, she felt safe and secure. There was a transcendental comfort in being warm and dry while nature wreaked havoc outdoors.

Two hours later, Peach gazed into the dying embers of the fire, feeling more at ease than she had in months. The time had passed in a lively discussion about the magazine's future.

"I'd like to do an article about the political corruption in the valley," Arye was saying, referring to the counties that bordered the Rio Grande.

"We've never done anything like that," she demurred.

"I know you like *Inside Texas* to keep a low profile but I'm not talking about anything with too much bite. However there are intriguing parallels between what's happening in the valley and the way politics were done in Arkansas when Bill Clinton was growing up."

"In what way?" Bella asked.

"In both cases, there's an almost incestuous relationship between money and politics. Everyone knows it but nobody talks about it."

"I'm sure I could open a few doors, get you to people who wouldn't see anyone else," Bella said.

Approval shone in Arye's eyes. "Spoken like a true journalist."

"Slow down, you two," Peach admonished. "Doing a story like that would mean a major shift in policy at *Inside Texas.* I've had too much wine to make a decision like that tonight."

Arye gave Bella a conspiratorial wink, then said, "But you will think about tomorrow."

The telephone rang before Peach could reply.

"Saved by the bell," she said, going to the desk to answer it.

The cultured Southern voice she had hoped never to hear again came on the line. "Is Peach Morgan there?"

For a long moment, Peach considered hanging up.

"Peach, is that you?"

Peach pressed the speaker button. She wanted witnesses to whatever the Sinclair woman had to say. "What do you want, Miss Sinclair?"

"I have good news, at least I hope it's good news. I have your father's book."

"Earlier today you said you threw it away. What kind of game are you playing now?"

"Please hear me out. I wasn't lying about disposing of the manuscript and the disks. To tell you the truth the material was so volatile, I didn't feel safe having it in the house."

"Then why are you bothering me? It's ten-thirty here. That makes it eleven-thirty where you live. Don't you need your beauty sleep?" Peach's voice oozed saccharine sweetness.

"Peach, you have every reason to hate me. For now though, I hope you can put your feelings aside. The night I threw the manuscript out, I was so upset, I hardly knew what I was doing. Your call today startled me. I wasn't thinking clearly. When I got home though, I remembered something I must have deliberately blocked out. I transcribed your father's book on an old laptop computer, one I haven't used since. I threw out the hard copy and the disks but I didn't erase the chapters from memory."

The implication weighed on Peach so heavily, she felt as though she couldn't breathe. "Are you sure?"

"The computer is on the table in front of me as we speak. Chapter One is on the screen. I can print *The Politics of Greed* out in a matter of hours—if you still want a copy."

Peach turned away from her loved ones and looked out at the storm. Her heart seemed to echo the roar of the wind. The safe secure future she had pictured shimmered in front of her eyes, then like a mirage faded away.

A few hours earlier she had reconciled herself to failing Blackjack. But she had made a promise to him and herself—and fate in the form of Jean Sinclair had given her a chance to keep it.

"Start printing, Miss Sinclair. I'll be there tomorrow. I'll let you know when to expect me as soon as I book my flight." She said good-bye and turned around to find Arye, Bella and Bert staring at her.

"Guess what, folks. The roller-coaster ride isn't over after all," she said with a feeble smile.

"You can't go to Washington tomorrow," Arye informed her.

"Why not?"

"Because I can't go with you. I have to finalize the December issue. I don't have to tell you what a disaster it would be if it came out late. In terms of advertising revenue, it's the most important issue of the calendar year."

"There's no reason for you to drop everything. I don't need a baby sitter."

"But you might need a bodyguard."

"Don't be silly. I won't be in any danger. No one knows about the manuscript except the four of us and Jean Sinclair."

* * *

Randolph Spurling sat at the desk that had belonged to Blackjack Morgan, opened the top drawer and took out a Partaga cigar. Although the building had been declared smoke-free, he'd be damned if he would stand out on the sidewalk with the peons. In his view, he paid enough rent to do as he pleased inside his own office.

He enjoyed the ritual of lighting up and took his time about it, puffed deeply, then held the smoke in his mouth a moment before releasing it into the air. There was nothing more soothing than the taste of a really good cigar.

Two more puffs and he felt mellow enough to make his weekly call to Peach Morgan's house. He loosened his tie, put his feet up on the desk and dialed Peach's number. Bella answered on the third ring.

After the hello, how-are-you amenities had been concluded, she said, "You almost missed me. I just walked in the door. Things are at sixes and sevens here."

"Is something wrong?" he asked with carefully calculated concern.

"Quite the opposite. I just came back from taking Peach to the airport."

"I had no idea she was planning another trip."

"Neither did she until last night."

Randolph's instincts for self-preservation were instantly aroused. He quivered like a bird dog on point. Peach's last two trips—first to the Outback and then to Washington—had caused him nothing but grief. "What happened last night?"

"Do you remember me telling you Blackjack had written a book?"

How could he forget? But for the missing manuscript, he'd long since have been free of the need to keep in touch with Bella. "To be honest, I didn't believe such a manuscript existed."

"Peach is on her way to Washington right now to pick it up."

Randolph's heart started like an antelope being chased by a lion. Blackjack's book was an equal threat to his well-being. He had paid a small fortune to the ex-DEA agent to locate and destroy it. When a man with his unique talents reported failure, Randolph had comforted himself with the thought that the book never existed. How could he have misjudged the situation so badly?

There would be hell to pay when his employers found out someone had the manuscript—and that someone wasn't him.

He could think of only one way to redeem himself in their eyes. He had to intercept Peach. With a little luck she would lead him straight to the manuscript.

"I just had a thought. Why don't you give me Peach's flight information so I can pick her up at the airport?"

The offer took Bella by surprise. She held the receiver away from her face and looked at it as if it had the power to explain Randolph. Surely he knew what Peach thought of him. Why would he offer to go out of his way for her?

"She's perfectly capable of getting a cab."

"It wouldn't be any trouble. I'd like the chance to convince her I'm not such a bad person."

The warmth in Randolph's voice didn't ring true.

"I don't think that's possible. Peach is very much her father's daughter. He was very angry with you when he died. Peach still is."

"I know, and I'd like to atone in some small way. Really, Bella, I'd be happy to pick Peach up."

His insistence troubled Bella. A chilling thought sent ice spurting through her veins. Peach had been certain someone was to blame for all their troubles, someone who knew a great deal about them. Could that someone be Randolph?

Bella could hardly conceive of such disloyalty. Why would he turn on them? For that matter, why had he turned on Blackjack? What had her husband known about Randolph Spurling that he hadn't shared?

"Bella, are you still there?"

A lifetime spent in the political arena stood her in good stead now. She could dissemble with the best of them. "I was just looking for Peach's flight information. I thought I put it in my purse but I can't find it."

"Never mind. Just tell me what airline she's on, what airport she's using and when her plane took off. I'll figure out the rest."

The more he persisted, the less she trusted him. "Surely you have better things to do with your time."

"Now now Bella, let me be the judge of that."

Bella had never missed Blackjack more than she did at that moment. She considered herself to be a competent woman, but she didn't have the cunning to deal with Randolph.

Suddenly she had the peculiar feeling that Blackjack was with her, looking over her shoulder and telling her what to do. "Let me think. It could have been Continental—or maybe United. Oh dear, I can't be certain. You must think I'm a scatterbrained old fool."

"Not at all, dear lady. Anyone would be upset under the circumstances. You certainly have aroused my curiosity, though. Who did you say had the book?"

"I didn't."

Bella dropped the phone with a clatter that surely hurt Randolph's ears, then knocked the receiver against the desk a couple of times for good measure.

"What's going on?" Randolph called out above the noise.

"I'm so sorry," she said sweetly. "The dog jumped up on me and I dropped the phone."

"Dog? What dog?"

"Arye Rappaport gave Peach a trained attack dog, a rottweiler as big as a house with teeth to match. I believe you met Arye in Washington. He thought Peach needed protection after everything that has happened."

While she talked, Bella took several pages of stationary out of the desk drawer and crumpled them next to the mouthpiece, mimicking the crackle of static on the line. She had seen Blackjack do it once when he wanted to get rid of an unwanted caller.

"I can hardly hear you. The phone must have gone on the blink when I dropped it. I'll call you next week," she said, then broke the connection.

She experienced a flicker of satisfaction at carrying out the charade. But the flicker faded fast. What if her suspicions were right? There's no fool like an old fool, she chastised herself as she thought of all the things she had told Randolph during the weeks she had regarded him as a friend.

He had known Peach's every move the moment Peach made it, just as he knew of Peach's trip now. She had to warn her daughter, she thought, picking up the phone and dialing a number she had never forgotten.

Randolph had listened to the noise coming over the line with growing impatience. A guard dog in the house? Trouble with the line?

The only trouble was that Bella didn't want to answer his questions—and that was trouble enough. It meant she didn't trust him anymore. Damn her to hell, he thought. The shit was going to hit the fan— unless he intercepted Peach.

He extinguished his half-finished cigar, mopped the sweat from his brow with a pristine monogrammed handkerchief and forced himself to control the panic that threatened to overwhelm him. There had to be a way out.

Bella said she had just returned from dropping Peach off at the airport. The drive back from Intercontinental Airport couldn't take more than forty-five minutes. Assuming Peach arrived the requisite half an hour before departure, her flight had left Houston at about nine-thirty. That put her in Washington around one.

He buzzed his secretary, told her a cock-and-bull story about a friend coming to town, and how he wanted to surprise him by showing up at the airport but didn't have the flight number. He told her to get busy checking all the airlines for Houston to Washington flights arriving around one, then sat back to wait.

Fifteen minutes later, he buzzed his secretary again. "Have you got that information yet?"

"I'm trying, Mr. Spurling. I was talking to American Airlines when you interrupted. They said they fly out of two airports in Houston. Do you know which one your friend used?"

"Just get on with it," Randolph thundered in reply.

An hour and a half passed before the secretary reported not one but four possible flights arriving within half an hour of one o'clock—two at Dulles, one at Washington National, and one at Baltimore-Washington.

Randolph gnashed his teeth in frustration. He might as well play eenie, meenie, minie, moe, for all the chance he had of choosing the right airport, let alone the right flight. But then he remembered Peach and her mother had flown into Dulles for the senator's funeral. Assuming Peach was a creature of habit, the odds favored Dulles.

The first flight was due there in an hour. He could make it if he tried.

A tail wind brought Peach's plane into Dulles ten minutes early. She took a small bag from the overhead compartment and hurried up the jetway. She had five hours to get to Annapolis, pick up the manuscript and return to the airport to catch an evening flight home.

She hurried past people heading for the departure gates. Her stride never slowed until she stepped onto an escalator going down. A hubbub drew her attention to the escalator heading in the opposite direction. A man who looked enough like Randolph Spurling to be his twin was practically climbing over people as he made his way upward. He was so intent on getting where he was going that he didn't even see her.

It was Randolph, she realized with a start before she turned away. Was he meeting someone or leaving on a trip, and why did he look so angry? She hurried outside to a long line of waiting cabs, took the first one, gave the driver the Annapolis address and sat back.

The drive took an hour, most of it through gently rolling countryside dressed in fiery fall colors. However Peach was unable to enjoy the scenery. She couldn't think about anything but the book—and the woman who had it.

Jean Sinclair lived on a tree-lined street near the Naval Academy. Four-over-four windows and black shutters complemented the house's elegant Federal Style. It reminded Peach of the home her parents used to own in Georgetown.

Had Blackjack bought this one for Jean? she wondered as she paid the driver and exited the cab.

Just then a tall, a silver-haired lady with a slender figure and an erect posture opened the front door. Peach had been expecting a *femme fatale,* not a woman of a certain age with her troubles written on her face.

"I'd know you anywhere," Jean Sinclair said, "From the pictures your father showed me."

Peach was too polite to ignore the hand Jean Sinclair extended. She shook it briefly.

"Won't you come in," Jean said, leading the way into a handsome entry hall.

Peach looked around, approving of the woman's taste if not of the woman. From her vantage point, she could see a small living room and a dining room furnished with good antique reproductions.

"You have a lovely home," she said.

"I inherited it from an aunt and have always considered myself more of a caretaker than an owner. I plan to leave it to the city to use as a museum."

So Blackjack hadn't given her the money to buy it. It was small comfort.

"Did they give you lunch on the plane?"

"I wasn't hungry."

"I fixed us an old-fashioned English tea."

"Look, Miss Sinclair, I'm not here on a social visit. I'd like to get down to business."

"In good time. First though, we're going to have tea. It settles the stomach and soothes the mind. You look as though you need both."

Jean Sinclair led the way to a small family room at the back of the house, overlooking a tiny but lavishly landscaped garden. A tea tray sat on a coffee table in front of a loveseat. Jean Sinclair sat down on the loveseat and removed plastic wrap from plates of delicate sandwiches and scones.

Not wanting to sit next to her, Peach took an adjacent chair. The spicy aroma of Constant Comment floated on the air.

"Lemon or milk?" Jean asked, filling a cup.

"Lemon."

Jean Sinclair may have looked at ease—but her hand shook when she handed Peach the cup. She offered the sandwiches and then the scones and smiled when Peach took one of each.

"You're much thinner than you looked in the pictures your father showed me. It's very becoming."

"I lost my appetite when he died."

"So did I. When we were working on the book, I used to fix lunch for him a couple of times a week. After we finished, I—" She paused as though to compose herself. "I enjoy cooking, but not for one person."

I'll bet that's not all you fixed, Peach thought, choking on a mouthful of scone.

"I can see the thought of your father being here upsets you. It might help if you knew I would never have heard from him again if he hadn't needed someone he trusted to type his manuscript." Jean's clear-eyed gaze met Peach's. If the eyes were truly the windows of the soul, the woman didn't have a guilty conscience.

"If that's all there was to your relationship, why didn't he tell my mother?"

"When we started working together, he wasn't sure he'd be able to finish the book let alone sell it. He didn't want to disappoint Bella—and he certainly didn't want to put her in danger."

"Are you saying he didn't care about you?"

"He may have a very long time ago—but not the way he cared for Bella. She was the only woman in the world for him."

"If you knew that, why did you tell her you were sleeping with him?" Peach blurted out.

"I would hate to be judged on that incident alone. I was young, terribly in love, and very foolish."

"You came close to destroying a lot of lives."

"Including my own. I've regretted it more than I can say. Fortunately your mother was far wiser than I. She ignored your father's peccadilloes and in the end, they were together."

"Peccadilloes! Is that your euphemism for habitual infidelity?"

Jean looked hurt. "Of course not."

"I'll never forgive my father for what he did." Peach didn't realize how angry she was with Blackjack until the words flew from her mouth.

Jean put her teacup down. "I'm not condoning your father's behavior—or mine, but I would like to try and explain it. He was a handsome, powerful man. He didn't have to pursue women. They pursued him." She cleared her throat. "He used women to help him forget."

"Forget what? His family? His obligations?"

"The war. He did some terrible things in Vietnam. The memories made him doubt himself."

"I don't believe that. My father was a supremely confident man."

"He put up a good front but he didn't like himself or the things he'd done. It's all in the book. That's one reason writing it was so hard on him."

"That doesn't make sense. He said it would clear his name."

Jean sat even straighter. "You know that's not true."

"I was there. He asked me not to let the bastards get away with it."

"Your mother tells a different story."

Apparently, Jean Sinclair's effrontery had no limits. "My mother would never talk to you."

"You're wrong. She telephoned me this morning."

"I don't believe it! Why would she? You're the last person she'd want to talk to."

"She's worried, Peach. She told me what Blackjack said to her before he died. She also told me about the apartment fire and the break-in at your house. She asked me to call and let her know you arrived safely. If you'll excuse me, I'll do that now," Jean concluded, taking a portable phone from the coffee table.

Nineteen

Although Peach couldn't hear her mother's end of the telephone conversation, she could figure out what Bella was saying from Jean's replies.

"Peach got here fifteen minutes ago," Jean said.

"I should have called you sooner but we got to talking."

"No, she's not giving me a hard time."

"She's a lovely woman, very much like her father in some ways."

"Of course you can talk to her. I'll put her right on."

Jean held the phone out to Peach.

"I bet you never thought I'd call you there," Bella said. It wasn't like her to be so blunt. She sounded breathless too, as though she been in another room when the phone rang and had run to answer it.

"You could say that," Peach replied cryptically, knowing Jean could hear her every word. "Why did you?"

"I'm worried about you."

"There's no need."

"I'm afraid there is. You see, Randolph Spurling telephoned this morning."

"I didn't know you were still talking to him."

"He calls once a week to ask how we are and what we're doing, and if there's anything he can do for us."

"Good old Mr. Helpful. You should have told me."

"I didn't want to upset you. Our conversations seemed perfectly harmless—at least they did until this morning."

"What happened? Did he say something to upset you?"

"That's putting it mildly. I made the mistake of telling him you were on the way to pick up your father's manuscript."

"Oh Mother—" Peach didn't finish the sentence. She couldn't fault Bella for trusting a man she had known for thirty years.

"You don't have to tell me I made a mistake. I haven't been able to think about anything else."

"What happened when you told Randolph?"

"He insisted on picking you up at the airport. The more he persisted, the more nervous I got."

Goose bumps prickled Peach's skin. "I thought I saw him at the airport. I was on the escalator going down when he passed me going up."

"I didn't give him your flight number," Bella rasped in a strangled voice, "but he knew I had just come from the airport. He must have made a lucky guess about what flight you took."

"He must have," Peach agreed. "He certainly was in a hurry. If the plane hadn't landed ten minutes early, he would have been waiting for me."

"Perish the thought. You were right not to trust him. I see that now."

"He was looking for me. I'm sure of it."

"Now I really am terrified," Bella quavered.

"Did you tell him where I was going?"

"I'm not that dense, honey."

"Then you don't have to worry. Randolph will never find me here."

"He's a very clever man. What if he checks the airlines for your return flight?"

"They don't give out passengers' names."

"He could pretend he's your husband or something."

"He can pretend anything he likes. It won't do him any good. Arye suggested I take the precaution of flying under an assumed name. I thought he was being overly careful at the time. Now I'm glad I listened to him."

"What name did you use?"

"Peach Rappaport." She grinned. "To tell you the truth, I sort of like the sound of it. I even charged the ticket to Arye's credit card."

"He's one in a million. I hope you appreciate him."

"Believe me, I do." Although Arye was two thousand miles away, the mere thought of him made Peach feel better, braver, more sure of herself.

Bella sighed. "I just hope—. Never mind what I hope. This isn't the time."

"Don't leave me in suspense. What do you hope?"

"I hope you and Arye have the sense to get married. There, I've said it!" Bella smiled. "And I must say, I feel better."

Strangely enough, so did Peach.

"Promise me you'll be careful when you go back to the airport. Wear sunglasses and a scarf on your head. You remember the way Jackie Kennedy used to wear hers. She's the only woman in the world who managed to make a babushka look chic."

Peach couldn't help laughing. Only her mother

would come up with a stylish disguise. "Sure thing, Mother. Please don't worry. I'll be perfectly safe. See you tonight."

Randolph Spurling arrived at the departure gate in time to see the last stragglers coming off the plane from Houston. None of them bore the slightest resemblance to Peach Morgan. Catching up with her had been a long shot at best, however he wasn't used to failure.

Although he knew it was a wild-goose chase, he ran down the jetway to look in the plane. Two stewardesses stood side by side in the door.

"You're not supposed to be here, sir," one of them said.

"I'm afraid I missed my wife," he gasped. "I got caught in traffic. Can I look in the cabin?"

"It's empty. We're the last to leave. Have you checked the baggage-claim area? She's probably there," the other stewardess suggested.

"She just had a carry-on. We had a fight before she left. She'll never forgive me if she has to take a fifty-dollar cab ride home."

"I don't see how we can help you," the shorter of the two women muttered, her charm worn thin by the three hour flight.

"She's in her early forties, about five feet three, a little on the plump side, and she has lots of long red hair. Did you see her?"

The two women shrugged in tandem.

"The only red head on the plane had a pixie cut. She looked to be a size five and I don't think she's anywhere near her fortieth birthday," the shorter one said. "Now, if you'll excuse us—"

They closed the cabin door and walked around him, trundling their luggage and chatting a mile a minute as they disappeared from sight.

He sagged against a wall of the jetway, took his handkerchief from his jacket pocket and mopped his brow. He'd been so sure Peach would be on this flight that he hadn't made a contingency plan. Even worse, he hadn't informed his superiors about her locating the book.

Still wheezing from his useless race, he made his way back up the jetway and into the airport, ignoring the crowds eddying around him as he grappled with the problem at hand.

Peach was the key. If she were out of the picture, he'd have no trouble manipulating Bella. The thought brought a brief smile to his lips.

But first, he had to find Peach, he mused as he drove back to the city. Locating her in a place the size of Washington would be akin to Diogenes' search for an honest man. But she was bound to return to Houston in a day or two. And when she did, he would have a lethal welcome arranged.

He returned to his suite, ignored his secretary's astonished expression at seeing him walk in without his friend, shook his head no when she asked if he wanted his messages, and closeted himself in his office. Trembling at the thought of what he was about to do, he dialed the now-familiar Houston number.

He'd never ordered a hit before. It gave him a real rush.

"Spurling here," he said, as soon as the connection was complete. "I have another job for you."

"I can always use a paycheck. But no more fires. My sinuses were plugged up for a week."

"It's not a fire. And it will pay well enough for you to go on a long vacation," Randolph replied, knowing his bosses would happily spend the funds for the job he had in mind.

"I'm not in the mood for twenty questions," the ex-DEA agent grumbled. "Get to the point, Spurling."

"I want you to get rid of someone."

"Wet work?"

Randolph nodded, then realizing the man couldn't see him, said, "I believe that's the current euphemism."

The sound of laughter startled Randolph. "You're dreaming. There isn't enough money in the world to make me do that sort of job."

"What's the matter? Aren't you man enough?"

"If you have any doubts about it, I'll be happy to pay you a little visit to discuss it."

Randolph squirmed at the implied threat. "If you can't do the job, perhaps you can recommend someone who—"

Before he could finish the question, the line went dead. Of all the unmitigated nerve! He had half a mind to call the man back and read him the riot act.

Instead, he sat still a moment and thought better of it. He dialed the number of his Washington contact. "I'm afraid I have bad news," he said to the person who picked up.

Their conversation was brief and to the point. Either Randolph took care of the problem, caught up with Peach and destroyed the manuscript or that pile of money in the offshore account, the money he'd planned to use for a lavish lifestyle, would vanish as though it had never existed. The man on the other end of the line said something about Randolph vanishing, too.

Of course, Randolph didn't believe that last part for a minute. Congressmen and senators might lie and cheat and steal, but they didn't get people killed—did they?

"I couldn't help overhearing your conversation," Jean Sinclair said after Peach put the phone back down on the coffee table. "Is someone following you?"

"That's really not your concern, Miss Sinclair."

"If I hadn't called yesterday, you wouldn't be here. If you're in danger, it's my fault. Your father would want me to look out for you as though you were my own."

"I find that rather insulting."

"Have you ever been in love?"

The question took Peach by surprise. "What does that have to do with anything?"

"I loved your father beyond reason. I lived for the moments we were together and died a little when we were apart. Do you know what that feels like?"

"Yes," Peach admitted. Did she ever. She felt the same way about Arye.

"Then you know how easy it is to lose control, to say and do things you never imagined yourself capable of. I know how much I hurt your mother. I also know I wasn't the first nor the last woman to do so. Although that doesn't excuse my actions, it doesn't make me your enemy. I'd like to be your friend—and right now, you need one."

Peach had too much common sense to disagree. Under the circumstances, she needed all the help she could get.

Besides, it was impossible to be furious at a woman who looked and acted like Jean Sinclair. There was something terribly sad about her trying to make a social occasion out of an uncomfortable encounter— going to the trouble of fixing delicate tea sandwiches and homemade scones for a perfect stranger. She must be lonely, Peach thought.

"May I ask you a personal question?" she said.

"Certainly."

"Were you ever married?"

Jean nodded. "Before I met your father. My husband and I had a baby, a little girl."

"What happened to her?"

"She died in her sleep when she was six months old. Now they call it crib death but in those days, everyone thought the parents were at fault. My husband blamed me. I blamed him. Our marriage couldn't withstand that much pain."

Although Jean spoke in a matter-of-fact tone, the tears glistening in her eyes told Peach how much the telling had cost her. She took a tissue from the pocket of her slacks and dabbed the corners of her eyes.

"I'm sorry. It's an old story and I'm not usually this emotional about it. I'm afraid it's due to our meeting after all these years, and knowing you're the same age Beth would have been. How I used to envy your father for having you alive and well at home."

"I don't know what to say except I'm terribly, terribly sorry—for everything including the way I acted when I arrived. I'd like to start over."

"I'd like that, too. Why don't you begin by telling me who you think is following you?"

"A man named Randolph Spurling. He used to be my father's executive assistant."

Jean had been sitting back against the sofa. Now, she straightened up. "I'm not going to let you out of my sight until I put you on the plane."

"From your answer, I assume you know him."

"Only by reputation. Your father talked about him a great deal, though."

"Do you know why Blackjack was so angry with him?"

Jean nodded. "And so will you when you read the manuscript. Randolph Spurling is a terrible man, and a dangerous one. He belongs in jail and there's a good chance the book will put him there."

Peach's scalp tingled. The hair on her nape lifted. "That sounds so cloak and dagger, like something that would happen in a Grisham novel."

"I've worked in Washington for a long time, both in and out of government. Nothing that happens here surprises me anymore."

Jean rose, went to a small cabinet tucked in an alcove, and took something out. Peach's eyes widened when she realized the something was a gun. "Do you know how to use that?"

"Since I live alone I thought it was prudent to take lessons at a shooting range."

"I took lessons too but guns still make me nervous," Peach said as Jean returned to the loveseat and put the revolver down on the coffee table.

"Randolph Spurling makes me more nervous."

"I'm not very fond of the man, but isn't a gun over-kill?"

"Blackjack taught me to never underestimate the enemy. Mr. Spurling is a formidable opponent. But your father didn't think he was acting alone."

"Can you give me any names?"

"No, and they're not in the book either. Blackjack was certain they existed—and that he saw them every day in Congress."

Peach let go a nervous laugh. "The last thing Dad said to me was, *'don't let the bastards get away with it.'* I thought he was talking about the media. God knows, they never gave him a moment's peace."

"The media didn't help. But they were only part of the power structure that brought your father down."

"Are you saying the stories in the papers and on television were part of a master plan?"

Jean nodded.

"I don't believe that! I'm a member of the media. I own a magazine and I control what we print.

"You just proved my point. Have you ever wondered why some stories get huge coverage and others disappear?"

"I suppose so," Peach said, recalling how quickly certain Washington scandals were squashed and how the stories about her father had lingered on long after their news value wore thin.

"Most newspapers and television stations are owned by large corporations. Those corporations have their own agendas."

"What about freedom of the press?"

"What I'm talking about is much more subtle than outright censorship. Most Americans don't realize the interlocking power structure that really governs this country. Your father did. He tracked legislation from the congressmen who proposed it to the lobbyists and PACS who influenced them, to the business interests that reaped the benefits. That's why he decided to write the book."

Peach had been holding her breath. She let it out in a rush. "Where is it?"

Jean got up again, slipped the gun in a pocket and motioned for Peach to follow. She led the way back to the foyer and up the stairs, past a couple of bedrooms to a bath at the back of the house. She stooped in front of a clothes hamper, rummaged beneath the laundry and pulled out a plastic bag.

"I got so nervous after I printed the manuscript out yesterday that I hid it here. I figured no one would think to look in an old lady's dirty clothes." She removed a thick stack of paper from the bag and put it in Peach's hands.

Peach looked down to see "The Politics of Greed by Senator John Morgan" on the front page, and tears welled in her eyes. Loss throbbed in her chest as fiercely as though he had just died. What she wouldn't give to spend another hour with him. She had never told him how much she loved him and now she never would.

"Are you all right?" Jean's voice seemed to come from a long way off.

"I'm fine," Peach replied although she felt as shaky as a baby just learning to walk.

"Let's go back downstairs where we can be comfortable," Jean said, taking her arm.

Peach was grateful for the support. As they returned to the family room, the manuscript weighed far more heavily on Peach than its actual weight accounted for.

"Would you like more tea, or perhaps a brandy? I kept a bottle of Courvoisier for your father. I haven't touched it since his last visit."

"Brandy, please."

Jean left the room briefly. She returned carrying a bottle and two delicate snifters. Peach fought back tears for the second time that afternoon, as she realized the last person to drink the brandy had been her father.

She took a bracing swallow as soon as Jean handed her a glass. "I didn't expect to feel so—so sad."

The expression in Jean's eyes grew even more serious. "I'm afraid the worst is yet to come."

"Are you referring to Randolph Spurling?"

"No, dear. I'm thinking about the book. There are things in it that may hurt you."

"If you're talking about the women in Dad's life, mother filled me in."

"That wasn't his only sin, Peach."

"I can handle it," Peach replied. "I've got an hour before I have to leave. Would you mind if I started reading the book here?"

"I don't think that's a very good idea."

"Why not?"

"Blackjack was very concerned about your reaction. He intended to have you and your mother read the book together. It was very important to him."

"And that's what you think I should do?"

"It was your father's wish."

Peach took another sip of brandy. "Do you have any idea how long I've looked for this manuscript?"

"I know it's been months."

"And now you want me to wait until I get home to read it."

"It's not what I want," Jean said softly. "It's what your father wanted."

Twenty

Peach arrived home to find Arye on the front lawn, throwing a ball for Sleepy. The two of them seemed oblivious to the fact that it was nine in the evening and quite dark outside.

For the first time since seeing Randolph Spurling at Dulles, she felt completely safe. Home had nothing to do with four walls and a roof, she mused, and everything to do with the heart.

Man and dog stopped the game when she pulled up and hurried to greet her. Sleepy woofed hello while Arye swept her into his arms and held her close. When his lips found hers, the world and all its troubles slipped away. For one sweet moment, she forgot everything but the magic they made together.

"I'm so glad you're here," she said when he let her go.

"Where else would I be?" Emotion thickened his voice. "I've been worried about you."

"You needn't have bothered. I had my own armed guard. Jean Sinclair and her .38 revolver were with me until it was time to board the plane."

"Bella told me about Randolph Spurling's call. She said he almost caught you at Dulles. I wish I'd been there."

Arye's voice had so much repressed anger in it, she couldn't help feeling sorry for Randolph if their paths ever crossed.

"I love it when you talk tough," she replied, "even though I know deep down, you're a pussycat."

"You sure do know how to turn a phrase. But the only pussy I'm interested in is yours."

"Promises, promises," she said with a giggle.

He picked up her bag, put an arm around her waist and headed for the front door, curbing his long stride to match her shorter one. "I'll make you another one. Randolph Spurling will have to go through me the next time he catches up with you. I moved in."

"Would you repeat that?"

"You heard me, Peach. Bella, Bert, and I talked it over and it's all settled. I'm going to stay in the guest room until your father's book is safely in David Keller's hands."

The fear that knotted in her chest when she saw Randolph Spurling coming toward her in the airport let go a little. "You won't get an argument from me. I know I'm being ridiculous—Randolph couldn't possibly have known what flight I took home—but I half expected to see him in the plane and I kept on checking the rear-view mirror when I drove home, to see if anyone was following me."

"It's not ridiculous. Someone set fire to your parents' apartment. Someone shot Bert and killed Herbert. Someone ransacked your house. That someone could have been Randolph Spurling."

Peach shuddered. "He certainly has gone out of his way to be aware of our every move."

"Are you cold?" Arye asked, his arm tightening on her waist.

"No. Just scared."

"I hate knowing—having you go through—oh hell—" He dropped her bag inside the front door and told her with his mouth, his arms and his body, what he hadn't been able to express in words.

The message was as clear as though he'd written it across the sky. She was his woman and he would do whatever it took to keep her safe. She clung to him, thinking how lucky she was to have this man in her life—and in her corner.

"Your mother and Bert are in the den," he murmured. "They're almost as anxious to see you as I was."

"If Bert kisses me the way you just did, we're all in trouble."

"I suspect he's kissing your mother as we speak," Arye answered with a soft chuckle.

Arye was right. Bella and Bert broke apart like guilty teenagers when Peach and Arye walked into the room. Their greeting was almost as effusive as Arye's had been. Even the normally laconic Sleepy got into the act, running from one human to another and letting go little yips of pure doggy joy.

"That was some welcome," Peach said when things finally settled down. "I ought to go away more often."

"I don't think my nerves could take it," Bella replied. "I feel so guilty for confiding in Randolph Spurling all these months. I've been a nervous wreck since I hung up on him."

"Jean Sinclair took good care of me."

Arye led Peach over to the sofa and pulled her down beside him. "Did you like her?"

"Not at first. We got off to a rocky start."

"You should have realized she'd be a special person," Bella interjected. "Your father had very good taste."

Peach looked askance at Bella. "Have you forgiven her?"

"I was very upset the first time we talked about her. Things have changed a lot since then. I hope you didn't say anything to hurt her feelings."

"Can we forget about Jean Sinclair's feelings for the moment," Bert declared, his gaze settling on Peach. "I want to hear about Blackjack's book. Was it everything you expected?"

"I haven't read it. Jean said Daddy wanted Mother and me to read it together. He planned to be with us. Since he can't, I'm awfully glad you and Arye are here. I'd be grateful if you stayed and read it with us."

"Where is it?" Arye asked.

"In my bag."

"Do you want me to get it?"

She nodded. "I didn't realize how tired I was until I sat down."

"I'll fix coffee," Bella volunteered and left for the kitchen.

"I'll help," Bert chimed in.

Peach watched the three people she loved most in the world—besides the twins—walk out of the room. Although they were within the sound of her voice she felt very alone.

Sleepy must have sensed her mood because he rose from his favorite lounging spot in front of the hearth, prowled from one end of the spacious room to the other, then walked to the French doors, growling deep in his throat.

Peach froze. She had never heard him make a sound like that. Panic welled up in her throat. She had the strange sensation that someone was out there in the shadows, watching her. Just watching.

"What the hell is the matter with Sleepy?" Arye asked, returning with the manuscript in hand.

"He seems to think someone is outside," she said past her chattering teeth.

"Do you have lights in the backyard."

She pointed at a switch by the French doors.

Arye turned it on and the patio appeared as though it had been conjured up by a magician. Beyond, the swimming pool glimmered like black satin.

"I don't see anyone," Arye said, gazing out into the night.

Apparently Sleepy didn't agree. He pawed at the door until Arye opened it and he bolted past Arye, his growl increasing in volume until it thundered.

Peach jumped to her feet as Arye followed the dog.

"Be careful," she warned.

She heard Sleepy crashing through the shrubbery.

"Sleepy, get back here," Arye shouted.

"Arye, are you all right?" she called out in a thin voice she barely recognized as her own.

Her eyes strained to penetrate the blackness at the rear of her property. Nerves tap-danced down her spine as a darker shadow coalesced from the surrounding night, a form of monstrous proportions.

She opened her mouth to scream.

The shadow moved inexorably closer.

Suddenly, she realized it was Arye holding Sleepy by the collar. Chalk one up to her imagination, she mused. She had done a very thorough job of scaring herself to death.

Arye walked through the French doors and let

Sleepy go. The rottweiler didn't waste a second returning to his place by the hearth.

"There wasn't anyone out there," Arye said.

"Some guard dog," Peach muttered in disgust. "The one and only time he wakes up long enough to do his job, it's a false alarm. I thought you said he had been thoroughly trained."

"Just because I didn't see anyone doesn't mean someone wasn't there," Arye cautioned, taking time to lock the door and then test the lock.

Randolph Spurling drove past Peach's house and circled the block a couple of times, studying the layout of the property before establishing his surveillance. Seeing Peach's Jaguar parked by the garage told him she had beaten him back to Houston. The front of the house was dimly lit, as though she and her mother had retired for the night.

He got out of his car, a nondescript Japanese sedan he'd rented at the airport because nothing distinguished it from any other car, and crossed the street. He cast a furtive glance up and down the sidewalk to make sure no one was watching, then skulked along the bushes that divided Peach's property from her neighbor's.

When he reached the brick wall that protected the backyard and saw a metal ladder propped against it, he took it as a sign from God. He climbed up, teetered on top of the wall and half fell onto a thick cushion of grass inside the backyard.

His heart thundered so furiously that for a moment, he couldn't hear anything else. He tiptoed up to the house, putting one foot in front of the other as though he were walking on eggs. One cautious step followed another until he turned a corner and saw the light streaming from a pair of French doors.

A quick look revealed Peach alone in the den. At least he thought she was alone until a massive fur ball hove into view like a battleship on patrol.

He made an executive decision and ran for the nearest shadows. They happened to be at the back of the yard. The next thing he knew, someone opened the French doors and the fur ball charged toward him.

That's when he decided discretion was indeed the better part of valor. Fear gave his feet wings. He hadn't realized he could jump a six-foot wall with the agility of a kangaroo. However, the dog provided plenty of inspiration. Thank God Peach's house backed up to a bayou or he might have landed in someone else's yard. And heaven knew what canine horrors might have been lying in wait for him there.

He slithered down a steep slope to the edge of the sluggish water, tearing his trousers and ruining a brand new pair of Bruno Magli shoes on the way, then set off toward a streetlight he saw glimmering through the trees. Cicadas serenaded his passage.

Was it true that alligators lived in the bayous? God forbid. He trudged along the muddy bank until he came to a place where he could climb back up to the street without trespassing in someone else's yard, cursing Peach Morgan with every step. But for her, he would be safe in his office instead of risking life and limb.

After her trip to Washington, he'd spent hours on the phone telling certain gentlemen they need have no further worry about Peach Morgan. Perhaps he had played his hand too confidently when he had assured them he could handle her with one hand tied behind his back. She had proven to be a far more tenacious adversary than he had imagined.

Although he exercised regularly, his calves protested at the strain of propelling his body up the bayou's sloping side. His chest heaved with the effort to catch his breath. He'd spent his entire adult life at a desk and didn't have the qualifications or the temperament to be a man of action.

A final step delivered him safely to the street. He looked around to get his bearings, then set off in his mud-caked shoes. He almost had a heart attack when a police patrol car came cruising by. Fortunately he was dressed well enough to look as though he belonged in the neighborhood. He gave the officers a jaunty wave and marched off purposefully, like a man who knew where he was going.

Two blocks later, he realized he was headed in the wrong direction. By the time he found his car, his wet shoes had raised blisters on the back of his heels. He climbed in and slumped behind the wheel, wondering what to do next.

His bladder decided for him. How did policemen on stake-out drink coffee for hours on end without having to take a leak? he mused as he started the engine. He drove south toward a cluster of bright lights, praying they would lead him to an all-night gas station.

He took care of his needs at a mini-market, bought a chocolate bar for energy, and returned to his vigil. By then, no lights were on in the Morgan house. He ate the candy, kept watch for fifteen minutes and decided to call it a night. Although his aching body and stiffening muscles craved the Houstonian's proven luxury, common sense dictated he stay someplace where he wasn't known.

An hour later he lay on a sagging bed in a no-tell motel, wishing he were anywhere else in the world. The effluvium emerging from the air-conditioning unit was damp, dank, and almost as warm as the outside air. The only thing keeping him on a mattress that smelled of old lust and broken dreams was the money deposited to his name in the offshore bank. He'd kill to hang onto money like that.

Tomorrow, he mused as he drifted off to sleep, he might have to do just that.

"What was all the commotion?" Bella asked, returning to the den with Bert.

"Sleepy thought he heard someone in the backyard," Peach replied.

"More likely, he heard something," Bella replied, putting a laden tray down on the table. "He's been having a running feud with a raccoon who comes up from the bayou to scavenge in the trash. Where's the book?" she asked as she poured for all of them.

Arye gestured at the bar. "Over there."

"I don't think we should start reading until we finish eating," the ever-practical Bert said.

"Perhaps we shouldn't start at all tonight," Bella responded. "Once we do I doubt we'll want to stop."

"I don't know if I can take the suspense much longer," Peach replied.

"Bella's right," Arye agreed. "You look exhausted. From the way you reacted when Sleepy growled, your nerves are shot. A good night's sleep will do you a world of good."

Peach got up and marched over to the bar. "I've waited months to know what my father wrote. I'd like to go over the first chapter tonight."

Half an hour later the four of them sat around the game table with the thick manuscript centered on the polished oak.

"How are we going to do this?" Peach asked.

"You go first," Bella suggested, "and when you finish, pass the page to me. I'll give it to Bert and he can give it to Arye."

Wondering if she was about to open Pandora's box, Peach picked the manuscript up and set it down in front of her. The title page was followed by a dedication that brought a lump to her throat. *To Bella,* it read. *No man ever had a better wife or deserved her less.* She passed the page on.

A page of acknowledgments followed the dedication. Peach scanned it quickly, pleased to see her father had remembered to thank Jean Sinclair. Again, she passed the page to Bella. Next came Chapter One.

Peach's hand trembled as she picked it up. She breathed deeply like a diver going off a high board, then looked down and began to read.

The noted English historian, Lord Acton, was one of the first thinkers to be concerned about the threat to liberty inherent in modern democracies. In 1887 in a letter to a friend, Acton wrote, "Power corrupts and absolute power corrupts absolutely."

My career in politics—three terms in the House of Representatives and three in the Senate—is a testament to Acton's acuity.

Peach blinked hard, as if doing so would make the words disappear. But when she looked down, the damning phrase was still there. She could almost hear Blackjack's rich baritone saying the words.

If I were the only sinner in Congress, the only politician to misuse my power and position, I would bow my head and accept the opprobrium of my peers.

I didn't write these pages to lessen my guilt by revealing the names of others who are equally guilty of wrongdoing but rather to prove Lord Acton's point. Power does corrupt.

I have never met a newly elected Congressman who has taken the financial risk of running for office—of seeing his private life held up to intense media scrutiny—for the sole purpose of milking the Washington cash cow and enriching himself. Men and women run for office because they want to ensure a better country for themselves, their families, and their constituents.

When they arrive in Washington they learn the first order of business is raising enough money to pay off the campaign debt they accrued in the process of getting there. In the first month's frantic round of parties, these Beltway virgins quickly learn all sorts of people want to help them—lobbyists for Pacs, multinational corporations, national and international interest groups, wealthy individuals seeking preferential treatment, Hollywood stars who want to burnish their image.

The new legislators' most noble aspirations are quickly submerged in the need to swim in an invading ocean of infinite possibilities. I know how seductive the siren song can be. I've heard it—and surrendered to it.

Peach's gaze drifted away. She stared into space. The chapter had certainly gotten off to a strange start. But sooner or later, she felt certain she would read the words that would clear her father's name.

An hour later, she passed the last page of Chapter One to her mother, then sat back, her mind drifting as she waited for the others to finish. The first chapter hadn't contained the material she had hoped to find. The discussion of term limits, a line item veto, a balanced budget, revamped immigration laws, campaign reform, and a more aggressive trade policy read like a compendium of Blackjack's speeches.

"Well, what do you think?" Arye asked, seeking Peach's hand as he put the last page down.

"It was pretty much standard fare. Dad has talked about all those things before."

Arye's brow lifted. "You sound disappointed."

Peach looked from Arye to Bella to Bert. "I am. Daddy begged me not to let the bastards get away with ruining him. I don't see how the book is going to do that."

Arye's grip on Peach's hand tightened as he wondered if she would ever be able to face the truth about her father.

"Be patient," Bella counseled. "We've only read the first chapter."

"How can we be sure Daddy wrote it?"

"I used to proof all his speeches in the days before he paid someone to write them. I know his style, the way he strings words together. I have no doubt those are your father's words."

"You don't care about him anymore," Peach declared.

The anger in her voice startled Arye even more than what she'd said. He had never been close to his own parents and couldn't fathom the complexities of Peach's and Bella's relationship.

"I care about Blackjack and I always will. You can't be married to a man for forty years and have his children and then erase his memory from your mind. But

I'm much more concerned about what all of this is doing to you. I'd rather burn the book than see you hurting the way you are now."

Contrition softened Peach's features. "I'm sorry. I didn't mean to bark at you."

"You're tired, honey. We all are. I think it's time to call it a night."

Peach nodded. She looked so defeated that Arye wanted to pick her up, carry her upstairs and put her to bed the way he would an exhausted child. Only, he knew he wouldn't be able to treat her like one if he took off her clothes. And she needed to sleep much more than she needed to make love.

Bert rose to his feet, said "I'll see you two in the morning," and headed for the door.

Bella caught up to him and they left together. They made a handsome couple.

Arye could hear her saying, "Would you stop for donuts on your way over tomorrow? I like jelly donuts and Peach prefers glazed."

Peach got to her feet, too.

"You look dead on your feet, boss lady," Arye said.

"Gee, thanks for the compliment," she said, giving him a poor excuse for a smile.

"You know what I mean. You've had a hell of a day. Go on up to bed."

"Not without you. I don't think I can go to sleep if I'm alone."

Peach couldn't have been more wrong, though. By the time Arye opened her bedroom door after talking to Bella for a few minutes, putting Sleepy out one last time, and then checking the locks on the doors and windows and arming the alarm system, Peach was sound asleep.

He kissed her on the forehead and breathed a silent prayer for her, for him, for Bert and Bella, and for their shared future.

Twenty-one

Peach's eyes felt like sandpaper and she knew they were red. The strain of reading nonstop all day yesterday and then getting up early this morning to read some more ached through her whole body. The one consolation was, she had almost finished. Hurrying, she scanned the last page and put it down. But the words reverberated through her mind.

The Constitution and the Bill of Rights were the product of citizen legislators. Both documents reflected the will of the people. Now, two hundred and nineteen years later, an omnipotent federal government rules over the people.

It is easy for citizens to point the finger of blame at their elected officials. But the blame extends far beyond Washington into every city, hamlet and town. In a nation where more people go bowling every year than go to the polls, the silent majority goes unheard.

Less than thirty-six percent of registered voters go to the polls to choose a congressman, a senator, or a president. But it's not too late to change the course of our great nation's history, to rid the body politic of men like me.

The power to do it doesn't lie in the hands of politicians who promise change. It lies in the hands of the people. The vote can be wielded against corruption. It can bring down a

*government that no longer listens to any voice but its own.
The public can be heard when it finds the will to speak.*

Noble sentiments, Peach mused, from an ignoble man. Her most cherished beliefs had been shredded by the manuscript. She felt as though she had been trapped in a surreal dream where up was down and yes meant no.

Reading *The Politics of Greed* had been an exercise in futility. The experience had proven to be even more painful than watching her father's coffin being lowered into the grave. She had buried his body then. Now she buried his soul.

During the reading, her emotions had ridden the familiar roller-coaster ride, soaring and plummeting between elation and despair, pride and anger. Ultimately despair and anger prevailed.

Her father's *mea maxima culpa* had left a bitter aftermath. She had trusted him, believed in him, risked her life to clear his name. How could she have been so blind to his faults, so trusting? Had he really imagined that by writing a book in which he detailed government's transgressions—the flagrant waste and disregard of the public's welfare—he could make up for the things he admitted to doing?

Her father had lived a vainglorious life devoted to self-interest. The book would forever shackle her family, her sons to the man he had been. At that moment she didn't know who she despised more—herself for measuring every man against Blackjack's standard—or him for fooling her so long.

"The Politics of Greed" was a painfully honest assessment of Congress's inner workings, one only an insider could write. But it revealed truths about Blackjack she had never known. The manuscript would destroy the Morgan name rather than restore its luster. Arye had been right all those months ago when he warned her of the danger of tilting at windmills.

She emerged from her reverie to find him staring at her.

"You were shivering. Are you cold?" he asked

"Not on the outside." She gnawed her lip. "I wasn't thrilled to learn my father was a liar and a cheat who took a huge bribe from a Japanese corporation because he had a cash flow problem—to say nothing of the way he betrayed Caitlin Pride. He plotted to ruin Cait so the Japanese could buy her cattle ranch below market value, hired Carroll Detweiler as his accomplice and then stood by and watched Detweiler take the blame.

Her stomach clenched as she recalled her stay at Pride's Outback and how Caitlin Pride thought of Blackjack as a savior, when in reality, he had done everything in his power to ensure she failed at transforming her family ranch into a resort where endangered species would have a haven. With friends like Blackjack, Caitlin Pride hadn't needed any enemies.

"It's true your father did some terrible things," Arye said, "but I don't think writing the book was one of them. I can't help admiring him. He could have resigned like Nixon did and the charges against him would have faded away."

"I don't agree. The story would have come out sooner or later," Peach argued. "Randolph Spurling found out about the bribe and used it to blackmail my father. In time the media would have uncovered the story, too. As far as I'm concerned, Daddy wrote the book to put the best possible spin on a very sordid situation."

"I think you're on the wrong track," Bert said in a soft voice that commanded attention. "You're concentrating on the small picture rather than the big one. Blackjack performed a real public service by writing the book. He pointed out enough waste, fraud and pure pork to reduce the national debt."

"You know what they say about it taking a thief to catch a thief," Peach replied.

"I'm not saying your father was a saint," Bert went on, "but he went through a real epiphany after Detweiler's death. It made him take a long hard look at himself. He was determined to change as a man and a public servant. He knew no one would believe the things he had to say about what really goes on in Washington unless he told the truth about the things he'd done himself."

Bella nodded. Tears gleamed in her eyes. "I have never been as proud to be his wife as I am right now."

Peach couldn't believe her ears. "This is so ironic. When I set out to clear Daddy's name six months ago, I was all alone. It seems I'm all alone again. I think writing the book was a horrendous mistake, one Daddy would have regretted if he had lived. As far as I'm concerned, publication is out of the question."

"Aren't you forgetting something?" Arye asked.

"What?"

"Randolph Spurling. You'll be a threat to him unless and until the book is published."

"That isn't fair. I despise the man. But he wouldn't have gotten away with blackmail if Daddy hadn't accepted the bribe. The whole thing makes me sick. I just want to forget all about it."

"At the moment, what you want isn't as important as what Spurling thinks."

Sympathy and concern shone in Bella's eyes. "Honey, I know what you hoped to find in the book. I'm so sorry you were disappointed. You've spent your entire life looking up to your father, expecting perfection of yourself and those around you because you saw it in him. Now you know Blackjack had a lot of frailties. He wasn't perfect. However he wasn't a monster either. He was just a man. In the end he had the courage to stand up and be counted. In a way the book is his last will and testament."

"Are you saying you want to see it in print?"

"That's not my decision to make," Bella answered so quickly, Peach knew she must have been expecting the question.

"Of course it is!" Peach declared. "You were his wife. The money from the sale will be yours."

"I have enough money. Your father left me long before he died but he never left you. You are his true heir, Peach. The decision is yours," Bella insisted.

Arye took Peach's hand. "You don't have to decide today. David Keller doesn't know we found the book. He doesn't ever have to know if that's the way you want it."

"But you think that would be wrong?"

"What I think doesn't matter."

"It does to me."

His eyes met hers. She saw nothing but love in their brown depths. "You have a tough choice to make. I have every confidence you'll make the right one."

She wished she could be as certain. She gazed out the window while self-doubt crowded close. An uncomfortable silence settled over the table. Bella busied herself stacking the manuscript pages in a neat pile. Bert filled his pipe. Arye took a sip of cold coffee.

Bella finally broke the quiet. "We've been cooped up for a day and a half. It's a beautiful morning. Why don't we take Sleepy for a walk."

"I have a better idea," Arye countered. "I always go for a motorcycle ride when I'm trying to think a problem through. And I know a terrific little restaurant out in the country where Peach and I could have a late lunch."

The suggestion took Peach by surprise. She knew why Arye preferred a bike to a car, but he never asked her to ride with him and she never volunteered. Doing sixty astride a Harley didn't strike her as relaxing.

Arye gave her the special smile that deepened dimples. "Take a chance, boss lady. Ride with me. I promise you won't regret it.

Her resolve weakened. "Where in the country?"

"Round Top."

"That's two and a half hours away!"

"That's the whole idea. You need to put some distance between yourself and the manuscript—and it's a great ride with lots of winding roads. You'll be so busy hanging on, you'll forget everything else."

"Getting away does sound nice. I'd rather go in the Jaguar, though."

"You know how I feel about cars. Besides, the world looks different from the back of a bike. It's liberating in a way nothing else is."

"It sounds wonderful," Bella cut in.

"I don't have biking clothes," Peach stalled.

"All you need are jeans, some sort of boots, gloves, and a leather jacket if you have one. I carry an extra helmet."

"Really, honey, you ought to go," Bella encouraged.

"Aren't you all forgetting something? What about

Randolph Spurling? He could be in Houston this very minute. It doesn't seem smart to split up. Isn't there an old adage about safety in numbers?"

Bert got up from the table. "Bella won't be alone. I'll be with her every minute."

Peach was about to say he hadn't been able to protect himself from a drive-by shooting, then thought better of it.

Bella gave her a reassuring smile. "You know Randolph, honey. He wouldn't do anything that would mess up his clothes."

She got to her feet, put her arm around Bert's waist, whistled Sleepy into consciousness, then nailed Peach with a sharp look. "We're going for that walk and I don't expect you to be here when I get back."

Arye rose, took Peach's hand and tugged her to her feet. "You're outnumbered, Boss Lady."

Fifteen minutes later, Peach came downstairs dressed in a pair of faded jeans she hadn't worn since the twins were in grade school, Western boots, and a leather jacket that was far too uptown for the rest of the outfit. She found Arye waiting for her in the foyer, helmets dangling from his hands.

"I feel claustrophobic," she said after she put hers on.

"You'll get used to it," he replied cheerfully, leading the way outdoors. "The helmet has an intercom so we'll be able to talk to each other.

He had moved the Harley from the garage to the front of the house. To her critical gaze, the two-wheeled vehicle looked unstable.

"This will probably sound stupid but what keeps the motorcycle from falling over when it isn't on its stand?"

"The driver—and a little law of physics called precession. Don't look so worried. You're much too important to me to risk your safety. And there is an added bonus. You can hang onto me all the way."

He walked over to the bike, pushed it off its stand, got on, and started the motor. She took a second to enjoy his appearance, thinking how sexy he was with his broad shoulders covered in black leather and his thigh muscles straining his jeans as he straddled the Harley. Sexy and a little dangerous.

He had certainly accomplished his goal. The last thing on her mind was her father's book.

Randolph sat behind the wheel of his rented car, cursing the misbegotten fate that had delivered him to this time and place. Damn all the Morgans to perdition. Damn the DEA agent too.

After spending fourteen long hours watching Peach's house yesterday—hours punctuated by trips to the nearest gas station to relieve his bladder and then to the closest fast-food emporium to refill it with execrable coffee—Randolph had surrendered his pride and telephoned the former agent.

He only meant to avail himself of the man's professional expertise, to pick up a few tricks of the trade as it were. But the agent broke the connection the minute he recognized Randolph's voice.

The trouble with people like that was their lack of loyalty, Randolph mused. He slumped out of sight when he saw Bella strolling down the drive accompanied by the furry monster and a dapper man he couldn't identify. Either the man had arrived before

Randolph resumed his surveillance at eight that morning—or the man had spent the night.

Randolph snickered at the thought of Bella taking a lover. The senator would be spinning in his grave if he knew. It couldn't happen to a more deserving corpse.

Determined to perform his unaccustomed duties in a professional manner, he took a small notebook from his jacket pocket, jotting down the time and a quick description of the stranger and the canine. He wrote *sixtyish male—fabulous wardrobe,* and *dog—lots of teeth.*

He continued watching as the threesome headed off at a brisk pace. When they turned a corner and disappeared from sight, he resumed his vigil. Fifteen minutes later an engine roared to life out of his line of sight. A moment later he was amazed to see a man and a woman heading down the drive on a motorcycle, and even more amazed to identify the woman as Peach and the man as Arye Rappaport.

He took a second to consider his options. He could try and break into the presumably empty house, then decided he better not presume anything where Peach was concerned. Considering his recent run of bad luck, he'd set off an alarm system and get arrested for breaking and entering.

On the other hand, he could follow the bike. After all, Peach was his quarry. If he stopped her dead in her tracks, his worries would be over.

The word *dead,* reverberated in his head, sending a chill through his body. There was a vast difference between blackmailing the father and murdering the daughter. Blackmail was a white-collar crime. Murder conjured up visions of blue-collar thugs with large muscles. Although he couldn't picture himself among them, he'd come too far to turn back.

He started the engine and burned rubber as he set off after the bike. He didn't have a plan other than learning Peach's destination. When had she taken up riding a bike? Didn't she know how dangerous it was? People were always getting killed on them.

Killed on them. Killed on them.

The thought burned his brain like acid etching glass. He didn't need the damn DEA agent to get rid of Peach. He didn't need to dirty his own hands either. All he had to do was make sure Peach and Rappaport had a fatal accident.

That shouldn't be too difficult for a resourceful man who prided himself on his ability to think on his feet. He lagged a couple of cars behind as he tailed the motorcycle out of the city, then fell back even further when tall buildings gave way to suburban sprawl. He hadn't worried about being noticed in the city. When the bike exited the highway and turned onto a quiet country road, he wondered what the hell he would do if Arye realized they were being followed and he really gunned that big bike.

"You were right," Peach said into the microphone mounted on her helmet. "Now I've got the hang of it, I love riding with you." She let go of his waist, lifted her arms high and shouted, "Look! No hands."

"Take it easy on my eardrums," he replied. "Would you like some music?"

"Not if it means you're going to serenade me. I've never heard anyone sing so off-key."

"The bike has a radio."

She chuckled. "Does it have a bathroom, too?"

"It's good to hear you laugh again. I love your laugh."

"More than my boobs?"

"The only thing I love more than your boobs is your you-know-what." He reached back and caressed her thigh. "Have you ever had sex outdoors?"

"No. Herbert was afraid of fire ants."

"Maybe we can find a nice deserted hilltop where we can explore the situation."

"Hills? We're going to be riding in hills?" she asked, thinking she had just become accustomed to riding on the flat prairie surrounding Houston.

"You haven't enjoyed biking until you've ridden on a road with lots of twists and turns. Trust me, Peach. You're going to love it."

They rode on through a series of small towns, each one more rural than the last. Homesteads with tidy houses and pastures occupied by cattle speckled the land in between. The bucolic serenity banished Peach's tension.

Although the first hills appeared on the other side of Bellville, she felt too relaxed to be concerned. She did what Arye had told her when they started out, leaning into turns rather than unbalancing the bike by trying to sit up straight.

He had warned her not to look at the asphalt which could seem ominously close as they dipped into a curve. Instead she kept her gaze fixed on the onrushing countryside, breathing in the scents of mown hay and dank humus.

She slid her hands up under Arye's jacket and reacquainted herself with the even more intriguing landscape of his chest. The events of the last few days had taken her mind off their relationship. Now the euphoria of being in love and being loved, returned like an answered prayer.

No matter what happened, no matter what she decided about the book or where that decision took her, she promised herself she would never let that feeling slip away again.

Arye's pectoral muscles flexed under her fingers as he guided the bike around the twists and turns. Her hands moved down to the washboard of his abdomen, then lower still until she touched his sex. "Are you really comfortable in those tight jeans?" she purred, "because if you're not, I'd be happy to help you out of them."

"Stop fooling around," he said sharply.

"Why? No one can see what I'm doing."

"You're wrong, boss lady. Someone has been following us since we left Bellville."

Twenty-two

Arye's warning shattered Peach's newfound tranquillity. She turned to look over her shoulder and felt the bike shimmy out of balance.

"Sit straight or we'll go down," Arye cautioned.

She obeyed at once. "All I can see in the rear-view mirror is sky. Are you sure we're being followed?"

"I wouldn't have mentioned it if I wasn't."

It felt strange to be talking to each other in normal tones while the wind tore at her helmet and whipped wisps of her hair against her face. "What kind of car is it?"

"A tan Toyota."

"Then it can't be Randolph Spurling. He wouldn't be caught dead in something so plebeian. Can you see the driver?"

"No. I'm trying to keep some distance between us."

"Couldn't it be a coincidence?"

"Not many people live out here, boss lady. We've turned onto three different farm roads so far. The odds that someone would be taking the same route are pretty damn slim."

"How far is it to the nearest police station?"

His harsh laugh didn't reassure her. Neither did his

words. "Too far to be any help. Hang on. I'm going to try and lose him."

She wrapped her arms around his waist and locked her hands together. Her thighs gripped his hips as though he were a wild stallion she meant to tame. Under other circumstances, it would have been sexy. But there was nothing remotely erotic about the experience. It was one thing to go for a leisurely ride in the country, and quite another to turn the winding farm roads into a Texas version of Le Mans.

She had never been more frightened. Still, deep down she admitted she thrilled to the danger. Gone was the society matron who did her husband's bidding. She had been replaced by a wild woman who took a perverse pleasure in clinging to her lover's body as they raced down a narrow two-lane road.

Randolph Spurling had been so preoccupied with keeping the bike in sight that he didn't have the vaguest idea of his location. Somewhere in Texas was all he knew for sure. Thank God he had the foresight to fill the gas tank last night. If he lost contact with the bike—

He let go the thought as he realized the Harley was pulling away. What was the expression he'd heard on NYPD Blue? Arye must have *made* him.

Randolph depressed the accelerator and felt gratified when the Toyota responded like a much more expensive car. At least he didn't have to worry about keeping up. What he'd do when he caught the bike was another matter. His plan depended on the terrain. He counted on finding a place in the road with a severe drop-off on the right, then hit the Harley from behind and send its passengers flying on a one way trip to eternity.

Although cold air rushed in through the open window, droplets of perspiration dotted his brow. He had no training as a race car driver—let alone an assassin—and didn't know how long his nerves would be up to the job. What he did know was he couldn't return to Washington to report a failed mission.

He kept his eyes open wide, barely daring to blink as he pushed the accelerator to the floor. If he succeeded, he'd damn well demand a bonus.

Not *if*, he reprimanded himself. *When*. And it had better be soon, he fretted as the difficulty of catching a motorcycle on a twisting asphalt ribbon became ominously apparent.

Suddenly they were in a little town—a real one-horse burg. He caught the name, Industry, out of the corner of his eye. Mercifully, there was no traffic at noon on Sunday. No traffic lights either. Put the pedal to the metal, Spurling, he ordered himself. He was no more than a few car lengths from the bike as he followed it back into the countryside.

"Up yours, who ever you are," Peach shouted at the driver of the Toyota, blissfully unaware that anything above a normal speaking tone would hurt Arye's ears. "Eat dust and die!"

Arye grinned in spite of the danger. "Don't you mean eat dirt and die?"

"Whatever," she replied.

Peach never ceased to surprise him. Instead of shaking with fear, she seemed to be taking their precarious situation in stride. She might not be willing to admit it but a full measure of Blackjack's piratical boldness flowed in her veins. The real enigma was how she had repressed her true nature for so long.

The demands of driving at high speed reclaimed his attention. The driver of the Toyota was a maniac. As the car skidded around a turn, any lingering doubt Arye had about being followed evaporated. With a sudden burst of speed, the Toyota came close enough to make out the driver's face.

"Hell, it's Spurling," he muttered under his breath, twisting the throttle in a demand for even greater speed.

"Spurling, as in Randolph?" came Peach's mechanically amplified voice.

"The one and only. I thought he was a wimp."

"He is."

"He doesn't drive like one."

"Isn't a Harley faster than a Toyota?"

"Yeah." Arye didn't add that the bike's superior speed wouldn't help them on the winding farm road.

So far Peach hadn't uttered a word of complaint. But he felt the tension in her body. He should never have suggested the ride. For the second time in his life, he had misjudged the enemy. If anything happened to Peach because of his stupidity—

He shoved the thought away. He hadn't been able to save his wife but he was damn well going to save Peach. The Round Top restaurant was only a few miles away. They would be safe there. He doubted Spurling packed a gun—and even if he did, he wouldn't use it in front of witnesses.

If he read Spurling right, he was going to try and kill them before they reached the safety of another town. The only weapon in Arye's arsenal was his knowledge of the countryside.

He'd ridden this road many times and knew all its twists and turns. Being able to anticipate them gave him a slight edge. His hand tightened on the throttle, letting the speedometer reach seventy on the brief straightaways, pulling away from the Toyota a yard at a time.

"Is it much further to Round Top?" Peach asked, her voice surprisingly steady under the circumstances.

"Just a few miles." He didn't tell her they would be the most dangerous as the road ribboned along the crests of hills and plunged into the valleys between.

The need to concentrate on driving kept him from saying more although there were so many things he longed to tell her, like how much he loved her and how he had never loved anyone more.

He hadn't said it half enough. Later, he promised himself, he'd say all that and more. He'd take time out for love—and not just the sexual part. Time to really experience all the feelings. To share them.

He felt the back wheel slip as he took a turn too fast. It took all his strength to keep the bike upright. A quick glance in one of the mirrors told him Spurling was having even more trouble.

Another curve loomed ahead, a long one that sent the road into a sharp left hidden by shrubbery. On his first few rides to Round Top when grief still held him captive, he had used that particular curve to test his skill, leaning into the turn so hard he could touch the asphalt, challenging death to take him.

Now he knew just how much speed he could carry into the corner. He drove the fine line between control and disaster, praying as he had never prayed before. He had just completed the turn when he saw a bulldozer lumbering toward them, its blade at half mast, looking more like a prehistoric monster than a machine.

The bike missed the blade with inches to spare. The driver's wide mouth spewed curses as they roared by. Arye was looking in one of the mirrors as the Toyota screamed into the corner, traveling on the left-hand side of the road.

He shouted a warning. But the only one to hear it was Peach. She started as his voice blasted in her ear.

Spurling never had a chance. He had to be doing fifty when he slammed into the dozer with a metallic shriek like a thousand banshees howling at the moon. The smell of hot steel, burning rubber and radiator fluid filled the air as Arye braked the bike to a precipitous halt.

"What happened?" Peach asked anxiously, vaulting out of the back seat and yanking the helmet off her head.

"An accident," Arye called out, removing his own helmet as he dismounted.

He took a moment to heave the Harley onto its stand, then ran toward the disaster. The sound of Peach's labored breathing told him she was at his heels.

At first, the bulk of the bulldozer hid the Toyota from view. Thank heaven the dozer driver had emerged from the accident unscathed. His denim overalls and John Deere cap marked him as a farmer.

"What the hell did you damn fools think you were doing?" he called out as Arye and Peach ran by him.

Arye didn't take time to answer. He swore under his breath as he got his first look at the Toyota. The hood had accordioned. The engine had been pushed back. The doors hung crazily askew and all four tires were flat.

Spurling was sitting straight up, not moving except for his hands which fluttered aimlessly. A thin stream of blood oozed from his mouth. If he hadn't been wearing a seat belt, he would have been thrown out of the car and killed, Arye thought as he sprinted the last few feet to the car.

When he got there he realized it wasn't the seat belt holding Spurling in place. It was the steering column. It had been driven into his chest, pinning him to the back of the seat like an insect to a specimen board.

Just then, Peach and the farmer joined Arye. Peach took a quick look in the car, gasped and turned away.

"We've got to get him out of there," Arye told the farmer.

A moan floated from Randolph's mouth on a spray of blood. "Don't touch me."

"I'll get help," the farmer said. "My house is just down the road. Christ, I was just fixing to dig a stock pond and now this." With that, he took off running.

"Peach, I want to talk to Peach," Spurling said.

"You've hurt her enough. Talk to me," Arye answered grimly.

"Sorry. Tell her I'm sorry. Bella, too. She's a good woman."

"Why did you betray the Morgans?"

Spurling's eyelids fluttered closed. The single word, "Money," emerged from his battered lips.

"Did anyone pay you to do it?" Arye's voice sounded overly loud in the quiet countryside.

Spurling's eyes opened again, only halfway this time. "Yes."

"Who were they?"

"Don't know. Didn't care as long as they paid me."
He paused, fighting for breath. The flow of blood from
his mouth had increased. "Can you give me last rites?"

"Sorry, pal. I'm a Jew."

"Doesn't matter. I'm going to hell anyway."

Peach had been standing a few feet away. She moved
closer to talk to Spurling. "Did you set the fire to
mother's apartment and ransack my house?"

"Hired someone," Spurling replied with blunt honesty. Of course, he didn't have a hell of a lot to lose.

"Why? My parents were always good to you."

Randolph's lips moved but Arye couldn't hear his
answer. Arye leaned into the car and bent his head to
the dying man's mouth.

"Power," Spurling said on a long exhalation that
ended with a rattling sound.

Arye felt the pulse point in his neck. It fluttered a
couple of times, then stilled.

Peach had been wrong. Randolph Spurling had
been caught dead in a Toyota after all.

Home never looked so good, Peach thought as the
Harley pulled up in the drive. Her muscles ached from
the hours she'd spent on the motorcycle. She could
barely lift her leg over the back of the bike. Arye
reached to steady her as she dismounted, then got
down himself.

"I want to take a hot bath and afterward, I want you
to hold me for a very long time," she said, pulling off
the helmet and handing it to him.

He didn't meet her eyes. She had never seen him

look so serious. "You've been through hell and it's my fault."

"How can you say that? You saved my life."

"It wouldn't have needed saving if I hadn't insisted on going for a ride."

She caught his upper arms, stood on tiptoe and gazed directly at him. "Don't you dare feel guilty. Randolph would have caught up to me sooner or later. I hate to think what would have happened if he did when I was alone."

Just then, Bella and Bert came pelting out of the house.

"Honey," Bella cried out, hugging Peach hard, "oh honey, thank God you're all right. When the sheriff telephoned and told me what happened, I couldn't believe my ears. I know Randolph was a dreadful man but I never once imagined he'd try to kill you."

"As you can see, he didn't succeed." Peach tried to smile but her lips refused to cooperate. She couldn't rejoice in her own survival while memories of Randolph's death still caromed through her head.

On the long ride back to Houston, Arye had played the sort of soothing music she'd heard piped into hospital elevators. But it hadn't banished the dreadful images carouseling through her mind.

She couldn't stop reviewing the events of the preceding months, from her father's death to the hair-raising chase that had culminated in shattered glass, crumpled metal, and Randolph Spurling's broken bloody body—wondering if she could have done anything to prevent any of it.

Time and again, she might have chosen a different path, one that wouldn't have resulted in the final confrontation. But she had insisted on doing things her way and far too many people—her mother, Bert, Arye, and even Randolph—had paid the price. She had disliked and ultimately feared him—but she never once wished him dead, not even when she realized he was trying his level best to kill her.

"You seem so distant," Bella said, putting a supportive arm around Peach's waist and helping her into the house as if she were an invalid. "I know the sheriff said you weren't hurt physically, but you could be having a delayed emotional reaction."

"I'm just worn out. It all seems so unreal, like something I saw on a television show rather than something I experienced."

"When I think what could have happened—what did happen to Randolph—I just want to sit down and bawl," Bella replied.

"No more tears," Bert said sternly. "You've cried enough for one lifetime. Peach and Arye are home safe. Nothing else matters."

Bert left Bella's side long enough to give Arye a bear hug. "I never told you this before, but you're like a son to me. I'm happier than hell to have you back."

"The feeling is mutual," Arye responded. "I hope the three of you won't think I'm dancing on Spurling's grave but we ought to be celebrating. I'm so damn glad we lived through the day, I could leap tall buildings in a single bound."

"That isn't the only reason to celebrate," Bella said with a sly smile as she led the way into the den.

Peach collapsed onto the sofa and put her feet up on the coffee table, not caring if her boots marred the polished surface. "What are you talking about? Did you change your mind and call David Keller?"

Bella's mouth gaped open. "I'd never do something like that. I told you the decision was yours to make."

"I hope you'll agree with me."

"Does that mean you've decided what you want to do?" Bella asked.

"Unless you object, I'd like to telephone David Keller right away and tell him we found the manuscript."

"Are you sure?" Bella probed.

"Very sure."

"When did you decide?"

"The moment I realized Randolph was willing to kill us to prevent it."

Bella sighed. "His death left so many unanswered questions."

Arye had been helping himself to a Dos Equis from the refrigerator behind the bar. He carried it over to the sofa, sat down and addressed himself to Bella. "Before he died, Spurling admitted he had hired someone to set fire to your apartment and ransack this house. Apparently he was after the book from day one. He also said he'd been paid to do those things."

"Who—?"

"He didn't know," Arye interrupted. "Either that or he wouldn't say."

"Does that mean the danger isn't over?"

"Not yet. But it will be as soon as the book is in the mail."

"What about Bert's shooting and Herbert's accident?" Bella probed. "How do they fit into the picture?"

"They never did. The police were right to attribute them to random violence."

Peach nodded, then snuggled closer. The warmth of Arye's body, the love that surrounded her, helped dispel her disquiet. "I'd like to forget all about Randolph for a while. Mother, you said we had something to celebrate. I certainly could use some good news."

"I hope you'll still feel that way after I tell you what Bert and I decided while you were gone. I know I told you I would wait until Christmas to make up my mind about getting married. After what happened today—knowing things can go very wrong when you least expect it—Bert and I agreed we didn't want to. We're going to get married as soon as possible."

"Thanksgiving at the latest," Bert said, beaming as though he'd just won the lottery.

Peach felt tears pooling in her eyes. She got up, went to her mother and gave her a hug. "I'm so happy for you."

"I'll second that," Arye said. "Congratulations Bert. You're a lucky man."

"I'd like you to be my maid of honor," Bella told Peach.

"And I'd like you to be my best man," Bert said to Arye.

"There isn't much time to plan so we want the wedding to be a small affair, just a few close friends," Bella explained, then leaned close and whispered in Peach's ear, "I hope it gives that man of yours ideas of his own."

Twenty-three

Peach drove home from work at the end of a December day to discover Christmas lights blazing from windows like beacons of hope. While she had spent the weekend grappling with the first of a series of articles about influential Texans, her neighbors had decorated their homes for the holidays. She loved everything about the season from the hurly-burly of shopping, to the good-will-towards-men ethos that transformed human behavior for a few glorious weeks.

During the twins' childhood, new family traditions had piled on old ones until there didn't seem to be enough time to carry them all out. She had baked dozens of cookies, filling the house with the aroma of vanilla, cinnamon and nutmeg, shepherded the boys and their friends on ice-skating and shopping expeditions to the Galleria, and spent the evenings at the elegant parties that were *de rigeur* on the Houston social scene.

This holiday season would be very different from the ones that preceded it, quieter and more contemplative. She had no one to bake for and no parties to attend, other than those given by companies who advertised in the magazine.

With Bert and Bella on their honeymoon, Arye

spending time in the valley chasing down the political corruption story, and so many members of the magazine staff absent due to the flu, she'd had neither the time nor the inclination to decorate the house.

Not that she begrudged Bella and Bert the two weeks they planned to spend in Santa Fe and Taos. And she was excited about the new policy she and Arye had hammered out vis à vis the magazine even though it meant Arye would be out of town from time to time. Nor had she objected when the twins, having spent extra time in Houston at Thanksgiving to attend the wedding, wanted to go skiing in New Hampshire over Christmas.

She was happily anticipating the annual party she gave for the magazine staff, having Christmas dinner at Bert and Bella's, and quiet evenings by the fire with Arye.

Things had worked out despite all the stumbling blocks fate had put in their way. Blackjack's book would be published during the white heat of the ninety-six presidential campaign, Bella had found true happiness with Bert, and one of these days, Peach felt certain Arye would get around to formalizing their own relationship. Considering the fuss he'd made about when and where they made love the first time, she had no doubt he was quietly planning the most romantic proposal.

She could hardly wait, she thought, as she pulled into the drive and parked in front of the garage. She took her briefcase from the passenger seat, got out and looked toward the empty house where the lights she had left on that morning made her homecoming seem less lonely.

She took a moment to look up at the sky, enjoying

the sight of the stars before making a wish on one. The same wish she had made since Blackjack's death—that no harm would ever again come to those she loved. Then she headed for the door.

Suddenly she thought she spied a flash of movement out of the corner of her right eye. But when she looked that way, all she saw were the thick bushes that divided her property from her neighbors.

Get a grip, she told herself. She didn't have a reason to be afraid, not anymore. Randolph was dead and the men who employed him had nothing to gain by frightening her now that "The Politics of Greed" was in the publisher's hands.

Her peripheral vision picked up the movement again. She whirled to get a better look and saw a woman moving toward her from the side of the drive. The single light over the garage didn't illuminate the woman's face well enough to make out her features until she came closer.

With a rush of relief, Peach called out, "Cindy, what are you doing here? Someone at work told me you called today to say you had the flu."

"I'm much better now. Before this night is over, my recovery will be complete."

What an enigmatic answer, Peach mused. But then, she'd never claimed to understand Cindy. "You must have discovered some sort of miracle drug. Everyone else who has had the flu has been out for a week."

She rooted in her overstuffed purse for her keys. When she looked up again, Cindy had moved closer. "Hey, would you mind backing off a little. With Bert and my mother on their honeymoon and Arye spending so much time out of the office, I can't afford to get sick."

"You don't have to worry about catching anything from me. You won't live that long."

"Is that some sort of threat?" Peach demanded, thinking the strange encounter had gone on long enough.

"It's not a threat. It's a promise." Cindy reached in her purse, pulled out a gun and aimed it at Peach.

In Peach's teens, Blackjack had insisted she learn to handle firearms. "You never know when you'll need to be able to defend yourself," he had said. The gun they had used at the firing range had been a .38. The one in Cindy's hand looked similar.

Her father had been right about her needing to know how to defend herself, Peach mused. However he hadn't told her what to do if the gun was pointed at her.

"If this is supposed to be some sort of joke, it isn't funny.

"I'm not laughing. Are you?" Cindy's eyes glittered with cold heat as she maneuvered between Peach and the door.

Peach felt blood draining from her face. Fear weakened her knees. But she refused to give Cindy the satisfaction of knowing it. "If you have any hope of keeping your job, I suggest you get the hell out of here."

Cindy shook a finger under Peach's nose. "You shouldn't have threatened me. I planned to kill you nice and quick. Now though, I think I'll enjoy making you suffer first. I hear a bullet in the gut is a real bitch."

Peach fought the scream rising up her throat. Why was this be happening now, when happiness seemed within her grasp?

"You'll never get away with it. People in River Oaks

aren't used to gunfire. Pull that trigger and someone will call the police."

"I'm not stupid enough to shoot you out here." Cindy looked toward the house, then back at Peach. "Those stone walls look pretty thick to me. I doubt anyone will know if I kill you inside."

"Why don't we go in now?" Peach said, edging toward the door.

Cindy didn't budge. "You'd like that wouldn't you? But I know all about your dog. When we go in, you're going to call him and lock him in a closet."

"He's a trained attack dog," Peach countered. "All I have to do is give the command and he'll tear you to pieces."

Cindy cackled, a crazed sound that echoed from the stone. "You seem to forget how well I know you. I've heard you talk about the dog and from everything you said, he's about as dangerous as a chihuahua. The only reason I want you to lock him up is so he won't get hurt. I like dogs."

"Why are you doing this? Is it because I didn't let you complete my training?"

Even as Peach asked the question, she knew how silly it sounded. During the weeks she had spent with Cindy, there hadn't been any love lost between them.

At least she had the satisfaction of knowing her intuition had been right. Cindy was as crazy as the Mad Hatter. Not that the knowledge gave Peach any satisfaction.

"I didn't give a shit about training you," Cindy replied in a voice as cold and unforgiving as the grave.

Keep her talking, Peach told herself. As long as she's talking, she won't shoot. "I can see you're very upset. If I've offended you in some way—"

Cindy didn't give her a chance to finish. "Everything about you offends me. You have it all, a big house, expensive clothes, lots of money, a family who loves you."

"You're a beautiful woman. You could have anything you want," Peach asserted, wondering if it was possible to reason with a maniac.

Cindy caressed her own face with her free hand, exploring her features with a peculiar seeking touch, as though she wasn't used to the feel of her face. "Do you really think I'm beautiful?"

"Of course. Everyone does. You've done so much to improve yourself."

"He gave me everything I wanted but your eyes."

Peach couldn't begin to follow the bizarre turn in the conversation. "Who gave you everything? Was it a man? Someone who loved you?"

Anger metamorphosed Cindy's carefully constructed prettiness. "Your husband didn't love me! I paid through the nose for everything he did."

Peach wasn't surprised to learn Herbert had been Cindy's doctor. Herbert may have had his faults as a husband but no one matched him in an operating room. "Do you think Herbert overcharged you? Is that why you're so angry?"

"He wanted to use me, to tell everyone what he'd done to me. I couldn't let him get away with it."

"That doesn't sound like Herbert. He was very good at keeping professional secrets. Why, he never once told me you were his patient."

"He didn't know my real name. And I made sure he never found it out."

Bile rose up Peach's throat. "You made sure? What does that mean?"

Cindy leaned close enough to whisper in Peach's ear. "It doesn't matter if I tell you the truth tonight. You won't live to tell anyone else. I killed Dr. Strand."

"My husband was the victim of a hit and run."

Cindy cackled again. "I know. I drove the car. We made a date to jog in Memorial Park. I made sure to get there first and hit him from behind. He sure did fly. He looked so damn funny, I laughed until I wet myself."

Cindy's humor was even more terrifying than her anger. "How could you?"

"Easy. It was a real rush. I felt terrific afterward—but not as good as I'm going to feel when you're dead."

"Since you seem determined to kill me, the least you can do is tell me why," Peach said, stalling for time and wondering what would happen if she made a grab for the gun.

Bang, bang, she'd be dead. That's what would happen.

"You know why."

The smile on Cindy's face had nothing to do with happiness. Despite her perfect features, she reminded Peach of a grinning gargoyle on a medieval cathedral. "I swear I don't."

"He was in love with me until you and Bert got in the way."

Dear God, she had to be talking about Arye. "How did Bert get in the way?"

"He was always in my face. But I fixed him good."

Peach trembled as she realized what Cindy meant. "You shot him?"

"He deserved it."

"Arye and Bert are just friends."

"Bert never liked me. He kept Arye away from me."

Cindy's voice was rising. If Peach could make her talk even louder, the neighbors might hear and call the police. Whereas if Peach screamed the way she'd been wanting since she saw the gun, Cindy would be sure to shoot her.

"If Arye really loved you the way you claim, wild horses couldn't have kept him away."

"He loved me until you seduced him with your money and your big house," Cindy cried out angrily. She looked around, then lowered her voice. "You're trying to trick me into making a lot of noise but it won't work. I'm much smarter than you think. The voices tell me what to do."

Voices? Cindy was even crazier than Peach imagined. "What voices?"

"The ones I hear in my head. They told me how to make myself beautiful so Arye would fall in love with me. But you and Bert poisoned him against me."

"I never talked to Arye about you," Peach replied, hoping to lie convincingly for once in her life.

Balefire burned in Cindy's eyes. "I saw you whispering to him, telling your lies. You took him away from me. So you see, I don't have any choice."

"Believe me, I know what it feels like to lose someone you love. I know how much it hurts. But Arye was never yours to lose. Did he ever once ask you for a date, take you to dinner, kiss you?"

Cindy trembled. The gun wavered in her hand. "You're trying to confuse me."

"I'm trying to help you. I meant it when I said you're a beautiful woman. One of these days, someone is going to love you. Give yourself a chance. Give life a chance."

"When you're dead, Arye will love me." Cindy

spoke with paranoid certainty that brooked no argument. She poked Peach with the gun again, using it to push her toward the door.

"Arye will never rest until he knows who murdered me. When he finds out it was you, he'll hate you. Is that what you want?"

Cindy gave Peach a hard shove that almost sent her sprawling. "Shut the fuck up. Arye is going to love me and you know it. Open the goddamn door and call the dog."

Peach had run out of options. Her mouth felt so dry, she couldn't have said a word even if she managed to think of something profound that would save her life. She held her key ring up to the light, found the right key and inserted it in the lock. A strange sound, a sort of low rumble that reminded her of the surf, came from the other side of the door.

"What's that noise?" Cindy asked.

"I guess I forget to turn the television off when I left this morning," Peach was quick to answer.

Praying she was right about the true source of the sound, she turned the key in the lock, pushed the door open, and whirled on her toes, stepping aside like a matador evading a bull's charge.

In a blur of black fur and white teeth, Sleepy charged past Peach and launched himself at Cindy. The gun went off and Peach saw a gout of crimson burst from Sleepy's shoulder.

"Oh, no," she cried out. "You bitch. You shot my dog."

Despite the pain, Sleepy pressed the attack home, taking Cindy's gun arm in his mouth and clamping down so hard, Peach could hear the bones break.

Cindy dropped the revolver and shrieked in pain.

Peach scooped the weapon off the floor.

"Call the dog off," Cindy cried out as Sleepy stood over her, dripping blood and saliva and still making that ominous rumbling sound.

"I couldn't if I wanted to. I don't know the right command," Peach replied truthfully. She turned her back on the macabre tableau and crossed the foyer to the telephone, trusting Sleepy to keep Cindy occupied while she dialed 911.

"Someone tried to kill me," she quavered.

"Are you hurt?" asked the calm voice on the other end of the line.

"I'm fine. But please send an ambulance for my dog. He's been shot."

Peach didn't break down once during the entire time the police spent questioning her. She didn't let herself cry when an officer helped her put Sleepy in the back of his car for a siren-wailing ride to the nearest emergency veterinarian. She even controlled her emotions when the doctor told her Sleepy would make a full recovery although she could have wept with relief.

Peach didn't let the tears come until she saw Arye's Suburban heading up her drive. Then a veritable Niagara poured down her face.

She had telephoned Arye in Brownsville to let him know what happened and told him he should stay there to finish his interviews. However she hadn't argued when he said he'd head back to Houston at once.

She had positioned one of the chairs in front of a window in the living room so she would know the minute he showed up and be at the door to greet him.

But her legs refused to cooperate. Unable to move, she heard Arye use the housekey she had given him.

"I'm in the living room," she called out as he opened the front door.

"Peach, oh Peach," he murmured, crossing the floor and lifting her to her feet, "I saw blood in the entry."

"It's Sleepy's blood. And Cindy's."

"Thank God it isn't yours." Arye held her so close, she could feel the beat of his heart.

It wasn't close enough, though. She burrowed against him like a terrified animal. Her throat was too dry, the lump in her throat too big, the recent insult to her senses too outrageous to be reduced to mere words. But her body language told him how frightened she had been.

He didn't talk. He didn't let her go either. They clung to one another for uncounted minutes while Peach wept out her terror, soaking his shirt with her tears.

"Don't cry for Cindy," he said.

"I'm crying for Sleepy," she answered between hiccupping sobs. "He was so brave. When I think of all the bad things I said about him—"

"Is Sleepy going to make it?"

"He's fine," she replied, fighting for control. "The vet said I might even be able to bring him home tomorrow."

"What about Cindy?"

"Sleepy broke her arm in four places. They took her to the hospital. One of the officers said something about her being arraigned in a couple of days. He said not to worry about her getting out on bail, though. Oh Arye, you should have heard her. She actually boasted about killing Herbert and wounding Bert. Her one regret was not killing me."

Now Peach had found her voice, she couldn't stop talking. She recounted every detail of her confrontation with Cindy, from the time she saw Cindy in the drive to arrival of the police to their departure several hours later. When she finished, she felt cleansed, as though she had purged herself and the house of the lingering miasma of Cindy's madness.

Arye held her close the entire time. It felt so good to be in his arms, to feel his strength replenishing hers. "Remember what I said about the women at the magazine falling crazy in love with you. I never meant it literally. Cindy was so certain the only thing standing between the two of you was me."

Arye's gaze was steadfast as he looked in her eyes. "I never gave her any reason to feel that way."

"I know." Peach tightened her hold on him. "I can't help feeling sorry for her. She will probably spend the rest of her life in a mental institution."

Arye nuzzled her neck. "One of the things I love about you is your ability to care for people even when they don't deserve it."

His lips felt so good on her skin. They would feel even better on her mouth, she thought, turning her head to capture a kiss. She forgot to worry about Sleepy or feel sorry for Cindy, forgot how frightened she'd been. She forgot everything except the man in her arms—and later, in her bed. Their lovemaking was fraught with the knowledge that once again, they'd come close to losing each other.

Morning came too swiftly and with it the demands of the real world. They showered together, enjoying a playful moment before dressing to meet the day.

"I've never felt so close to anyone as I do you," Peach said over coffee in the breakfast room.

Arye's gaze lingered on her face as though he couldn't bring himself to look at anything else. "The feeling is mutual."

"I've been thinking about the future," she said.

"In general, or do you have something specific in mind?"

"Very specific. I've been thinking about us."

"So have I."

"Have you come to any conclusions?"

He nodded.

"Don't keep me in suspense."

"You know you mean more to me than anyone in the world," he began, looking far too solemn for a man who was about to make her the happiest woman on earth.

"You certainly proved it last night. Three times."

He opened and closed his mouth a couple of times as though he were at a loss for words. Men were so silly about popping the question, she thought fondly.

"I've been waiting for the right time to say this."

"The way you waited for the right place to make love the first time?" she asked with a husky chuckle.

"Peach, I'm not very good at this sort of thing."

"Let me make it easy for you. I know what you're going to say. And the answer is yes."

"You are one in a million," he exclaimed as the tension left his body. "I thought you wouldn't understand."

"Why not?"

"It is asking a lot of you."

"That depends on your point of view." A frisson of doubt tingled in her brain like a distant alarm bell.

She stared at him. "We are talking about the same thing, aren't we?"

He smiled that special smile that never failed to melt her. "I don't know how you figured out I wanted a leave of absence. All I can say is I'm damn grateful you did. It makes things a lot easier."

It took a supreme effort not to let anguish show on her face. "When did you make the decision? Before or after we made love?"

"Before."

Somehow that made it even worse. "How soon do you want to go?"

"I know how much you love the holidays. How does the beginning of the new year sound?"

Awful, her heart cried out. It wasn't some sort of cruel joke. He meant it. He actually planned to leave her here in Houston while he went off God knew where doing God knew what. She'd been such a fool, thinking he was going to propose. She felt more hopeless than she had facing Cindy's gun. Cindy had the means to kill her—but Cindy could never defeat her.

"How long will you be gone?"

"That's the worst of it. I don't know." He looked askance at her. "I can't believe you're taking it this well."

Taking it well? She was a better actress than she thought. "Is it too much to want to know why you have to get away?"

His smile faded. "Since you figured out everything else, I thought you figured that out, too."

"Humor me, just in case I've got it wrong," she said, clinging to her dignity.

"I want to spend the rest of my life with you—"

She interrupted. "And you plan to prove it by leaving."

"You are angry, aren't you?"

He reached for her hand.

She snatched it away.

"Angry? That's an understatement. I thought you were going to ask me to marry you—not to let you go."

At least he had the sense to look shame-faced. "I've made a mess of things."

"You sure have, buster. Why don't you tell me the truth? I can handle it. If you don't love me, just say so."

"This doesn't have anything to do with what I feel for you. I want to marry you. And I wish I could do it tomorrow. But I have some unfinished business to take care of first."

"Unfinished business? What's her name?"

"Helen," Arye replied quietly. "Her name was Helen. I can't start a new life with you until I end the one I had with her."

Despair slumped Peach's shoulders. "I could fight a living rival. I can't deal with a dead one."

"She isn't a rival. I've never loved anyone the way I love you." He paused a moment, as though he wanted to be sure the words sank in.

"Do you mean that?"

"With all my heart. But that doesn't change things. I should have stayed and nailed the bastard who killed my wife. I couldn't cope with my grief so I ran. It's been eating at me ever since. Don't you see, Peach? I have to know. I won't be able to sleep through a single night with you in my arms until I do."

His anguished confession smothered her anger as

surely as a vacuum smothers a fire. Arye was an honorable man. He would never walk away from a debt or an obligation. "All right. Go back to Phoenix if that's what you have to do. I'll go with you."

He shook his head. "I can't let you."

"You can't stop me."

"Peach, please, if you love me, this once you'll do as I say. I cannot—I will not endanger your life again. Besides, you have to think about the twins. They lost their grandfather and their father. They can't afford to lose you."

"The twins are grown up," she argued. "They don't need me. I hardly see them anymore. They have their own lives."

"Everything you say is true—except one thing. The twins will always need you. Then there's Bella to consider."

"She has Bert."

"You aren't making this easy."

"Why should I?" she challenged.

"What about the magazine? *Inside Texas* could be a real force for good with you at the helm."

"I don't care about the magazine."

"You don't mean that. You have the makings of a first-class journalist."

"When you find Helen's killer, it's going to be a big story. We could write it together."

He dropped to his knees in front of her in a cruel parody of a proposal and clasped both of her hands in his.

"We can spend the next four weeks arguing about it and really get pissed-off with each other—or we can enjoy the time we have left," he said with flawless male logic.

She couldn't think of a single argument that would sway him. The man she loved, who swore he loved her, had made up his mind to walk out of her life and there didn't appear to be a damn thing she could do about it.

Merry Christmas indeed!

Twenty-four

"I can't believe Arye's really gone." The quiver in Peach's voice betrayed how deeply she'd been hurt.

"I can't believe you *let* him go," Bella replied.

"He didn't give me any choice."

"A woman always has a choice, honey."

They were sitting in the parlor of Bert and Bella's home in the Heights on a fine Sunday afternoon while Bert put the finishing touches on supper.

For a couple in their sixties, Bert and Bella certainly had a nineties approach to marriage. They shared everything from their work at the magazine to the care of their home. Seeing them so happy would have been cause for rejoicing if Peach hadn't been so depressed.

"Mother, you know Arye's reasons for leaving and not taking me along. I have to respect those reasons."

"Men don't always know what's good for them. Sometimes they need a little guidance before they see the light," Bella answered with a peculiar gleam in her eyes. "Do you remember the day Randolph died?"

"How could I forget?" Peach couldn't imagine why her mother would bring up such an unpleasant subject when Peach felt terrible as it was.

"When you got home that evening, I told you a white lie. I said Bert and I had decided to get married as soon as possible." Bella leaned closer and lowered her voice. "The truth is if I had waited for Bert to propose, we'd have been in wheelchairs in a rest home by the time he worked up the nerve. I asked him if he wanted to marry me and he had all sorts of reasons why it wasn't a good idea. He was worried about the reaction of the media and what my friends would say. I think he even said something about marrying in haste and regretting it at leisure. That's when I told him after everything I'd been through, I didn't give a damn what anyone said. Then I took him straight to bed to make the point."

"You didn't," Peach gasped.

"I most certainly did. I wanted Bert to know I meant business."

"You are incredible, Mother."

"And you're my daughter."

"Meaning?"

"Meaning you shouldn't have let Arye out of your sight."

"She's right," Bert said, appearing in the parlor like a genial genie. "Frankly Peach, you disappointed me. I didn't think you'd have trouble dealing with Arye after the way you handled Cindy."

"Do you think he meant what he said about coming back?"

"Oh, he'll be back all right. One of these days. The trouble is there's no knowing how long it will take him to nail the bastard who murdered Helen. Arye could get himself in a great deal of trouble along the way."

"Do you think he's in danger?"

"It's hard to say. It wouldn't hurt to have someone watching his back."

"Could I be that someone?"

"You certainly could," Bella cut in. "The last few days, Bert and I haven't talked about much else."

"But I'm not an investigative reporter," Peach burst out. "I don't even have a college degree."

"Being an investigative reporter isn't something you can learn in college," Bert shot back. "A professor can teach you how to do research and how to write a declarative sentence. But no one can give you a nose for the news. You can't learn instincts from a book. You're born with them."

Bella was quick to reinforce what Bert said. "You saw through Randolph Spurling from the very beginning. And you had doubts about Cindy months before she showed her true colors."

Peach had been so focused on her own narrow viewpoint—the one that concluded she was too old for Arye, too unattractive, too inexperienced in and out of bed to hold him. She had been so unhappy, she hadn't attempted to look at the situation from any other perspective.

"You've certainly given me a great deal to think about."

"You've done nothing but think since he left," Bella declared, "and it hasn't gotten you anywhere. Don't just think, honey. Act!"

"It isn't that simple."

"You're the one who makes it complicated."

"How does Arye sound when you talk to him?" Bert asked.

"I don't know. Lonely, I guess."

"Of course he's lonely." Bert seemed to relish explaining the male psyche. "Any man would be, living in a hotel room after spending so much time with the woman he loves."

"If only I could be sure he did. But a man doesn't walk out on a woman he loves."

Bert looked as solemn as a wise old owl. "Sure they do, all the time. Some men are more scared of making a commitment than they are of going to war."

Peach cocked her head and looked at him, thinking what a wonderful father he would have made and half wishing he were hers. "You know Arye better than anyone else. What do you think I should do?"

"The situation calls for bold action, something that will shake Arye right down to his foundation and make him reconsider all the givens he has been relying on," Bert replied.

"What sort of givens?"

"Arye had a very old-fashioned upbringing. His father brought home the bacon and his mother cooked it. Although he believes in women's liberation on an intellectual level, deep down in his gut he thinks it's a man's duty to protect his mate and keep her from harm."

"How can I change his mind?"

"That's your call, Peach, not mine," Bert answered.

He certainly picked a fine time to clam up, Peach fretted, then turned her hopeful gaze on her mother. Bella had been through so much. She was so wise about life in general and men in particular. She'd be sure to have the answer Peach sought. "What do you think, Mother? What should I do?"

Bella gave her a radiant smile. "Look deep in your heart, honey. That's where you'll find the answer."

Peach did something she would have considered socially unforgivable just a year ago. She ate and ran.

But she knew Bella and Bert understood. She spent the better part of the night doing as Bella suggested, looking deep in her heart. All she saw there was Arye.

By morning, bleary-eyed from lack of sleep but happier than she'd been in days, she knew what she had to do. She made her plans as carefully as a general going into battle and spent the next two weeks carrying them out.

Although she and Arye talked every night, she never once mentioned her intentions. Surprise was an important part of her scheme. She rolled into Scottsdale on a fine Friday afternoon, registered at Arye's hotel, carried her luggage up to her room and laid out the clothes she planned to wear.

She took a last look a the black leather jacket and skin-tight pants, said, "Smoking!" then returned to her Jaguar and the trailer she'd towed all the way from Houston. After removing the cargo she returned the trailer to the nearest U-Haul.

By five, the hour when Arye usually telephoned her at work, she had dressed for the occasion. She lurked behind a potted palm in the lobby to await his return. Her pulse quickened when she saw his familiar form backlit by the sun. A second later he strode into the hotel.

He looked preoccupied. Formidable. And yes, lonely. Although several female heads turned to watch his progress, he projected such a hands-off aura that none of the bodies they were attached to tried to intercept him.

He headed straight for the elevators without glancing left or right. She waited until one swallowed him up before emerging from behind the greenery. Although she felt as though she were wearing a costume, no one seemed to notice her outfit as she walked to the elevators, stepped into one and pressed the button for Arye's floor.

The elevator's mirrored walls reflected a sexy-looking leather-clad woman with a dynamite figure and a naughty gleam in her eyes.

That's me, Peach thought in wonder. She'd come a long way, baby.

She pressed a hand against her thundering heart, took a deep breath, then winked at her own reflection. Bert had advised bold action. It didn't get much bolder than what she had in mind.

She exited the elevator on Arye's floor, made her way to his room and knocked on the door.

"Who is there?" he called out.

"Room service. I have a special delivery for you."

Before the last word left her lips, Arye had yanked the door open. For a moment he just stood there, his eyes traveling from the top of her head to her boot-shod feet.

His mouth opened and closed a couple of times before he managed to say, "Is that really you, Peach?"

"In the flesh."

"How did you get here?"

"I drove."

"But it's fourteen hundred miles and I just talked to you at home last night."

She had certainly taken him by surprise, she thought with glee. "I have call forwarding."

He shook his head as though he couldn't believe the evidence of his eyes and ears.

"Aren't you going to ask me in?"

"Sorry. It's just that I can't believe you're here."

He opened the door wide and ushered her into the

room. She took a quick glance around, thinking how sterile and lonely a hotel room could be. A few flowers would do wonders for the ambiance.

"Now I'm here, I wouldn't mind a kiss."

Arye didn't have to be asked twice. There was nothing tentative in the way his lips met hers, or in the embrace that went with it. One hand held her close to his chest. The other cupped her leather-clad derrière, pressing her against his manhood. At least that part of him hadn't taken long to get used to the idea of her being there.

She returned the kiss with equal enthusiasm, mating her tongue with his in a dance as old as time. "Are you glad to see me?" she asked when he paused for breath.

He pressed her even closer. "Can't you tell?"

"One part of you seems to be thrilled. What about the rest of you?"

"I haven't been this happy since I left Houston. I love you, Peach. Nothing is ever going to change that."

So far things were going exactly as planned. "Aren't you the least bit curious about the special delivery?"

"You're all the special delivery I need."

He tried to take her in his arms again but she danced away. They had all the time in the world for making love—a whole lifetime if she had her way.

"I brought you something besides me. It's downstairs in the parking lot," she said, taking his hand and tugging him toward the door.

He paused long enough to snatch his room key and wallet from the dresser before following in her wake. "Don't tell me you brought Sleepy with you. I don't think the hotel lets guests keep dogs in their rooms."

"Sleepy is at home with Mom and Bert. They're so crazy about him, we'll be lucky to get him back when we get home," she explained on the way to the elevator.

"What's this about *we?* I couldn't be happier to have you here for a few days, but you can't stay. It's too dangerous. The situation here is beginning to heat up."

Peach was glad to find the elevator empty when it arrived. She stepped in with Arye at her heels.

"For once in your life, will you consider the possibility that you don't have all the answers. You're potent—not omnipotent."

He grinned. "You sure know how to put a man in his place without hurting his ego. Can we talk a little more about the potent part? After three weeks alone, I'm feeling potent as hell."

"Later," she answered airily, dismissing his sex talk even though she couldn't be more turned on. "I have something to show you first."

"It can't be better than the sight of you in tight leather pants. You look like a biker's babe."

"If the shoe fits, wear it," she answered cryptically.

"What is that supposed to mean?"

"Wait and see."

"Are you playing with my head, Miss Morgan? If that's your game, there are other things I'd rather have you play with."

Before she could respond he kissed her again, putting his heart and soul into it. They were still kissing when the elevator doors parted on the ground floor.

An elderly gentleman walked up to Arye, tapped him on the shoulder and said, "Son, the bedrooms are upstairs."

Peach Morgan-Strand would have been mortified at getting caught in so compromising a situation. The new Peach laughed throatily, thanked the man for the advice, and marched off the elevator with her head held high. As she headed for the front door, the fringe on her leather jacket swung with every step. She felt like a gunfighter, preparing for a shoot-out.

"Don't keep me in suspense," Arye said, taking her hand and rubbing her palm with his thumb as they walked out of the motel.

A sensual tingle ran up her arm. She came to an abrupt stop. Lord, she was tempted to go straight back to his room. "Close your eyes and I'll guide you the rest of the way."

His immediate compliance proved the depth of his trust. She led him around the side of the building to the place where she had parked the Harley. "You can look now."

His eyes opened, then widened as he took in the cycle. A grin seamed his face. "How the hell did you get my bike here?"

"On a trailer."

"But I left it in my garage."

"In case you've forgotten, you gave me your housekeys." Peach's heart thundered in her chest. So much depended on the next few minutes. She prayed she could pull it off. "Now the bike is here, would you like to go for a ride?"

His brow furrowed. "I didn't think you would ever want to get on the back seat of a bike again."

"I wasn't planning to."

"Then forget it. You just got here. I don't intend to leave you alone."

Peach chuckled. "You misunderstand. I plan to take *you* for a ride. That's why I'm dressed this way."

"I value your hide far too much to risk it."

She reached in her pants pocket, pulled out her motorcycle license and held it under his nose. "See. The State of Texas doesn't think there's any risk."

He couldn't have looked more surprised if she had done a striptease then and there. "What—how—?"

She ignored his sputtering, walked over to the bike, took two helmets from the boot, put one on and offered the other to him. Then she pushed the Soft-tail off its stand and got on. It was a big bike for a woman, but the Harley salesman had given her lessons and had assured her other women rode the same model. He even produced a couple of them to teach her the fine points of bike handling from the female perspective. One had been a stockbroker, the other a waitress. Now they were her friends.

She put the key in the ignition, revved the engine a couple of times, then looked at Arye. "Don't tell me you're chicken."

"To tell you the truth, Peach, I'm dumbfounded. Are you sure you know what you're doing?"

"I've never been more sure." She gave him a thumbs up signal, then pointed to the back of the bike. "Hop on."

Arye shook his head as if to say they were both crazy, then mounted behind her.

Her thigh muscles quivered with the strain of balancing the bike until he settled in place. If she hadn't spent hours practicing with the six-feet-tall teacher in the second seat, she couldn't have managed. Now though, she felt confident as she put the bike in gear and eased it forward.

The home-bound evening traffic had thinned by the time she turned the bike onto Scottsdale Road. She had vacationed in the area, had studied a map back in Houston, and knew where she wanted to go.

"How does Papago Park sound?" she said into the mike.

"You're the driver," he answered in a strangled voice.

She could feel the tension in his body just as he must have felt it in hers the day they went to Round Top. "I guess you never rode second seat before."

"Never. I like being in control."

"You can't always. Sometimes you have to put your trust in someone else."

She turned the radio on to the same sort of soothing music he had played for her on the way back from Round Top, then concentrated on enjoying the drive and the cool crisp air that felt so different from Houston's humid climate.

Forty minutes later, she brought the two of them—safe and sound—back to the motel parking lot. Arye dismounted first, then helped her off although she could have managed just fine by herself.

"Well, what do you think?" she said, making the question a challenge.

He stared at her as though he'd never seen her before. "If you wanted to impress me, you've succeeded. I think you're the most amazing woman I've ever known."

"Good. That was my intention. I wanted to show you I'm not going to settle for the sort of sit-by-the-fire life I had before. I want to explore my abilities, to be challenged every step of the way, to kick a little ass."

"You can get hurt doing that."

"It would hurt a lot more if I didn't try. I was scared to death the first time I drove the bike by myself. If I had let fear rule my actions that afternoon, I would have missed out on learning to do something I love."

"You're not just talking about riding a bike, are you?"

"You catch on quick. I'm talking about you and me. You've let your fear control our relationship. It's not fair to either of us. I missed you."

His eyes glistened. "I missed you too, boss lady."

Her own tears were very near the surface. "I'm not afraid of life with you. But I am terrified of it without you."

"What are you suggesting?"

"A marriage. One with shared risks and shared joys."

"Is that a proposal?"

"It certainly is."

"No one's ever proposed to me before."

"That makes two of us. I've never asked anyone to marry me either. How long are you going to keep me in suspense?"

Although a tear rolled down his face, he gave her that special smile, then took her in his arms. "The answer is yes—to everything, boss lady. It always has been."

"Words to live by," she said. And she intended to spend the rest of her life doing just that.

This book had its beginning three years ago with the writing of *Lawless*. I was fascinated by the character of the villain, Senator Blackjack Morgan. Over time I started to wonder if such a man could be redeemed. *Seasons of the Heart* is the answer to that question. It may be naive to believe that love can overcome the hardest odds, that it can lift men and women from the depths to the heights, but that became my answer. It's still my answer.

For readers with inquiring minds who want to know the resources I used in developing the political under-pinnings of the story, my resources included *Boiling Point* by Kevin Phillips, *The Lobbyists* by Jeffrey H. Biernbaum, *Scandal* by Suzanne Garment, *A Call for Revolution* by Martin Gross, *Adventures in Porkland* by Brian Kelly, and *The Politics of Rich and Poor* by Kevin Phillips. Special thanks are due Denise Little for trust-ing in my ability to combine romance with politics, to Richard Curtis for believing in the book, and to my husband Bill for putting up with my polemics.

One last word to my readers. Love can heal—and please, please vote!

Alexandra Thorne

**If you liked this book, be sure to look for others
in the *Denise Little Presents* line:**

PUT SOME FANTASY IN YOUR LIFE—
FANTASTIC ROMANCES FROM PINNACLE

TIME STORM   (728, $4.99)
by Rosalyn Alsobrook

Modern-day Pennsylvanian physician JoAnn Griffin only believed what
she could feel with her five senses. But when, during a freak storm, a
blinding flash of lightning sent her back in time to 1889, JoAnn realized
she had somehow crossed the threshold into another century and was
now gazing into the smoldering eyes of a startlingly handsome stranger.
JoAnn had stumbled through a rip in time . . . and into a love affair so
intense, it carried her to a point of no return!

SEA TREASURE   (790, $4.50)
by Johanna Hailey

When Michael, a dashing sea captain, is rescued from drowning by a
beautiful sea siren—he does not know yet that she's actually a mermaid.
But her breathtaking beauty stirred irresistible yearnings in Michael.
And soon fate would drive them across the treacherous Caribbean, toss-
ing them on surging tides of passion that transcended two worlds!

ONCE UPON FOREVER   (883, $4.99)
by Becky Lee Weyrich

A moonstone necklace and a mysterious diary written over a century
ago were Clair Summerland's only clue to her true identity. Two men
loved her—one, a dashing civil war hero . . . the other, a daring jet pilot.
Now Clair must risk her past and future for a passion that spans two
worlds—and a love that is stronger than time itself.

SHADOWS IN TIME   (892, $4.50)
by Cherlyn Jac

Driving through the sultry New Orleans night, one moment Tori's car
spins out of control; the next she is in a horse-drawn carriage with the
handsomest man she has ever seen—who calls her wife—but whose
eyes blaze with fury. Sent back in time one hundred years, Tori is falling
in love with the man she is apparently trying to kill. Now she must race
against time to change the tragic past and claim her future with the man
she will love through all eternity!

*Available wherever paperbacks are sold, or order direct from the
Publisher. Send cover price plus 50¢ per copy for mailing and
handling to Penguin USA, P.O. Box 999, c/o Dept. 17109,
Bergenfield, NJ 07621. Residents of New York and Tennessee
must include sales tax. DO NOT SEND CASH.*

DANGEROUS GAMES (0-7860-0270-0, $4.99)
by Amanda Scott

When Nicholas Barrington, eldest son of the Earl of Ul-
combe, first met Melissa Seacort, the desperation he
sensed beneath her well-bred beauty haunted him. He
didn't realize how desperate Melissa really was . . . until
he found her again at a Newmarket gambling club—being auctioned off by her father to the highest bidder. So,
Nick bought himself a wife. With a villain hot on their
heels, and a fortune and their lives at stake, they would
gamble everything on the most dangerous game of all:
love.

A TOUCH OF PARADISE (0-7860-0271-9, $4.99)
by Alexa Smart

As a confidence man and scam runner in 1880s America,
Malcolm Northrup has amassed a fortune. Now, posing
as the eminent Sir John Abbot—scholar, and possible
discoverer of the lost continent of Atlantis—he's taking
his act on the road with a lecture tour, seeking funds for
a scientific experiment he has no intention of making.
But scholar Halia Davenport is determined to accompany
Malcolm on his "expedition" . . . even if she must kidnap
him!

FUN AND LOVE!

THE DUMBEST DUMB BLONDE JOKE BOOK   (889, $4.50)
by Joey West
They say that blondes have more fun . . . but we can all have a
hoot with THE DUMBEST DUMB BLONDE JOKE BOOK.
Here's a hilarious collection of hundreds of dumb blonde jokes—
including dumb blonde GUY jokes—that are certain to send you
over the edge!

THE I HATE MADONNA JOKE BOOK   (798, $4.50)
by Joey West
She's Hollywood's most controversial star. Her raunchy reputation's brought her fame and fortune. Now here is a sensational
collection of hilarious material on America's most talked about
MATERIAL GIRL!

LOVE'S LITTLE INSTRUCTION BOOK   (774, $4.99)
by Annie Pigeon
Filled from cover to cover with romantic hints—one for every
day of the year—this delightful book will liven up your life and
make you and your lover smile. Discover these amusing tips for
making your lover happy . . . tips like—ask her mother to dance—
have his car washed—take turns being irrational . . . and many,
many more!

MOM'S LITTLE INSTRUCTION BOOK   (0009, $4.99)
by Annie Pigeon
Mom needs as much help as she can get, what with chaotic schedules, wedding fiascos, Barneymania and all. Now, here comes the
best mother's helper yet. Filled with funny comforting advice for
moms of all ages. What better way to show mother how very
much you love her by giving her a gift guaranteed to make her
smile everyday of the year.

*Available wherever paperbacks are sold, or order direct from the
Publisher. Send cover price plus 50¢ per copy for mailing and
handling to Penguin USA, P.O. Box 999, c/o Dept. 17109,
Bergenfield, NJ 07621. Residents of New York and Tennessee must
include sales tax. DO NOT SEND CASH.*